INHALED

Nathalie Guilbeault

FIRENZE BOOKS PUBLISHING

Copyright © 2022 Nathalie Guilbeault

Firenze Books Publishing

All rights reserved. No part of this publication may be reproduced, distributed, or transmitted in any form or by any means, including photocopying, recording, or other electronic or mechanical methods, without the prior written permission of the publisher, except in the case of brief quotations embodied in critical reviews and certain other noncommercial uses permitted by copyright law. For permission requests, write to the publisher, addressed "Attention: Permissions Coordinator," at the website address below.

ISBN: 978-1-7772810-6-9

Inhaled /Nathalie Guilbeault—2nd edition.
Editor: Christian Fennell

Any references to historical events, real people, or real places are used fictitiously. Names, characters, and places are products of the author's imagination.

www.nathalieguilbeault.com
www.firenzebooks.com

ACCLAIM FOR
Nathalie Guilbeault's
INHALED, First Edition

Goodreads Reviews:

"Compelling and raw, this book takes you on a disturbing journey into depravity and the hold that some men can have over us, no matter how strong of character we may be. This is about a wronged woman trying to heal who instead chooses poorly, and through her story makes you realise that this could happen to any one of us. I couldn't put it down!"

"I'm a police officer/crisis advocate/domestic violence and sexual assault survivor. These two characters are text book with what I've dealt with in both my personal life and in the field. To put it mildly.... this book triggered me. That's hard to do."

"I constantly had shivers while reading this book and truly felt like I could vividly feel the presence of each character."

"Inhaled is what I did when I finished this book. In this semi-autobiographic novel, the author takes us on a dizzying ride through a brief and addictive relationship. An intense tale where you are left wondering how can you fall in love with someone who loves themselves more than anything else."

Amazon Reviews:

"A rare and powerful glimpse into the dark power of abuse, the dependency that can fuel it, and the determination it takes to break free."

"Guilbeault has shed a very important, and necessary light, on the dangers, and ease, one can become trapped in a relationship with a sociopath, somatic narcissist."

"A beautiful novel reflective of the intricacies and realities of love, hurt and healing."

"Inhaled offers the reader an intimate glimpse into the dangers and consequences of an abusive, toxic relationship and the price we are willing to pay to quench our own loneliness."

"A dramatic intertwining of lust, dependency and sociopathy revealing the vulnerability of longing, and the cycle of manipulation that can take hold."

"This book was intense! I couldn't put it down."

"If your hand causes you to stumble, cut it off. It is better for you to enter life maimed than with two hands to go to hell." – Mark 9:43

Christian Peter,

Without you, this book would have never been.
Like us?
I am uncertain of this. I like to think that somehow, somewhere, we would have met, still, like we do every morning, surrounded by life, so much of it. I like to think that.
My words, all of them, the ones that came before, the ones that are and will be, all of them—for you.

With Gratitude

Katia
Alana
Romy

INHALED

Nathalie Guilbeault

FORWARD

Inhaled was first published in the fall of 2018 as a fictionalized memoir, under the pen name Isabelle Duval. One could say I hid behind the name, and I guess there is some truth to that.

Some.

Isabelle is my middle name, Duval is my paternal grandmother's maiden name. The hiding, if anything, was partial—a false hiding?

Perhaps.

A desire to be recognized?

Maybe.

Inhaled is about love gone wrong; a love wrought with subtle but relentless abuse—psychological, emotional, and sexual. I wrote about what it did to me, and what it did to my children. I wrote about how I clung to an elusive being in order to survive. How I let it feed me, and how I escaped through it. A show and tell made for voyeurs, untraceable to the real me, which is what I wanted. You see, when I first decided to publish Inhaled, my core, like a pillar made of shame, was weak, unable to keep me balanced. My pen name, a pseudo shield.

It took some time—three long years—to acknowledge what had unfolded, and to get acquainted with the term 'victim', which is what I was—apparently, and to understand trauma bonding, and its effects on the brain: my brain.

The type of abuse I describe in Inhaled is usually unseen, unlike physical abuse. And because it is invisible, it is often misunderstood, and yes, easily dismissed.

Just leave, they'd say.

Not that easy. But, hey, I did. And all alone, I did.

In hindsight, I wanted to try and give the reader a glimpse into a mind addicted to hurt and pain. A truthful accounting.

Like the abuse, I wanted to remain unseen, and undetected.

Over time, with proper help, support, and yes, medication, I climbed out of my hole and came back to—almost, brand new. Of course, I will not forget, I cannot, in fact, forget, the triggers are there, less and less, but they manifest themselves regularly. While I do the dishes, while I drive, when I hear my partner's notifications come up. The good news, I have come to understand that I need to befriend these triggers, as they are there to protect me. I like the thought of them not being too, too far away from me. I panic less often now when one surfaces in the middle of a nowhere, for I understand much more.

When I was first approached by Firenze Books, June of 2021, the head of the publishing house said he liked the book, and offered to re-edit it. And I said, well, yes, why not? And while I enjoyed the first version, this second edition offers additional answers, answers I wasn't able to provide when the book was first written.

And so, in the process of being reviewed by the editor, and myself, Inhaled has grown from *fictionalized memoir* to *novel based on a true story*, its author, from *Isabelle Duval* to *Nathalie Guilbeault*. It makes me laugh, this trajectory, a tip-toing that has become a brisk walk into the comfort of being me.

Another type of coming out, isn't it?

PART ONE

CHAPTER ONE

In her mind, and only in her mind, Isabelle Duval started to wander early in her marriage, revealing the permeability of its seal.

A seal that would hold for 23 years.

Until it would no longer.

A differing reality of the physical world, there, and waiting.

And one of the heart, too, for that is also true.

I turn my hand over and look at the fleshy part of it.

The pain, I think.

The days and the nights.

The …

… broken and wondering.

And here, now, quiet in the dark, I press down on that place, on my right hand, and I whisper—why?

"But, as I said somewhere, the human heart is indestructible. You only imagine it is broken. What really takes a beating is the spirit. But the spirit too is strong and, if one wishes, can be revived." – Henry Miller

I knew I was not the only woman who had had the safety of her world destroyed, the structure of her life disjointed, the foundation of her union blasted. Countless stories depicting evidence of marital crumbling are readily available to the insecure voyeur like me, seeking reassurance in futile comparisons. I wanted to share my story, not as a premise for revenge, but rather, to unburden myself from the encompassing guilt that had woven its way into my stomach. I needed to describe, in painful detail, the unexpected life passage I had chosen to walk, its fine line sometimes erased, or redrawn, oblivious to the hurt and destruction that would ensue. My desire to share was a function of survival, as I needed to finally breathe properly, dilute the shame and access the universe's forgiveness, and not be inhaled, any longer, by ways I did not understand then, and may never fully, yet.

Seated on the edge of her seat, Isabelle Duval fixed her eyes on the dining room floor, pondering something so out of character; so daring—in fact, so dangerously reckless, it sent shivers up her neck. She needed to offset imposed earthquakes with controlled ones. She needed to shield herself from the waves of grief that kept coming at her, violently and consistently, like eternal tides tightly bound together, leaving her with barely time to breath.

For somewhere, over the endlessness of a vast blue sea, her moon had gone rogue, and had lost its ability to ground her, and she felt confused. She felt lost.

Do I want movement, or do I want stagnation?

She wondered more, her eyes still fixed to the floor.

Do I want freedom from this pain? A pain she did not seek. A pain she did not ask for.

Or deserve.

Enough, she thought, and she looked up, for she knew her answer. Her way forward.

CHAPTER TWO

The decision to marry came rapidly, most likely out of a fear of being alone; a fear rooted in my past. I had decided, almost unilaterally, John was going to be the one. I didn't see any of it coming, even when the clues telling me to go came rushing over me.

The pre-honeymoon phase took a nosedive one week prior to the ceremony. My married life, in its infancy, had set its own beat, and I heard nothing, or so little of it. I was deaf to it all. Oblivious.

I remember the morning of the wedding, telling my maid of honor, I couldn't go through with it. It was a gorgeous day for an exquisite fifty guest lunch affair held in one of Montreal's landmarks, a quaint little Inn, located where the International and Universal Exposition had taken place in 1967. John and I had planned the wedding together, and the venue had been carefully scouted. There was an unbelievably beautiful rose garden, coupled with a country ambiance, that made a small, inexpensive wedding feel grandiose and regal.

At 28 years-old, fresh from a seven year relationship that had ended badly, I had fallen in love with a man who would prove immature his whole life. At first, I had been seduced by John's tenacity, his perseverance in courting me. That someone was able to keep up with my abrupt and cynical side had stoked my curiosity, as each of my genuine pushbacks had been met with such nonchalance and humor.

From the beginning of our relationship, the sensations I extracted from my time spent with him were sensations that filled me with unconditional acceptance–or, what I thought was unconditional acceptance. And that was my opium, the need to be seen. For the duration of my entire marriage with John, I would rely on this feeling to legitimize my union with him, and to tolerate the many deviant behaviors that would come to mark our relationship. So yes, the way I thought he fully accepted me, the whole of me, complete with my curvy personality, and sharp edges, had seduced me. He truly wants me, and this I thought, is what love is supposed to feel like.

John and I met at a private party in Montreal, and I would later understand that his emotional inadequacy was responsible for what I perceived as his tenacity. I remember vividly the B-52's song, Love Shack, blasting, the crowd dancing, as he introduced himself.

"You train often," he had yelled to me with the wave of a hand, and beady, glassy eyes that told of nothing I wanted. Not too far from us, stood a tall, redhead, slim and elegant. She seemed paralyzed in the corner, before the large window, beer in hand, playing with the *Claudine* collar of her white *chemise*. I remember thinking as I scanned the whole of her, the way girls do with impunity, the verdict harsh and final, this girl looks as if she is wearing a collar made of dollies. Sometime after, I would find out he had attended the party with his then girlfriend—the tall, slim, and elegant redhead. Oblivious to her presence, and oblivious to my reticence, John had planted his index finger to my side, deep into my flesh. I had pushed his hand away from my body, pulled my tank top further down. Nothing, my eyes had said to him, you are nothing. That night, he had followed me to the taxi, running behind me, begging for my phone number, which I had declined to give him.

Eventually, after three months of incessant phone calls left with my secretary and my roommate's boyfriend, I gave in. He had touched something. Marylin Monroe's saying was starting to ring true—if John could handle me at my worst, I could give him, at the very least, a glimpse of me at my very best.

Somewhat handsome, at 5 feet, 11 inches, his body, although, still lean, showed signs of impending doughiness. Our lovemaking had allowed me to touch and feel the potential for his body to become fleshy. I understood that he probably had peaked physically a few years earlier, his trained body then the subject of an intense sports regimen. I would discover over time, how my slow disinterest for all things sexual would correlate with John's inability to care for himself, body and soul. Weaved into the us we were, inside the slow dysfunction of our ways, the desire to feel and touch—to be touched—was alive. I wanted John in a way he could never be. Slowly, so very slowly, my abdication for all things sexual, unfolded, leaving the seeds of intimacies behind.

Armed with her answer, Isabelle left her home in a state of shock, not knowing her destination. Not knowing where the night might lead her. Aware only of the possibilities of her needs, now surfacing, and stalking, in every possible way, and wanting to be unleashed.

She hastily packed an overnight bag, one betraying her intentions—the irrefutable proof of her premeditated plan: a pink lace nightgown, two G-strings, a hairbrush, a toothbrush (complete with tongue cleaner), some medication, and a laptop and charger. Together, totaling the incriminating evidence pointing to her desire to escape.

Anywhere.

With anyone.

CHAPTER THREE

The thirteen months preceding our wedding had been blissful, even though John was, I soon discovered, prone to sudden, strange temper tantrums, often punctuating very normal, quiet moments. There were other red flags I willingly ignored. Explosions of rage because socks were put in the dryer, because bagels were burnt, because of anything and everything. Nonetheless, I had decided it was time to marry.

I had chosen my groom.

John and I were living in one of the most romantic places Canada has to offer, Old Montreal, the American Europe. The architecture, reminiscent of the start of the area's colonization, created the backdrop for the beginning of our story. The sound of horse-drawn tourist carriages rolling along the rustic cobblestone, non-stop waves of visitors basking in the European ambiance, and a majestic port with its busy boardwalk, provided an idyllic springboard for our young love.

Following our wedding, we stayed a second and final year in Old Montreal. I was starting a master's program in management at Montreal University's Ecole des Hautes Etudes Commerciales. John was working as a financial advisor for a well-known international consulting firm.

From there, we moved to downtown Montreal, the corner of Sherbrooke and Stanley, to a small Victorian-looking house. I had had a miscarriage and had decided to pursue my master's thesis on a part-time basis. The miscarriage had left me shaken and depressed. Suddenly, the pursuit of a full-time master's degree seemed irrelevant. My failed pregnancy had transformed itself into the perfect pretext to leave Montreal for two months and accompany John to Paris and Marseilles for his work as a financial consultant. From there, I decided, I would research my thesis.

My daughter Catherine, was born two-and-a-half years after we married, followed by her sister, Alice, three years later. I had now accomplished a deep want I had held in my heart. I had become a mother. The pull of motherhood had succeeded. The visceral knowledge that, somehow, part of my mission in life was to bear children and touch them with my truth, had been confirmed and accomplished.

The fulfillment I felt during those first few years, while somewhat energizing, was not enough to offset the overwhelming feeling of it not being enough. This feeling of quasi-fulfillment, shifted my definition of balance, my sense of it, including, rationalizing not returning to work for the sake of the children's well-being. Moreover, deep at the core of my being had settled a monstrous truth. Shamefully, like a little girl caught in her mother's unambiguous world, the place where flowers rot and slowly die, the place where women hold one place—second place, I had let John's needs superimpose themselves on mine, morphing my needs into his. I remember thinking, the price to pay in order to not have it all, when family becomes your only bearing, is to not have it all, and to not have it all means life is divided in morsels that you see, and hear, but cannot ever fully taste.

Isabelle had been chatting online with three men, and had in her possession, four or five pictures of herself that she considered good ammunition. When she pulled out of her driveway at 11:00 p.m., well-coiffed and dressed to close her deal, she still did not know where she was heading, as not one of the conversations had reached a satisfying conclusion. Nevertheless, she left hoping to get a drink at the local bistro, and pursue matters further from that location.

The bistro was closed for the evening, and she felt deflated. In fact, everything in downtown Northampton appeared to be closed. She had deployed so much energy to get this far, and she was now left with the option of either returning home, or heading to her local Holiday Inn Express.

Parking her car in a nearby parking lot, she headed to the local pub, which, thank God, was still open.

She walked into the pub, flaunting a fur poncho and suede knee-high boots, strutting in front of the college students who were watching some sports event on the big screen. She sat down on a stool, ordered a rum and Coke, and checked her phone. She only had 14 percent power left, and a message from one of the three men interested in meeting her. She had barely finished her drink, before heading to her car. From there, she charged her phone, called her newfound blind-date, and made sure she entered the right address into her phone. He lived one hour and 45 minutes away. It was now 11:30 p.m.

All that mattered now, was that she had a destination. A place where she could escape the reality her life had become.

A place, she thought, where she could seek her revenge. And she would. All of it.

No matter what.

She started the car, and she drove into the waiting dark, on this night of her revenge.

CHAPTER FOUR

The thoughts circling in my mind were challenging to ignore, as I considered the tasks involved in moving to Taiwan. Prior to the move, my migraines and widespread body pain had notably increased. The eight months preceding our departure had been filled with mixed emotions, as leaving behind family, but mostly good friends, provoked a vertigo-like sensation that had enmeshed itself in my body, altering my already delicate sense of balance.

Nothing, however, hurt more than abandoning my growing coaching clientele. I had been building that clientele since the children were eight and eleven years-old, following my decision to slowly reintegrate into the workforce. Somehow, I had understood the need to lean into my professional self, acknowledging my hunger for recognition.

Nonetheless, my apprehension quickly gave way to excitement. I had rationalized the move as the right step to take to provide my family with some unity and stability. John would be available to help with Catherine, now fourteen years-old, whose mental health issues were becoming more evident. John's assistance could create an equilibrium in which we could possibly redefine ourselves, as a family, as a couple.

Our house was put on the market in February 2010 and was sold that April. On July 30th, we were taking off for Taipei, Taiwan, full of hope and promises. While John had been commuting between Asia and Montreal for fifteen years, the move to Taiwan represented my first contact with Asia, an unbuffered contact whose impact I felt the minute we landed in Taipei.

The taxi ride to The Grand Hotel, Taipei, Taiwan, was a quiet one. The exhaustion we felt was unknown to our bodies, our systems shocked by the harshness of the voyage. Twenty hours of traveling—Montreal to Toronto, Toronto to Hong Kong, Hong Kong to Taipei—coupled with twelve hours of time difference, had taken its toll.

When I had proposed we move to Taiwan, I was aware any move would be unsettling for Catherine. Moving to Taiwan, I rationalized, would be good for all of us, but mostly for Catherine. I thought it would provide her with an unequaled growth opportunity. Up to this point, she and I had been quite close. I had been the very present parent in her life, as John had mostly concentrated his efforts with our company. Yes, Catherine and I had a strong bond, a close understanding of one another, one which I had used in order to legitimize our move to Taiwan. Under the assumption that, I, the competent parent, understood her needs more than anyone else, I had set the stage to test her limits.

Have I gambled on the mental health of my fourteen year-old daughter? I asked myself, as I stepped into the taxi leading us to Juifen. I was bitterly realizing I had consciously not calculated the probabilities of a win. Holding Alice's hand, trying my best to hide my worries from her inquisitive eyes, I stared in disbelief at the dashboard in front of us. It had been profusely decorated with potted plants, a Taiwanese 'thing,' I would quickly discover. I turned my head toward Alice and looked at her gaping mouth. My eleven year-old daughter's small face had distorted into an expression of such surprise; her round, brown eyes were almost as big as her mouth. Her reaction immediately refocused my attention on the moment, highlighting its incongruity. As if on cue, we both exploded into an uncontrollable, fatigue-fueled laughter. There, in the back seat of the garlic-smelling taxi cab, I tightened her hand, brought it to my lips and kissed it with immense gratitude, as I closed my eyes.

The urban heterogeneity of Taipei was quite startling, but somehow equally refreshing. We had arrived in a strange land where beauty and hideousness coexisted in a tamed harmony. Absorbing it all, we checked into our rooms, physically unable to articulate our concerns. My stomach was churning, and my head was throbbing.

The Grand Hotel was a huge pagoda-shaped structure built, according to the locals, under the supervision of Chiang Kai-chek's wife, Mei-ling. John had chosen to introduce us to Taipei via this old and stinky landmark, where carpets and walls seemed to release a constant flow of mold-like odor into the Chinese five-spice laden humid air.

Located far from the city center, it proved to be the wrong location from which to fight the jet lag we were all feeling. Unable to distract ourselves from our fatigue, and overwhelmed by the lack of western cultural references, the children and I felt trapped. Nonetheless, we spent our first six days at the hotel, waiting for our container to reach our new home in Cedar Village, a small compound located at the base of Yangmingshan National Park. Slowly, recuperating from our travels, and preparing our new house for the arrival of our belongings, we braced ourselves for the official launch of this adventure.

We finally moved into our house up on Yangmingshan seven days after having landed in Taipei. Overlooking a valley, our new home was an immense three-story structure located within a private sixty house compound. Upon entering the house, the children had immediately felt at home, as if reassured by the luxurious and inviting feeling the space provided. It was a sharp contrast to what they had observed thus far.

I, too, had been reassured by our new home's design, charmed by its Asian simplicity, but mostly by its inviting layout. The path through the house was a jade-colored, carpeted slicing through the wide open space. It seduced me. The novelty of it, so calming, so reassuring. Entering from the third floor, we would make our way down to the first level, greeted by a luscious garden and an in-ground swimming pool. Much of our time would be spent there, seated on the bench, holding hands, observing the serpent eagles circling above our heads, scanning for prey. These moments of quiet mornings, late afternoon teas, and brimming glasses of wine, should have been enough.

But no.

They were not.

Isabelle looked at the tall branches overhanging the small road, the tall, majestic trees etching a military-like salute, guiding her on toward Lowell, MA.

Toward freedom.

Away from her pain and sorrow. Hate and spite, the pillars of her revenge—a guiltless revenge she would master and feast upon, and worming now into her heart.

She would apply herself. She would allow herself to let go. The darkness of the night pure, the air thickened by a light fog. Yes, she was afraid, but she would pierce the blurry curtain until reaching the highway—until reaching him.

Yes. Revenge. The unlikely key to her freedom.

Or, so she thought, as she drove on, lost to her thoughts.

Lost to her escaping.

CHAPTER FIVE

Thanks to an incredible neighbor, who quickly became a good friend, I joined an international choir for expatriates and local Taiwanese women. I would soon understand how my French heritage had molded my social norms and rapport. Frankness, spontaneity, and humor are modes of expression that are typically encouraged and displayed in my culture. It can feel overwhelming to anyone coming from a more conservative background. My singing ladies' mode of communication contrasted with mine. Norway, Sweden, Holland, Australia, Britain, Japan, and of course, Taiwan, were countries that seemed to value self-containment. Ironically, the singing class provided a space for some to let their inner diva out, while allowing my own self-containment to live. Amongst them, I did not have to perform. I just had to blend.

Being part of a women's-only group was a new experience for me, one that acted as a soothing balm to my loss of bearings. The weight of the move had felt light, until it did no longer, until the full significance of what I had created had settled firmly into my stomach. The intimate space we created during our singing practices had a healing component. It held the power to momentarily suspend our respective worries, allowing our voices to quiet each, and everyone's, untold sorrows, and secret wounds. Because we all have them, don't we?

Living in Yangmingshan provided John and I with the opportunity to hike one of the world's most beautiful landscapes. Taiwan is a small island offering an abundance of opulent vegetation and a challenging terrain. Graced by the Japanese's sense of practicality, the hiking paths they created while occupying the land for fifty years were accessible through interminable sets of stairs available everywhere throughout the island.

The national park offered a multitude of trails catering to both beginner and expert hikers. But the children, while compliant the first three months, quickly disengaged from this family activity. They unknowingly helped John and I carve a space we would learn to love, as it allowed our bodies, but mostly our minds, to rest from our lives' challenges—the children. They were in a disequilibrium like I was, with no recognizable rail to hold on to. While Alice didn't worry me so much, resilience planted in her core, Catherine did. And she should have been with us, shaking her anxieties away. With me.

I quickly came to understand Taiwanese also cherished the outdoors, perhaps a consequence of living in tight spaces, but also a manifestation of their love for nature. It was a love central to their focus on living a well-balanced life. Nothing was ever more uplifting for me than to cross paths with a local hardcore hiker, fully geared up, wearing a head scarf, holding a walking stick in each hand and carrying a radio hanging from a lunch, and water-filled, backpack.

The sound of traditional Chinese music coming from the radio would linger as we continued on our respective paths, marking our journey through the mountains, leaving us bewitched, and uplifting my spirits. The high pitched mandarin tones and traditional Bayan instrumental gong-filled music further anchored the realization that my life was now unfolding here, between the bamboo-filled jungles and the silver-grassed mountains.

Our family dog, a French spaniel named Jackson, also enjoyed the hikes. He had traveled with us to Taiwan, providing some leverage with our children to help them "buy into" our overseas adventure. Hiking with Jackson remained, by far, the main event on our hikes. Taiwanese loved their dogs—their small dogs. They would dress them up in Mandarin outfits and proudly display them in single or double strollers. But on the mountain, Jackson, often running ahead a quarter mile, would startle and elicit yells from the local hikers, as his large scruffy body would appear out of nowhere. We would hear the uproar from afar, each time sending John and I into a complicit laughter that would momentarily weld us fully together. I remember those moments, as my proximity to John would be heightened, then and only then, while basking in a lightness I was eager to feel and taste. Hiking became a drug—my drug.

John and I loved to see Jackson run full steam through the buffalo meadow up on Qi Xing Shan, the "seven-star mountain," located near our home. This meadow, my favorite hiking destination, where actual buffalos lounged and grazed, would attract local picnickers who feasted on chicken, pork, and soup contained in plastic bags. Often, Jackson would swiftly grab one of the plastic soup bags and run in circles with it in his mouth. The dumbfounded Taiwanese would watch in disbelief as our dog pierced the bag, lapped the soup-drenched grass, and eat the plastic. Of course, we would run after the dog, screaming out his name and trying to grab him as he would speed by. All the while, we would apologize profusely, in our tentative Mandarin, on behalf of the soup thief. Finally, we would crumble to the ground in laughter, waiting for Jackson to join us.

By far, my most memorable hike took place well into my second year living in Taipei. From the village where we lived, we could access a hiking path that ran alongside a water canal. It offered a full two hour hike, so I often selected it when pressed for time. Once you passed through the rubbish-filled lands where locals would burn their garbage, the flat hike would lead you through a series of orange groves that would welcome you into Mayan-like stepped fields. A path bordering the fields would lead to a promontory, where, on a clear day, my favorite landmark, Taipei 101, could be admired in all its iconic splendor. There, I would stop, remove my Beats and let myself be hypnotized by the singing cicadas and the bristling tree leaves. Drenched in sweat, I would stare ahead and breathe out any discomfort, that, and so many other worries.

On that particular day, I lost track of Jackson sixty minutes into my hike, when his brown and white furry body disappeared in the distance. Already upset by the fact he had just drowned a poor squirrel, mistaking it for a willing playmate, I increased my pace. I quickly caught up to Jackson, but nothing could have prepared me for the scene unfolding before my eyes.

There, in front of me, was a cobra with its head fully raised. Jackson had found a new friend, one who, unlike the rodent he had just chased and killed, was not going to run from him. Tail up, staring straight at the snake, Jackson stood immobile, focused on his new toy. The back of the cobra's head was facing me, so I did not feel I was in immediate danger. But my dog was. Standing at least six feet from the snake, I barely remember picking up a small rock and quickly aiming it at the scaly creature, and hitting him. I must have hit him, but I do not remember. All I could declare with confidence was this: I was capable of frightening cobras, something no one should ignore.

Uncertain of the persistent woman who had pressed him into giving her his address, Isabelle's blind date had purposely given her the wrong house number, securing him enough space and time to assess the color of her skin, the size of her body, and the features of her face.

Isabelle was nervous, and she tried to settle herself before getting out of the car and walking toward the stairs leading to the porch.

She stopped and looked up, and she saw him, standing on the porch with his arms crossed. A handsome Latino, and she was pleasantly surprised. No, in fact, she felt as though she had won the lottery, having always had a fascination with Latino men.

She realized then, this man had tricked her into thinking he was northern European. His picture had not been that revealing, and the name on his profile was misleading. Her Ulrich, would turn out to be named, Patrick.

She climbed the stairs and she stood on the balcony, unsettled by the ardor and newness of the moment.

He invited her into the house, and she stood in the living room, trying to still herself—to orientate herself, to understand where exactly she had landed. A striking odor of spice was floating in the air, startling her nostrils, adding to her disorientation. The man standing in front of her was dressed in a tight fitting V-neck shirt that clearly defined his muscled body. His black afro was cut military short, leaving her no other choice but to focus on the structure of his face. He had a square jaw and high cheekbones. His nose was wide, with flaring nostrils, indicating some African heritage. His wide eyes were framed by gently defined brows. He plucks them, she thought, smiling to herself. But it was the mouth that drew her in, with lips, pink, plump and soft, extending an unapologetic invitation.

His gaze, serious and armed with intent, destabilized her, unsettling her sense of security.

He must be feeling uncomfortable right now, she thought, disregarding her own discomfort, ignoring the uneasy feeling in the bottom of her stomach. Instead, reminding herself why she was there—to fuse her body with that of a stranger's.

Their attempts at communicating were strained by her clumsiness, his limited knowledge of the English language, and the thickness of his Spanish accent. He took a firm step toward her, and she stiffened, uncertain of what was to follow. She had dressed in black velvet skinny pants with a tight-fitting asymmetrical black top. He scrutinized her face, kissed her neck hastily, and quickly stepped back to analyze her reaction. The look of approval on his face told Isabelle, he also, felt he had gambled successfully.

CHAPTER SIX

In addition to singing and hiking activities, tea drinking had been added. In fact, it became an obsession. I researched the types of teas Taiwan produced, spotted all the teahouses I wanted to visit from Taipei to Kenting, and organized tea-tasting sessions in my own private tea room. The addiction, like all addictions, I think, was rooted in the process. The ritual. Moreover, I became addicted to the moment it revealed, the grounding ceremony that brought me mindfulness, the true and honest savoring of the moment.

Despite these activities, the healthy solitude I had learned to cultivate was quickly fraying into shreds of loneliness. It frightened me. John, now working from the office he had set up on the third floor of our house, was overwhelmed by the flow of work to which he, himself, was addicted. His work had taken over our home, spreading into our everyday life. And so, traveling, those continuous escapes to so many other 'nowheres', became my panacea.

Catherine's state quickly became of concern. I knew she suffered from anxiety, but never suspected the depth of her mental challenges until I was faced with the display of her disturbing behaviors and choices. Early into our move, it had become clear Catherine would not fit into the British school system. She rejected all—its hierarchies, its boundaries, its coldness. She, too, had found a way to escape to 'nowheres' she thought she would tame, wanting to belong somewhere, to someone as well—just not to her family.

Her school was proving to be a fertile playground for teenage delinquents, girls and boys wanting to experience complete freedom, including, squatting in abandoned army houses, urinating in our pool, anonymous phone calls in the middle of the night, and fights instigated with local Taiwanese gangs. Yes, worries were starting to pile up, picking up speed, and it would become clear, soon enough, that I would lose the race.

The objective reading of her predicament was self-explanatory, and one we felt ill-equipped to confront. We had no friends truly capable of helping without judgment, no family to rely on, a health system using outdated mental health practices, and a culture that still viewed mental illness as taboo.

The inevitable happened. Catherine disappeared for a weekend without a trace, not answering our phone calls. We decided we had had enough. We flew-in two juvenile escorts from Los Angeles to bring Catherine to a therapeutic boarding school located in Chili, a choice we had made with the aid of an educational consultant.

This had not been part of the plan. I had moved to Taiwan to create a solid base from which we could all grow together, while providing John with the ideal conditions in which to sell his business, and to bond with his family. Instead, I was removing my eldest from our family, denying Alice access to the sister she loved, but most importantly, I was losing my eldest child, my beloved Catherine.

Mentally unprepared, psychologically confused about the adequacy of our decision, and physically drained, I let the incommensurable guilt invade my heart and mind, paralyzing my body. We had consciously injected trauma into Catherine's life. A legal kidnap, a new age reform school, that could possibly leave scars of the kind that teases the spirit at night, incessantly, making sure one will never forget, possibly forever. My only salvation lay in the belief that I must have saved her, that our actions had, in fact, prevented a catastrophic conclusion from unfolding. But decisions in life, like all wagers, contain hopes that are too often untouchable, unattainable, and remain all they can ever be—greased up filaments of hope.

Following her departure, my headaches multiplied in frequency and intensity. I lost my voice. I lost my will to move. I felt myself become stale, from the inside out. I had become catatonic. For two weeks, I stayed curled up in a fetal position in my bed, waiting for life to return.

One of Catherine's issues was with impulse control, mainly concerning alcohol and drugs. John's immediate family had displayed, overtime, a fair share of functional alcoholism, and John, over the years, had subtly fallen into the same trap of numbing himself through the use of alcohol. Alcohol had stealthily inserted itself into his everyday life. Bottles would accidentally be discovered everywhere in the house, including, buried deep in the back of his office cabinet. It had become quite evident that he needed to stop.

Catherine's struggle was the trigger, but I was the one who pulled it. I told John unambiguously: quit drinking, or I leave. For the next eighteen months, he stopped completely, giving us what I think now were the best years of our lives. But he could not resist the pull soirées and the likes of them had on him. It took one event. The first domino. One event filled with laughter, a laughter that must have told him, all is all right, all will be okay.

This was the beginning of my beginning. My real beginning. The prologue to my next life, there, and written, signed even, at the bottom of all the glasses he drank that night.

He overestimated his ability to control his intake, slowly reintroducing the substance into his life—into mine, Alice's, and Catherine's.

We were now in the middle of our fifth year in Taiwan, and sadly I had pulled further away from John. What were my choices? My marriage, eroded by a lack of admiration for the father of my children, and stunted by the cruel absence of desire, felt unsafe and at risk. In this context, I decided we should return to North America. We had been away from the western world for three years longer than we had initially intended. Moreover, John's failure to sell the company, his main goal, had troubled me. I felt the time to resume our lives elsewhere—anywhere—had arrived.

He had offered Isabelle a glass of red wine. She accepted. Barely having had time to swallow her first sip, he took her hand and led her across the dining room to his bedroom door.

She followed, haltingly, unsure of the accelerated rhythm and pace, and very much feeling as if she was about to jump off a cliff.

To her, it looked like she stepped into another country, or even another era. The bulky bedroom furniture with a colonial Spanish air about it, an orange Himalayan salt lamp on the center of a long dresser table. The light from that lamp responsible for the fiery glow splashed on the walls. The plastic wallpaper, frayed here and there, almost meshing with the flower motif at the heart of its design.

In the corner, to the left of the dresser, a flickering candle. A wooden cross placed in front of it. She approached the cross and studied the picture pinned above it. A tall, black woman, flanked by two boys, standing stoically, looking at the camera.

"My mother," he said. "She died six years ago. I promised this candle would be lit for her endlessly until my death." She doesn't know what to make of the shrine, but will recall reading something about the close bond between Latino men and their mothers. Promising herself to read more on the subject, she turned to him, searching for a cue, a signal, something to alleviate her fear.

With surprising ease and fluidity, he removed his clothing, his lack of modesty somewhat destabilizing her. She sat on the bed, watching him undress, struck by the strangeness of the moment, and her own reckless behavior. Seeing his body before her, threw a veil over her concerns, obscuring whatever common sense she had left.

And yet, she thought, the man standing naked before her was extraordinarily perfect in all his handsomeness. His bronze glowing skin holding the promise of a satiny feel. His muscular chest, arms, and legs, evidence of a physically active lifestyle. His stomach, however, betraying a love for food, and a small aversion to crunches, but still, the alluring body before her was a godsend to her senses. She continued her gaze, stopping at his erect penis of average, to below-average length. It doesn't fit his body, she thought, surprised by her own educated opinion. Although, she thought, with relief, its width should be filling.

Silently and swiftly, he pulled her top over her shoulders. She offered no resistance. What she had started in motion, was now generating a force independent of her control. Even though she was now exposed to a stranger, she began to feel no vulnerability, fully understanding the meaning of her presence in that Latino den. She was there to break and annihilate her past, so she could heal. She was there to renew herself. She was there, to fuck until the numbness subsided.

He removed her bra, revealing her small breasts. She closed her eyes, understanding the point of no return was fast approaching. Upon reopening them, his eyes met hers with a hard stare that clearly expressed negotiating an exit was now impossible. He removed her panties with one hand and threw them over her head onto the grease stained off-white carpet.

Naked, fully present, she stretched out on this man's bed, waiting to be pounded into healing. His eyes locked onto hers, he moved toward her, gently taking hold of her one breast, while acknowledging the other with his strong, wet mouth. One of her nipples, vigorously being kissed, while the other one was pinched with savvy.

She longed to feel his mouth on hers, with an expert and sensuous tongue capable of feeding her hunger for seductive tongue play. A pleasure she had been denied for the past twenty years. Wanting to be properly kissed was an obsession of hers throughout her marriage. "Teach me how to kiss," her husband had often asked. It was an impossible challenge, and one that troubled her throughout her union with him. The best kissers are connected to their emotions and can let the current of those emotions transport them. That was never going to happen with her husband. His kisses always failing to ignite a fire between her thighs, feeding only her frustration and discouragement.

She was eager to discover this man's mouth on hers, to renew sensations central to her. She closed her eyes, suddenly filled with angst and a desire to scream her relief. With their first kiss, long and deep, her visceral wish was granted, indulging in exploring the lusciousness of his lips, testing their apparent softness—a softness that quickly turned to a slow and violent suction, whereby her lips and mouth were taken with rage. He gathered a profuse amount of saliva, only to force it into her mouth for her to swallow, a move that startled her. He then nibbled on her lips, stretching them delicately with his white teeth, until the soft pull became unhinged, leading him to engulf her mouth entirely.

Satiated, he paused to look at her. Her red and pulpous lips seemingly mesmerizing him. His eyes studying every detail of her face, as if he was seeing her, in her entirety, for the first time. He fixated on her lips, her green excited eyes, her jawline, her perfectly oval face, her curly, auburn hair. In an almost dream-like state, he commented on the soft, smooth texture, and whiteness of her skin. She began to tremble, and he plunged his tongue into her mouth, while letting her freely caress his taut body, the type of body she had desired to feel for so long. She stroked all she could, his large chest, his strong arms, his bouncy ass, his muscular thighs, all while restraining her desire to touch him there.

That could wait.

This moment is dedicated to me, she thought, soaking in every square inch of his satiny, brown body.

Quickly, he proceeded to move down on her with vigor.

True, she thought to herself after thirty minutes of pure delight, Latinos love to suck and lick with passion. He focused on the color of her labia, her small lips, and the taste of her, a taste that had always seemed to please men. He looked at her, firmly spreading her thighs. The message being clear, do as I want. This was the moment she had anticipated, and dreaded at the same time. The intersection where John's fuck up would be met with hers.

The thrusts, at first, tentative. He closed his eyes, seemingly to get a visual map of her insides, then, opening his eyes, changing the rhythm that would gradually become deliciously intrusive and forceful. He told her, she has the body of a 23 year-old. The breasts of a teenager. He stopped, taking her to the edge of the bed, raising up her legs, inserting himself.

Having secured his view of their lovemaking, she followed suit. For the first time in her life, she included herself as an observer. Never had she felt the urge to watch herself in the act of having intercourse. More importantly, she had never made eye contact with her past lover.

Her husband.

The scene unfolding before her was profoundly arousing. She watched him looking at her, rhythmically moving in and out of her, a greenish vein emerging across his forehead. He looked at her with deep, fiery eyes, full of lust and desire. With one arm, he artfully switched her onto her stomach, and reinserted himself from behind her.

New sensations flooded her body, as she sustained this position, one she had avoided with her husband. He collapsed on her back, his body shaking uncontrollably, his feet doing a funny little dance that startled her.

He's been electrocuted, she momentarily thought to herself, as his shaking arms tentatively held her. Or, she thought, he's having a seizure.

They kissed again, with abandonment, repeating all that they had done, with one added twist, he asked permission to take her anally. She was surprised by this, never having had anal sex. She refused this with her husband, having withheld this option from her sexual life up until then. She looked into his eyes, somewhat panicking, looking for a reprieve, a supplication for him to not press on.

She told him, hesitantly, "No, not tonight," but he ignored her request, as he had ignored her plea to use a condom. And so, she decided not to push back, as if hypnotized by his will.

He manipulated his way into her by first teasing the area with his penis. This act sending new sensations to her brain, quieting the tension that threatened to stiffen her body. Giving in, she let him feel the virgin contours of her rectum. There was violence to the passage, and some forcefulness. She had, however, the imperative to remain still. A compliant hostage, saving her life.

He authorized her to move, trusting she'd stay with him, and within the moment. She correlated the intent, the foundation for allowing this part of her body to be kidnapped.

She laughed, overwhelmed by this new physical sensation she had discovered in this stranger's bed, escaping her head, her pain, her life.

Is this what mindfulness was all about? she asked herself. Being acutely present to oneself?

Sadly, her moment of chosen irresponsibility would disappear as suddenly as it had emerged, leaving the full weight of what had happened, anchored to her. No, being in the moment should make her feel whole. It should make her feel as though she was being held together by a steel thread, holding a concentrate of herself, her essence. In contrast, she felt diluted. Her sense of self exploding all over the walls and cheap bedspread of the dimly lit bedroom. She was outside the moment, one million miles away from herself.

CHAPTER SEVEN

I plunged headfirst into our new project, establishing ourselves for two years in Northampton, Massachusetts. From this American east coast town, John would operate his hedge fund, while Alice would attend a small International Baccalaureate school in Deerfield, where she would board during the week. The school offered advanced Mandarin classes, giving Alice the opportunity to pursue the study of a language she had started to master in Taipei.

Once again, our imperfect family was to begin a new adventure. John and I, trying to rally, to form 'a team'. Eventually, adjustments to the marriage would have to be considered seriously, but now was not that time. Catherine's mental health issues were still unresolved, and she was now joining a gap year program in Argentina. Alice, however, was showing mounting distress at the thought of losing the friends who had stamped her five years in Taipei with unbelievable depth. There would be no time for John and I to work on our marital challenges. After twenty-two years of marriage, that was the harsh reality.

And so off I went, me, the all-encompassing, loving mother whose decision held the higher needs of the family, and that of her husband's.

Waiting for us in New England was an architectural faux pas, a hiccup only the 1970s could have produced. The house was a small, almost windowless square, encased in brown bricks and greenish metal siding. Deciding to live there was a huge compromise. As tasteless as it was, it was the only house available near Alice's school.

Catherine had decided to join us from Buenos Aires to help us unpack and settle into our newfound home. I had been missing my eldest, but the daughter I had known was nowhere to be found. Depression had molded her presence into nothingness, a nothingness I had to contend with while John was away working in Asia.

The thinness of her limbs and body met me always in that house, in many ways, it felt as she was stalking me. She followed me everywhere, wherever I was, unable to tackle her aches, unable to make sense of them. What I saw scared me. She had lost most of her long black hair—a grown up doll, abandoned, or lost. Her body now but a wire tweaked with random curves that surprised with the incongruity of their presence. Catherine had lost movement. Her hands always so cold, like her gaze, absent, uncaring. The human in her seemed gone. I remember the nights, living nightmares where she roamed the narrow corridors, silently, stealthily. And she knew I was watching her. I would see her from my room, her shadow, resembling that of giant praying mantises, one that sprayed their presence on the walls.

The house itself, maybe Catherine's state as well, should have acted as deterrents. Its decrepitude, its lack of luster, its soullessness, were all warning signs that John and I ignored. But, it was when Alice started to have panic attacks that we should have fled.

Three weeks into the school year, Alice complained about tightness in her chest that would emerge at night, preventing her from sleeping. She had been prone to bouts of minute anxiety before leaving to board at school, but now these moments had morphed into portions of time suspended in hardcore nocturnal despair. She was suffocating, where only breathing should have been felt. I, on the other hand, was now finding the ability to breathe again, where previously, only stale air had met the lungs. A slow process of intoxication had started.

My first reaction was to have Alice consult a therapist, hoping that alone would help her adjust at school and would soothe her symptoms. John had returned from Taipei for a week, with our dog Jackson. I hoped maybe zoo therapy would operate its magic. Despite all these changes, including Catherine's tentative return to Buenos Aires, we had come to realize the only way to alleviate Alice's distress would be to remove her from the boarding school.

At the time, I did not fully understand the significance of that decision, how its impact on my immigration status would alter my life as a whole. What I did understand was that, with Alice no longer boarding at school, I would need to stay full-time, or almost full-time, on American soil, to look after her. My life's sole purpose was going to weave itself around her needs. My wish to reconnect with Montreal would have to wait.

John reassured me all would be fine.

And I believed him.

At 6:00 a.m., nestled in his arms, Isabelle felt her blind date slip into sleep, and she stayed there, her head on his thick torso, haunted by flashing images of her husband's indiscretions. Ready, it would seem, to do anything, to make those images disappear.

When she opened her eyes, she saw him seated by her side with a teacup in hand.

"Drink," he said.

She pulled herself up and placed a pillow behind her back. She stared at him, observing how the daylight shone on his bronze colored face, revealing him in all his splendor. She had spent the last twelve hours with this man, a man whose house she had crashed without restraint or impunity.

She brought the teacup's rim to her lips, star anise and cinnamon. Scrutinizing his face, her eyes lingered on his mouth.

"You like?" he asked, pointing to the tea.

"Yes, I like. I like it a lot," she replied.

Together, still in his bed, they tentatively shared bits of information that were meant to add a layer of intimacy to their time together. She was uncertain this was necessary.

Why bring John here? she thought. Why bring twisted fragments of my past into a place I'm only using to shun that past?

She decided to let him talk, observing him leisurely, as she drank the Latino concoction.

She learned he was from Nicaragua. That was surprising, given his tall stature. He was also a war veteran. He had been part of the Coalition of the Willing, a United States-led multi-national force meant to support war efforts in Iraq in 2003. He had trained to be part of Spain's special force unit, and had been deployed four times to western Asia.

A military man, she thought, now understanding the physique she had played with all night. He proudly showed her pictures of his two tours, pictures of him, his companions, and also, oddly enough, graphic pictures of his victims. She chose not to enquire, unsure what to think. He was in the military. He was trained to tolerate the intolerable, after all, she rationalized.

After Spain's withdrawal from the Coalition in 2004, he explained, he returned to Nicaragua and abandoned the military to attend law school.

"I hated it," he shared with her, his eyes squinting. "The students, their cockiness, their lack of modesty. I had to quit. I didn't belong."

She observed him, detailing his arched brows, gently caressing the bridge of his nose with her index finger, as he added that he had then, immediately left to immigrate to the United States.

"My future is here," he stated, while biting her finger.

Placing her cup on the floor, she reached for his neck, interlocking her fingers around its nape. She pulled him in closer and, eyes wide open, kissed him softly.

She wanted more, and once again they slid violently into one another, for what felt like a luscious eternity. He loved her backside. The sight of her marbled white and red ass caused him to almost instantly release. As for her, the added intensity of it all had now swallowed her vagina, most likely excised her clitoris, and inflated her inner lips.

The roughness of their lovemaking was taking its toll on her body. To welcome any type of roughness was atypical for her. It was foreign to her fantasies and absent from her sexual playbook. She was now discovering her ability to cling to pain as a gateway to pleasure, and seemed to need it more than she had ever needed anything.

The more her nerve endings were awakened by the pain, the further she stood from her complicated life.

He climaxed uncontrollably over her back with what would become his signature warning sign, a softly held hissing sound. It paved the way to his escape, as well as hers.

Their heads were both spinning, and she could sense their infatuation with one another setting in. They could have shared more information about themselves, but what would have been the point? They would have retained nothing.

They emerged, naked, from the bedroom, and walked through his house. Isabelle now seeing it in all its ugly tastelessness. He lived on a street called Blackwell. Looking around, she wondered if he had taken the theme a little too far. The inattention to color, décor, and aesthetics conveyed a clear message, this was a funeral parlor, or at best, a man-cave. Evidence of disorganization was everywhere, from the mismatched tableware inside the glass kitchen cabinets, to the tools scattered on the floor and stacked on an old wooden dining room table.

Aside from the bathroom, the outdated kitchen was probably the most disconcerting space in the house. The brown cupboards were filled with an array of Goya products and canned processed foods that had been carelessly placed on the shelves. The stainless-steel refrigerator was marked with grease and dried-up food. Isabelle had an urge to open it. Inside, a display of equally unkempt products, almost certainly alive with bacteria. Repulsed, she quickly closed the door.

In lieu of curtains, thick brown cloths covered the only kitchen window, preventing any light from piercing the room. She opened them, wanting life to warm the coolness of the space.

"I hate my neighbors," he said, closing them back firmly. Startled by the contempt he displayed, she turned away from his eyes and sipped from her water bottle, dismissing her unease.

Choosing to ignore the repulsiveness of her surroundings, she let him lift her up and sit her, still naked, on the kitchen counter. Her physical discomfort was immense. Every fiber of her body was paralyzed by the cold air, the backs of her thighs resisting the iciness of the surface they were resting on. From this vantage point, she took him in, studying every detail of his naked brown body. He was standing facing the kitchen sink, displaying himself in only sandals. She bit into a slice of apple he handed her from the tip of his knife. His eyes had changed, holding nothing she could translate, appearing only to exist. She sustained them, as fright somewhat resurfaced and fed her growing nervousness. For a moment, she felt the need to get dressed, take her overnight bag and flee.

As she swallowed her apple slice, he playfully took her hand and led her to the living room. She could see his brown leather couch waiting for them. He placed a dry towel on the couch, as he had done on the bed the night before. Then, he laid her down on the protected couch and positioned her onto her stomach. She obeyed, knowing she wanted this as much as he did. This was now purely sexual fun, exactly what she had signed up for.

As he slowly kissed her neck, the roughness of his hands teased her thighs. He whispered to her that he had not been with a woman in ten months. Motioning back and forth with her knees and forearms digging into the cushion for stability, she kept wondering how such a potent sexual being could have possibly withheld his carnal hunger that long.

The edge of the afternoon transformed itself into dusk. They had now showered and were contemplating their next steps. Her lover had offered her to stay another night. Deciding to stay was easy, and easy was all she wanted. That, and food to sustain her physical activity.

CHAPTER EIGHT

What about a getaway? I asked John. Cape Cod or New York? It would be good for us. We could leave Alice at Pauline's and leave for four days. I smiled at this man, my husband, sitting there, across the table, me wanting more.

Desire. Fluidity. Movement.

Please, soon, a river of it.

I sipped my coffee and looked at him. I noticed the bags under his eyes had darkened, blueish half-moons that won't leave anymore; panda brown colored eyes framed by bristle-like lashes and sparse brows that gave his face an albino feel. I took him in, the sight of him now, and the sight of him then—when we'd first met, younger, vibrant, athletic, and promising of a life, a full one. A fair one.

Slouched behind his computer, he typed on, impassible, placid as always, the obvious there to see—the way he barely moved, unresponsive to what I was really asking him. Are you aware, John, that we are here standing at this invisible junction, of what is waiting for us if you look away? Will we survive our story, its destination? His eyes, an obsession of mine, almond shapes that pressed against his cheeks like a finger pokes risen bread dough. Just below them, touching the back of his ears, his parotids, glands overactivated by the use of alcohol. Not a chipmunk, I thought. More like a bullfrog.

And I stayed. Because even crumbs of love does its thing and tethers you to the relevant past, the good of it, to memories that are meaningful. Valuable.

I had them still.

I demand that you care, I thought, about me.

Don't leave us.

Behind his computer, I saw his head lift, his fingers stretching to touch his Blackberry. All right, he said, Cape Cod.

We sped along the I-95 through a morning that felt loaded with more than mist, fog, and tentative sun rays. John's hands were glued to the steering wheel. I caught sight of his knuckles. They were of a yellow that faded into specks of white. Had I scrutinized his jaw, I would have seen it just as compact, and just as stiff. But I didn't.

Are you tired, my love? I asked.

He looked at me, no, he said.

Jet-lagging was his only true sport, I reminded myself, the only one he excelled at. That's what he did best, move and travel to places that would remain unknown, like him, never really landing anywhere, finding comfort in zones so broad and so loose it allowed him to belong to nothing.

To no one, and to remain out of sight.

So he thought.

The bed and breakfast was located mid-Cape, facing the not too far away sea. The house that greeted us as we turned into the driveway was covered by grey shingles that meshed with the sky's gloominess. As I stepped from the car, my eyes caught a glimpse of John, phone in hand.

Business, he said.

I dawdled to the door, feeling rested, breathing in the salty air. I smiled to myself. Finally, some time alone, together.

And maybe …

We climbed the stairs, luggage in tow, and reached the door to our room, number 11. As we entered, I started to laugh. We can't afford to fall off, I told John, pointing to the bed. We both stared at the height of it, its massiveness, and he joined me in genuine laughter. The mattress and its box spring, four feet from the ground, were framed by a pale wooden structure, each bed post, almost touching the ceiling. The bed cover, blue toned and dotted by a myriad of pink-colored flowers, barely reassured in its frivolity. I placed my carryon on the bed, noting how narrow it was.

A double bed. It made me smile.

Okay, said John, as he stepped out of the washroom, time for lunch, Province Town.

The getaway lasted three days, a time filled with clam chowders and lobster rolls and walks by the beach and long drives when at times, my hand held his, and his mine. This time together, as humans bonded by children who loved us, friends who looked up to the strength we exuded, mothers and fathers and sisters and brothers who believed in us—this time, together, as a couple, would be our last.

That night, the window was opened, the curtains pushed by the soft breeze coming from the sea. I slid closer to John whose back was staring at me. I let my hands glide to the warmth of his groin, slowly, wanting him.

He gently removed my hand, and whispered goodnight.

Before leaving for pizza that evening, they felt the need to renew their sexual play. Disbelieving her own obedience, Isabelle let her body collide with his, absorbing her escalating physical tension. His weapon of choice, his untamed, powerful, and unforgiving mouth. She drew him back into herself, guided by the softness of his directive touch. To her surprise and delight, she let him penetrate all of her, wherever possible. Why had she avoided, with such disgust and apprehension, the sensory pleasure of having her backside filled entirely by a man?

Toying around his penis with her tongue, she lapped the leftovers of his passage into her, surprised by his extreme saltiness, a novelty to her palate. She stroked, licked, and sucked with purpose. She had a desire to execute and the want to please at any cost. She lifted her head and brought herself on top of him, sliding herself onto him, rocking to a rhythm she was now setting. There she stayed, squatting in motion, playing with herself. She was unaware, careless, and unhinged, until she came.

Flipping her onto her back, he plunged his mouth between her legs, tasting with abandon the juice she had produced, her milk, as he would call it. There, she lowered her arms, fully extending them towards the top of his shoulders, letting her hands linger across the length of his trapeze, mindlessly rubbing against a deep indent her curious fingers had discovered. Suddenly, she felt his muscles stiffen, as he lifted his head to meet her eyes. "Never, ever scratch my back again," he let out in between his teeth.

"Scratch?" she asked, disconcerted. Had I not simply caressed his skin? she thought, wisely keeping it to herself.

"Yes," he simply stated. "I hate it." He then brought his face back to hers, opened his mouth, and unloaded their mixture into the bottom of her throat, shutting her up, and shutting her out. She stared at him, her own stranger. However odd this man appeared to be, he was hers to toy with, hers to play with, hers to use as a means to get even with John.

Surrendering to their rhythm seemed her only option. At this point, with intruding images of her painful reality imposing themselves on her, all she could think of was to fuck away the pain and compel the healing to start. She had become the main character of a Lars von Trier movie. She was Breaking the Wave's new heroine, fucking her pain into oblivion.

Shaken by the thrust of her new lover, she was seeing sex as a celebratory healing power. She identified the need to be brutalized as a way to protect her own physical and mental sanity. Her insides were burning and tingling, and even though they were swollen and red, she wanted more.

She wanted to fuck into obscurity. Pound into darkness. Until feeling, if ever possible again, the touch of different days coming.

But would they? The sun upon her face ...

She touched her face.

A hope, she thought, that lasts.

A hope, that does not fade away.

CHAPTER NINE

Alice, before leaving Taipei, had collided with a new truth—her own, in fact. At the end of her academic year at Taipei American School, she discovered the theater and recognized she had a penchant for acting. More importantly, her undeniable talent for this newfound passion had been acknowledged by her theater teacher, surprising both John and me.

Alice had decided on her career path, she would study theater and focus on becoming an actor.

A choice that made me happy–more traveling, more time with my girl.

New York and London were immediately targeted as cities with theater schools we would consider. The upcoming American Thanksgiving break from school was offering Alice and me an opportunity to visit London, "a window to better breath", whatever that meant. I also had realized that one of John's favorite bands, Simple Minds, was playing at the London O2 arena. During our stay in Taipei, we had followed their tour, playing around with the idea of attending their concert in Berlin, Munich, Amsterdam, or Paris. Animated with pure joy, I went ahead and bought three tickets.

Before leaving for London, a certain lightness, a euphoria even, had settled in my stomach, caressing its insides. The turmoil that had so far marked the onset of my arrival in New England, was soothed by a feeling of softness that startled me, not because of the rarity of its experience, but because of the premonition I felt it carried. It was the promise of a change, I, so far, did not know I had desired.

We arrived in London for eight days of visiting campuses, shopping, sightseeing, and catching up with some old friends we had not seen in over five years.

Our travels in London would be punctuated by an outing with our good friends, Laure and Beatrice, an outing that would reveal a desire that I had never acknowledged before. One night, while Beatrice and Alice decided to stay in and prepare their own meal at the Chelsea flat, Laure and I opted to eat at her local pub just three minutes from the flat. The night was a cool one and the rain had stopped and I remember taking Laure's arm and bringing it tightly to my side. I must admit I had missed her, her spunkiness, her French abrasiveness, her arrogance. All of it.

The pub we entered was filled with animated voices, alive with the myriad of human connections taking place. The air was hazy, with an almost ethereal quality. I was convinced sparkles of human energy were floating in the air, as if enveloping our bodies with warmth.

The pub was a local establishment, a place meant for people to share and bond, a focal point pulling the members of a community together, to meet, rejoice, and bereave. There, I felt a sense of belonging anchoring within me. A sense of belonging I had missed dearly.

I had removed myself from its embrace when I had left Montreal, and, to a lesser extent, when I had left Taipei. Aching for its healing touch, I was immediately seduced by the convivial atmosphere of the pub. I felt high on life. There in London, with a good friend, I felt worldly. And still, that feeling of desire that tormented my stomach, a sensation that I had been transporting, was ever so present. This time though, it screamed a little louder, a little longer, tugging at something, firmly.

We chose a table not far from the bar. The menu was a classic one, comparable to any Parisian bistro. Its alter ego. I ordered monkfish on a bed of lentils, as did Laure. Laure was the eternal dieter, calculating her portions, her calories, her pleasures. I could not resist and ordered a bottle of Beaujolais.

To hell with the migraines, I told myself as I looked up at the waiter serving me my plate. Tall, lean, dark-haired with dark brown eyes, he had to have been Italian or Spanish. And there it happened. I sustained his glance, much longer than I wished, much longer than I thought myself capable of doing. A moment that surprised me. What had he seen? My initial reaction was to make light of this non-verbal interaction Laure had discreetly noticed. Seated diagonally to the bar, I caught a glimpse of him, his silhouette, drying glasses. I could not resist and gave into the pull, the pull to slightly turn my head in his direction, while feigning to be a good listener to Laure's family issues. Finally, he lifted his head and met my gaze. The desire that emerged whipped me, not by its violence, but by the familiarity of its violence, its meaning remaining opaque. Chaos filled my head as I tried to decipher what his smile held. The smile I returned would remain there, at the bottom of my stomach, the place where my secret wants accumulated

Sitting on the toilet relieving herself, feeling unsettled by her lack of bearings, Isabelle heard him say, "Are you hungry?"

She looked at him, standing diagonally to her, washing his penis with peroxide. Something she had never seen a man do before. How odd, she had thought.

"Sure," she replied, realizing she had barely eaten anything all day. She quickly washed up, slipped on her clothes, and hopped into his 2003 silver Mazda 3.

As they drove, she began to discover the streets of his working class Latino neighborhood. What a contrast to her reality. Everywhere she looked, tightly bound and unfinished houses welcomed her eyes, their ungroomed cemented yards, a vision of very real poverty. Some houses were missing sidings while others had been protected by plastic tarps in lieu of windows. Old cars displaying their twisted metal frames seemed to abound, sharing their space with overfilled garbage cans. As they drove to the pizza parlor, she understood that she had landed her posh ass in a ghetto. A Latino one. For a moment, feelings of anguish resurfaced as she repeated to herself that this place was not for her and that this improvised voyage into a universe she didn't know existed was simply a transitory event meant to mute her fears. Yet, walking into his favorite pizza joint, she felt at ease. It had a simplicity and an anonymity that somehow felt appealing. She had been seduced by its simplicity

She stayed by his side, standing, resting her head on his shoulder, listening to him order their pizza. She lifted her head and stared at him, tired, while feeling his sperm come down between her inner lips and land in her panties. No longer able to resist his physical pull, feeling flustered, she walked to the bench facing the counter and sat down. She observed him interact, move and talk with the cashier. Her lack of sleep, excitement, adrenaline, and desire were all mixed together, making her dizzy. Her cheeks, flushed with unmistakable redness, were warning her, she most likely would be facing another sleepless night.

When they got back to his house, they set the table, poured themselves some red wine and ate their pizza in relative silence. She could tell his eyes were dissecting her, the way she held her pizza, the manner in which she held the stem of her glass.

"I love your hands," he suddenly blurted out, with seriousness. She looked at him, her mouth full, ignoring how to integrate a compliment no one had ever given her before.

"You want help with the dishes?" she asked, while finishing her last bite.

"Nope," he said, standing up, taking her hand firmly.

For the better part of the night and most of the following day, they barely exchanged any words. When she was finally ready to leave, she gathered her things and walked with him to her car. Evening had set in, the darkness firmly implanted in the sky. He kissed her softly goodbye, gazed into her eyes, and closed the car door.

The goodbye was a natural one, offering the promise of nothing. A tacit understanding that their meeting had been just that—a meeting of two bodies. And yet, her heart tightened.

She suspected his did as well.

As she drove, she thought, falling in love—falling in lust, even, had not been the purpose of her getaway.

INHALED

But was she?
Either one of those things?
She didn't know.
She did know, she couldn't stop thinking about him.

CHAPTER TEN

The familiar cold I missed so much while in Taipei was now manifesting itself in Northampton, confirming December had finally arrived. That morning, I woke up feeling rested, after a rare, uninterrupted sleep. I knew my body had benefited from this undisturbed flow of deep sleep, as I felt the thrust of newfound energy within the sensitive fibers of my muscles.

I had suffered from chronic migraines and fibromyalgia for the last ten years, a condition, that, while in Taiwan, had been exacerbated by the country's humid weather. There, pain had defined my existence, gluing me to the bed one third of the time, when I was not hospitalized to treat my status migraines. Taipei Veterans General Hospital became my second home, a place where my visions of a welcomed death and the flow of suicidal thoughts were halted by the administration of dexamethasone delivered though intravenous therapy. Gradually, once I had moved to Northampton, my pain, while still part of my everyday life, had become manageable, rendering me almost functional.

Magically, that morning, the usual aches and pain greeting me at the onset of each day were temporarily absent from my body, and would not, I hoped, interfere with the promise of an active day. My back felt supple, my neck was mobile, and my head was pain free. The challenge was to not overdo it.

John was scheduled to arrive in three days, after a six-week trip to Asia. This last trip had been unusually long, considering he had already spent so much time there prior to our move. It occurred to me, that since our arrival in North America, at the beginning of August, he had spent a total of twelve weeks away from home. These separations had become constants in our lives, but this time felt different. I knew he had to meet some important work deadlines, and it was understood, this was going to be the last big push, before a lengthy separation would be imposed on us.

The twelve weeks spent alone with the children had been particularly difficult ones. I had managed to finalize the move with little, or no help. Plagued by daily fatigue, I assisted Alice, then sixteen years-old, in adjusting to a new school, and had also cared for Catherine, helping her with her anxiety and depression. I was feeling overwhelmed.

That morning I rushed to the spa in Hadley, a town adjacent to Northampton. I had to tend to that bushy bikini line of mine. Even though sex was declining in quality and quantity with John, I had thought, who knows, maybe a little spark will hit my stomach and a desire to fuck would follow.

Driving back to Northampton, I felt that same high reemerge, the high so difficult to understand, the floating sensation that had been with me, intermittently, since October. It was a feeling of aliveness I did not want to question, as it, too, was a feeling I had seldom experienced. I primarily lived alone with my daughter, in a strange place, while my husband was mostly gone, far away. I had not made time yet to establish myself, develop friendships, discover the surroundings, or partake in any of Alice's school activities. It was then, while appreciating the fullness of the moment that I decided now was going to be the starting point of my new life. I headed to one of the many local coffee shops, armed with my laptop, alert, attentive to my surroundings, acutely connected to my mind and my senses.

The coffee shop was a small, locally-owned venue serving perfect macchiatos, and homemade pastries. I had just discovered the shop's existence the previous day, while familiarizing myself with Northampton's quaint downtown establishments. With unexpected lightheartedness, and yes, flirtatiousness, I placed my order with the young student at the cash register. I remember thinking this was a good feeling to draw from.

INHALED

I opened my laptop in the coffee shop, like I had done so many years ago while writing my thesis. I was finally giving myself permission to try something new. I was finally carving myself a space to live, and maybe even thrive. I was allowing myself to play with the writing ideas I had briefly explored while in Taiwan.

Two hours into my first day as a writer, I checked my watch. It was now 3:00 p.m., time to pick up my daughter from school.

Driving was now becoming an enjoyable activity. I was traveling sixty miles a day on Massachusetts roads, transporting Alice to and from school. I had no choice but to tame my fear of driving, especially my fear of driving at night. Living in the country where deer sightings were part of everyday life, John and I had decided on the purchase of a Mercedes Benz truck, a logical choice that granted me the feeling of safety and protection. This car would become my true sanctuary, a place where music would become my only faithful, and non-judgmental companion. The songs were my sanity, paving the way in, unleashing the debris that clogged my thinking, allowing me to better understand their meaning. There, in my Mercedes truck, music would make sense of my life.

Driving home with Alice, I was now speeding through an obscurity that had transposed itself inside the car, caressed by the soft pinkish glow of the car's interior ambient light. The chat between Alice and I was light and happy, interrupted only by our renditions of the Christmas music being played on the radio. Her voice brimming with relief, she described how she was satisfied with her overall performance at school and shared her delight at the thought of spending Christmas surrounded by the whiteness of snow. Purchasing a real Christmas tree was going to be the highlight of the upcoming week. For that, we were going to wait for John's return.

To celebrate the end of her first semester, we decided to dine at the Chinese restaurant located on Main Street. Alice and I both missed Taiwan—its vibrancy, its people, its food—and mostly, we missed John.

That evening, a delicious mother-daughter outing unfolded peacefully. We laughed and shared memories of our lives in Asia. I knew I had wanted to synchronize myself to John's reality, whatever reality was unfolding for him at that exact moment in time. Dumplings, tofu, and fried rice had become, childishly, in my mind, a gateway to him and his life. I had consciously decided to seek his rhythm, his pulse, his heartbeat, while one million miles away from him, certain of the magical power of my intent. Little did I know how far from the truth I had been standing, how my life's direction was forever going to change.

Arriving in the driveway, a burst of anger emerged from within me, gripping me at my throat, recognizing, yet again, the singularity of my situation. I felt the stings of isolation poking at my vulnerabilities. I cursed my husband for relying on me so heavily, and myself for explicitly condoning his absence.

As Alice and I entered the house, Jackson greeted us, expecting to be fed. In typical fashion, my daughter, ignoring her dog's needs, rushed to her room, eager to charge her iPhone. I dived into my Facebook page, telling myself I would attend to Jackson in a few minutes.

Quickly scanning my newsfeed, stopping only where I deemed necessary, I noticed I had received a message request from a Mandarin account. The Mandarin characters spelled the name, Xiao Hua: Little Flower. I got up to make myself some tea, returned, and accepted the message. I did not think anything of it, as I had many Taiwanese friends, and had coached a few people in Taipei as well.

As I brought the celadon cup of tea to my lips, two collages, totaling 16 photos, appeared on my screen. Cup in hand, I stared, not understanding what I was looking at.

I do not know how long I stayed seated, coat still on, fixated on the images. Time had not stopped, no, it had delicately overstretched itself until it had finally snapped. I must have called for Alice. I do not really remember, but that is what she would later tell me. When she came in and looked at the screen, her reaction was instantaneous, loudly inhaling through her mouth, her gasp crystallizing the truth in the present, realizing what I had failed to understand. She fled to her room, while I remained sitting at my computer with the on-screen images assaulting my eyes. Once I realized she had fled, I quickly ran to her room. As I opened the door, I shrieked at the sight that greeted me, she had buried her face in a pillow to buffer her cries, blood everywhere on the white bedding. It was flowing from her nose, where the capillaries, unable to sustain the pressure—the new added pressure—had burst. Guttural sounds inundated the room. Stunned, I stayed there, paralyzed, still uncertain of what had just happened.

I gave Alice a sedative before trying to reach John. It was 8:00 p.m. Friday. That meant it was 9:00 a.m. Saturday in Taipei. I felt a rush of adrenaline coursing through my veins. At the same time, I felt my breathing become shallow, constricting my chest, feeding a newly felt sense of dizziness. Frantically, I walked through the house in circles, retrieving a phone only to set it down and misplace it again. Finally, after thirty minutes, my hand shaking, I dialed John's number. He did not answer.

I emailed my Montreal friends. They were my pillars. Their presence had cut through the distance imposed by living in Asia. They had been there for me when Catherine's ordeal had shaken my life, providing me with an emotional outlet while in Taipei. Here again, I let them know what had occurred. I let them know another shitstorm was possibly pointing itself across my horizon. Even the most compassionate of them could not settle my mind. They knew, just as I did, that there was only one way to interpret what I had seen.

It was not until the next morning that John finally called back. That call became the start of a long, tedious, and frustrating process, marked by the trickling down of information. Even then, when faced with the opportunity to correct the faulty process that fueled the impending disclosure, my husband chose to distort and omit vital information.

On the morning of December 14th, Alice left for school, leaving me three hours to brace for my husband's return from Taipei. In those three hours, I mindlessly cleaned the house, took a shower, dried my hair, and put on some makeup. I even took a selfie and hash-tagged it on Instagram as #freshwound. It was my first hashtag, and it served to highlight my uncertainty, and apprehensions. I felt the need to capture the moment, to immortalize my pain, to document my own social study of it. I knew I needed to remember the visual consequences the fear of his betrayal painted on my face. When John arrived at the front door, the dog greeted him with great excitement and affection. It was a sad contrast to my demeanor. And John, from the sixteen hour flight, thirteen hour time change, and three hour drive from the airport, was drained of all color. My physical appearance, with my puffy eyes and dried, peeling lips, was not much better. I had been crying without restraint, unable to stop. As he made his way inside with his bags, I focused on making tea, using my favorite celadon cups. Together, and not so long ago, we had bought those cups at the oldest teahouse in Taipei. Celadon pottery had truly caught my attention when we were traveling throughout Southeast Asia. Its satiny finish, brightness, and fragility made tea-drinking an even more enjoyable experience. Its ritualistic components had been associated with a pull to surrender, with the need to sink into the present, something I was unsuccessfully trying to achieve, there with John. I chose to brew my favorite tea leaves, Oriental Beauty, an odd selection considering the context. Absentminded, I had failed to catch the irony my choice was revealing. While the sweet honey-like flavor of this tea had always seduced me, it would forever now be associated with grief and despair, and ironically, John's own personalized version of oriental beauty. Bitterness was setting in.

I placed the tray carrying the small iron kettle and two cups on the dinner table beside the computer. I instructed him to sit, and demanded he explain himself, suddenly feeling grounded. The story he fed me was that the pictures I had seen were taken by a barmaid who had been smitten with him.

"You know how they are," he told me. "They love to take pictures of anything and anyone, at any time."

It was true. Nowhere else on the planet could you witness individuals so obsessed with capturing moments they were barely even experiencing. This phenomenon, just emerging in the western world at the time, was already rampant in Asia.

"So, OK," I had thought to myself, "fair enough."

John continued, claiming she had sent me the pictures in retaliation of his apparent refusal to date her. A few obvious questions popped into my brain. How did she know my name? And more importantly, what led her to think dating my husband was ever an option?

For a moment, I felt the story was a plausible one. I could have believed his version of events entirely, had I not seen the pictures. I did smile at the thought. The man said he avoided all presence on social media. John, the fake account owner, the denier of progress, the pretender, would be betrayed by his own fear.

Those pictures offered a different account of the alleged events, suggesting the existence of an alternative narrative. For that reason, I asked to know the context within which each photo had been taken. I saw my husband entertain the thought of pushing back for a split second. He had paused, looking into my eyes, his discouragement embedded in his own. I gave him no choice but to explain himself, to shed some light on the "mystery".

The first picture was clearly taken on a train. The selfie showed her pressing her chin against his right shoulder, their foreheads slightly touching. "Think nothing of it," he said. "We were on our way to a hotpot in Schinshu with a group of Taiwanese friends."

While not completely incriminating, the physical proximity they comfortably displayed was unsettling to see. The second picture was similar to the first. It seemed to reveal evidence of a bond between them—a warm, enveloping bond. He told me the photo was taken outside of the bar she owned: The Pink Lotus. "A fucking bar," I repeated to myself. "Of course, that would do the trick." I was starting to understand, looking at John. The third picture, another selfie, showed them posing together, joined affectionately at the temple. She was wearing Asian-trendy fake eyelashes and bright pink lip gloss. My husband, donning the George Clooney scruffy-look, displayed soft eyes and a genuine smile.

John's explanations at this point were no longer important or relevant. My brain knew the truth, only my heart was now fighting. The fourth picture put a sword in my heart, and because of its existence, because of its revelation, my life's course would be permanently altered. Artfully captured by the photographer, it was a black-and-white photo of an intimate, tender moment between John and the woman, a glimpse into a sanctuary belonging to two lovers oblivious to the world around them.

"Explain?" I asked firmly, pointing to the devastating photo.

"We were both drunk," he nervously replied. "The conversation around us was rapidly paced," he continued. "Someone in our group asked a question, and we simultaneously gave the same answer. It's the custom to rub noses when this happens," he added, sternly.

I stared at him, trying to wrap my head around this novel cultural ritual that had apparently escaped me while living in Taipei.

I skipped the fifth picture depicting him with a bird on his shoulder in what, I assumed, was his apartment. The sixth picture featured the woman alone in a heavily edited selfie. She was lying on her back, wearing a blue hoodie, with her hair tied in two ponytails. Her lips were painted a pinkish orange and her skin was shiny, devoid of any imperfections.

"Flawlessly photo shopped," I thought. The arrogant bitch had placed that picture in the middle of the collage as if to tell me she was now the heart of John's life, the central presence responsible for the mayhem that she had unchained.

"Where was this picture taken?" I asked, irritated.

"Inside her apartment," he replied instantaneously.

"What do you mean, her apartment?" I screamed. "How the fuck would you know?" I asked him, feeling a sudden warmth travelling to my face. I knew that I had to stay calm, that I had to stay alert. I took a deep breath and willed some form of quietness into the whole of my body. And so, with momentary restraint, I observed him. He looked straight into my eyes and paused. I could feel the energy leaving his body. I could see his strength fading into a dark corner. I could detect panic seizing him, seizing his chest, his throat and his mouth. He purposefully let the silence rest on his shoulders, allowing himself a moment to think. He was trying to buy time, not allowing enough for it to become the counselor time had the potential to be.

"I had a fling," he blurted out, eyes unflinching.

"A fling?" I asked, understanding quickly I had been right all along.

"Yes. A small one," he whispered. "We kissed three or four times."

A small one.

As if.

Livid, I directed my eyes back to the collage. Instinctively, I knew his confession was false. I got up slowly, looking for something, needing to shake the unsettling feelings assaulting my brain. My eyes spotted the baseball bat. I picked it up without hesitation and started to walk around the living room under John's fearful gaze. I quickly scanned the room and sketched the path of destruction I wanted to follow.

All John's beloved art pieces were displayed in the den of our shitty plastic house. My first target was the cheap-looking, but expensive pair of gold-plated Chinese lions we bought in Yingge. I then turned to a bamboo-framed cherry blossom tree and readily smashed it to pieces. I then shattered a Taiwanese trinket, the tacky kind only an uneducated tourist like John would buy. The shards of glass were now raining down onto the den floor and sliding across the floor's synthetic finish.

Ironically, the week before, I had watched a Japanese movie where the heroine saw a picture of herself cut in identical squares and randomly repositioned to form a Picasso-like mosaic. It had struck me as an attempt to communicate the advent of change, an indication that somehow, somewhere, a point of no return had been reached, life permanently altered, demanding a decision, commanding an action. In this reformatting of reality, I had seen the configuration of a new perspective, a new life statement. I was drawn by the novel point of departure it held, pulled by the potential for change it carried, inspiring me to create my own change. I thought of our large wedding photo portrait tucked away in the garage, encased in a flowery, golden Victorian frame. In this photo, I was tenderly holding my husband's arm, our eyes lovingly gazing into the photographer's aperture. I had planned to go to my local arts and crafts store and get the material necessary to execute the rearrangement of this portrait. I, too, would cut the picture into identical squares and redispose them into a message of marital dissatisfaction, a plea to renew ourselves, our marriage, our commitment.

I had intended to surprise John, by using art as a means of communicating, and using my creativity to devise a therapeutic moment. Instead, I calmly walked to the kitchen and retrieved the Japanese knife I had bought for myself in Tokyo. Returning to the den after retrieving the framed wedding picture from the garage, I stabbed its heart violently, sending more glass fragments to the floor. I felt nonexistent.

I made it quite clear that John was not going to sleep at home and that we would conduct our discussions away from Alice's ears. He would stay at the Holiday Inn Express located five miles from our house and from there, clarity would hopefully emerge, shedding light on the drama.

During the three days following John's move to the hotel, his alleged groupie, Xiao Hua, called him to assess the damages she hoped she had caused. He shared with me the content of her inquiries in the hope it would showcase his newfound transparency.

"How can a few kisses justify such a presence in his life, such an intrusion still?" I asked myself, confused.

I went on living in a continuous daze, interacting with my daughter with surprising calm and contained emotions. I was not sure how she was holding up. She kept silent, her observant self in full mode, fiercely ignoring John, watching me navigate through a pain I was managing to internalize. I knew I had to wait for the right moment to address her feelings. I guessed that horrendous collage had been rapidly filed in a virtual drawer inside her mind. She would need to open it, sooner or later.

Lying on my bed, I phoned my husband at his hotel. I had, in front of me, the photos sent to me by his "want-to-be" girlfriend. I kept analyzing each and every detail they contained.

"I just kissed her three times," I recalled him telling me.

Crying heavily, I said to him, I suspect there's been more between the two of them.

"I assure you," he said, "there was nothing more than three or four shared kisses."

Not convinced and still crying, I hung up, curled myself into a ball, and tried to find sleep.

The next morning, my mind was still racing over the meaning of those pictures. I put on my bathrobe and went outside to call John again. Alice was inside, and I wanted to protect her from the distress I knew my voice carried. I was again probing my husband for better answers, pressing him for more information. And, finally, the abscess was pierced.

"I had a six month affair," he revealed from the safety of his hotel room.

How ironic that even though he had come back home to Northampton to divulge his affair face-to-face, I was still informed by phone. He claimed that was the very thing he had wanted to avoid. That was John though, always landing beside the target.

Through the tears, the sobs, and the curses, I slipped back inside and rapidly climbed the few stairs to my room. I put on a pair of pants, threw on a coat, got into my car and drove to the hotel. On my way there, I called the only person I could think of at the time, my mother. Somehow, I managed to drive through the veil of flowing tears, while informing her of what had happened. She was set to arrive by plane the next day to celebrate Christmas with us. It was a trip that had been planned since November.

"I will be there for you," she had said. "You'll see. I'll give him a good shake. He'll listen to me."

Whatever, I had thought to myself. "He may listen to you, but it is I who will no longer listen—to anyone."

When I got to John's hotel room, I launched at him with fury. All the rage, the hurt, the disbelief I felt was channeling through my hands, my fingers, my nails. The strength I suddenly had, momentarily seized my attention precisely when my fingernails tore into the flesh of his neck.

He screamed.

I punched, I screamed, then scratched the side of his face. Homemade souvenirs that would never leave–tattoos made of betrayal that would never fade.

I kicked the hotel furniture. I threw random items at the wall and cried without restraint or concern for the other hotel guests.

Hurt legitimizing hurt.

Knowing I was coming, John had arranged a call with a psychologist he'd sought out during the three days he was at the hotel. Evidently, he had expected the truth to surface and hit me.

And it did.

The psychologist tried his best to make me understand that whatever pain I was feeling was due to the trauma I was experiencing.

"Really?" I mockingly asked him.

"Yes," he said, in an attempt to normalize my reaction.

My suffering, however, was annihilating my mind. I could not breathe properly. I could not focus. Assholes, I thought. Both of them—ignorant assholes.

It was 9:30 p.m. Sunday evening when Isabelle arrived home, having been gone two nights.

These nights of her awakening.

Revenge, she told herself.

She walked into the house, Alice and John were watching the Golden Globes, and she sensed the mood was unnaturally silent, but she welcomed it with relief, feeling certain no one would upset her. Her husband had tried reaching her throughout the weekend, and she had reassured him through text that she was safe and secure, somewhere in Massachusetts.

"Where did you go?" he asked.

"Cape Cod," she lied to him. "A small bed and breakfast by the beach."

"Funny," he retorted sarcastically. "There's no sand on your high heel boots."

She bent down and looked at her suede boots. There, where no one could see her face, she smiled. She looked up into his eyes and demanded he stop asking questions, containing her urge to laugh. "You can accept my answers or ignore them," she replied, with a straight face, going on to insist that she would not be harassed or bombarded with further questions.

Her dog Jackson, whose brain wires were exclusively connected to his nose, offered a different challenge, as he kept planting his snout in her groin. Busted by her dog, in front of both her daughter and her husband, she feigned to ignore him. Nonetheless, she pushed him away firmly as she rambled on about the winners and losers of the Golden Globes. But, he kept coming back. Ignoring John's reaction, she quickly grabbed her overnight bag and brought it upstairs to her room. There, she undressed, put her clothes in the laundry bin and firmly closed its top. She walked into the bathroom and locked the door. She ran hot water into the bathtub, and stepped in.

She hated the thought of having to scrub away the smell of her sexual encounter, the souvenirs still lingering on her skin. But, she had no choice, as she began to reconnect slowly with the signals her body had tried to send her in vain over the weekend. Her lower belly was aching from the ardent pounding it had met, his unbridled thrusts inflaming her insides. During the course of her escapade, she had barely eaten, but worse, had not hydrated herself sufficiently.

As she stepped out of the bathtub to relieve herself, she felt her urine trickling down slowly and painfully. Dark and smelly, she knew she had contracted a nasty urinary tract infection. Furthermore, her vagina was raw, in excruciating pain, unable to withstand contact with her underwear. She felt like a locked-up Ferrari, one that has just been rediscovered, and given the opportunity to perform to its potential. Although her engine had felt rusty, the breaks had been the real problem. They had failed.

Stepping out of the bathroom into her bedroom, she caught her full reflection in the hallway mirror, and jumped at the sight of her bruised skin. There was the indisputable evidence of his teeth on her neck, her shoulders, her back and her arms. She started to laugh uncontrollably, almost madly. She had never had, nor given, hickies. Turtlenecks and scarves would be her chosen attire for the week. Winter, her ally.

CHAPTER ELEVEN

I felt as though I had stepped outside of my body, only to see myself as a discarded piece of human material. It was as if I was melting into a black hole, disappearing, unable to keep together the pieces of my existence. Deep down, however, I knew that even if I could have held them together, it was now pointless. These parts of me could no longer fit into the puzzle that my life had now become, not that I had any idea what this new life was going to be like.

I was experiencing, with abrupt honesty, the multi-layers of pain and grief that had been drilled into my body. I was mourning my sense of reality, my sense of truth. Parting with the perceptions I held about the solidity of my union, letting go of the innocence that was lost to all the members of my family. I was bereaving each and every element I thought structured my commitment to John, striking at my balance. Pulling me to the edge of my worst apprehensions, was the visceral, blood-chilling fear of pursuing my life alone. At that moment of realization, I had wished, with all my heart, that I could dissociate from my mind, my body. I had hoped that a feeling of numbness would gain momentum and disperse itself through every part of my body.

Give me numbness, or give me death, I had prayed. Those had become my only Christmas wishes.

I had originally been waiting for John's homecoming before adding the final touches to our holiday plans. Catherine was remaining in Buenos Aires to spend Christmas with her new Argentinian boyfriend and his family. At that point, she was unaware of the family drama unfolding. Still very much fragile, there was no reason for me to share what would most likely crush her newly acquired sense of balance. I had meant to compensate for Catherine's absence by including her grandmother in the celebration, wanting to please my mother and respond to Alice's desire to fully delve into a white Christmas. Our first in five years.

After the disclosure of the affair, all thoughts of Christmas were lost. My daze lifted somewhat after my mother left and it was then I realized that, at least for Alice's sake, there had to be some form of joy, despite the doomsday atmosphere reigning over the house.

"New York," I said to John. "Let's go spend Christmas in New York." With it being so accessible from Montreal, I had visited New York numerous times in the past, but never at Christmas. The minute we stepped out of our hotel onto Fifth Avenue, Alice and I were transported into the magical atmosphere of the street. John was in tow, not far behind, unable to hide the sting of rejection we were inflicting upon him. An objective observer would have never known he was traveling with us. I kept reminding myself that we were in New York to escape the suicidal atmosphere of our house in Northampton, and to somehow offer Alice a decent Christmas. The challenge of remaining polite, discreet, and restrained seemed very difficult for John, but in all honesty, it proved far more challenging for me. I was locked in a stupor.

The bitterness and anger I was now carrying exceeded my emotional and physical strengths. Poor Alice would regularly scream for us to shut up from her side of the suite, in a failed attempt to silence her mounting frustration. She could not escape the numerous discussions that would emerge from our room with the speed of a flash flood, unleashing their unsavory content on her innocent mind.

My lack of control highlighted my feeling of parental incompetence, exposing my imperfect, flawed self. The guilt of not being able to provide exactly what your child needs was alien to me. I had always thought of myself as a good and responsible mother. I was a conduit of sound values and principles, and had always been accessible to both her and to Catherine.

But the difficulties I faced now seemed insurmountable. I needed to constantly restrain myself, while the sight of my husband made me gag. An impossible task.

I must shamefully admit that when I learned of my husband's affair, I felt jealousy amidst the predictable feelings of betrayal and deception. This jealousy was not aimed at the mistress, as one might think. No, I was not jealous of her, not that much, anyway. John had given himself the freedom to experiment with, and feel, the excitement of discovering a new mind and new body. I was not jealous of Xiao Hua, no, I was jealous of John.

As I had been left to care for my children in a less than ideal context, I could have used the distraction and the soothing nature of an affair. Now, while in New York, I was overcome, more than ever, by the need to be validated as a desirable woman. I needed a physical soundboard to somehow gauge my worth.

That need was challenging for me to ignore, there in a city like New York. Attentive to the passersby, acutely aware of my surroundings, I walked through the streets and sidewalks with the desire to touch and meet new flesh. I felt overwhelmed by the emergence of a need I now knew had been buried and forgotten for the better part of my time with John. I now knew I had settled for it to be stored away, most likely forever.

On our second day in New York, while John was busy reading the paper, and Alice was watching a movie, I discreetly managed to register myself on a few dating apps. I was scared, but my curiosity superseded my fear of the unknown. Not only had I not dated in 24 years, but I knew nothing of the new landscape awaiting a neophyte like me. To my complete surprise, I quickly drew some attention—a lot of attention.

How easy. How playful, I had thought to myself, while scrolling through profiles, swiping my screen rapidly left and right. Impressed with my new found popularity, I eased into chat mode. I enjoyed the natural flow of the conversations with all the sexual innuendos they contained.

Something inside me had changed.

My slow descent into visible irresponsibility had officially begun, as my daughter, Alice, caught a glimpse of me making quick sweeping motions across the screen of my phone. Seated in the back of a New York taxi cab, even the driver, winking at me with unequivocal complicity, had somehow figured out what was unfolding in the backseat of his car. My only response to the twisted expression on Alice's face was a shrug and an embarrassed smile. Knowing that she would keep this information from my husband barely registered with me. I continued checking my phone throughout the day, letting the addiction take root.

I succumbed first to an Indian man, whose muscled and toned body seemed to extend an easy invitation. The conversation with him quickly turned sexual and fueled wild and novel thoughts in my head. I chatted with him incessantly, while eating, shopping, and sightseeing with Alice and John. I wanted to skip our Central Park skating plans and meet up with my new Indian beau. But, no, I centered myself, closed my phone, and headed out to the Central Park rink. Even though I was tired and weary, I convinced myself that exercise would keep my mind off the pain…and the temptations.

The weather in New York was absurdly warm for December, marking a balmy 75 degrees Fahrenheit on the thermometer. The rink was filled with tourists and locals wearing only T-shirts and shorts. The sight of all those novices trying to stand on blades was unexpectedly lifting my mood. The men, of course, caught my attention. Tall, athletic men reeling about, ankles turned inward and almost touching the ice. The virility they seemingly wanted to project was offset by the physical vulnerability their unsteadiness betrayed. It was simultaneously endearing and laughable. As a Canadian woman who had grown up practicing winter sports, I was entertained, and momentarily distracted from my own vulnerabilities. And I welcomed it.

The day unfolded slowly into the evening, punctuated by poorly restrained blowouts and altercations between John and myself. Alice was, unfortunately, exposed to these outbursts, as I was unable to dissimulate the contempt I felt for John. The sight of him, together with his misunderstanding of what he had provoked, were too overwhelming for me to digest. Still, we had to eat, feed our bodies, ensure our existence, and function. The three of us headed to a restaurant the hotel concierge had recommended, a Mediterranean venue across from our hotel. There, we sat, eating in silence, amidst the effervescent crowd and the abundant laughter emanating from the adjacent tables.

After dinner, we walked back to the hotel, dawdling, and making a detour to stop by the Rockefeller Centre to take in the majestic beauty of the famous Christmas tree. As we passed in front of St. Barthelemy Church, we tacitly decided to climb the stairs leading to its front doors, from where we noted the church's quasi emptiness, an invitation in itself. There were only a few randomly dispersed visitors seated in the pews. Quickly, I chose to sit on a pew located in the middle of the sacred establishment, noticing the visitors mindlessly playing with their phones, while the kneelers seemed to pray with apparent authenticity.

A voice, carrying with it an ethereal quality, emerged, singing a beautiful rendition of Ave Maria. My eyes watered as I saw John's lower lip quiver. "I will climb this mountain," he told me. "I will win you back." I turned my face away from his eyes. I could not stand to look at him, or to listen to, his whiny, whimpering attempt to lure me back into his life.

How could he dare expose his hurt and try to place it above my own?

Alice remained seated, in obvious discomfort. She played with her hair, not quite knowing what to make of this impromptu religious layover. It then struck me. It was Christmas Eve. I had forgotten, as the warm weather, combined with the sadness we were all carrying, had completely obliterated the purpose of our presence in the city, let alone the church. Half-drunk from the red wine I had carelessly drank at the restaurant, I stared at the statue of Christ suffering on his cross. Suffering, such a sine qua non condition of my faith. How ironic the society I lived in pushed hedonistic values as a way of escaping that very suffering. I wondered if Christ, watching over us, was satisfied with the impact his suffering had on his followers. What a bunch of dilettantes we make, I thought, looking over at John.

Our walk back to the hotel was marked by my intent to step away from John. I could not bring myself to walk by his side. It was a place I had held for twenty-two years, faithfully, diligently, and with authentic commitment.

How easy it was, I was now realizing, to break away from this pattern. How easy it was to simply let go and let myself be entertained by the thought of meshing my body with that of a perfect stranger's.

Back in the hotel room, I undressed away from his eyes. I wanted to distance myself from his hopeful stare. His desire to touch me was evident and off-putting. Quickly, I slipped under the duvet, eager to check my phone, its constant vibrations, a firm reminder of another world's existence. When I opened my phone, two matches stood out from the twenty appearing on my account. Only one profile really interested me, that of a thirty year-old doctor from South Carolina who was visiting in the New York vicinity for two days.

The exchange rapidly became heavy with warm and suggestive details of the possibilities the night held.

Have you been with two men? he probed. Do you often seek younger men?

His perspective on 'my goods' and the value I could add to his collection of sexual experiences, became evident to me. He was totally turned on by the fact I had not been with anyone, other than my husband, for the last twenty-two years. I must have appeared to him as the Virgin Mary, another version of the symbolic purity she carried, albeit, a redefined one. He wanted to fuck, I read, startled by the imperativeness of his statement.

Aroused by the unfolding opportunity, I did the unthinkable, and I dressed on the spot. I told John I needed to have some time to myself, not to worry, I would return in two hours. His distraught look did not hold me back. Alice was sleeping, unaware of my impending departure from the suite. Detached, curious, and my blood filled with adrenaline, I left. The agreed upon meeting point was about three blocks from the hotel. Omni Berkshire Place Hotel, room 817, was my destination.

He wore loose-fitting jeans and a black shirt, arrogantly half buttoned, to reveal his well-muscled torso. Statuesque and lean, he knew how to expose his goods. His beautifully structured face, which was neither round nor fleshy, encouraged me to touch him. Unable to resist, I slowly caressed the contour of his face, while examining his smiling brown eyes and stroking his curly black hair. He was as attractive as the pictures he had posted revealed to be and possessed a raw refinement that made my stomach clench. "Come in," he said, his voice grave, walking toward the middle of the suite. Observing his movements from the doorway, noting his studied nonchalance, I felt a rush that momentarily dizzied me. "Enter the fucking room," I heard myself whisper. "Just enter."

To step into a space filled with sexual anticipation was seductive, yet, extremely frightening. How I had missed the feeling of wanting someone, the desire to seduce and to willingly be seduced.

He had dimmed the lights and opened a bottle of Laurent Perrier. The Perrier sat on a tray that had been placed on the bedside table, while on the bed, rose petals had been randomly placed. Romantic, yes, but then something else from around the bed caught my attention. I had to squint to focus while my eyes adjusted to the dim lighting. Tied to the four bedposts, black restraints were dangling, the leathery material unfolded on the carpet. The evasive look that momentarily flew over his face gave him away. His inability to make eye contact, alerted me. However hungry for flesh I had become, my despair had limits.

Out of here, girl, I heard myself saying to myself as he stood there, assessing my reaction, quickly taking a step to catch me. Fortunately, he did not move fast enough, and I ran out of the room, ignoring the elevator, heading toward the staircase. He followed me to the emergency exit marking the floor's number, eight, but stopped short when he heard other hotel guests coming up the stairs from the seventh floor.

An hour and a half had passed since I had left John and Alice at the hotel. As I walked back in, shaken, I could see John's worries dissipate and transform into a heartfelt relief. I was almost touched by it. Curiously, I was still filled with a strong urge to fuck, felt the need to come, to let go. I changed into my nightgown and slid beside John, who was more than happy to oblige, unaware that my desire had been fueled by the thought of fucking another man. It turned out to be an incredible release for me, as he did with his tongue what I thought he did best. I would miss that, yes, but I had trained him. I could train someone else.

Our third day in New York was spent shopping at Forever 21. It was Christmas Day and it was insanely crowded with last minute shoppers intent on getting their shopping done. The store was filled with young people buying their Christmas and New Year's Eve party outfits. It made me feel good, normal, as if my life had remained the same, filled with the joy I hoped my purchases contained, promises of glee that quieted my torments–all our torments. Seated on a bench, brushing against mannequins dressed in startling red sequin outfits, I observed the New Yorkers' sense of style. How they choose their clothing items with such flair and savvy, I remember thinking. It was New York, after all, and for a moment I loved something— felt something, other than pain.

We dropped our purchases at the hotel and headed for a quick dinner off Broadway before catching the musical Allegiance. That particular play had been on my radar for quite some time. I have never been a fan of Star Trek, or even a fan of my fellow Canadian, William Shatner, but George Takei's spirit had reached me, somehow. Takei's Facebook post had surfaced on my feed. His kindness, authenticity, and contagious generosity caught my attention and made me want to see the musical in which he was now starring. While Allegiance reviews were mixed, I was drawn by the subject matter, the creation of Japanese camps inside the United States, following the bombing of Pearl Harbor. Tragedy, mingled with some form of lightness, seemed the right mix for me at this time.

In fact, I had thought, isn't it a reflection of my own reality?

The notion of honor, including its composition and timelessness, grabbed me without warning. The relevant question of belonging, so central to the play's theme, was hitting its mark with me repeatedly, until I could no longer withhold my tears. They were streaming and causing undulations of their own inside my mind. It was there, in this Broadway theatre, that I fully felt the enormity of John's betrayal.

When I left the theater, with my face marbled red and my eyes swollen, it became clear to me that I needed to infuse some levity into my life. An emergency infusion had to be self-administered. I somehow needed to counterbalance the ripple effect John's indiscretion was creating at the core of my being. These waves, I knew, would now rock the rest of our lives. Their eternal but subtle presence would forever frame my horizon with uncertainty and anguish. It was bound to have the same effect on John.

How he had miscalculated the impact of his decision to stray away from us. From me.

Our final moments in the city were spent having dinner with good friends we had not seen in six years. I was elated to see them again, as I equated their presence in my life with vivid occasions of pure joy, punctuated by long periods of separation.

To appear centered and somewhat joyful was challenging, but I managed to incarnate the lie I needed to be, as did Alice. I watched John rekindle his friendship, and I noted his ability to deceive, something that had escaped me throughout my time with him. The poker player in him was there for me to now clearly discover.

The talk, small and superficial, was barely tolerable, contrasting with the seriousness of my reality. Each time I felt the need to speak, I feared I would inadvertently blurt out my truth, vomiting its content on the red and white checkered tablecloth. The live wire I felt myself becoming would be cut when the time to say our goodbyes finally would arrive, freeing me from the mask I had been wearing. And when it came to be, both relief and sadness gripped my heart.

I was relieved that I did not have to continue performing, extenuated by the weight of an act I was ill equipped to sustain, but saddened because I knew I would never see these friends again. They had been meaningful friends to me, but they were John's friends and they would stand by him, unconditionally. Another casualty stemming from John's indiscretion.

One of many more to follow.

New England, with its valleys, mountains, and coast, had always attracted her, and electing to live in Northampton had not been a random decision. She had chosen it carefully to ensure both Alice's and her needs would be met, while also being charmed by the knowledge Boston could easily be accessed. Sharing with Patrick her desire to visit the city, a city she barely knew, a city located only thirty miles from his house, they decided to have dinner at a seafood restaurant located near the Quincy market in Boston.

As they walked into the restaurant, she saw, with dread, a similar reception to the one they had received on their previous outing.

A peacock would have been less noticeable, she thought, walking behind him, amused by the arrogance of his trot. Arriving at their table, he pulled out her chair. Seeing that she was cold, he placed his coat on her shoulders, kissed the nape of her neck, and took his seat. His eyes quickly scanned the crowd. He wanted to show her off, and that was fine. She had not been treated with such adoration in a long time, if ever, and, in all honesty, she enjoyed the stares and the attention. Even the waiter's obvious annoyance at Patrick's theatrics, entertained her. It left her with the opportunity to study the collision of two cultures. She was conducting, she realized, a quasi-anthropological study of the Latin and American cultures.

After dinner, as they got lost on their way back to Lowell, she observed Patrick, apprehensively. Her husband normally gave in to fits of impatience when confronted with such scenarios. His outbursts over the years had traumatized and transformed Isabelle into a very anxious passenger. Patrick, on the other hand, kept quiet as he tried to figure his way out of Boston. It was unsettling, as she anticipated an explosion of curses and a cascade of uncontrolled and unproductive emotions. She braced herself on the edge of her seat, as Patrick quietly fixated his gaze on the road, while holding Isabelle's hand and profusely apologizing for getting them lost. She turned to look at him, seduced by this newfound display of attentiveness, and she sank into her seat and let go.

Back at Patrick's house, he again, meticulously placed a towel under their bodies. This time, a bottle of baby oil, placed in proximity on the bedcover, was included in their play. With her legs firmly parted, he proceeded to insert his fingers, slowly, his eyes filled with almost childlike curiosity. She could tell he was intent on gauging the width she could sustain. Her discomfort was emerging, settling inside her stomach, but she kept quiet, wanting to please him.

"Wait a second," she heard him say, leaving to go to the kitchen. When he returned with a plastic bag, she was completely surprised by the item it contained. From it, he pulled out a vibrato—a huge one. Her sexual experimentations with John had been limited, if not, non-existent. And so, the item Patrick was planning for them to use, startled her. Although its life-like attributes; its tactile resemblance to the male genitalia impressed the neophyte in her, its massive size sent her into a moment of pure shock. Measuring twelve inches in length, and displaying a circumference of four inches, the sexual device was now included as a new option in their night's scenario. Staring at the penis shaped vibrator, she suppressed a smile. Its tip, red colored, towered over a lengthy skinned colored base. To her, it suddenly looked like a long index finger whose long nail had been painted red. Her laughter took him by surprise, but it was not contagious. This, to him, was a serious matter. An experiment of the unfulfilled teenage kind, she presumed.

She watched him with apprehension and concern, as he coated the device with a copious quantity of oil. She did not think any amount of oil could secure the insertion of that monster inside her. She said nothing, letting him glide his oiled hands around her labia and inside her, with expert softness. She closed her eyes, certain of him, confident in his capacity to assess her physical limits. But, no. With an abruptness that can only be explained as an aim to hurt, he pushed the large object into her violently. She instinctively retreated and closed her legs. He immobilized her, first with his left arm, then with his eyes. "If you relax," he told her, coldly, "it will be painless."

Time had stopped.

The pain was real.

The disbelief, brutal.

"What the fuck just happened?" she demanded to know, as he pressed his lips on her forehead. She could see his eyes pleading for clemency. "An apology," she was thinking, as she turned on her stomach and used her hands to soothe her inner thighs.

"Come with me to my sister's," he suggested. "I need to discuss matters concerning my daughter."

She had forgotten the pink room located beside the bathroom. He had a daughter, she was reminded. Where has she been for the last two weekends? she wondered.

"No, I will stay here," she told him. "It's 2:00 a.m." It was absurdly late to settle matters of any kind. More importantly, she wanted to avoid formalizing her presence in his life, as she knew she would eventually leave him. She decided not to ask about his daughter, either. The less involved she became, the better. Still, she wanted more of him and feared his family would see through her, immediately understanding the shallowness of her intentions for Patrick. The obvious cultural and social class, incompatibilities impossible to ignore. Anyhow, meeting his brother was more than enough for one day. And honestly, even if she had wanted to accompany Patrick to his sister's, walking would have been a challenge.

She headed to the shower, shaking her head. This weekend with him, she momentarily thought, should be the last. The thought that she might be wasting her time and his was troubling. But, within seconds, she knew it would not be troubling enough for her to change course.

She needed her revenge, and she would have it.

And more of it, still.

CHAPTER TWELVE

Upon returning from New York City, on December 26th, I decided to leave Northampton again and celebrate the New Year in Montreal with friends. I needed a New Year's celebration without my family, away from the alarming transformations waiting to reshape my world. In all honesty, over the years, my New Year's celebrations with John had been acceptable, but unremarkable. John had never taken the lead on an occasion, any occasion. The socializing aspect of our lives had over time fallen solely on my shoulders, something I had come to despise him for. His inability to bond outside the confinement of work had showcased this inaptitude, gradually scraping whatever admiration I had felt for him. To his credit, he did organize my 40th surprise birthday party. I was born in February, and the party did not occur until June. So yes, in this instance, I had been surprised.

This year, I was opting out after suddenly remembering the place we had celebrated the year before. We had been invited to a party at the Grand Hotel in Taipei. The hotel had a firm policy to deter would-be cheaters from booking a room there. Upon arriving at the reception desk, it was said that any local Taiwanese couple would have to prove they were legally husband and wife. Mei-ling, wife of the leader Chiang Kai-chek, having repeatedly been the victim of her husband's meandering ways, had taken it upon herself to be the gatekeeper. She would ward off infidelities. I now knew, for sure, John had not taken Xiao Hua to that establishment.

But it was of no comfort.

My state of mind was unstable, to say the least, as I arrived alone at the hotel we habitually checked into in Montreal each summer. All those familiar faces—the valets, the reception employees, the concierge—they were all genuinely happy to see me, and of course, all inquired about Mr. John.

"He is busy in Taiwan," I lied, as I hurried to the elevator, nestling in a corner, wishing the swift closing of its doors. There, engulfed by feelings of shame and loneliness, I wished I had died.

The suite I walked into was the same one we usually booked. It was a newly, but poorly, decorated room. The city noise, the Febreze smell, the sight of over-bleached sheets, all assailed me as I settled into the room. Five years of summer memories flooded my stomach with acid. Five summers that bridged my North American life with that of my Asian one.

More poignantly, I recalled the multiple episodes of physical suffering I had endured here. I had often felt nailed to the bed in the room, paralyzed by status migraines and debilitating fibromyalgia. I had suffered so much here, so much. Now, another layer to that suffering was being applied. Hopefully, the top and final coat.

My friend's New Year's party was a welcome distraction, but it was odd to reunite with close friends without John's presence by my side. I sensed everyone's uneasiness around me. I heard their well-meaning, but clumsily chosen words, and I saw their body stiffen as I approached them with a smile meant to be reassuring. Their sincere sorrow for me grabbed my heart. Off centered by the schizophrenic sensations imprinted on the moment, a moment where effervescence and despair strangely fused unapologetically, I tried to breathe, and just be.

While it was good for me to spend New Year's in Montreal, nothing about the trip was easy. Even crossing the border back into the United States proved difficult. I was a Canadian citizen, with an official residence in Taiwan, living in the United States of America. None of the answers I provided to explain my situation satisfied the agent.

Intrigued enough by my unusual profile, the border agent pulled me to the side, motioning me to park my car in the parking lot adjacent to the U.S. Customs building.

"I will meet with you inside," he said sternly.

Within the walls of the Vermont Highgate Springs Port of Entry, I was relentlessly questioned. My living arrangements concerned them, as I appeared not to conform to the U.S. immigration policy. In spite of the turmoil I felt, I was able to act stoically and control the feeling of panic that had readily emerged the previous times I had been pulled over for the same reasons.

Have my eyes betrayed my angst enough to elicit empathy? I wondered. Had my smile unwittingly pled for mercy? Whatever the case, the gingered-mustached agent agreed to let me in, seemingly acknowledging my right to stay on American soil, given my situation. I was, after all, the sole parent, the only adult available to Alice, a daughter who was now attending school in Deerfield, Massachusetts. "We are not in the business of splitting up families," he said candidly as he handed me back my passport.

Right.

Returning home on Interstate 89, I was aware that my state of mind was fragile, aware that my stay in Montreal had been nothing more than a filler of time, a failed attempt to distract me from the unavoidable. To counter my fears, I tried to keep my focus on the landscape. I sang to all my favorite songs. I practiced fake smiling. Nothing would do.

When I reached my destination, I was utterly tired, wounded, and experiencing more than ever, the bitter taste of having been blindsided. I headed to the bathroom, planted my head in the toilet, and expelled whatever was left of the stale bagel I had ingested for lunch.

John was lively, welcoming me home with a huge smile, and seemingly, very happy to see me.

He still did not get it.

Isabelle's lover, her intended boy toy, had reached his tentacles inside her mind and her body. He had ignited a desire in her that was challenging to contain. Stored memories of their lovemaking sessions inhabiting her brain, and intermittently intruded in her days. She had flashes of his eyes, with their agonizing desire, staring at her inner thighs. Trickling sounds of water would transport her to countless moments of climax. Thoughts of their ardent gazes, sustained during their sexual exploits, made her quiver. But, no feeling was as intense as the firm way he held her hands above his head, signifying her abandon and surrender to the will of her dictator. These sensations now held her hostage. The thought of not seeing him again, of losing it all, of losing her newly discovered senses was too much for her to bear. She was distraught, and she had lost her footing.

Confusion was poisoning the heart of all of her. She feared everything. Her undeniable loneliness, her emerging weaknesses, her inability to understand herself. All that grounded her was Alice, who was unaware of her own light. Only she could keep her focused on the essentials of day-to-day living.

But, she knew, Alice could feel her unsteadiness. She had to keep reminding herself that she could not, nor should not, understand the depth of the wound that had been inflicted upon her by her father's indiscretion. She had to protect her and she had to protect herself. This might mean she would need to abandon the one thing she wanted most, unbridled sexual experiences in the embrace of a warm body. She had to keep looking ahead, hiding her distress.

The physical and emotional space she craved was unattainable. Her house was not conducive to Alice's, or her well-being, to what they needed to cross the storm that had hit their family. With its plastic floors, plastic ceilings, plastic counters, and plastic bathtub, it was a synthetic house that welcomed and exposed a love for John that had long ago morphed into its own form of synthetic composition.

CHAPTER THIRTEEN

After I had received the incriminating pictures, my husband had assured me that all had been divulged. It was essential for me be told all, without exception. Experts offer varying advice on how to disclose all elements leading to an affair, or the affair itself. Some women want a broad picture painted for them. Others, like me, wished to gather sufficient information, so they could move on after learning the truth. Now, my challenge laid in defining what was sufficient information. I was greedy. I wanted to know everything, the slow build-up of desire that led to him deviating from that sense of right and wrong. I wanted to know the texture, the sound track.

I was about to find out that all was not as transparent as it had been made out to be.

Two weeks after initially seeing the pictures, John finally confessed to having signed a lease with Xiao Hua. From my hard, and relentless questioning, I learned that my husband had not been living with his business partner, as he had maintained all along. Having needed an official address for tax purposes, and apparently, because of some legal issues, having not been able to use his business partner's address, John's response had been simple and practical—he had signed a lease with Xiao Hua, and moved into an apartment with her, an apartment they had scouted out together in September, five months earlier.

To save money.

"Cheaper than paying for a hotel room," he had rationalized.

And how stupid do you think I am, John? I thought to myself.

In reality, the idea of living with his mistress had first come to him in the form of a document she had emailed him prior to our move to Northampton, sometime in July while we had been traveling to Central America. Now in January, standing in the laundry room, the only room somewhat capable of protecting Alice from our virulent discussions, he brandished that document in front of me, slicing the air with a swishing motion, gesticulating mindlessly. At first, I could not understand him, or make sense of his story, where the words lease and agreement were repeated non-stop.

Irritated by the confusion of the moment, I grabbed the document and read it as John stood watching me, bracing himself for the inevitable. This document laid out the terms of their union, suggesting ways by which they could better their relationship. Upon reading the lengthy text, I was unable to stifle my laughter. She had listed her demands, instructing him to, among other things, lose weight, exercise, stop drinking, and take good care of her.

However, two points on her long list of demands gave me pause. Moving in together was one, and leaving his wife within six months was the other.

I gasped.

For more privacy, John and I moved the increasingly volatile discussion from the laundry room to the truck. John was fighting to save his dignity, belittling the importance of the document, and the true impact it would have on our future relationship. The hate that filled my heart at that very moment was indescribable. All I knew was that I needed to remove myself from his presence, so I could breathe again. True hate, I was discovering, was like poison. Only one question remained for me. Was vengeance a better alternative?

I woke up the next day demanding John call Xiao Hua in my presence. I wanted to hear him tell her that he would not pay his part of the rent, as she was now demanding. He claimed they had had a verbal agreement, that in the event of a break-up, Xiao Hua would be solely responsible for the rent.

How ridiculous. It was obvious he was legally bound to the lease. Verbal agreement, or not, I made it clear to John that there was no way in hell my money would be spent on his mental patient.

"Your little flower can pay for her own fucking plastic pot," I told him quietly, my words as hard and icy as I could make them.

We drove downtown, parked in front of the local CVS pharmacy and walked to my favorite bakery on Market Street. Back in the truck, sipping coffee in the passenger seat, I observed John closely as he used the truck's Bluetooth to phone her. Xiao Hua answered and started talking, unaware of my presence. I could see John's demeanor stiffen, his persona slowly slipping into a character he seemed unwilling to adopt. I could only imagine how his small, small hands were sweating profusely, and soaking the winter gloves he wore. I knew my man.

By contrast, the calm I felt surprised me as I witnessed the obvious closeness they still shared. I knew my presence was leaving him no other choice but to assert himself, and firmly tell her he did not love her. That had been my main goal, to strike a final and definitive blow.

She repeatedly asked John if he still loved me.

"Yes," he simply offered, in a soft voice.

"Will you leave her? Will she leave you?" she insisted.

"We are working through our issues," he stated.

Her voice became high-pitched, and I could feel the effort it was requiring her to contain herself. She softly started to cry, intermittently stopping to tell John that his wife was smart—very smart. She then pursued the crying with more abandon.

You can cry all you want bitch, I thought coldly. You lost. And, you got it right. I am smart.

That incriminating document was revealed to me on January 4th, 2016. On the days following that discovery, all I did was read and reread its content, point-by-point.

Promise to do everything to make me happy. Workout. Bring me to all your business travels. Learn Mandarin. Leave your wife in six months..

Leave me in six months, by the summer of 2016. It was unbelievably hard to absorb, painfully challenging to imagine. Ironically, this document had more soul than my twisted marriage contract, more depth even than the cookie-cutter vows we had promised each other at the altar. Nonetheless, her demeanor betrayed her despair. It was a despair that pervaded with so many Chinese and Taiwanese women when they were securing their marital status. This woman's fool-hardiness, her own inner-fed enemy, was unleashing destruction to capture her lover.

She had failed.

I had never before been the victim of malicious behavior. But now, I was the one with malevolent plans. Xiao Hua and I had blocked each other from Facebook. When I realized she was still calling John, despite the last phone call to which I had been privy, I decided to act. I sent her an email from an anonymous account I had specifically created for that reason. I wanted her to stop calling John, to leave us the fuck alone. I reminded her that while men may want to fuck women like her, they would never marry them. I also told her what John had shared with me, and that I had foolishly believed, that each time he climaxed into her, he had thought of me, his wife.

I had touched a raw nerve. Yes, I could have refused the new message request when I received it. But, I did not. Quickly, I recognized the purpose of her message was to expose the crucial elements that had marked their relationship, and to also get even with John. Armed with revenge and the desire to see me bleed, she unveiled every single detail of their six month liaison. I was finding out, yet again, that John had omitted important segments of his story with Xiao Hua. Had I not sent that email, I would have still been fooled by my husband's distortions and omissions about his life, the truth of it. While describing, with excruciating details, their six month relationship, one event stood out, a Bangkok trip, complete with unsavory sexual escapades. Reading this passage of her message, I closed my eyes and I imagined her standing in line with John as they registered their luggage at the airline counter. I snapped.

Armed with my phone, messenger text opened, I flew into John's office. I confronted him, but I was unable to listen, let alone hear him out. I spoke incoherently, shaking, my face hot as an iron. These last revelations were unbelievably challenging to read, to assimilate. There was no way to tiptoe around the issue that was emerging again, more clearly than ever, I was not going to bear down and move forward with my husband. Whatever possibilities of reconciliation I may have momentarily entertained to that point, were now shattered in that very moment.

We took one last trip to the truck, the space where all was permitted, and spewed without impunity, away from Alice's presence. There, my mind capitulated to the pain, giving in to the pressure it applied on the whole of my being. The instant of realization, that I was never going to get over his betrayal, came through as a stream of tears and hysterical screams.

I heard myself yell at him, "You had such a good girl! You had such a good girl!" And as trivial as it may sound, articulating those words underscored the very important fact that I had been good to him to the core. I had been a straight arrow, a pillar, a rock, a purpose-giver, a good and functioning compass for the better part of our twenty-three years of marriage. Where had it led me?

Still seated on the passenger seat of the truck, I barely lifted my head, unable to contain myself anymore. How I wished for the sound of my howls to exorcise my demons. Looking at the spit that had landed on John's cheek, spit that had a purpose, spit that had a soul, I knew then I had to leave.

What I did not know from that departure, was that my life would capsize.

Isabelle rang the doorbell, and with his shy and hesitant smile, he greeted her. A brief dry kiss in the private door entry followed. He then pulled away and led her to the dining room, where a tall, beautiful young man was eating his dinner.

"Meet my son," he simply said. "Alejandro." She did not understand the magnitude of that moment, until she was told, later that night, that she was the first woman to have ever set foot in his house. Even Alejandro's mother, Desiree, had never entered Patrick's home.

This is wrong, so wrong, she told herself. She could not be the first one. She could not be the only woman to make it past the threshold of this tightly-guarded, masculine household.

That evening, Patrick and Isabelle caught a late night movie. It was midnight when they got back to his home. She thought for a moment to not text John, but he had a plane to catch the next day and a part of her wanted him to sleep without worrying about her return home. She also had to think of Alice, as her anxieties had returned, infusing sleeplessness into her nights.

She texted John that she was fine and not to wait up. Her next reflex was to turn off her phone, so she could avoid reading a sad, or confrontational response. She was not quick enough.

I cannot do this anymore … was the last thing she read before shutting down her phone. For one moment, she feared for him.

As if on cue, Patrick came from behind and embraced her, held her waist and kissed the side of her neck. She slowly turned to him. She brushed her lips against his, teasing the lower part of his mouth with her teeth, before responding fully to the inviting tongue he was extending. All her concerns instantly vanishing. All would be fine. Under the glow of his orange light, they both undressed. Like previous times, he kissed her with the seemingly pure intent of swallowing her whole. He flipped her face down on his bed, pushing her up and digging furiously with his tongue everywhere he could, while smelling, suctioning, and licking his way up her back. He lifted her to an upright position, and stood behind her. Holding her with one hand, he placed his other hand firmly on her breast. She twisted her head to meet his mouth. The taste of her assaulted her palate, and his saliva inundated the well that her mouth had become. "How juicy you feel," he whispered. He pulled her to the ground, ordered her to her knees and proceeded to insert himself, everywhere. "Push your culo down," he ordered. She complied, lowering her ass, only to then feel his foot being placed on her neck. He had her head on its side, completely immobilizing her.

"You know," he whispered in her ear, "my son, Alejandro, is obsessed with you. I've caught him masturbating with your underwear. I've found two pairs of them under his pillow," he added quietly, as he stroked her back with his hands. Drenched with his sperm, his words barely registered. Fleetingly, she noted one curious fact, she had just met Alejandro. I don't really care, she told herself, as she indulged in the violence that had been introduced to her. The sex was rough, animalistic, and almost dehumanizing, but it was a novelty for her, and at this point in her life, she decided it was better to get fucked, prisoner style, on a grease stained carpet, than to drink tea with John.

CHAPTER FOURTEEN

John's affair was to be forever kept secret, its content to be stored in the safe memories of the two lovers living at the other end of the world. But all had surfaced. The incriminating details of his betrayal were revealed with potent vividness. Those images had pierced through my chest and tattooed themselves on my brain. I envisioned Xiao Hua's silky black hair caressing John's face as they fucked wildly. I imagined their bodies blending seamlessly while the enticing odors of jasmine and lotus flowers poured from her skin. I imagined their scotch-filled nights warming their embrace as they walked through the nauseating city smells to a cheap hotel only fools in love would consider. The soundtrack to the movie I had produced in my mind was gut wrenching. The noisy scooters, the Mandarin tones, the bristling movements of bamboo leaves superimposed over the humming of bicycles rolling alongside the Danshui river. All these sounds were echoing inside my head, dizzying me.

In the backdrop of my story, stood the majestic Taipei 101. That tall, iconic building should have been a warning sign for John. Taipei 101 was built on ground ill-suited for the building's heavy weight. Taiwan was prone to frequent earthquakes and typhoons and Taipei 101 sat 660 feet away from a major fault line. Did that not symbolize what indulging oneself was all about? Braving the odds, challenging all logic, taking risks to fill some void, confirming your sexual self-worth?

Taipei 101, with its bamboo-like ridges, seemed to promise pleasure, pain, and release. It is such a sexual symbol, in its pretension, in its arrogance, in its defiance of Mother Nature. White men came to Asia and related instantly to these promises. Gone were their vulnerabilities, their restraints, their weaknesses and deficiencies. All was allowed, and all was legitimized, by the simple anonymity that emanated from the sea of humans flowing freely through the streets.

So, yes, when I presented John with that last Facebook message from Xiao Hua, terrifying disbelief had taken hold of my husband's sad face, a face twisted with belated remorse, disfigured by the impossible thought of losing me forever. The valiant effort he had deployed to minimize the content of that last message was simply impossible for me to comprehend.

I got back home the next afternoon at around 4:30 p.m. When I entered the house, the music was blaring. John was alone in the kitchen, eating an apple, seemingly waiting for me. He looked up at me, his face gray, his eyes, two little beads recessed in their hollow sockets.

His relentless questioning struck a nerve. It infuriated me. I kept recalling how he had conducted his affair, comfortably, out of everyone's sight. It had now been two weeks since I had started to see Patrick. I was tired of lying, of distorting and manipulating information, of camouflaging my physical desires. It took focus, consistency, agile planning, and so much energy to excel as a deceiver. Would I be a pain reliever? Would I be a pain inflictor? If I decided to bring my own truth to the foreground of this obvious transitional phase of our lives, whose interest would I serve?

I decided to disclose. His guttural, blood-chilling sobs and cries for help were extremely challenging to witness. Kneeling on the floor with his head on a chair, he was throwing up, unable to stand, let alone walk to the bathroom. I tried holding him, but he stepped back, recognizing the leper in me.

Thankfully, my daughter was spared John's emotional departure for Asia, as she was away at school preparing for her ACT exams. Alice was keenly aware that quite a change had taken hold of me. I was no longer behaving like her mother. I was now the mother whose eyes dilated at the sounds of incoming emails and texts. I was now the mother who slept with her phone close to her chest. I was now the mother who was going to see her lover, after sending her daughter to an impromptu weekday sleepover.

Yes, her mother had gone ... she had left.

What started as a one-night stand—a night of sensual and animalistic pleasure, had now become a tense and thrilling month-long ride. Some of her best friends offered unexpected, uncalled for, and untimely advice from their comfortable, safe positions, of ignorance and judgment.

How dare they? she asked herself, as she continued to drive home from Lowell, bruised by their lack of understanding, the specter of abandonment floating around her fragile heart.

Fuck them. Fuck them all.

This was her revenge for the taking.

If that's what it still was? She didn't know, and she looked out at the night, and she let herself be taken by it—the music in the car, and feeling timeless in the present; in the dark; in the quiet, and yet, there was something lurking just beneath it all, taking her back to something her father had one said to her, about how her mother despised her grandparents.

Your parents? she had asked her father.

Yes, he had continued, your mother felt too good for them, constantly belittling their modest origins. Being seen with simple farmers, stained the bourgeois image she had painstakingly cultivated. A fucking snob. A failed sycophant. That's what she was to me, her father had said. To the world.

And much more, Isabelle had thought to herself. You always referred to her as Madame la Baroness.

Madame La Baroness, he whispered.

She had waited for her father to speak more. More of what she knew was coming.

To me, looking back at it, the only reason I married her—the flaw that made me fall, was her beauty. Nothing more. Just that.

Beauty, Isabelle thought now, and she said, yes.

She remembered looking at her father, watching him disappear, the arch of his brows unleashing skeletons still cutting into him.

One fall day, he had said, as we were driving to see her parents, I told her that we would be making a quick stop at my parent's farm, just to say hi. A very small detour. She immediately pushed back, said no, that she didn't want to, that it was out of the question. She hated them.

Why?

Because they couldn't stand her.

She had watched him pause, to gather himself.

I ignored her and continued on to my folk's place. As we were approaching the farm, she started to scream, and to scratch my face with her fingers. Fucking wild, that's how she was. I had no choice. I slapped her. Hard. Her head bouncing off the edge of the half opened window. There was a short reprieve, not long, and she regrouped, something she always did. When I looked at her, I saw it. You remember that look, the zoning out, that moment of calmness that preceded chaos as much as tranquility? With her, there was but one outcome possible. Fucking delusional craziness. The look was one of defiance. And she did defy me. She grabbed the door handle, and said that if I continued, she would jump out of the car. I looked at my odometer—I was doing 70 mph, and I could no longer hear what she was saying, something about me never taking care of her, I think. I slowed down, as I drove past my father's farm. She had threatened to do the same just the week before. He had paused, and looked at his daughter. I had no choice. I had to give in. She was five months pregnant with you.

On the road, driving, to home that was no longer a home—if, in fact, it had ever been, Isabelle grabbed at her belly and clutched her flesh, unleashing her own nails, as she remembered more of the conversation. When you were born, her father had continued, your mother felt she had lost what little place she held in my life. From the moment you were conceived, you had become her competition. My favorite, according to her, even when compared to your sister, Helen, whose existence never provoked such bizarre behavior in your mother. It took me some time to realize what was going on, and by the time you were two, and Helen seven, it had become clear that I had to oversee her when she was with you. He had looked again at his daughter. Leaving home for work was so difficult …

Isabelle's lids dropped while she let her mind unlock images that strobed, that were of screams, of kicks, of bloody noses and swollen eyes. She opened her eyes, and she steered back from the shoulder of the road, her heart racing. She looked in the rear-view mirror. She was the only car on the road, thank God. Her mother's hands, she remembered, were her obsession, as she looked at her own, white-knuckling the steering wheel. The use of pans, fly swatters, and buckled belts, all extensions meant to protect her damn hands from the strain of hitting her daughter. She could feel her tears rolling down her cheeks as she drove on in the dark, alone and wondering— remembering, the fetid smell oozing from her mother's dry mouth, the red lipstick barely clinging to her chapped lips, a Craven A there, hanging, the smoke curling around her, covering her painted face. The Yves St-Laurent turban. The Cossack boots.

A fucking clown, Isabelle spoke out loud. She then realized, she had seen her father, for the very first time, that day.

Because new eyes give new life, she thought. Her new life now.

The final curtain had been lifted when her father, a talented photographer, had digitized some old slides of Isabelle's younger years, and had stored them on an USB key, and given it to her the Christmas before. One-by-one, she had studied the photographs that had been freed from the past. Photographs of fishing trips, snowmobile hikes, winter picnics up in James Bay, baseball pitch and catch, Montreal Formula 1 Grand-Prix races. Her eyes had watered at the sight of one particular picture from her early childhood. Malibu beach with her father, 1967. A timed shot capturing her father's playfulness, as well as her mischievousness. She had stared at the two of them for a very long time, in awe. What she saw reframed a lifetime of perceptions her mother had intently manipulated. Planted in her. He never loved you, she had said, and never will he ever love you. She saw herself now, in that photograph, a small, fragile girl, sitting in the sand, her pink and white polka dot bikini, the ruffles blowing in a warm wind, her goodness inscribed in the small creases of her eyes. All so clear and shiny, she thought. Driving, she cried more, large gulps of quiet, evening air, the question remaining, its uselessness worming inside her mind, sometimes steeped in the depth of her pain, other times skimming at the forefront of an overloaded heart. What had been there, inside of me, for my mother to want to hate and crush me so much?

Why?

And just then, driving on in the dark, she found the answer.

A coward.

A fucking coward.

And like all abusers, her mother had made sure the porous child she had created would carry her own pain and guilt. A cute human garbage pail dressed up in the latest of fashions, a tiny soul hidden inside the cashmeres, the silks and the lace that reassures the commoners—a child you leash up, and train, walk, and display.

And she knew, she would never have allowed any of these men in her life, if she hadn't been conditioned to minimize the foulness alive in humans, to swim happily in its ocean, seeking it—this comfort of pain. Its nemesis never too far, but unattainable.

No more.

And there, driving through the night, she felt a need—a yearning, to a come back to the reality of loving.

Real love.

A love that does not harm, like a parent once did, to a young child, on a beach now, her face turning to the feel of a warm breeze blowing over her.

And she cried more.

PART TWO

CHAPTER ONE

John was parking his car in the driveway, just as I arrived home from Lowell. He had been gone for two weeks. Two very long weeks. We both walked into the house in silence, Jackson providing us with our only glimpse of normalcy. The discomfort was acute for us both. It was uncomfortable for him because he could not stomach the fact that someone other than him had touched his wife. It was uncomfortable for me because, more than anything else, I wanted to be elsewhere. I wanted to be in Patrick's dungeon-like home.

It was rapidly becoming clear that we could not sustain living under the same roof, let alone be in the same room. We were not to be trusted. We could not control the direction our arguments would take, nor the sound level our voices would reach. Our daughter seemed to hear everything, and was extremely sensitive to any perceived change of tone. We both agreed I would leave mid-week, for a five-day stay, anywhere I wanted.

Cape Cod in February must be beautiful, I thought to myself, understanding the opportunity that was presenting itself. Well, who took his mistress on a seven-day trip to Bangkok? I asked myself, as I happily included Patrick in my plan. My objective was very simple. Because it was winter, I knew Patrick had less work. I would offer him some time alone with me, and away from his dreaded town and bleak home. I informed him of my intention to book a beautiful bed and breakfast located in the mid-Cape area. His response, while positive, was equally opaque. I went ahead, reserved and paid.

This quaint bed and breakfast was located within 200 feet of the beach. Its sun-washed wooden siding hinted at the summer sun's intensity, offering a sharp contrast to the carpet of white snow surrounding it. The small Inn had seven spacious rooms, each having been decorated in the Cape's unavoidable ocean theme. The room I was given was spacious and beautifully lit, and according to the on-duty manager, was the best room the Inn had to offer.

I had arrived on a Wednesday, and would be the only guest there until Friday. I had our room booked until Sunday, so I was eager for Patrick to be there with me. I was so eager, that I let my imagination script various erotic scenarios that were surfacing in my mind. Energized by my anticipation, I headed to the dining area where I made myself a tea. I then chose a table by the window, plugged in my phone and computer and started to write. I texted Patrick five times and called him three times. It was now 6:00 p.m., and I was starving for both food and the fulfillment of my pressing desires. I wanted to know about our dinner plans, so I called him, yet again, but only got his automated voicemail. It was then I received his text explaining he was at the Market Basket, paying for his food. I called back, astonished, and finally reached him.

"Baby, I can't go," he blurted out. "I have too much to do. You should see the state of my refrigerator. It was so dirty, and there was no food. When I opened the door, I just couldn't help myself…" he kept on rambling, as I shut down. It seemed cleaning his refrigerator was a better option than spending four nights in Cape Cod with me.

Unbelievable. I should stay, I told myself. The promise of quietness was assured here, and peacefulness felt within reach. Sweeping my eyes across the dining room, I suddenly sensed the weight of my choices falling on me. I got up to make myself another cup of tea and to grab a few cookies. The solitude I knew necessary to my healing was at bay, carrying with it the possibility that my nervous system would be tamed, if not soothed. Here, far away from Northampton, Lowell, and Montreal, I could better absorb the impact with which I had been crushed.

INHALED

The pull was not strong enough. My weakness for him, I convinced myself, was essential to my healing. I had to go.

I had paid in full for my stay at the Inn, but had only been there a total of four hours. Those four hours would cost me eight hundred dollars. I was a crazy woman. I went to my room, with adrenaline pumping through my body, packed my bags, and found the innkeeper.

"Something has happened in my family," I shared. And I did share, almost everything, concentrating on the topic of my separation. For my own sake, I needed to weave some truth into the story. She confided that she, herself, was a widow, and therefore, somehow, understood my pain. I stared at her. She must have been beautiful in another life. I could see she had withered away, transforming into the incarnation of some form of resignation, the antithesis of what I wanted to become. My stomach tightened, as I walked to my car with my overnight bag in tow. I suddenly wished John had died, too. It would have been easier. There would have been no feelings of humiliation and betrayal to combat each day, only the reverence of a fulfilling union.

Patrick somehow insisted I grab a meal on the way back to town. I stopped at a McDonalds, somewhere near Boston, and ordered at the drive-thru. I parked in the lot and proceeded to unwrap my meal. Turning my head to the right, I noticed another car, parked maybe 10 feet away. In it was a very tall lady. Her hair was thick and appeared to cascade down to her mid-back. As my eyes now concentrated on her face, I could distinguish her features more clearly. A man caught in the body, the mind and the soul of a woman. man. A feeling of fright suddenly surfaced in me, twisting inside my throat. Clarity has a funny way of manifesting itself.

My life now was in sharp contrast to the life I had lost. I, Isabelle Duval, was now parked in a dingy area of Boston, eating a Mc-something. I had left my husband for a poor Latino lover who had stood me up at a luxury bed and breakfast I had already paid for before I fled. My eyes swelled. The tears rolled down my face as the 'dressed-to-kill' stranger walked toward me, having somehow noticed my state of despair. As recklessness had somehow become the general theme of my life, I let her enter the car. Being murdered would somehow befit my story, I thought. Yet, somehow my fear rapidly lifted the minute she slid onto the passenger seat. We both stared at each other and smiled.

Janet, this tall trans woman, had just left his wife of ten years for a lifestyle she could not share. I listened, momentarily taking in someone else's pain and hopelessness. We must have stayed there holding hands for an hour, listening to a tacky, adult, contemporary, nostalgic music station–Celine Dion?–while staring at the houses before us.

And being blinded by the unapologetic light coming from ill-placed lampposts surrounding the parking lot, the only light to brush against both our tears.

Another stranger, to hold.

CHAPTER TWO

Overnight bag in tow, I climbed the stairs to Patrick's front door. Remembering the doorbell was broken, I knocked repeatedly. Quickly, the door opened, and Patrick appeared wide-eyed and with a frozen smile. As swiftly as he had opened the door, he kissed me and ushered me to the dining area. As I stepped into the room, I was unexpectedly greeted by a full house of people. The contrast whipped me, and I felt an internal shift of some sort that pierced through my stomach. I had left the safety and solitude of my Cape Cod Inn to enter a zone devoid of bearings. The bare rawness of my setting, the brownness of it all, the stammering rhythm of the Spanish language, spat out at a velocity that made the words undecipherable to me, dizzying my senses.

Hugging me tightly to his hip, it was obvious he was proud to introduce me to these people. Alejandro was setting the table, welcoming me with his timid eyes. I was introduced to Patrick's niece, Sabrina, who was sitting at the table, mindlessly playing with her phone, and a friend, named Romero, who was preparing a pasta-based meal with sausages, vegetables, and that little kick most Caribbean dishes offer.

Why had Patrick asked me to eat something beforehand? I asked myself, feeling the fullness of my stomach. To be polite, I partook in what I thought was a pleasant, albeit light, conversation. At a certain point, Patrick made it clear to his guests that it was time to leave.

It reminded me of a dinner I had once attended in Montreal. The dinner had been held by a wealthy and eccentric investment banker, who at 10:15 p.m., once desserts had been served, had proceeded to call taxis for all his guests. He had wanted them to leave before his predetermined bedtime. It made me smile, as I rejoiced at the thought of being alone with Patrick. It was true, I was going to Patrick's home because I wished to see how he lived, but I could not fool myself. I was also in dire need of escaping Northampton, John, and the house. I wanted a soothing warm body to cling to, and a place to hide in. Walking into the shower that night, I felt certain of one thing. Sex would be the weapon of choice. That and food.

Coffee was on my mind the moment I opened my eyes the next morning. I stepped into the kitchen, suddenly remembering that neither Patrick nor his son drank coffee. I needed a coffee to avoid the onset of a migraine. I quickly dressed, so I could drive to the closest Starbucks, and to stop at the Market Basket on my way back. I had decided to serve boeuf bourguignon for dinner. I was wired with the desire to please.

Patrick was pacing upon my return. He frowned at my two-cup-a-day coffee 'addiction'. Furthermore, he thought I should have shown appreciation for the tea he had made available for me in his house. Coffee withdrawal was a foreign concept to him, it seemed. Ignoring his agitation, I placed the groceries on the counter, realizing I had forgotten the main ingredient, burgundy wine. I decided to walk to the nearby wine store to purchase a bottle. The expression carved on Patrick's face was one of growing irritation. He insisted I take my car, but I firmly told him that, no, I needed to exercise. I did not know why he was so annoyed. Somewhat perplexed, I left by foot as planned.

When I returned with the wine, I was excited to begin the execution of my culinary project. I had been missing that zone where, under the pressure of nothing but the sole pleasure of cooking, I could feel tranquil. Chopping my vegetables to the sound of jazz, I meditated on the moment, and briefly, just before he waltzed in, I touched on it, happiness–some dwarfed form of it.

Grabbing me by the waist, he pulled me toward the bedroom, despite my protests. I still had much to do for the meal to be ready on time, but my will was weak and, as usual, I gave in. Of course, by the time we were done playing with our bodies, it became obvious the meal would not be ready on time. I had warned him of that and thought he understood the consequence of adding more sex-fun to our day.

The concept of opportunity/cost was all so foreign to him, I was soon to discover. His mood changed, his gesturing became abrupt and he launched into a long diatribe meant to squash me into nothingness.

When he gets like this, where exactly does he disappear to? Where does he retreat to? I wondered with surprise.

His inability to think rationally was evident, as there in his kitchen, he was directing his festering anger at me. Leftovers from the previous night would not suffice and Patrick was steaming as he and his son scrambled to find some rice to make an impromptu chicken stir fry. Looking at me sideways, his eyes, two little beams radiating spite, he ordered me to set the table, prepare the salad, and make some tea. The sinner I had apparently revealed myself to be needed to be punished.

He christened my first official, albeit makeshift meal, with a very strange rendition of Grace. The sternness he displayed removed any possibility of his blessing reaching its intended target. I, for one, did not feel blessed one bit. In fact, one blessing from him would assuredly mean I would hit a deer or two on my way back to Northampton.

To fit in and avoid any additional discomfort during dinner, I took it upon myself to fill any awkward silence by directing the conversation and orchestrating its flow. Alejandro, responding well to my efforts and recognizing my valiancy in thrusting the conversation forward, was answering my questions, but with obvious restraint. He was eyeing his father at the same time, looking for some kind of feedback.

Our conversation touched on many subjects, including, his classes, his girlfriends, politics. I was starting to feel better, regaining my confidence and finding the balance that had escaped my body. Then it happened, taking both Alejandro and me by complete surprise. Violently, Patrick slammed the palm of his hand on the table. "In this house, we are to keep quiet at mealtime!" It was apparently a worldwide held protocol. "Haven't you been well educated?" he added, looking straight at me, his chin down, his eyes lifted.

Dumbfounded and shaken, I stared at my plate. Staring was now threatening to become my full-time activity. In shock, I tried reviewing the few options that were coming to my mind.

Yell? Leave? I considered.

Patrick frowned at his son with obvious disappointment and reminded Alejandro that he knew the rules and should not have encouraged the conversation. "We talk once dessert is served," he reminded Alejandro, with fury. "And only then."

I stared, still in disbelief, at Patrick. The discomfort was unbearable. I needed to escape this hellish moment.

I told him I had to call my nephew, as it was his birthday and he would be going to bed shortly.

"It is impolite to do so at this moment. You know this," was his response. For the next five minutes, I stayed seated, breathless, unable to quiet my heart, until I finally decided to get up, without a word. I cleaned my plate and left rapidly for the bedroom. I sat there, on the edge of my playground, and started to cry.

What fucking place is this? Who the hell is this guy? I was screaming in my head.

Charlie. I needed to speak with Charlie.

From the moment Charlie and I had met at our daughters' ballet class, ten years earlier, we had immediately fallen into a deep friendship. Slender with brown, shoulder length hair, signature bangs that framed her large brown eyes, she naturally drew you in with her boundless energy and striking beauty. Charlie stunned me, in every sense of the word, exuding a level of elegance I had rarely been exposed to before in my life. While intimidated at first by the creature of luxury she clearly incarnated—logos, jewelry, and furs melting into one unapologetic vision of abundance—I was quickly seduced and reassured by her affability, her genuine kindness, and mostly, her capacity to listen, to really listen.

I tried to dial her number, but with my vision blurred by raging tears, I could not even see my screen. Just as I was about to press send, Patrick came rushing into the bedroom, his wooden rosary now halfway emerging from his white shirt.

"What's wrong?" he asked, eyes shifting. His surprise astonished me.

I lashed out at him. "What the fuck, Patrick? Who doesn't talk during a meal?" I snapped. "Where on earth did you get the notion that you don't talk before dessert is served? What type of woman do you really want to share your home and your life with? Because the type of woman you wish for will never put up with these phony rules of yours!" I was sobbing uncontrollably, my face distorted by an overbearing feeling of sudden inadequacy. Before I realized it, he had me in his arms and was rocking me to the sound of his continuous apologies.

For the rest of the night, I stayed nestled in his arms, until exhausted, I fell asleep. He undressed me slowly, slid me under the bedcovers and tucked me in, like a child—like a child.

The next morning, I was still uneasy. The wound was fresh and raw. How would I go about my day considering what had unfolded the night before? I walked to the bathroom and examined my face, discovering, as expected, how reddened and swollen my eyes had become. I headed to the shower and tried to regain some composure, letting the hot water wrap me in a tentative blanket, while I contemplated my next step. As I dried my hair, I considered leaving his house, imagining the short-lived satisfaction it would grant me. I did not want to go back to John and Alice, as my own house offered a different type of unease. I quickly decided I needed to step out for some coffee. I thought everything would somehow start to make sense once I tasted that first soothing sip.

I left, barely acknowledging his presence. He was busy filling out some documents for a work permit of some sort.

He projects self-control and emotional detachment so well, I thought. I knew I wanted to discuss with him what had unfolded. I knew I wanted to know, and to understand, the mechanics behind his behavior. But, I could not. I feared him, his reactions, his lack of control. I chose to keep quiet and pretend all was all right. I was in dire need of coffee.

    I had to go.

CHAPTER THREE

My boeuf bourguignon was finally being served. It had been forgotten in the oven the night before, but saved in extremis by Patrick's son. I could not believe I was back at this table from hell. Despite the abundant compliments on my dish, I did not say one word. I would give him what he wanted. Still, the topic of when to speak resurfaced. I held my breath and listened. "Isabelle," he said, "you are allowed to speak after you have finished your first serving. Then, and only then, are you permitted to talk."

I pinched myself. My story with Patrick was evidently no longer light and easy. But, I had no perspective anymore. I was emotionally caught and tangled in my own wants, captured by the desire and the refusal to see things as they were, or could become.

Patrick had not noticed, but at the end of the afternoon, following a short call to my sister for my nephew's birthday, I packed all my belongings and placed them in the corner of his room. I had decided that if I was still feeling awkward after dinner, I was leaving for good. Yet, while washing the dishes with this man, the debate was still going on inside my mind.

Maybe I should conduct a search on the subject of dating Latinos? Maybe I'm missing something?

Back in his bedroom, we magically regained a kind and intimate interaction, with a rhythm that immediately soothed me, its change of pace confusing me almost.

While nonchalantly playing with the clothes inside his closet, he proposed we go see a movie. I looked at him, surprised again by his change of tone and demeanor. Suddenly, I buried my plans to leave. Assessing my appearance, he chose shoes and a shirt that would match my black outfit. He noticed my dress hanging off the door frame, but he did not say anything. He had told me numerous times that he wanted a simple girl. I would definitely not wear my Diane Furstenberg dress to catch a movie at a local theatre. I would remain dressed as I was with black velvet pants and a black laced Victorian blouse. Black—the color of choice.

Inside the car, I did not ask which movie he had chosen for us to see. I just wanted to be guided, I just wanted to follow. There with him, despite him, I felt grateful. I was grateful for being able to postpone my return to Northampton. I was grateful for being able to escape Patrick's house.

Still carrying with me the fear of being verbally assaulted, I kept silent. We were heading toward Boston, and I resisted the urge to ask where exactly it was we were going, as the theatre was only 20 minutes away, in Lawrence. He must have felt my unease. Tilting his head toward me, he told me softly that we were going dancing. Feigning indifference, I smiled to myself. It seemed staying had been the right choice.

Latino night at Vincent's, he said.

A surprise, it seemed, maybe a gift, a reflex to please–a plea to be forgiven?

That's promising, I thought to myself, walking into the large establishment located in Randolph, 15 miles south of Boston. I felt at ease instantly. The rhythms of Merengue were quick to send shivers of pleasure up my legs. This new insight into my lover's life was feeding the growing sense of disorientation I had been feeling from the onset of our relationship. But, dancing was something I loved, something I had mastered. Here, I would have some footing.

It was the voluptuousness of the feminine bodies, responding to their male counterparts, that I first noticed. Their dancing was like wavy fusions meant to exorcise life's vicissitudes, the Latino way. The lounge-like atmosphere was electrified by the energy of the crowd. I looked down at my boots. I was wearing knee high boots with rubber soles. Patrick should have demanded I change into the proper clothing, including the proper shoes. Remembering how meticulously he had chosen his clothes, it was apparent his personal comfort had been his sole concern. I let it go.

We headed to the bar, where Patrick ordered a rum and Coke for me and a vodka and cranberry juice for himself. From there, he took my hand, proudly showing off his skinny, white companion to the Latino community. We slowly started moving together to the Bachata beat playing for the dance-hungry crowd. The high voltage ambience was jolting me back to life. I felt as though I had landed in heaven, there in this newly discovered universe. Patrick and I moved in synchronicity. He kept repeating to me how I was a wonderful dancer, his awe sincere. I was hoping my own fluidity would be as seductive as his movements. I wanted to immortalize the harmony I was in dire need of, a feeling that kept escaping me, its nemesis pulling me down into a well of insecurity-filled emotions.

I was hypnotized by the savvy moves he displayed, the natural ease with which his body responded to the Latin beats bedazzling me. I observed and felt his body move with such flow, such subtle moves, that were yet so masculine. I was subdued, as we locked eyes and he pressed his body against mine. His hands guided my hips gently as he moved in closer, his head approaching mine, allowing my temple to rest against his forehead. I closed my eyes. We both did.

He led like no man had ever led me before. He was guiding me, teaching me how to let my body pulsate the Latin way. He pointed to my hand, telling me to look up and hold *that* position, as he gently held my right hand with his left. His competent, gentle, and protective guidance, touched my soul, whipping me mindfully into the moment.

He directed us near the center of the floor for all to see, now comfortable to display our version of a Bachata dance. When the sole of my boots stuck to the floor, causing me to lose my balance, he was there to catch me, effortlessly. How could this possibly be the same man I had spent the last 24 hours with? I wanted more of him, I wanted to stay longer, wanted Patrick to stay with me, be with me, needed the person he had become, there amidst the crowd, the glare of the spotlights, and the soothing sounds of the Latino music I loved to move too. But the establishment had to close. We left the club sometime past 1:00 a.m., and headed back to Lowell.

Police were patrolling the road, so we drove slowly. Inside the car, I thanked him profusely for the impromptu evening. I was overjoyed.

"You did well," he said. "Extremely well. I am so proud of you. You are the perfect woman." The compliment felt forced, useless and laced with condescension. But, I let it go.

"Thank you," I responded, feeling the sudden weight of his despondency. Still, with a smile, as he grabbed my hand, I pointed to my boots. "Not the proper equipment to be swayed in," I told him.

He started laughing, just then recognizing how much my agility and swiftness must have been impeded by the highly adhesive nature of my kinky boots.

But he must have known, I told myself. He had to have known.

The minute we entered the house, I felt it again, the heaviness of his presence—an absence. The feelings of playfulness I had been filled with earlier were annihilated by his sudden and unpredictable detachment. There would be no shower, therefore, no sex. The distance that he had abruptly imposed was wide and its timing incomprehensible. I felt panic surfacing, squeezing the air out of my lungs.

After trying to sleep with him awhile, I got up from the bed. Unable to sustain his indifference, I headed to the brown couch, seeking refuge on its cold surface. Folded into a fetal position, I rocked myself to sleep. The gloom I felt was palpable. It would follow me until my departure the next afternoon. No salty skin would be licked until the following day. Valentine's Day.

CHAPTER FOUR

Patrick was the combination of all the men I had wanted and desired, but did not get to have the opportunity to be with, before marrying John. He represented the footballers of my college years, with their chiseled faces and hard, youthful bodies. The difference now was that I exuded a confidence, independence and maturity, that translated into attractiveness. But, the self-confidence I projected hid the uncontrollable lust I felt for Patrick. It made me feel weak. It told me I needed to tame the vulnerability lying at the core of my being.

My week had been a miserable one. Patrick was returning none of my calls, sending me into an acute state of angst. When he did text, breaking the silent treatment he was deploying, the text would be cryptic, crumbs of opacity. His behavior stemmed from something I still failed to understand. We had last seen each other the previous Wednesday. I had gone to the Taiwanese consulate in Boston to renew my Taiwan residence permit. I had proposed we meet for dinner for a short two hours, as I had to go back home to pick my daughter up from school. I had also mentioned my need to pick up my hairdryer and some expensive hair products I had left behind.

I needed them, I explained, for my daughter's upcoming play. Somehow this had infuriated him.

As he slid into the passenger seat of my car, he apologized for being an hour late. He had gotten a haircut at the busiest barber in Lowell, he said. For a moment, I felt like laughing. He took himself so seriously—too seriously, I now realized. I looked at him. His head was neatly shaven from his receding hairline and emerging bald spot to the back of his neck. I was suddenly reminded that the weekend before, I had become aware of some of my lover's insecurities. While applying a special scalp lotion he usually ordered off the internet, he had shared his plan to get a hair transplant. He also revealed the use of the black hair dye in his bathroom closet and the tweezers for plucking out his chest hair and eyebrows. It seemed Patrick dedicated much time to the maintenance of his appearance. The round magnifying mirror sitting majestically atop his bathroom counter should have warned me, at the very least—I had landed myself a metro-sexual of the Latino kind, a lethal combination.

We decided to have dinner at his local Chinese buffet restaurant. The idea was to eat rapidly, so as to efficiently manage the little time we had. It was now 8:00 p.m. I had to pick Alice up before 11:00 p.m.

Back at his house, we undressed rapidly, exceptionally skipping the shower and dove into bed. Again, our bodies were moving in synchronicity, a shared rhythm so compelling, it rendered me speechless. The passion emanating from him felt real, as he used his mouth to possess me and violently mark me. On many previous occasions, I had playfully tried to push his lips away from my neck, pleading him to stop. This time was no different and would yield nothing new. Upon hearing my demand, he lifted his head and told me that, until I lived with him, under the same roof, these markings would serve their purpose.

"I love you," he added, as he bit the inside of my right palm, bringing me to the edge of bearable pain.

"I love you, too," I replied, momentarily stunned by the violent gesture. This ritualistic component of our lovemaking had started to create a permanent wound on the palm of my hand. But somehow, I ached for that pain, wanting more of it, each time.

The cumulative effect of his repeated biting was that the wound created a sensor, a direct pathway to him. I would either press on the tender point to imagine being with him, or the pain would surface on its own, mentally transporting me to him. Either way, he had now physically etched his presence onto my body.

I kissed him goodbye. With a funny smirk on his face, he reminded me to take my hair products.

Once home, I hurried and headed for the bathtub, feeling the urgent need to soak my bottom in hot soapy water. I could feel solid particles had slid into my panties. Sitting in the tub, the filth from our lovemaking was evident by the little brown bits floating in the water around me. It reminded me of the turn my sex life had taken, of my slow descent into depravity, of something that was slowly settling into me, surfacing, other pieces of filth, hugging, this time, the mind.

I stepped out of the bathtub to dry myself, suddenly feeling tired, seeing my reflection in the mirror. The deep purple markings around my nipples and along my collarbone had returned, forming an odd constellation whose meaning and influence had yet to be determined. But I knew, deep inside, that their presence on my body foreshadowed the implosion of its main star. This constellation was a dark constellation.

"Shit, shit, shit," I thought. I wrapped a bath towel around myself, then opened the door, popping my head out to make sure Alice was in her room. I swiftly entered my room and changed into tight fitting pajamas.

Alice suddenly came into my bedroom and informed me that, the following day, day four of spirit week, was a 1980s fashion-themed day. She was donning a high side ponytail, and wearing the tiger-striped leggings, neon pink leg warmers and headband I had purchased for her in Boston. Pointing to the knot tied on the side of her left hip, she asked me if, during the 1980s, that was how they wore their sweatshirts.

Suddenly, hope reentered my life, as her tone and demeanor uplifted me. She was smiling at me and my heart melted, as I felt a reconnection with her. With a mix of candor and eagerness, I asked her if she had seen the movie, Flashdance.

"No," she replied.

"Well," I said, suddenly feeling energized. "Jennifer Beal wore her sweatshirt off the shoulder like this," I said, as I proceeded to demonstrate.

I had lost my vigilance and forgotten about the marks, as I would countless times to come. They would become evolving tattoos. A classless mother is what I had become.

"Nice hickies, Mom," Alice stated, unable to hide her disappointment. And then she left the room. I remained seated on my bed, mouth agape, awkwardly stunned into silence. And I started to cry.

The weekend preceding my birthday, at the end of February, was punctuated by my daughter's three drama presentations. There was one on Friday evening, Saturday evening, and Sunday afternoon. I saw these events as lifelines to help me find our new state of balance together. I intended to grab each and every performance firmly. I would be attending the first two alone, while John would be joining me for the third one.

I received a text from Patrick just as the lights had dimmed for the Friday evening performance.

Call me now, it read. Instantly feeling giddy, I got up and called him.

"I need to see you, baby," he said. "Get in your car tomorrow morning and leave at 6:00 a.m."

Always flattered to be this wanted, I smiled to myself. "OK," I told him. "Let me call you after the play." Excited, I returned to my seat, convinced everything between us was going well, trusting his eagerness was a sign I could seek comfort from. To my complete surprise, at the end of the show, I found out he had wrongly expected I would call him back 15 minutes following the end of our conversation. It had become obvious that, my Latino boyfriend's English needed some good tweaking. I am not exactly sure how me saying, "I will call you back after the play," was misunderstood for, "I will call you back in 15 minutes," but apparently it was. After the play, he ignored my calls and texts, making it impossible for me to understand how just two hours before, I had been a wanted woman.

Two days had passed since my last exchange with Patrick, infusing my state of mind with much turmoil. I drove to Montreal for my birthday, carrying a weight I couldn't comprehend–I just knew it wasn't normal. It felt as if I was being erased from something, from someone's life. I arrived in Montreal nauseated, shamefully displaying my feelings of infatuation everywhere I went, for everyone to see. My phone was glued to the inside of my hand, its heat prompting me to obsessively open it. I had become a slave to its ringtone and vibrations, in despair each time I realized Patrick had not surfaced. I hid my lack of concentration by retreating into untimely silences and zoning out of ongoing conversations. I was aware I had slid into a very uncomfortable space, and more than ever, it frightened me. It had now been a week since I had heard his voice.

And still no calls or texts from Patrick.

His hurtful silence had been overwhelming, especially on my birthday. I had moved back from Taiwan to reconnect with the western world, specifically to reconnect with portions of my past, to expose the newness of me within a known context. Patrick was the obstacle to it all, the ultimate hurdle I had placed in the middle of my life.

The evening before leaving Montreal to drive back to Northampton, he finally texted me. The phrase stunned me. Do you want me to stop texting you? it had read. There, in Montreal, seated on my friend's living room couch I stared at my phone. I understood nothing of what was unfolding, I had no reference, no understanding of the man's behavior. I felt the panic rise to my throat and I called him, my heart racing. On my second try, he answered, sounding irritated. My voice must have carried with it a plea. I do not remember, but I had been heard.

Biting nervously on my lips, and with a taste of iron in my mouth, I drove to him the next day, wondering how our meeting would unfold. To be near him, however painful to bear, was all I wanted.

I had purposely left Montreal early to ease into a constructive state of mind, catching a movie before I saw Patrick. I felt the need to transition to him, to dilute the feelings of neediness so foreign to me. Toward the end of the movie, my phone's vibrations alerted me. Nervously, I pulled it out of my coat pocket and saw I received a text from him asking me to meet him at the coffee shop next to the theatre in 45 minutes. There is no privacy at my home, he had written, no room to discuss.

My efforts to ground myself were useless, as fear interjected itself in an instant. Discussing, he had said. And yet, discussing was something he avoided. How many times had he repeated those words to me? Unable to concentrate on the movie, I left my seat knowing I would watch the ending some other time.

But I never would.

I needed to move, to physically walk the feelings outside, into the cold air. I headed to the coffee shop, ordered a tea and called Charlie.

She was not impressed with me.

What a lost cause Isabelle has become, was what I sensed she was thinking. In fact, this friend, the best listener in the world, who was never judgmental, and always expressed her opinion in a tactful and timely manner … well, this person was now speechless. I had incarnated her limit.

I tried to prepare myself for the pain and relief I was about to feel in massive doses. Humiliation was what made me the most apprehensive. He was ending this crazy relationship. He was initiating the process. He was the human incarnation of chaotic thinking. He was the singer of the nonsensical anthem that reunited all the unstable lovers of the universe.

He was going to leave me.

He walked in, obviously annoyed, scanning the coffee shop, evaluating the crowd. His attire was almost comical. Casually dressed in sweatpants and a cheap hoodie, I caught a glimpse of his feet. I blinked at the sight. His bare feet had been slid into fluffy beige slippers. The absurdity of it saved me, helping me regain some composure, helping me put my potential loss in perspective.

He kissed my cheek, but barely. Oh, but still, a kiss. He sat down and looked at me straight on with inquisitive eyes.

It is I who should demand answers. It is I who should display anger, an emotion forbidden to express in your presence, I was thinking.

The discussion we had was filled with incongruous versions of hard facts. His recollection of the events leading to my departure for Montreal were senseless, but without appeal. I had to bite the bullet.

He decided to move our discussion to his car, invoking yet again the need for more privacy. There, filled with a renewed sense of self-confidence,

I told him I was not the girl for him. In fact, I told him the girl he wanted did not exist.

He stared at me, wide-eyed.

"No skinny white bitch will ever put up with your antics," I told him.

I could see he was torn, caught between hardwired principles directing him to get rid of me, and the sense that I could be the girl he had waited for. For a moment, albeit too brief, I did ask myself if I wanted to be that girl. I did not really care anymore. I had managed to secure my place by his side for the upcoming night, which was the essential part—the quintessential fix.

I understood his hesitancy in bringing me home with him that night. When we got there, a little brunette was seated, waiting for us, in the living room. Patrick introduced her to me as Jocelyne, the four-year-old daughter who lived with him on the weekends. Slowly walking toward her, I wondered what Patrick had done with her for the last two months. Where had she been on the weekends?

I knew of her existence, the product of a one-night stand with a young illegal immigrant from Guatemala, but I had become accustomed to her absence, an absence I had failed to question. As I kneeled to introduce myself to her, I was distraught by the sight of her hair. It was strikingly scant, betraying what I suspected was malnourishment. With an already apparent athletic build, a bouncy little derriere and well-balanced facial features, she was the carbon copy of her father.

My first contact with her was cold and tentative at best. She observed me with obvious mistrust, and hesitantly moved to the brown leather couch, pretending to watch her favorite movie, Frozen. I joined her on the couch and we stayed there together, taming one another's presence until Patrick put her to bed at midnight. It seemed inappropriate to put her to bed so late, but I knew better than to voice my opinion at that time. Why compromise the consumption of my carnal meal?

The alternate self he presented, yet again, was hypnotic, fueling my hunger for his hands, for his mouth, for him. The intense energy from our argument was now being transferred into our hips, effacing the uncertainty that had threatened my sense of balance hours before.

That night, our lovemaking would be marked by undeniable synchronicity. My orgasm triggered shivers in me that cascaded throughout his insides, evidently surprising both of us with a simultaneous feeling of pleasure. Then, his eyes opened up a little more, his sand-paper-like hands moistened the inside of mine. Something had startled him.

He got up early, to feed Jocelyne. He gave her milk to drink and began force-feeding her the Latino breakfast he had prepared, a mushy mixture made of oats. It was disconcerting to observe how he fed her. He placed her on his lap and shoved spoonful after spoonful of food into her obviously full little mouth. I noticed, with dread, that she was complying, clearly out of fear. I said nothing, eating my piece of toast quietly, sipping my cinnamon and star anise tea. I watched Alejandro as he, himself, was busy observing me integrating what I was witnessing.

"Don't worry," he said with a strange seriousness, "you will get used to this."

I sustained his look, unable to reply, frozen by the oddity of the comment.

What exactly was I going to learn to adapt to?

At this point, my interaction with Patrick had returned to its default mode, an unbearable staccato rhythm of monosyllabic interjections. He had changed.

"Ven aca," I heard him command from the living room. I walked across the dining room, careful to close behind me the French doors dividing both rooms and, as instructed, sat on the sofa diagonal to him, clueless as to what would unfold. Off-balance and perplexed by his tone, I watched his eyes fix on a void. Still looking away from me, his words poured out with a surprising flow. "Last night was my first time feeling like love was made," he confessed. I swallowed what little saliva I had left inside my dry mouth. These words, as flattering as they were to hear, were unexpected. "I want a home," he continued. "I want to build a home with somebody who is serious about being part of my life."

Is this a ploy to get me out of his life? was the first question that came to mind. I thought he must have known how I felt about our prospective future together. That we, whatever we were, were not sustainable. Our respective differences in culture, education, and social class all pointed to a profound mismatch. I knew it.

Yet, I heard myself say, "I want the same thing." That was what actually came out of my mouth. Staring at me, the expression on his face unchanged, he got up, kissed me fully on the mouth and said that it was all settled. Stunned by this turn of events, we both rushed out and got into our respective cars.

While driving on Interstate 90, I received a flood of texts from Patrick, reaffirming his love for me. The incongruence that had emerged inside my gut would stay with me the rest of that day.

CHAPTER FIVE

Alice's March break had arrived, and she and John were preparing for a trip to Taipei. I had initially thought of going with them. I had many good friends there to see, many places to revisit. But I decided against it at the last minute, as I had to think of my health. For one, my migraines and fibromyalgia seemed better controlled in North America. For another, the sixteen hour plane ride and thirteen hour difference in time zone would be a lot for me to manage for a short two-week stay. It did not make sense to me. Sure, the freedom and accessibility to Patrick may have played a small role. But in all honesty, I needed to challenge myself, by facing the loneliness and solitude I felt were necessary to my healing. I was slowly coming to understand what Patrick was all about. He was a light and pleasant distraction. Still, I wanted more of that.

Before leaving for the JFK airport, John looked at me as I discreetly prepared for Patrick's nightly visit to Northampton, to me, his first. His hurt and pain was so palpable it shocked me to a halt. He looked at me with an odd tandem of resigned sadness and desire.

"Can I take a picture of you?" he asked tentatively. "You are stunning." I stood there, unable to articulate a response. I stared back at him standing in front of me. "Isabelle," he added, "I don't have a picture of you on my phone. I never did." I looked at him, unable to speak, paralyzed by his sadness, understanding his despair, the lust in his eyes, a weight I felt ill-equipped to absorb.

"Sure," I finally said, "go ahead." Suddenly, I was reminded of those sixteen selfies of him and his mistress. Yes, I thought, as much as you want, take your pictures, my gift to you.

I hugged my daughter tightly. I knew she had wanted me to go with her, but I also knew this trip was essential in helping her reach a new equilibrium. She had been exposed to the turmoil of her parents' unraveling, and she had witnessed my descent into indecency. I had been sucked into a vortex of pain she could see, but not understand. Taipei would provide her with the soothing reassurances of her past, while giving me the space to exhale my fetid breath without provoking further collateral damage. Nonetheless, I felt my heart sink as I saw her get in the car with her father. This was her first trip alone with him—and without me.

I was quick to put on some music, feeling the need to fill the now empty space. I began slowly setting my table, being careful not to deter my expected guest with an overwhelmingly flawless display. The huntress in me understood I had been chasing an animal through careful traps and set-ups. This mindful adjustment was just another one. An overabundance of luxury and perfection had proven a hurdle for us in the past. Stark simplicity was going to be my new religion.

When Patrick arrived, rapidly bringing us upstairs, he seemed most drawn to the personal items in my bedroom. He manipulated my statues with care, examining them from all angles, as if looking at artefacts. It was the childhood album my father had created for me, fifteen years prior, that was, by far, what pulled him in the most. With evident composure, he flipped through the pages, pausing repeatedly to focus on some aspect of an image. He then walked slowly around the furniture, taking mental notes of the framed pictures of me, my friends, and my children hanging on the wall above my dresser. His feigned detached study of my environment was betrayed by the fascination his face expressed. My world intrigued him.

He approached me with calculated indifference, still, and smiled. Returning the smile, I slowly bent down and pulled out a box from under the bed. It held ropes, vibrators, butt plugs, and a candle, from which the melted wax could be used as massage oil. His eyes widened, sending me into a heartfelt laughter. I had meant to teach him the art of slowing down, but he hastily undressed and started to unbutton my shirt. The slowing down part would have to wait.

My aim had been to command the pace of our evening. In spite of his innate sexual abilities, he did not understand my body, the demands it communicated. His kissing me now amply compensated for these deficiencies. His lips, my weak point, the ultimate fire starter, dictated a surrendering I could not deny myself. I let him wet my mouth with his. I let him remove my clothing and place my body under his.

He had introduced me to anal sex and I had become fixated on returning the favor. I had tried numerous times before, but always had been met with his resistance. This time, I would succeed.

Leaving my straddle, I kissed his mouth and licked my way down, stopping to cover the width of his chest, gradually circling down to the base of his shaft. There I hovered, letting my hair dangle, brushing against his soft testicles. Once lubricated by the inside of my mouth, I slid up and down him with generous attention to the tip, carefully suctioning, while slowly rubbing that space he loved so much. But my descent stiffened him. He was pulling my finger away from this forbidden place I had tried to access. I pushed back, but I could feel his resistance. It was becoming obvious that his criteria for manhood associated anal sex with homosexuality. It would have to wait, I told myself, caressing his shaved pubic area. Patience would win him over.

I had hidden the restraints under the mattress, restraints purchased for him, wanting to surprise him. It was he who discovered them accidentally, as he pulled my head from the pillow. His surprise matched mine, as I had forgotten about them. The weapons meant to subjugate him were now going to be turned against me. He carefully attached my wrists and ankles to the legs of the bed, evidently careful not to hurt me. What was meant to be a playful scenario was now becoming a very serious one, to him anyway. Unable to hold back my laughter as he hovered over me, I simply asked him to remove the bonds. "We don't need these," I concluded with a soft smile. "We are so much better without them."

And as I laid on my stomach and faced the wooden floor, him asleep by my side, miles away from me, from this room, I became aware, more, of my thoughts—the center of them. Words, so often, aren't enough to reveal the depth of who we are—simple touches, uncontrived touches, better at bridging one body to the other, one soul to the next. I looked at the artillery of sexual toys sprawled on the floor. They made me wonder but for a moment. About where I was in this life, in a quest to experiment more—a certainty—but to what purpose? And I felt his hand reach for mine, fatigue easing its way behind my eyes. I took it and tucked it between my breasts. How the pleasure of the flesh, with all its heat, tantalizes even the spirit, I thought. It does for me. My eyelids dropped, my mouth opened, soft and spent, and from it flew, doubts about my choices, about why I was letting recklessness weave itself into me. Anais Nin came to mind, the mindfuck behind her life, mostly, and how that life had led her to ignore her boundaries, a choice to try and heal the unhealable. She had lived her life unhinged. She had allowed herself to be, and do, with impunity. A passage she had written, ringing inside my ear, words that were striking a fragile cord.

"I disregard the proportions, the measures, the tempo of the ordinary world. I refuse to live in the ordinary world as ordinary women. To enter ordinary relationships. I want ecstasy. I am a neurotic—in the sense that I live in my world. I will not adjust myself to the world. I am adjusted to myself."

Anais, I whispered to myself before falling asleep, is this really sustainable?

Is seeking passion the only path to wholeness?

And I wondered, and I wondered more.

And I slept, and I slept well.

The light in the room hinted to the morning's arrival. The splash of rays that highlighted Patrick's body was irresistible. I had to capture the moment. Standing over his body, camera in hand, I froze images of his back, focusing on the scars I still had not been allowed to play with. Immortalizing the passage of this man in my life, I hoped our day would unfold without any problems. I had noticed that the mornings following our lovemaking had become marked by a disturbing lack of proximity. I wanted to reverse these tendencies, prevent them from rooting themselves into our time together. Clicking away, I hoped I would succeed.

Still, he seemed to withdraw more than usual that morning. It took me a moment to make sense of that and not to give in to the bitter sensations I felt at the perceived rejection.

The equilibrium was brought back, as usual, in the shower, the ritual bringing peace and harmony as we washed, or specifically, scrubbed our bodies. He spoke of how his mother washed his body, scraping the skin into absolute cleanliness.

She has planted the OCD seed in him, I was thinking. And, my God, I cannot escape her. She watched over us in his bedroom, while he took me from behind on the carpet, and now the shower. Would it have been better or worse had she still have been alive? I wondered.

Through the rigid personae he chose to display in order to establish, I presumed, his authority, he playfully flipped me in the kitchen, incapable of controlling his urge to show his happiness. I was touched by his failed efforts to hide his affection for me. His vulnerabilities moved me, his flaws seducing me into submissiveness. And, that was my problem. I forgave and hoped with such ease. What would be the cue that I would finally notice, that would tip the balance in the proper direction?

He snapped the visor down and asked me to look at my eyes reflected in the mirror.

"See how green they are," he said with fascination. I turned to him to acknowledge the look of enticement I had provoked in him. He took my face between his hands and kissed my mouth, my forehead, my cheeks, painting my face with his saliva. I got out of the car. He rolled the window down. "I'm getting my passport. Soon," he said, "we will go to Montreal."

I looked back and smiled.

CHAPTER SIX

One week had passed since Alice and John left for Taipei. The house was mine, and my view of life at that time was wallpapered with images of bronze and white body parts tightly bound and rolling in dripping bodily fluids. I was consumed with desire. It was evident. Fuck, to be honest, I could not think straight.

But, he was not there for me to hold onto at the moment. He had refused to let me stay with him in Lowell for the last week of Alice's March break, blaming his work schedule.

To try and prove his point, he sent me a picture of his dining room table, filled with roughly, ten file folders. This was meant to convey the message that he was overwhelmed with paperwork. It was the end of March, and it was tax time and he was setting up his construction company. But, I could also clearly see that some folders were empty. Insulted, I insisted I was coming, and I texted him that I was leaving for his house in the next 15 minutes. It was 11:30 p.m. I had been drinking, not heavily, but still too much to drive. His reply sent me into disbelief.

You know I cannot concentrate when you are close to me, he said, a line I was hearing more and more. At first, I was flattered, but after rereading the pleasing words he had written, suspicion emerged, stirring more unease. It was a strange line. He specified that if I were to come I had to arrive after 1:00 a.m., and leave before 8:00 a.m., that same morning. He was expecting me to drive almost two hours for a six-hour cuddle. Stung by his display of childish absurdity, I started to gather my keys and my purse, preparing to drive to his house, one last time, and tell him I had no intention of further pursuing this type of unfulfilling relationship. With my hastily written script in hand, I left, fuming.

I was now in the comfort of my car being soothed by the melancholia of my music, by my mood, and by the Xanax I had just ingested. Alcohol and drugs were threatening to become my default mode of coping.

How commonly vulgar you have become, Isabelle, I told myself, as I backed out of my driveway.

What I saw, when I entered his house, was comical. He appeared to be sleepy, his eyes half-closed, wearing an old knitted hat with the word, Chicago, written on its rim. The hat was really more of a rag, a dirtied woolly garment precariously placed on his head, leaning to the left, as if just about to fall. Not wanting to waste time, I immediately lashed out, like the Isabelle I knew; the Isabelle who was specific, to the point; the Isabelle who was regaining her integrity, her sense of right. She was back. She was in control.

And then, I sensed it happening in slow motion. First, the threat of a loose bowl movement, and then the tightening of my throat. My voice suddenly became unsteady and hoarse. I continued though, encouraged by the nervous symptoms Patrick himself was displaying. His throat was obviously parched and he spoke in an agitated tone. It did not stop his discourse, though. Patrick was agile at turning the tables on me. Suddenly, I was the one showing disrespect, and not understanding the pressure he was under.

"I cannot work while you are close to me," was his only defense. He repeated this phrase over and over, while he paced across the dining room, pointing at all his folders.

His Latino display of emotions impressed me, freezing me on the spot. The confusion I felt was now seated on my chest. He had me convinced that I was the one at fault, and I could now hear myself clumsily apologizing for my rudeness and insensitivity.

I had crossed his line. We were now in the middle of a stormy discussion, and that, to him, was paramount to sinning. I knew this relationship was unsustainable. I knew it. I knew it. But still I decided to lie by his side on the bed, fully clothed. He remained, of course, distant, milking my faux-pas as much as he could.

I wanted to flee, to regain some form of dignity, and to send him a message. I made a move to leave. I tentatively got up but was unable to walk out of his room, to leave his house. I had come to him for a reason. I wanted to be held. I craved his touch. I needed his body. Like a beaten puppy, I slid in beside him again, still clothed, and inched myself closer to him. At least I felt the heat—his heat, as vapor steaming my body. It was better than nothing.

I did not sleep, but neither did he.

At 5:30 a.m., he turned around to face me. Unable to sustain my pleading eyes, he looked away as he removed my clothes, swiftly, thereafter, penetrating me. This was the fix I had come to collect. Slipping inside of me, silently, he lifted his head, looking to meet my eyes. My tears were plentiful. They streamed down, wetting the satin pillowcase. His face brushed against mine, and he ignored the fresh warmth of my tears. He was slowly motioning in and out of me, while effectively striking my clitoris. He looked at me and told me never again to shake our relationship.

"Never again," he repeated as he ejaculated profusely inside me. "For the next time will be the last," he added, as he withdrew. He then got up, showered, slipped on his long johns, jeans, and a black turtle neck. He kissed me, and he exited the bedroom to make us some tea.

I needed to keep feeding this facsimile of a relationship to determine the extent to which I was willing to take it. I needed to find a way to test myself. The March break should have provided me with that opportunity, but Patrick had pushed back, blaming his work. He commanded the pace at which the relationship was allowed to develop. That left no room for my needs and wants to be addressed. I could not understand how he failed to see that we had lost momentum. The rejection stung.

My own paralysis was also unsettling. I was afraid to assert myself, and clearly state my boundaries. Capitulating to his requests and impositions in exchange for a void was distressing. I was not recognizing the person I had metamorphosed into.

No one would have recognized me.

Whatever I was becoming, I could not withstand the edges loneliness was sharpening. To counterbalance the void I was carrying, I had to provoke and shape my destiny, or at least a shadow of it.

I decided to leave for another trip to Quebec. I carefully prepared Patrick for the thought of me wandering the streets of Montreal on my own. How ironic. He pushed but couldn't handle the consequences of a push, on me, on him—on us. It had become obvious that the idea of his prized possession straying from his sight was enough to provoke tides of anguish in him. This was a paradox, considering he had declined to let me spend time with him in Lowell. His vivid imagination, I now knew, played wicked tricks on his mind. I was becoming the victim of his paranoia. I was also the target of long periods of emotional abandonment, feeling his silence through the absence of texts and phone calls.

The fragments of neglect I wanted to flee, reconstituted themselves during my drive to Montreal. There, within the confined space of my car, I acknowledged their existence, but my will to examine them was lacking. The moment I stepped outside of my safe haven of a car, anxiety and unsteadiness always awaited me. There, in Montreal, I would face perplexity and ambiguity with unflinching grace. I foolishly believed, all would be well.

Again.

When will I learn?

How will I learn?

I did manage to momentarily flee my pain, by spending a lot of time with my Montreal girlfriends. From my friend's house, where I was again staying, we coordinated dinners, booked spa services, and headed out to restaurants. There, in my hometown, I was seeking the antidote for the crushing loneliness I felt. I had come to Montreal to regain the unshakable stability I used to feel with my friends.

Unfortunately, I felt rootless.

On my last evening with the girls, we decided to eat in Old Montreal, at le Garde-Manger. This restaurant had been a culinary destination of mine, ever since I had come back to North America. The chef there was amazing. He had even managed to dethrone Bobby Flay in the Iron Chef competition. I took selfies and sent them to Patrick.

Despite the constant ache I was carrying inside, I managed to enjoy myself. I was soaking in the love and affection of my friends, aware of the rarity of those feelings back in Northampton.

I wanted to feel fully replenished. I wanted to capture and deposit every single bit of kindness I could find.

It was a question of survival.

The next morning, my friend had gathered the girls for a farewell brunch. The discomfort I felt was unbearable, as I listened to them voice their displeasure over my involvement with Patrick.

"Cute and funny in January," they all said, "but now it was time to leave him." Not only was he below my social class, but he could jeopardize my divorce settlement. This had been tugging at me, too. Part of me did not feel like ceasing my relationship with Patrick. On the other hand, he was proving to be more trouble than anything else. He might not be worth the price to pay, should John decide to hold the liaison against me.

Deep inside, I believed John would do the right thing no matter what. I could not believe John would intentionally hurt me, even monetarily. The ugly reality though, was that our prenuptial agreement did not favor me. I would leave with whatever assets were under my name, and John would leave with whatever assets were under his name. Bluntly put, that meant I had nothing. Why, on earth, I had agreed to sign such an agreement was beyond me. And the girls, half of them lawyers, had me in a state of panic.

The truths of my life, that I had avoided on my way to Montreal, were now difficult to ignore. I had crafted the very opportunity that made meeting Patrick possible. I was responsible for that fateful Friday night. I had formulated my own relationship rebound therapy. The moment I stepped into Patrick's life, our incompatibility was evident. His working-class neighborhood and poorly furnished house had not deterred me from focusing on tending to my sensual needs. But, I should have left after that first weekend. The mantra, slow and steady, repeating itself like a keynote gone mad, was now calling me home.

Preparing to leave for Patrick's home, I was thinking about the disturbing text I had received from him that morning. It was a photo of my bra and panties spread out on what appeared to be Alejandro's bed. This was not all that surprising. Somehow, after each shower, I would come back to Patrick's bedroom looking for my panties. Nine times out of ten, I would not find them. I would return home, either wearing no panties, or wearing an extra pair I had brought with me.

In our bedroom conversations, Patrick kept bringing up the subject of Alejandro's fixation on me. He would mention how beautiful Alejandro found me, and how my skinny body allured him, filling his fantasies. I could see Patrick's discomfort, but appreciated how he had chosen to manage the delicate situation.

While unusual, the fact that Alejandro found me attractive had not really bothered me. I felt Patrick's competent patience, as he guided Alejandro through his teenage fixation on me. With these thoughts in my mind, I was driving to Patrick's house for a spontaneous visit, improvising a midweek layover.

When I arrived, I met Patrick in his garage where he was repairing a car with his son and his brother. It was the first time I was seeing Patrick in his element. There was something so poignant about the scene, as the bond uniting the three of them was palpable. I felt envy and jealousy springing inside me, wishing my husband had been this close to our children, and been capable of transmitting his own set of abilities.

I spied on the three of them, indulging the voyeur in me, hoping for some sort of revelation to appear, until I decided to make my presence known, knocking on the side of the open garage door. Patrick pulled his head up and for a brief moment I saw the smile in his eyes—for a moment. It quickly was followed by such drastic self-restraint, it startled me. I could never get used to this persona, I thought. The character he would choose to inhabit was so authoritarian and dry. Apparently, the behavior he displayed in public was meant to demonstrate his sense of superiority, highlighting his mental toughness. It manifested itself as a cruel veil of indifference directed at me, his prized possession. I was quick to dismiss his hurtful attitude, so I headed to the house. All would be mended in bed.

I placed the angel food cake I had baked at home that morning, on a plate beside my freshly made strawberry and raspberry salad. There, in the middle of the kitchen, I wanted my lure to shine. Its hook, pointy, and sharp.

Patrick and Alejandro walked into the house, bringing with them a strange, oppressive silence. Patrick's intolerance of Alejandro had become more challenging to ignore. All was said in Spanish, but the tone did not lie. Spite would be on the menu tonight. That and rice.

Grace was said with the usual acrimony and the meal eaten in relative muteness. I had learned my lesson, I just wanted to blend into the tableau. Sitting at this stern table, I could not help but rationalize my insistence at being part of such a sad scene. I looked at Patrick, carefully examining his features, and somehow my presence here made sense.

I headed to the shower first. Wet on wet, I was thinking, feeling my body respond to the beginning of our ritual. I dried off quickly and jumped into bed dressed in my nightgown, as I had learnt not to take anything for granted anymore. He slid in beside me, naked, immediately pulling my nightgown off and meeting me as I had hoped he would.

It was during the third round of our lovemaking that his unusual request was formulated. In the midst of our caresses, while still inside me, rocking me gently, he started whispering his plan. He had devised a solution that would cure Alejandro of his infatuation with me, he told me between two breaths. His still virgin son was no longer functioning, he added. Smitten by me, he spent hours masturbating, anywhere he could.

"OK," I said, imagining pairs of underwear hanging somewhere in his son's room. Mental images of them emerged, starched by dried up fluid, rigid, stiffened with want. Beautiful pieces of art, sculptures, or better yet, modern mobiles distinct with black, white, and turquoise lingerie pieces, circling above his head to the sound of Ravel's Bolero. I imagined Alejandro's eyes glued to the middle part that absorbs my bodily secretions.

I imagined his nostrils alerted by the smell my hormones had leaked. But the moment failed to be light, the flattery had worn out, I now felt, as Patrick pursued with insistence, his quest for me to deflower his son. "If you love me," he continued, "I beg of you, take him now and satisfy his need to be with you. Help me end this nightmare I have been living with."

No longer sure what I was hearing, I blurted out my refusal to comply with his demand. "What are you asking?" I heard myself scream. "Are you insane? Are you fucking insane?" He slowed down his hip motions, pretending to recognize the nonsense, only to pursue the conversation. I came to understand that this plan was the result of numerous conversations he had conducted with his son over the last few dinners.

"You discussed this with him?" I asked with incredulity. "Like, in a structured conversation?" I continued, dumbstruck. The exchange continued on as we still were moving our bodies, somehow responding to these twisted thoughts. Even I was momentarily turned on—momentarily. He commented on the size of his son's penis: big, long, better than his. "If you love me," he said, "I can go get him right now.... He is waiting.... We both love you.... I know he is waiting for me to get him from his bed."

"If I love you, and because I do, I cannot go ahead," I replied, suddenly aware of the seriousness of his intent, its imminent fulfillment. "Understand that if this scenario of yours was to unfold, I would never return to you, physically, or otherwise—ever. In fact, let me go now," I suddenly said, disgusted. "Let me leave." I had had enough. The thought of Alejandro had sickened me to the point of escape.

"No, no," he said, nailing me solidly to the mattress. Amazed at the fact that I was still physically there, in the room, in this house, I pushed back until we somehow magically climaxed. I turned around quickly, with Patrick tightly holding onto my waist, knowing I would face another sleepless night.

Driving back to Northampton the next day, my mind was assaulted by the many unavoidable and troubling questions I knew I had to elucidate. Why did I believe this was only a father's overzealous way of providing release for his son?

"You are clean," he had reminded me. Yes, I had thought to myself, free of disease, approved and stamped by daddy's seal.

Trying to decipher the meaning of Patrick's fantasies, the main questions imposing themselves on my distressed mind, were surfacing with clarity. What portion of his reality was rooted in fantasy? What portion of his fantasy was rooted in reality? The intersection they formed held a space I did not feel comfortable living in. What, exactly, was breathing in that space? Or better yet, what was being bred?

But wanting to understand, the quest to grasp the unthinkable, is but a trivial wish, isn't it? To prostrate yourself to the altar of all unknowing, is the only religion.

CHAPTER SEVEN

Spring arrived, coinciding with Patrick's sudden willingness to spend more time with me. Maybe the change of season had modified his perception of our viability, exposing a potential he had chosen so far to ignore, or dismiss. Whatever had prompted his change in behavior could not be logically explained as I knew he didn't have more time to dedicate to me. His working schedule was filling out, his newly formed company starting to generate some interest.

"I am the best kept secret in the area," he now repeated giddily.

Instantaneously, almost overnight, his focus on me sharpened. The phone was now ringing in the middle of the night at random hours, intruding on my delicate sleep. Each time, disoriented, I managed to talk, to listen, somehow thinking Patrick was calling me from his home in Lowell.

"I am here," he would say in his familiar low voice. "Here, in front of your home."

These words echoing in my foggy mind would direct my attention, first, to Alice, followed by an awkward, and diffuse sensation, pointing to a hard fact, my space was no longer under my full control.

It would come as a complete surprise, and he knew it. He knew what he was doing. He understood the only way I would interpret his nocturnal apparitions was by giving into the—he must love me narrative. Yes, those late night calls made me feel unique and special and would charge my body with a shot of chemicals, so potent, it became a hurdle to my thought process.

His tardy appearances infused our lovemaking with new and uncomfortable realities. My dog, Jackson, was becoming quite a liability. Aching to socialize, to be acknowledged, he always wanted to be with us and, unable to control his excitement, would bark continuously at seeing Patrick.

Patrick's main concern was that Jackson would bite him in the ass, a thought that always made me smile, knowing Jackson's proverbial inability to fight back, even when attacked. Seeing Patrick, a military man, in fear of the dog was impossible to ignore, and would send me eventually into an unappreciated laughter. We tried to get the dog to sit during our lovemaking sessions, the furry incarnation of a sex therapist. But each time, we had failed. In truth, I did not mind my dog with us in the room. What I did mind, was a dog that stood in the way of my pleasure.

I did the unthinkable. The dog had become such a nuisance for Patrick, and thus, us—I began sedating Jackson with peanut butter coated Xanax. It felt so wrong, but I saw no other choice as Patrick's already volatile temper would continue to be fueled by the dog's inability to quiet down on his own. So, reluctantly, I would feed Jackson his roofied snack and, seated on the edge of the bed, I would witness the medication's effects spreading throughout his body, as he slowly reeled to a halt, his four legs giving in to his weight. Then and only then would I feel relief spread throughout my own body.

More importantly than Jackson, there was Alice's presence to consider. She had never met Patrick, but now that he was imposing his presence in our home, I had to hide him and muffle his moaning sounds. If they were ever to meet, I would have to sanitize the context in which it would occur.

Aware of the wall's thinness, I was caught between the urge of letting go and the imperative of limiting our noise-making. The liquids we were producing offered their own form of music, to the beat of my ass being slapped, no less. Withholding my orgasms each time, I prayed for Alice to be rocked to sleep to the sound of the white-noise makers I had recently purchased. To my delight, all the adjustments I made to secure my nightly activities yielded the desired results. Stealth lovers are what we had successfully become.

His nightly visits were now extending themselves into leisurely mornings when Alice was away either at school or at a sleepover I had devised. Twice a week, he would grace my sheets with an undeniable presence, providing me with a space to surrender fully. I was struck by the ethereal quality with which our moments together were now being imprinted. I liked to think they were promises of sustenance, as I felt my hunger for intimacy slowly being fed. His willingness to weave himself into my life was fueling my mind with images of the east coast home I had always dreamed of owning. These were images of new contrasting possibilities.

John, at the house in Northampton for a five-day visit, was trying his best to contain his jealousy. He was suffocating me with his futile attempts to reel me back into his vision of a renewed relationship. Everywhere I went, he was there following me with insistent pleas to come back to him. It brought my level of impatience to a new high. I felt his neediness, yet again, but I had no strength or will to manage the despair he so freely displayed for Alice and me to see. The only escape for me was to retreat to my bedroom. In the confinement of my room, I could hide my world, complete with its messiness and lack of direction. It was from this faltering shelter that I received a few disturbing WhatsApp texts from Patrick.

Lying on my bed, at the end of the afternoon, while John was downstairs watching television, I began reading with disbelief.

Who are you chatting with? he texted.

No one, I replied, quite surprised by the absurdity of the question.

Do not lie to me, he retorted. The cascade of ranting messages that began rapidly appearing on my phone was troubling to see. I had left my WhatsApp open and I now understood he thought I was chatting with some men.

How childish, how derisory, I thought. This is my opportunity— another one. His paranoid and controlling behavior was absolutely unacceptable. Exasperated, I finally told him to go fuck himself, that I had had enough of his abusive tendencies, and that I was the wrong woman for him. You need a maid and a mother to your children, I wrote with newfound assertiveness. Just like that, I had finally given myself the permission to close my phone, something I had never done for fear of Patrick's retaliation.

There must have been 20 of them ready for me to view. Lifting myself to a seated position, I brought my phone closer and analyzed what he had sent me. Pictures of vaginas wallpapered my WhatsApp string of texts. There were dysfunctional vaginas, diseased vaginas, vaginas disfigured by perforated abscesses and vaginas blackened by sickness. His aim, I was understanding, was to scare me into faithfulness. He was orchestrating a warning meant to slow my sexual ardors.

The images were laughable manifestations of his own diseased mind, yet, it amused me. He was a child, and a child would be easy to handle. A child could create the distraction so essential to the dilution of my rootlessness, providing me with lightness and a feeling of short-term purpose.

I had agreed, twice before, to see a marriage counselor. Twice, at the very last moment, I had changed my mind and declined couple's therapy. Both attempts had been feeble ones, propelled by the urgency a crisis would provoke. I had been in a state of shock, I knew that much. But the shock had mellowed into a feeling of comfortable unrest, a place from which I felt no desire to renew my relationship with John. John had devised the third attempt, but it did not inspire me to let go of Patrick.

I did consider it, for a small moment, until John asked me to sign an informal document stating that, should we both enter therapy, we were not to date anyone else. He was toying with the definition of separation, limiting its meaning to a physical separation with a twist, I was not permitted to get involved with anyone while we were separated. It would not hold. I would not hold. I did not want it to hold.

Maybe it was a reasonable demand under the circumstances. After all, if you were trying to save your marriage, what was the problem with committing to being faithful? But, I was not ready to fully let go of Patrick, it was now very clear. How shameful. I somehow did not value my twenty-two years with my husband enough to sign the proposed document.

Had I not sacrificed enough?

The notion of time also gnawed at me. Time. I did not feel I had that much to waste. My time was now—my time. Mine. Had I been ready to move on years ago? Had I decided to quiet my quest for a vibrant liaison in exchange for financial comfort? John, pressing me to consult a therapist with him, was only adding to the certainty of my decision to pull further away from him. I felt the weight of coercion where I hungered for the lightness of freedom.

Unsurprisingly, the third attempt with a therapist was a failure. Feeling the need to justify my desire to forgo therapy, I reminded myself of my husband's needs to delve into a lifetime of ignored suffering, unresolved fears, and destructive impulses. I held the certainty that I would be sucked into his world of pain, a black hole he had created and fed. Frankly, I felt I had given him enough of my time.

In the middle of a quaint café located on Leverett Road, in Amherst, I told him that, no, there would be no possibility of a reconciliation. He had asked me to reconsider, pleading not to let go of us, to give him the fighting chance he felt Patrick was depriving him of.

"No," I simply repeated.

At the end of the afternoon, as I watched John leave the house in tears, I felt unmoved by his despair, and relieved by his departure. I had needed to be clear in my intent. I owed him that much. But now, I, too, had a void to fill.

Patrick was on my mind.

Alice, concentrating on an art project she had to submit the following day, barely noticed my preparations. At first, seemingly oblivious to the effervescence coming from my bedroom, as I was trying on clothes to the sound of my music, she walked into my bedroom and stared at me, suddenly intrigued. I mentioned, nonchalantly, that I was going to a book club in Worcester, an hour from Northampton.

What a book club it must be? I could see her eyes commenting.

Yes. Quite an intellectual one, indeed, I was smiling to myself.

The drive was especially smooth, the April evening air, warm, with a hint of the typical coolness that can be expected at the beginning of spring. Anticipation was my sole companion, its intoxication inescapable.

I arrived, just as Patrick was preparing to shower. How timely. Comfortably seated on his bed, the orange light impregnating the room with an aura of sensuality, I used my phone to read the news. With a towel wrapped around his waist, his wooden rosary flaunted on his chest, he stepped into the room, easing himself behind me.

Pressing my head forcefully against the nook of his shoulders, he reached for my phone, and told me it was time to share its contents. I somehow managed to extract myself from his rigid embrace, and turned to face him. I felt the edges of panic carving themselves onto my face.

There were texts exchanges between my friend, Charlie, and me that I did not want to share. These texts included unimportant bits of mockery directed at him, as well as detailed evidence of my own insecurities that I wished would remain private—as they should. His eyes had become lasers converging to a point, a target, a prey: me. The look of a wild feline was etched on his face, assuring me there would be no way out. I would have to comply. Curiously, my texts were of no interest to him, only my pictures seemed to obsess him, pulling his fingers, making them scroll into my life, an irreproachable one. I remember sighing–my relief. The main question I avoided that night, the main worry, should not have been directed to my phone, its lack of relevant content. It should have been directed at what he owned—his two phones never too far from his reach.

It didn't worry me, because I didn't know.

Ignorance, the wicked bliss.

CHAPTER EIGHT

I had decided to exchange my Mercedes truck for a smaller Mercedes model. Common sense dictated I compress some elements of my lifestyle. To finalize the purchase, I drove to Montreal, where it would be done cost effectively. Motivated to downsize by my newly discovered sense of financial self-preservation, animated by a will to control aspects of my life I had delegated to John in the past, I headed confidently to my hometown. Quieted by the knowledge my stay would be a short three days, Patrick had blessed this third trip to Montreal with a loving kiss. This time, finally, visiting my city would be a peaceful experience.

My schedule had been filled with back-to-back activities, with art gallery openings and formal parties, occupying most of my time. Following a quick lunch, organized by a friend, I rapidly left for Northampton in the early afternoon, happily driving my new car. While waiting to cross the Canada-Vermont border, logistics over the upcoming summer plans were nagging at me.

Could Patrick remove himself from the responsibilities of his newly created construction company? Would he bring Jocelyne? Alejandro? Would I include Alice? Catherine? Preoccupied with the intricacies of my new familial concerns, I rolled to the booth and handed over my passport. I looked up at the gentleman, and once again, recited the elements detailing my living situation in the United States. I was a Canadian, accompanying my daughter in Northampton, while she finished her high school in

Deerfield. While mindlessly playing with my new car's fun little gadgets, I heard him tell me to pull my car over and meet with him inside. I lifted my head and looked at him, unsurprised, but concerned. His tone left no room for doubt. I was in real trouble.

The agent was unapologetically blunt. It appeared to him I was living in the United States, and this posed the dangerous possibility that I would establish myself permanently on American soil. He gave me five weeks to fix my situation. By May 30th I had to leave voluntarily, or I would be barred from his country.

I had moved to Northampton, Massachusetts so my daughter could complete her school IB program. We had considered returning to Montreal, but we had not found a school there of comparable caliber. The initial plan for Alice had been for her to board at school, giving me the opportunity to travel to and from Montreal. This would have allowed me to stay under the limit of 183 days in the country.

Alice had boarded, as planned, for the two first months of the school year, but then began having panic attacks. We had then decided she would live in Northampton with me and that I would drive her back and forth to school. In addition to these adjustments, the revelation of John's affair and the quick implosion of our marriage, I could now add this debacle to the turmoil.

I called John in a state of complete hysteria, the moment I crossed the border. Screaming and yelling, I was barely able to communicate what had just unfolded. The hurtful nonchalance that greeted me was like a slap in the face. For one brief moment, I felt sorry for myself. It was such a novel feeling, a violent reminder of the abandonment, still resonating in my heart. I was being engulfed by circumstances that appeared to be out of my control, and seemingly, John was oblivious to my distress. I hung up abruptly, unable to tolerate the high pitch of his feminine voice. My situation had become nightmarish. John said it was manageable. Clearly, it was not. I needed legal help, and I needed it fast.

Upon returning to Northampton, I dialed the number of a lawyer, a friend had recommended. The call was curt, to the point. She managed to reassure me, repeating, she had successfully extended the non-immigrant status of many of her clients.

"Great," I thought. But, there was a catch. I could leave the United States if I so wished, but there was no guarantee I would be allowed back. Leaving the United States would annul the Homeland Security demand, placing me at the mercy of the American agent assessing my re-entry into the country. Decisions made at the border would be final, with no possibility of appeal.

This was now April 2016. I would not receive my answer until September, as there was a four-month backlog. I had no choice, but to stay in Northampton with Alice. I could not jeopardize her school year, and more importantly her fragile mental state. All my parental guidance and motherly presence I had sprinkled over time could be diluted, if not invalidated by my escape to Canada, or anywhere else for that matter. The nightmare was real. I was stuck here. I could now see my summer unfolding before me, frightened by the loneliness that would envelop me, a loneliness sharpened by Patrick's presence. Of that, I was becoming acutely aware.

I quieted my fears, deciding to do my best to embrace the situation. I now ignored the financial insecurities my marriage contract had revealed. I told myself repeatedly, with probable self-deception, that I had to trust John. Desperate to avoid loneliness, I decided to fully explore what needed to be explored with Patrick. It was an uncomfortable relationship, but one I was willing to better understand, to observe and to learn from. I felt confident I could walk the fine line and safely delve into the summer project I had decided Patrick and I would be. Malignant optimism had started to root itself into my psyche.

Lying in the bathtub, letting the water cover my body with its protective warmth, my thoughts had stilled. Water, how I loved its soothing, cleansing of the body and mind. I bowed to its capacity to ease my pain, as I slid slowly, immersing my head in its care, completely face down, floating, protected as a baby in its womb.

I stepped out of the bathtub, shook the excess water out of my hair, and glimpsed at my phone. I had received eleven Tango calls, five WhatsApp calls, and six regular text messages. All were from Patrick.

Someone needs to talk to me, I thought, unfazed. I walked to my bedroom wrapped in my towel. I let myself fall on the bed and proceeded to call him back.

"Where were you?" he asked lightly.

"In the bathtub," I flatly responded, slipping into my jeans.

"Why didn't you answer?" he went on.

"I didn't hear your calls come in," I said, hiding my laughter.

"When I call, you need to answer. Tango me, please," he insisted.

"Now?" I questioned, amused by his behavior, but knowing far too well that this type of distraction had a clear expiry date. Just then Alice entered my room in tears. Unable to continue with Patrick, I hung up. Turning to Alice, I noticed her crying had evolved into unstoppable waves of hyperventilation.

Alice had been struggling with the adjustment to her new school environment, challenged by the difficulty of connecting with new friends. Her worldliness clashed with the American self-sufficiency she felt the students at her school patriotically brandished. The cultural mismatch, while objectively understandable, was interpreted as rejection by Alice. The weight of loneliness was proving heavy for her to manage, meshing itself into her growing sense of rejection.

Alice had asked me for permission to sleep over at her friend Robert's boarding school in Connecticut the following Saturday. The two had attended the same elementary school in Montreal and had been best friends since kindergarten. Robert had just come out as gay and needed Alice by his side to help him quiet his own anxieties about his disclosure.

"Come and hold my hand," he had told her. "I need you."

Given both their circumstances, I knew visiting Robert would infuse her with the emotional depth she felt was missing with her other friendships. I also recognized the other opportunity Alice's sleepover was creating. It would give Patrick and me the chance to spend some quality time together, something we had not indulged ourselves in for a while. The decision to acquiesce to her demand, therefore, was an easy one to make.

As I dropped Alice at Robert's school that Saturday morning, I reminded them, with humor, of the importance of studying while catching up with each other. Robert's mother, still unaware of her son's coming out, had been clear; her son needed to prepare for the upcoming math exam on Monday. They had both smiled at me, and with their feigned teenage seriousness, agreed that, yes, they would be studying that evening. I drove off the school premises, seeing their faces slowly disappear from my rearview mirror. The love I felt right then for Alice, was incommensurable.

I headed off to Lowell, and arrived at Patrick's house amidst major house renovations he had started in his dining room. Nothing he had in mind would ever transform his dump into anything aesthetically worthy of my approval. But, I kept my mouth shut. Why rock the boat and compromise another delicious evening of pleasure?

The wall separating the kitchen from the dining room area had been destroyed. It would not be entirely brought down. Instead, it would simply be replaced by new drywall. The area had been neatly sealed with plastic sheets, while all the furniture had been piled in the living room. I was surprised, even impressed, by the precision and swiftness with which he had executed the work.

The intelligence is there, I caught myself thinking, surprised by the sudden relief it brought me.

We ate our chicken, avocado salad, and rice, while seated at an old, unstable, metallic table in a makeshift dining area. The silence surrounding these reunions was always so uncomfortable for me to feel, not knowing if a storm was to come. Alejandro said Grace with so much weight and seriousness, it made me decide, from then on, to keep my eyes forever open during the mealtime prayer. I felt the need to study the actor who was invoking his master's clemency. I did appreciate the spiritual feeling I derived from these moments, when a heartfelt Grace was pronounced. But here, resentment and judgment were teaming up in the name of God, asking Him "to give bread even to those who are undeserving."

Patrick and I headed to bed at around 11:00 p.m. that evening, both tired, but still playful. The eternal orange glow of that Himalayan salt lamp greeted us, reminding me that this was our playroom, the room where the focus of our lives was clear, where there was no ambiguity as to why we were there. Yes, it was our playroom. And, playtime had arrived.

We spent the next two hours slowly rediscovering each other's body, with delight and curiosity. That night, somehow, our connection felt stronger, our interaction morphing into a fluid feeling only contentment could explain. Lying sideways in his arms, watching him read the news on his phone, I savored the moment. This was time we had concretely carved for ourselves, a space for our lives to intersect.

While glued to Patrick's back, looking over his shoulders, watching him now play a game on his Samsung phone, my phone rang. It was now 1:30 a.m. Startled, I bent to the floor where my phone had been placed. I took it to see who was calling me. A number from Connecticut appeared on my screen. I answered, expecting Alice to be on the other end of the line, calling from Robert's dormitory.

"Hello?" I answered tentatively.

"Hello," a masculine voice replied. "Is this the mother of Alice?"

Fuck, I thought. "Yes, it is," I mumbled.

"This is Officer McMillan," he stated.

I straightened up seated on the bed, realizing immediately that this was the call no parent wanted to get. My heart stopped, my mind emptying itself of any leftover images and sensations my night had held. With trembling hands, I wrote down the address of the hospital, my illegible writing betraying my state of anguish. Patrick, stoic, observed me strangely while trying to slow me down, asking me to sit and assess the situation.

What the fuck needs to be assessed? I wondered. "We need to leave now," I said firmly, regaining my composure and collecting my belongings. There had been a change of plans. There would be no cocooning up to my Latin lover tonight. I had to drive to Hartford, Connecticut. I had to drive to the Children's hospital.

INHALED

The ride was silent except for the few phone calls I had to place to Robert's mother, Jill, and, of course, to John. Jill was as baffled as I was, stunned into a deep sense of worry, unable to clearly understand the string of events that had occurred in the unfolding narrative. Sadly, John's concern had focused on me and my whereabouts, on the implications of my absence from Northampton.

"You are an unfit mother," he finally blurted out. "How could you allow this to happen?" Driving on the barely-lit empty highway, with Patrick seated by my side with his eyes closed, I felt the sting those words had meant to inflict. They had successfully scratched guilt into my heart, ensuring the scar would forever remain there, a permanent reminder of my failure as a mother.

"We will talk tomorrow," was all I could reply.

We arrived at the hospital at 4:00 a.m., tired but wired from the adrenaline flowing through our bodies, or in mine anyway. I did not know what to expect. All I knew was that Alice was still unresponsive, that Robert, surprisingly sober, had found her unconscious in a pool of vomit and blood on the bathroom floor of the dormitory. It appeared Alice had had a serious encounter with a bottle of Grey Goose vodka. Now, plunged into a deep alcoholic coma, her head would be scanned, her body rehydrated.

When we were finally reassured Alice was out of danger, we decided Patrick would return home to Jocelyne and Alejandro by Uber. I would stay with Alice until her discharge. While calling for the Uber, I was now noticing Patricks' quiet demeanor and remembering how he had insisted the nurse clean Alice's bloody nose. His attentiveness had been endearing, but his stance had appeared distant and cold.

"See," he said, staring blankly at her, "she is fine."

It had occurred to me then, as we were both standing by her bedside, that Patrick had now met Alice for the first time.

I could not make sense of what was happening between Patrick and me, feeling paralyzed by the loss of ascendancy over my own life. I would wait patiently for him to call, text, or visit me. He invited, disinvited, committed and cancelled, all the while regularly appearing at my door step, announcing only by a text or a call that, "I am here." These unexpected visits had an intoxicating aura, but the debilitating sadness and despair I would feel upon his departure were overwhelming. No, they were not overwhelming. They were hurtful.

I had ached for him to solidly plant himself into my life, to structure a routine onto which I could grip. The time spent with him felt calculated, as if tied to a quota, dosing his love, his caress, his sperm even. I was coming to understand that the wind had more staying power than his presence in my life. There was no room for me in this relationship. In fact, I wondered if I existed in his mind at all.

To celebrate the end of Alice's school year, Alice and I dined at her best friend's home in Petersham. Her parents, both chefs, had become good friends of mine over the course of my first year in Northampton. They often organized themed soirées, complete with costumes and ambiance. Italian food was the evening's theme, and pizza, from the outdoor oven, the star of our meal.

The late afternoon was a peaceful one, and the warm air enabled us to dine on our homemade pizzas outside at a picnic table. Standing at the corner of the table, tossing the salad, I stared at the lanterns hanging above me, and watched hummingbirds feed from the bird bottle adjacent to the outdoor chandelier. I felt happy to be there, mingling with truly intelligent people and partaking in stimulating discussions.

We were transferring the meal inside, escaping the bugs, preparing the tea and dessert tray, when Alice came to me, visibly annoyed.

"Your phone keeps ringing, Mom," she said, looking at me, embarrassed, her eyes pleading. I walked to the table where I had voluntarily placed my phone out of my reach. I heard its vibration, and saw the screen, displaying Patrick's name, yet again. Grabbing my device, I walked to the garden, away from the busy kitchen, and answered.

"Patrick," I said, infuriated by his persistent audacity. I was now faced with no choice, but to disclose to my friends a relationship I had so far kept secret. "I am with friends, dining at their home. Can I call you back later?" I asked, somewhat impatiently.

His answer was a surprisingly compliant, "Yes," followed by a quick, "I love you."

I had succeeded, it appeared. I had tamed my wild animal.

The house was dark and quiet. Alice had opted to stay in Petersham overnight. I brushed my teeth and washed my face, possessed by an almost disturbing tranquility. I kept rewinding my last conversation with Patrick. Finally, I smiled. I had set my boundaries and he had respected them. As I placed my head on the pillow, to my astonishment the phone rang.

"Open up!" he yelled. "I'm at the door." I complied without resistance.

"I need to know of your whereabouts, always. It is your obligation to inform me of your activities at all times," he said to me, upon entering.

I observed him undress, still shocked by his words, disbelieving he had driven at 2:00 a.m. from Lowell to pour his venom on me. Toothbrush in hand, foam freshly spat into the sink, he told me that I was a disappointment.

"You failed me. You failed us," he continued, wide-eyed.

"Fuck that!" I suddenly screamed, unable to contain myself. "Fuck YOU!" I specified with conviction and a strong need to defend myself. "Get a life," I added, not sure exactly who this sentence was aimed at. He must have gone off into that crazy mind space, only he could visit at will, because there in front of me, I saw his eyes dive into darkness.

"Shut up, you bitch," he shouted, as he then quickly sat down on the edge of my bed, blankly staring ahead, retreating into stillness. "You were like the Virgin Mary to me, Isabelle. Now, look at what you have done. Look what you have become," he added with disgust. Unsure of what his words meant, of their weight's relevance, questioning my own behavior, I scanned the evening events, searching for hints of missteps.

I saw nothing.

"Come lie beside me," I told him, pulling him to my side, understanding our storm was passing. He stretched his body along mine, remaining clothed, fixating on the ceiling. Looking at him, acknowledging the man's volatility, I knew the time had come, a decision had been made.

"I'm OK with us parting," I told him, while my head was nestled in the hollow of his shoulder. "Thank you for our time together. I now know what kind of man I need...and don't need," I said feeling grounded, the relief spreading through my body.

Upon pronouncing those words, I finally realized Patrick had been the obvious transition from John I had required before I could move on with my life, something friends around me knew. I no longer feared being alone, being away from Patrick, being away from home. Listening to me pronounce these words, he stayed silent, on his back, his eyes to the ceiling, impassible.

I got up. Breakfast had to be made.

I prepared the smoothie, the eggs, and the hot chocolate, mindfully creating a moment of happiness that would make the send-off painless, I thought, the lightness of my decision settling into my movements. I brought the food to the table I had quickly set and proceeded to serve him. Seated in front of his hot chocolate, he turned around in my direction, his eyes questioning mine and gently brought me to him.

"Ven aca, mi amor," he pleaded.

And I let myself be led. One last time I told myself.

Just one last time.

I had caved, unable to resist him. Positioning himself firmly behind me, licking the side of my neck, his mouth seeking to grab my lips, there was no fleeing the feeling I was his possession.

And I knew my self-indulgence to be the foundation of my self-sabotage.

"You will love me forever?" I whispered in his ear, spent.

He turned me around, lifted his head a bit more, squinting his eyes, as if to better examine my face. "Yes," he said. "Forever".

CHAPTER NINE

I spent the first weekend in June cleaning the house, with Patrick and his children. He had made notable improvements to his garage-like home. He had purchased a desk, from which he could now conduct his business, and placed it against the wall adjacent to the dining room. The dining room walls had been refreshed and new kitchenware and bathroom accessories had been purchased. His house was slowly becoming a home.

That Saturday we spent installing an old beige carpet on the living room floor and rearranging the boxes and equipment spread across his large basement. I was happy to be useful, wanting him to see me as a valuable asset to him, his life, his children.

Aware of his observant eyes focused on my hands, I held the carpet tightly, so he could cut the overhanging material. The complicity felt real; its presence hinting at the emergence of an intimate moment. Throughout the day, as we passed each other in the house, in the basement or in the yard, he would smile at me with amusement. He looked at me with such surprise, seemingly astonished by my petite frame's apparent strength, impressed by my stamina. I was in performance mode, ignoring the grease, the dirt, the sweat. I was aware of its impact on Patrick—and my body.

Tidying the bedroom and looking, yet again, for my underwear under the bed, I come across a golden-colored flip flop. Just one. Not the pair. I grabbed it and gently examined it, unperturbed by my discovery. I slowly made my way to Patrick, sandal in hand. "What is this?" I asked softly, showing him the golden find.

Seated at his new desk, he looked at me, unflinching. "I don't know," he said, continuing to work on his laptop. I now remembered the Victoria shampoo and conditioner on full display on the shelf of his bathroom cupboard.

"Who do they belong to?" I asked, suspiciously.

He stopped typing and turned toward me with instant stillness. "I repaired a client's car last week," he quietly stated. "He, his wife, and three kids came over and forgot some of their items. I tell you," he quickly added, "this woman…this woman always overspends." I looked at him, noticing for the first time how the desk's dimensions dwarfed his silhouette, minimizing his stature. The afternoon had been perfect, delightful, in fact. His explanation seemed plausible enough. Some kids had played in his room with golden flip flops.

Okay, I thought.

I left for Northampton the next day, confident and secured by the profuse tenderness I had received over the weekend. Furthermore, Los Angeles, with its beaches, its restaurants, its universe was waiting for me and Alice. All of a sudden, my life seemed brighter.

Before consciously knowing she wanted to act, Los Angeles had long attracted Alice. Now, her wish to visit this iconic location was coming true. We were planning to spend six days in Santa Monica, while visiting four colleges: California Arts Institute, University of Southern California, Chapman College, and AMDA, the American Musical and Drama Academy, in the heart of Hollywood.

We expected a lot from this trip. Alice and I had been steadily drifting apart, no longer able to hold meaningful conversations. My willingness to bond with her was weakened by my emotional unavailability, and strained by my inability to withdraw from Patrick. The change of pace in LA could provide us with bountiful opportunities to mend and solidify the link between us that was threatening to give way. Some uninterrupted time together would help establish that I, her mother, was still capable of focusing on her needs. My redemption was at hand.

John had offered to drive us to the Hartford airport, located 45 minutes from Northampton. I had hesitated, knowing each moment I spent with him would suffocate me with an overabundance of attentiveness. Still, I accepted, thinking Alice would appreciate the presence of a father she rarely saw.

As John was driving, I started receiving texts from Patrick. He was expressing his frustration at my being with John.

I want to be the one with you, Patrick was texting. I should be the one driving you. I should be the one there in the car. Amused and very much conscious of John's eyes on my phone, I tried resisting the urge to play the Spanish song Patrick had also sent me. "Tu Hombre Perfecto" by Marc Antonio Solis was the vessel through which he apologized for his shortcomings. I did not have the cruel audacity to play it for all to listen to in the car, but I must confess I almost did.

The week went by quickly. Alice, unsurprisingly, fell in love with Santa Monica, where we were lodging. I was happy to share with her my favorite spots on the beach, my favorite restaurants. Our college visits were well-spaced, so she had enough time to work on the online US history class she had to take to graduate from her school. It was mandatory, since she was Canadian.

Problems with Patrick started surfacing early in the trip. His reproaches were profuse, fueled by the obvious threat my independence exposed. I was not texting him enough, I was not calling at convenient times, and when I did there was too much noise in the background. All this painted in his mind the portrait of a neglectful novia, a girlfriend unconcerned by the imperatives of a balanced and cherished relationship. Annoyed by the flow of incessant and unfounded accusations, I decided to call him and clear up the mess. Two minutes into the conversation, he hung up on me.

You are not speaking softly, he had then immediately texted me. Impatient and hurt, I called him back, but he ignored my call. Confused, I went back to my motel room, understanding that to remove him from my head, I had to focus solely on Alice.

AMDA was our last college to visit in Los Angeles. It was Friday and Alice and I had decided to celebrate the end of our trip by eating at Sugarfish, in Santa Monica. Sushi had the same soothing effect on us both, so we indulged, invigorated by the moment.

The first texts that day rolled in at 10:00 p.m., Los Angeles time.

You have opened a Pandora's box, Isabelle. You clearly are not taking our relationship seriously. How is it that in the last six days you haven't been able to dedicate a decent five minutes to me. To us?

I stared, dumbstruck, at the words my brain was trying to absorb, elements of craziness etching themselves on my horizon. I felt it, the confusion he meant for me to feel, its tentacles tossing my thoughts around in my mind. I took my phone and started to text, demanding explanations, asking for a reprieve. It was ridiculous. I had to end the exchange. I had to end it.

Let's finish on a good note, Patrick, I wrote.

What do you mean by that? Specify, he quickly demanded.

Specify? I thought. But, I could not. I had the option of either stating that I had meant for the conversation to end on a good note or to confirm that I was alluding to the relationship. Unable to write the words required to convey my message, and convinced that the best way to end a relationship was not by text, I called him. He did not pick up.

Pick up, I ordered him by text. I called again and again, but he continuously ignored me. Fuck it, I thought. Goodnight, I wrote putting my phone on mute and hiding it far away from my bed. I had a plane to catch in the morning. I needed to rest, I needed peace.

Good morning mi amor, was waiting for me on my phone when I woke up. I will be picking you up at the airport, the next text said.

OK, I responded. I closed my phone, half in anguish, half in apprehension. But somehow I felt it again, the pull–like understanding of his craziness. Maybe, mine as well. And a forgiveness of all things strange and awkward, all that makes life's rawness inviting, so pure. So alive.

No one was there to pick us up at Hartford when we arrived.

I can't make it on time, he had written, but, I will meet you sometime during the night, he promised. Exhausted, we hopped in a taxi. We walked into the house at 1:00 a.m., after having texted Patrick that I would keep the front door unlocked.

I woke up alone, in the middle of my bed, at 10:00 a.m., somewhat disappointed, but mostly furious. My door had been left unlocked all night. Unimpressed, I went to the kitchen, shaking my head, to prepare my coffee. Checking my phone, I saw I had a missed call from John. I had forgotten that he had driven to Northampton the night before as we had agreed to discuss matters concerning both Alice and Catherine before his departure for Taipei the next day. I quickly dressed and drove to the Esselon café in Hadley, my favorite spot.

My feelings for John had changed substantially since January. The initial anger I had felt upon the revelation of Xiao Hua's existence, had morphed into a quiet friendliness, something John abhorred. He wanted more. He wanted me. But I had moved on to something novel, exciting and life affirming. I was just starting to enjoy it, and I was unwilling to forgo it.

Looking at John over my coffee, I saw his tears threatening to flow, the redness in his eyes indicating he had been crying on his way to meet me. Pretending not to see his distress, I focused on the children, providing him with a summary of my time in Los Angeles with Alice and asking about Catherine's state of mental health.

Catherine had halted all communication with me, rejecting my suffering, suspicious of the speed at which I had dove into a new relationship.

"If you had loved Dad, you would have fought for him and us," she told me. "You would have saved the family." Her warped understanding of the situation crushed me, the parent who had sacrificed her career, but mainly her health, to keep her child alive.

John and I navigated our respective sorrows as best we could, but in the end, we were unable to part unscathed. He had pressed me for a kiss, for a touch, and I had been unable to hide my repulsion. It was something he had been unprepared to see. I carried his despair with me, only until my return to Northampton. When I got home, I walked onto the front lawn, out of

Alice's earshot, and decided to finally call Patrick. Not expecting him to answer after the first ring, I was taken off-guard, unable to fully articulate my disappointment both at his absence at the airport and his absence from my bed.

"Sorry baby," he said, "I was so tired."

I sighed. "You do understand that I left my door unlocked all night?" I highlighted, perplexed.

Ignoring my question, he quickly changed the subject and inquired about my afternoon plans.

"Why do you want to know about my plans?" I asked, gingerly.

"Well, there is an afternoon party in Springfield I should attend. It's a business event. I would like to take you," he said.

This was a first. We never do anything, I thought. "Why not?" I replied.

"I will be there to pick you up in an hour and a half," he dryly stated and hung up.

He had established early on that the whiteness of my skin offered a welcome contrast to his nights. But now, as I walked to greet him in my driveway, I was struck by the way the sun's light contrasted Patrick's own flawless skin. For once, we were going to leave the coffin that was his house and expose ourselves to the light of day.

In so many ways.

"You cannot wear this," he said, as he took my hand to lead me to the bedroom. He closed my door, examining with newfound curiosity the maxi-dress I had chosen to wear. Without another word, he pushed me onto the bed and lifted my dress, revealing my thighs. He looked at me as he spread my legs, took his index finger and twisted it around the elastic of my panty. He proceeded to slide my lacy garment to the side, exposing my now plump lips.

"You will have to change your clothes," he expressed, plunging into me as I looked out, mesmerized. I could see his tongue move, playfully licking, but it was his eyes that caught my attention. The way they were eating me up, the way they focused attentively. It was his eyes, not his mouth, which truly lulled me into a trance-like state. No man had ever looked at me that way before.

Realizing we might miss his business meeting, we interrupted our lovemaking to get dressed.

"Isabelle," he repeated, looking in the bathroom mirror, "Please wear something decent."

I turned around to face my closet, playing with that word in my head. Decent. I love fashion. I love to dress. In fact, twice a year I meet with my stylist to reevaluate my wardrobe, to discard irrelevant garments and identify the must-haves of the season. I have been traveling the world, attending formal functions for the last twenty years. When I dressed with the subtle intent of exposing my skin, I always had done it with elegance, class and distinction, something Patrick failed to notice.

Staring at my options, I smiled. Let it go, Isabelle, I told myself, enjoy the entertainment and comply. Sifting quickly through the many options, I selected a flattering black-and-white striped pencil skirt and a black halter top decorated with white polka dots. My color choice had somehow epitomized the polarities carried at the heart of this relationship. Patrick hated anything and everyone that was black. His quest for pure whiteness was a manifestation of his aversion. I had unconsciously chosen a befitting outfit, an outfit whose obvious rebellious symbol I had not understood until I looked at myself in the mirror before leaving.

The unattractiveness of the surroundings was clear. Folding chairs had been randomly placed in the treeless yard, two large tables were strewn with half-emptied plates, and garbage was everywhere to be seen. Twenty people, maybe, were in attendance, all leisurely walking, chatting, and dancing to the sound of Latin beats. This garden party, held in a Springfield driveway, would be my first official introduction as Patrick's *novia*.

Upon our arrival, he took me by the hand, proudly bringing me closer to him, and, just as quickly, let me know we needed to part. He had a meeting with a potential business partner. Nonchalantly, I walked toward a group of seated women, while Patrick headed toward a younger crowd of men, seemingly waiting for him.

The women I met were lively and affable, insisting upon getting me food and wine, which I politely accepted. I had secretly taken my migraine medication before leaving Northampton and knew just one glass would not impact my sensitive head. The lady to my left, a real estate contractor, was a Nicaraguan who had established herself in the nearby Chicopee area twenty years earlier. Now, an American citizen, she flipped houses, renovating them to resell for a profit.

I could tell Patrick was observing me attentively, as he conducted his informal meeting.

"How long have you been with him?" my new friend asked, observing me as much as Patrick.

"Five months," I answered, as we both turned our heads toward him.

"Five months" she repeated very slowly, now focusing ardently on Patrick's silhouette.

"Be careful," she articulated. "Be careful."

I turned to her, head tilted, and eyes locking into hers. "What do you mean, be careful?" I asked with surprise.

"Just be careful," she said, staring ahead, her tone conveying firmly that the conversation had ended. Unsure how to follow such a statement, somewhat destabilized, I changed the subject and engaged with her husband, who was seated to my right. In the back of my mind, I knew I would need to wait for the right time to question Patrick on the matter.

Once Patrick's business meeting was concluded, he walked toward me, kneeled by my chair, took my hand, and while looking straight into my eyes, asked if I was ready to leave.

"Yes," I said, unable to add anything else, completely hypnotized. I got up, while he profusely thanked my new girlfriend for taking care of me. We quickly said our goodbyes, shaking hands and air-kissing each other. I then noticed how she was looking at him, again, and I listened to their Spanish exchange, an exchange charged with a strangeness I could not pinpoint. This woman was sixty years-old, maybe fifty-eight, and with her short stature and unremarkable facial traits, was not particularly pretty.

INHALED

I then remarked, again, in disbelief, that she was trying to seduce Patrick, shamelessly, unaffected by my presence. I watched incredulously, as she slid her hand slowly into his hand, gliding it back with the obvious desire to leave it there, inside of his.

Did she think she had a chance? I thought to myself, retrieving my smile. Maybe, she is the one who needs to be careful. And anyhow, how could she think he would ever consider her?

Back inside the car, as we drove, I suddenly became agitated. Unable to wait, I questioned him, probing, "Why would she tell me to be careful, Patrick? Why?"

Seemingly unperturbed, he started to laugh. "This woman is a whore," he stated. "She fucks around with all her workers."

I looked at him, scrutinizing his face. I had witnessed her move, her attempt at sending some form of message to Patrick, her lack of restraint, her lack of inhibition.

"Don't worry," he added while biting my palm, "no one is tastier than you."

I looked ahead, through the filth of the windshield, and wondered about me, him, and the rest of my life.

CHAPTER TEN

To Patrick's home, the morning drive was sublime. The sound track that now accompanied my car trips had evolved, as I would no longer let my emotions dictate my song choices. I did not seek comfort in overplayed songs or in songs that had already served their purpose, and for the moment, felt meaningless. I did not want to activate the imprints that lay somewhere in my nervous system, so I decided to let myself be surprised by whatever songs the radio had to offer. I wanted new stamps, new sensations, and new memories.

I wanted to let go.

And I asked myself, Can I let go too much? And what if I did? What would happen? Would I still stand? Would I fall? If so, where exactly would I land?

Patrick opened the door, his face sketching a soft smile. He had cancelled my visit the night before, stating his long day and tired state of mind as the reason. "I cannot give you the attention you deserve," he had said again.

The absurdity at the center of his explanation, like his frequent and regular changes of mind, were challenging. I was a planner. In contrast, Patrick was the king of the moment, never wanting to commit in advance to anything, always securing the many options he felt he required in order to breathe. Yes, plans, it appeared, suffocated him. I had not pushed back, but I had felt hurt by the sting of his perceived rejection of me.

The question remained in my mind, "Just how much instability can I withstand?" Feeling as though we were building a home during the constant perceptible shifting of tectonic plates, I kept walking the shaky ground, dismissing the existence of those quakes, feeding my nausea.

I walked inside the living room as Jocelyne and Alejandro were playing video games. Happy as always to see me, Jocelyne's welcome offered me a lifeline. Both his children created some form of normalcy for me. These two children, unlike their father, had integrated to the beat of the American culture, like I was trying to do, easing me into a reality we all could comprehend. Here, with them, I felt at home. With it, the feeling of being wanted and appreciated, something Alice's demeanor had failed to convey. Who could blame her? I had abdicated, hadn't I?

A pillar made of straw.

Me.

And yes, I wondered often about it, this pseudo surrendering of a motherhood I had desired all of my life. How easy it is to give to strangers, to be seen as a form of savior.

To them.

To myself.

Mother Isabelle.

But not to Alice.

Patrick and I headed quickly to his bedroom to do what we did best, with implicit impunity. Yes, it was wrong to spend three hours fucking, while his children were physically so close. Yes, it was wrong to enable Patrick's remorselessness. Yes, it was wrong to indulge ourselves. But if he did not care, somehow, I did not either. If he did not care, it made it right. We removed our clothes and wasted no time. I had started using Tango, a phone app, exclusively with Patrick. While browsing his Tango page a few months earlier, I had noticed the picture of a woman who, on every one of his few posts, had pressed the heart option. Alongside the derisory Spanish monologue post about the important place Christ held in his life, there had sometimes appeared two or three of these likes from her. This had bothered me.

Her name was Lydia Maxwell. She was a tall, white-skinned woman, in her mid-forties, with long, curly strawberry-blond hair, living in South Boston, a place most commonly known as Southie. A mother of four, three boys and a baby girl, her profile read that she worked as a web designer, a part-time food caterer, and a cleaning lady.

It reminded of Patrick's incessant push for me to clean his house. That must have been the deal closer, I thought, as I had scrutinized her appearance, trying to understand the physical attraction he would have felt for her, focusing on the fleshiness her body displayed. It had puzzled me. Patrick was drawn to thinness, obsessing over my petite frame, complimenting me continuously on my teenage-like body.

I quickly saw what had pulled him to her, her white skin, her white teeth, and her long, very long, hair. Her aquiline nose, while quite prominent, was interestingly balanced by eyes whose roundness and turquoise color mesmerized. While imperfect, she was still somewhat attractive, but stunning, no, she was not.

He most likely just settled for a few fucks with her. But why? I momentarily asked myself, intrigued. In truth though, I did not really care that much. Nonetheless, I probed, asking Patrick to define the place this woman held for him in his life. His answer had been simple enough. She was a woman introduced to him at his sister's party the previous Christmas. He had met her twice. It was nothing more.

Now, two months later, and five months into our relationship, I had started reanalyzing Patrick's Tango page, his paranoia evidently contagious. Seated on my bed, I felt guilt and shame, as I stared at Lydia's Tango profile, again. Yes, his past was his past, but why had he been evasive, and obviously intent on quickly changing the subject, the last and only time we had discussed her.

I had left the story alone for two months, but suddenly felt the urge to bring her up again. I wanted to know more. Am I not allowed to play the inquisitive, jealous girlfriend? I wondered, drawing for myself a new set of rules to legitimize a behavior I so despised in myself. The confident woman I had known myself to be had vanished. In its place, a woman apprehending the uncomfortable edges of insecurity, was forming. So, seated on the edge of his bed on that Sunday morning in July, I asked him again, about this woman.

His eyes shifty, his body appearing to stiffen slightly, he responded, "Well, you know, it was a girl I met at my sister's house a few Christmases ago."

OK, I thought. Consistency. Good. "Did you guys ever fuck?" I asked.

"Nope," he simply responded.

"Kiss?" I insisted.

"Nope," he answered again.

I observed all that I could during that short interaction. I had tried to identify a baseline from which I could tell his potential lies from his truths. While nothing really stood out, I kept asking myself, is the discomfort stemming from him, or me?

After that brief conversation, the day went on in a family-like atmosphere. He had much to do. There were trucks to repair and outside cameras to install. The house was now going to be filmed from the inside out, hints of paranoia slowly confirming themselves in his behavior. He had been in the military's Special Forces, I had rationalized, so maybe there were good reasons for him to feel he needed protection.

But for a few outings with Alice, my family life had become bodiless, virtually nonexistent. My desire to somehow integrate myself into a family structure remained strong though. Jocelyne needed supervision, and in providing this for her, I was also succeeding in my quest for Patrick's recognition. I enjoyed the feeling of being with his daughter, to be able to give this child access to an adult who cared and was available.

Patrick, his employee, and Alejandro, were all working outside, so I decided to take Jocelyne for a treat. The day was hot and dry, a perfect summer day. The multi-colored dress I was wearing featured a flowing skirt, a cinched waist, and a halter-type top, leaving my shoulders bare. I felt the soft, hot breeze caressing my skin, and most importantly I felt Patrick's delicious gaze on me.

INHALED

I took Jocelyne's hand and proceeded to the ice-cream parlor around the corner. Jocelyne was a sharp-minded, alert, and very talkative four-year-old. As we started walking, I asked her what ice cream flavor she wanted to eat.

We had walked about 1,000 feet when she decided on a chocolate sundae. She then proceeded to ask me a question. It was a question that to this day, I cannot quite recall. All I remember is her tiny, little face twisting, when she realized, too late, she had started her question by calling me Lydia.

A pasty feeling started to spread inside my mouth the minute I heard Jocelyne pronounce that other name. My throat was pulsating, rendering me speechless. In slow motion, I turned around, my unsteady legs somehow still holding the weight of my panic. Mindful of the worker installing the camera outside the window, I reached Patrick, stopping at his side in silence. I had no intention of causing a scene, but Patrick did not know that, and a scene was what he feared the most.

"Jocelyne just called me Lydia," I finally whispered in a breathless voice. Though I thought I had contained myself, I was unable to camouflage the drama now unfolding. His workers, his son, and the little one still clenching my hand all watched motionless, obviously aware of the palpable tension. I heard Patrick say something to Alejandro, in Spanish, adding to my uneasiness. Patrick and I then moved to the house, transferring the drama to the kitchen, our dark stage. He closed the starched, brown curtains, as quickly as I reopened them. I needed air, I needed space.

"She called me, Lydia," I repeated.

"Maybe it is another Lydia," he quickly retorted, looking straight at me. He held up my chin, kidnapped my eyes with his and with the power of concentration, he pulled me to him and took me in his arms.

I started to cry uncontrollably. "I so want to believe you. I so want to believe you," was all I could muster, my head resting on his chest. Suddenly, exhausted, I left his embrace to go to his bedroom and lie down on his bed. Flashbacks of John's indiscretion were assaulting my head, unleashing the all too familiar emotions I had been trying to flee, reigniting my wounds.

"There is nothing going on with this woman," he insisted. "There is only you in my life. No one else."

Hearing those words should have quieted my concerns and helped attenuate the disbelief that had settled inside me. I wanted to leave. I wanted to leave this man and leave this house. But looking at Jocelyne, who had joined me in bed, and was holding my hand, I knew I had to stay. She had inadvertently stirred the world her father had wanted unshaken, and I did not want to burden her further with my hasty departure. I decided I would leave at the end of the day. For her sake, the drama had to be halted, at least, for now.

Upon my return to the kitchen, I crossed paths with Patrick. His demeanor was odd—his smile, a triumphant air floating around his face. He looked at me, his own eyes seemingly about to burst into tears. I love you, he said, as he carried a box full of wires to the basement.

I was puzzled. Why didn't I feel relieved by the very words meant to soothe me?

From the front porch, I dialed Charlie's number. Just then, Patrick peaked his head through the door, inquisitively. "Charlie," I told him abruptly. "I am calling Charlie." He stayed there, hesitant, then retreated inside, unsatisfied, knowing he had no other choice but to share me.

"He has been put on your path for a reason, for a purpose," she had repeated each time I had called in distress. "You will leave him when you are ready. I trust your judgment." Listening to her words, yet again, I stared down, hypnotized by the patterns of the wooden porch. Her common sense did not reassure me this time. It was masked by her voice, a voice burdened by worry.

While on the call with Charlie, my cousin Cecil, a Canadian ambassador to Spain, had tried FaceTiming me. I put Cecil on hold, finished my call with Charlie, and immediately returned to Cecil, deciding to continue my conversation from Patrick's living room.

Cecil was the sister I wished I had had. My only biological sibling, the result of a warped attempt at welding my parents back together, was more devious than Mephistopheles himself. I had abandoned her years ago. Like my mother, my sister Helen, a psychologist five years older than me, had been cursed with a deeply rooted narcissistic trait. Her harshness was always ready to spring forth, a trait I knew she admired in herself. Manipulative and deceitful, Helen had often lured me into her life with her hidden agendas, and each time I had grabbed the bait with a full mouth, until I finally removed her from my life.

Cecil had filled the void, replacing the hurt and rejection with her two lifesavers, lightness and humor. Two years my elder, she was a pretty, strawberry blonde, whose freckled face always seemed ready to break into laughter. She had become, from a young age, my trusted confidante. Our own brand of sibling unity had been nourished by a scathing humor we both mastered. Yes, cynicism formed our tight bond.

I pressed to connect to her FaceTime call, noticing Patrick walking toward me, visibly annoyed by the attention I was receiving, and by the attention I was giving someone else. I ignored him.

Cecil's call lifted my mood. She somehow shifted my focus, entertaining me with her stories depicting the challenges of living in Spain, another Latino-type world. Spontaneously, I decided to include Patrick and motioned for him to come and join me on the call. He looked at me, considered my invitation, then proceeded to his room, only to reappear wearing a new shirt. He had chosen a white and blue striped T-shirt to impress Cecil, a rag he took five minutes to pick. I smiled.

He sat beside me, placing his arms around my shoulders and engaged with Cecil, whose Spanish was impeccable. He was impressed. I stayed there, observing them, sensing the tension leaving my body. Within a span of five minutes, I had transformed my doom-like moment into one full of hope and promise. As we said our goodbyes, Patrick, with much deference, retreated from our call, giving me and Cecil some privacy.

"He seems to love you, Isabelle," she said. "It is quite apparent." Her comment gripped me. We air-kissed, as we usually did, and I closed the call, leaving the echoes of her words resonating in my head.

Cecil's words had not quieted my suspicions. Playing mindlessly with my food, seated at that serious table beside Alejandro, thoughts stuttered inside my head. I was recalling the YouTube video Lydia posted, where she was actually advertising her cleaning services. In that video she also enumerated the name of her four children: Steven, Tristan, Julian and Emily. Julian, I was now remembering, was the name of a boy Jocelyne often referred to as her boyfriend.

Still unsure, and hoping my memory was failing, I decided to check if Julian's name had really been mentioned in that video. When Patrick stepped out to drive his worker back home, I logged into my phone and viewed her YouTube video again. I then waited for Patrick's return, unsure how to address my suspicions. I wanted to project detachment and control, but the minute he entered the room, I lost whatever control I thought I had over my voice.

"How can you not know of the presence of this woman in Jocelyne's life, a woman who incidentally is all over your Tango page?" I yelled. Slowly undressing in his bedroom, preparing to shower, he reminded me, in his own controlled voice, that because he avoided any contact with Jocelyne's mother, he did not know who his youngest child associated with during the week and that there was nothing going on with him and this Lydia girl. Naked, phone in hand, he left for the bathroom, locking the door behind him.

I looked at Jocelyne who had joined me on the bed, sitting on its edge. "I need you to wash my hair," she softly said. Yes, she needed it. And, I needed the distraction.

"Patrick," I said, "be quick."

He walked out of the bathroom, looked straight ahead of him, as if in a trance.

"There you go," he mumbled.

Okay.

While giving Jocelyne her bath, I could feel nausea slowly setting in, the acid burning the lining of my stomach. I tried, as best I could, to offer Jocelyne some lightness, but Patrick's denial of Lydia's existence in his daughter's life was unsettling me.

INHALED

The energy had drained from my body. I had more questions, so many questions that I should have asked while he was fearful of losing me. It was too late now, I thought, some form of expiration had stuck its head, and I could not inquire any further. His controlled demeanor had halted my momentum. My resilience was absent. If I pushed for more answers now, I knew I would be placated with vague responses. I felt weak. I felt weary. I needed to sleep. I looked over to Jocelyne, who was now playing with her Frozen doll, Elsa, in the middle of the bed. Driving back to Northampton was not an option, I was now thinking, sliding in beside Jocelyne.

"Jocelyne will sleep with us tonight," I told Patrick flatly, when he entered the room. He turned to me, eyes questioning, and saying nothing, except to acknowledge Jocelyne's excitement at the idea of sharing our bed. Protection, I felt, was something I needed from him and from myself. Jocelyne would have to provide it.

Before going to sleep, Jocelyne had insisted I give her a second bath. Following my own shower, I sat on the edge of the bathtub and let the water flow into the scum-covered tub. Water soothed me. It helped regulate my breathing, bringing me closer to myself. But here, with Jocelyne, water was failing me. Its flow was unable to ground me. Breathless, I took Jocelyne's little hand and helped her out of the water, wrapping her in a towel, as I had done so many times with Catherine and Alice. Carrying her to the bedroom, the gesture's significance hit me—I had fallen in love with this little girl. I had become her mother. I had been captured, willingly. A harder truth repeating itself. I had left Alice behind, willingly as well.

Upon leaving the bathroom, I saw Patrick, phone in hand, walking toward the kitchen.

"I need to make a call," he said. "My work schedule has changed, so workers need to be notified." Mindlessly acknowledging his words, I dressed Jocelyne quickly in her pajamas. It was then that I shamelessly thought of it. Without hesitation, I tapped into the information source his daughter had become.

"Jocelyne," I started, tentatively, wanting to validate my hypothesis, "can you remind me of the names of Julian's brothers?" Her little body stiffened, as her blistering answer popped out of her mouth. "I don't feel like it," she said. Stunned by a four-year-old's ability to respond with such virulence, I decided to change my strategy. I opened my phone and proceeded to show, with feigned indifference, pictures of my children, of me, of my dog. At the end, I slid a screenshot of Lydia's face on YouTube.

"You know her?" I innocently asked.

The distrust, now gone from her body, she happily exclaimed, "Lydia!" Absorbing her response, and with no time to react, I saw her bounce off the bed, look me straight in the eyes, and reach for the door handle. "I have a secret I need to share with Daddy," she said on her way out.

I was frantically getting out of my pajamas when Patrick entered the bedroom, stealthily, Jocelyne in his arms. I headed to the bathroom to collect my toiletries.

"What happened?" he asked, visibly concerned.

"I need to go home," I said. "Alice needs me," I lied. He seated himself on the bathroom counter, his towel casually wrapped around his hips, facing me, his back to the mirror.

"Nothing is going on with anyone," he repeated calmly, somehow knowing what had unfolded.

"Too late for that refrain Patrick. Jocelyne has confirmed that the Lydia in question is, in fact, the mother of her best friend Julian."

He looked at me and calmly repeated that he met her twice, and that he did not know how or why this woman was such a part of Jocelyne's life.

I cried, my head in the hollow of his shoulder, again. I so wanted his words to be true. He embraced me, softly, taking my face between his two hands. "There is nothing going on," he said. "Nothing."

Disbelieving my own malleability, I heard myself say, "Okay," as I slowly walked back to the bed. I removed my dress, slipped into bed, simultaneously alarmed and reassured. He placed Jocelyne on the wall side of the bed and positioned himself between us. He clutched me, as if to prevent me from falling off the cliff from which he had pushed me.

"You, Jocelyne, and me," he softly said. "My family."

INHALED

The time I spent driving home from Patrick's the next day, created the space I needed to think and breathe. Doubts were coming back, flooding my thoughts, knotting my insides. I knew nothing of Patrick. He was nowhere to be found on the internet. I lived almost two hours from him by car. What was it that I needed so much, that I could not let him go? As I pulled in my driveway, I decided I would have to get to the bottom of it.

Looking at my Google search results from the seat of my car, I never thought it would be so easy. There were so many hackers to choose from. And yet, I would be at the mercy of whoever I did choose. There was no way to distinguish the competent from the incompetent, the real from the fraud. Same dilemma, different context.

"My name is Isabelle," is what rushed out of my mouth the moment he answered my phone call.

His voice had a tough baritone like tonality, its staccato tempo clearly projecting a no-nonsense approach to problem solving. After briefly explaining my situation, his direct and relevant questioning hit me like a ton of bricks.

"When you confronted him, did he reassure you by offering you his phone?" he asked.

"No," I mumbled, realizing my mistake, my stupidity.

"Look, Isabelle. I can call you Isabelle? I've cheated before. I know the drill," he stated.

"But, he denied everything quite convincingly," I stressed, naively.

And I realized, then, the sadness of the moment.

Hacker therapy.

Reality check from an underground I never knew existed.

"Of course, he did. And he lives two hours from you? Look lady, leave this guy. I've been this person. I've used the same strategies. He's lying to you."

Still seated in my car, his words were ringing in my head.

"There is no need for me to do anything," he added. "Save your money," he finished.

Suddenly, the doubts I had fought on my way to Northampton had been lifted. Patrick was guilty. Someone had told me. A man. A man who had hurt a woman like me. Staring at my yard from inside my car, I dialed Patrick's number, looking at the gray sky, feeling the weight of the humid air. He answered after the first ring.

"You lied to me," I spat out. "Your job was to reassure me by handing me your phone. You never did," I sobbed, feeling childish, the words spewing out of my mouth with rage, humiliation and horrible relief. "No more," I thought. I hung up, blocked his number and entered my house.

Dinner with Alice that evening was uneventful. I ate in relative silence, listening to her speak. Her day had been a good one, I was pleased to hear, feeling hopeful. She offered to wash the dishes, as I cleaned up the rest of my neglected house. I had steadied myself, feeling my sense of integrity resurfacing. The urge to wash him off assaulted me, as I was climbing the stairs to my room. In the shower, where all seemed to converge and make sense, I rinsed off his liquid, still dripping from me.

I woke up the next morning with the compulsion to insult him. After dropping Alice at school, unable to resist the pull, I unblocked him. I needed to display my true indignation at being caught by such a con-artist. I texted him my frustration.

Why be so defensive if nothing existed between you and Lydia? I wrote. Why go through such precautions to hide her presence in Jocelyne's life? His responses were all the same, nauseating me with their constancy. He had seen her twice, that was it.

Ask anyone. There is no one, but you, he had again stated. Adding a new twist, he wrote, I cannot prove to you anything anymore as you are far away from me.

I ended the texting, confused, keeping his number unblocked.

After picking up Alice from school, we headed to Whole Foods. I missed normalcy, the soothing mundanities at its foundation, and there in the middle of the food aisles, I clung to them.

When we got home, I focused on preparing our meal, hoping the activity would distract me from my worries. Cooking something tangible, that pleased her, would be my short-term remedy. I could at least still feel productive. I could shed my human debris through the process of actually pleasing someone who could possibly appreciate my existence.

While washing the dishes, I felt Alice's gaze on me and turned to meet her eyes. My phone had started to ring. She looked at me discouragingly, as she caught the name appearing on my phone. Dropping my dish rag on the counter, I headed upstairs, like a teenager, and closed my bedroom door. The low-pitched, controlled voice, I loved so much, greeted me.

"Isabelle. You are everything to me You are the only one. If you shoot me now, I will be alone," he said, quietly.

What was I to say? He was pleading for me to come to him. And why it happened so quickly, I don't know. I felt myself slide into that other side I was trying to flee. His voice melted into my ear, and it did that thing to me, that thing that makes everything rational leave, as if kicked out by a want fastened to an imaginary world I never knew existed. In that space, the truths were reshaped by a state that spoke to me only. It said to go, to drop everything, to forget who I was all about.

And in a flash, amnesia set in.

I hopped in my car and drove the usual two hours to his house, just in time to slip in beside the warm body waiting for me.

Four hours into my deep sleep, I woke up to the sensation of being rocked back to life. He had slipped inside me from our spooning position, his hand parting my lips, toying with my clitoris. "I love you," he whispered, his breath, a warm caress.

After placing the covers over my tired body, he showered, dressed, and kissed me goodbye. Again, exclaiming his love for me. As I heard his footsteps steadily move towards the front door, I suddenly sat upright, my throat knotted. I realized I had forgotten to ask to see his phone. More importantly, I realized, he had not offered it to me, as he had promised me the day before.

CHAPTER ELEVEN

Alice was set to spend four weeks at New York University's, Tisch School of the Arts summer acting camp, a coveted program. She would be gone from July 10th to August 7th. This meant I was able to see Patrick as much as I wanted.

Beyond everything, I thought, we simply need more time to fully know one another, to tame our differences and to understand what adjustments are required for this relationship to finally take off.

After having dropped off Alice at NYU, I called Patrick from the road. While our chat was light and cheerful, no word was mentioned about him coming to see me upon my arrival home that night. I was secretly hoping for one of his impromptu visits, as now, more than ever, was the time to crash my nights. Unfortunately, Patrick had to comply with last minute contract changes, so my night remained blank—another void waiting to be filled.

The following day, I leisurely picked up around the house, tended to the yard with the gardener and made plans for the dog sitter to come and take care of Jackson. I had four weeks of free time ahead of me. The potential content of those four weeks had been floating around in my head, holding either promises of renewed closeness with Patrick, or threats of acute loneliness without him.

Should I have wondered if there were other choices? Possibly. But I did not.

At 4:00 p.m., I texted him that I was leaving for his house, and to expect me for dinner.

Unusually, he replied immediately. No sweetie, you can't. I'll be at work.

Who cares, I replied, stung by the rejection. Too late, I lied. I have already left home. Make sure Alejandro is there to open the door.

I arrived in Lowell just as Alejandro was leaving the house. He stopped and rolled down the window of his beat up, black Toyota.

"Hey," I said with a smile, "you mind opening up before you leave?"

"Sure," he replied, his arched eyebrows betraying the surprise my presence was provoking.

Clearly, he had not been informed of my visit. We both walked to the side door of the house.

"I have to step out and get some food," he said, promptly returning to his car.

As I saw him drive away, I suddenly realized, I had the opportunity to snoop and see, if, in fact, Alejandro had my underwear. My sexy panties, meant to seduce and titillate, each pair laced with uncompromising femininity, had been disappearing, about nine pairs, so far. I stepped inside his dark and messy bedroom, turned on the light and headed instinctively for his closet. I was kneeling to check under his bed when I heard the key opening the door. I somehow managed to turn off his bedroom light, run out of his room and stop in front of the dirty, stainless steel refrigerator, which stood just outside the kitchen area, diagonally from his bedroom door.

Out of breath, looking blindly inside the refrigerator, containing my laughter at the thought of the posterior view I was offering Alejandro, I stayed, pretending to look for something. I turned around and noticed, surprised, that he was oblivious to my breathlessness, as he, himself, was trying to contain his. His eyes were shifty, his body alert. Returning to the kitchen with some eggs I had chosen as a culinary decoy, I began making a frittata. I understood. We both had something to hide.

Somehow, living in Massachusetts, had provided me with a culture shock equal to the one I had faced when moving to Asia. In Taiwan, I had been met by a culture, imprinted with restraint, politeness and genuine kindness. Here in the United States, my country's neighbor, American harshness and self-sufficiency, combined with Patrick's obvious machismo attitudes, had transported me out of my comfort zone, as well. Still, I had chosen to embrace the space I had created for myself with this crazy Nicaraguan man, I knew was wrong for me.

From the sink where I stood, I saw Patrick pull up in his beat-up red Dodge Ram. I watched, as he parked in front of the house and stepped out of his truck. In a flash, I felt myself melt away. The whiteness of his T-shirt highlighted the tone of his bronze skin. His jeans were perfectly sculpting his body. All I could think of, at that moment, was how much I needed to mold myself to him. As he walked into the house, that feeling dissipated.

. Whatever lightness I had been feeling crumbled, as I now remembered his prompt refusal of my offer to visit him that night. We barely looked at each other or exchanged any words throughout the meal. Grace was said with renewed rigidity.

"This is a very good meal," he said flatly, staring at the zucchini frittata, the watermelon and feta salad, the garlic bread and the tzatziki on his plate.

He must have an invisible gun to his temple, I thought. That, or he hates me.

The night unfolded quietly, the sex uneventful. While lying beside him, hearing him, his breath, heavy and loud—undisturbed by me, my body, the heat of it—I knew then, I would leave the following day and head back to Northampton. I wanted to be with him, but I also wanted more. Dignity, the wanting of it, the feel of it, I was able to sense. Still, there was something else tugging at me, a diffuse feeling, a presentiment unable to anchor itself into my reality.

And just like that, July and August suddenly frightened me.

With Alice now gone to camp, I felt lost. Patrick had taken so much space in my head, I had not invested the required energy to shape a life for myself in Northampton, and I was now feeling this cruel truth. The only activity I had planned was a mindfulness class being held in downtown Northampton.

I felt the razor-sharp pain, stemming from my isolation, a sensation exacerbated by Patrick's busy working schedule. I kept reminding myself that he was starting his business, that all this was natural.

Wednesday arrived, promising nothing. Deadened by a feeling of gloominess I knew I needed to shake, I decided to look into the shows playing in Northampton and opted for Shawn Mullins, an artist I had never heard of before. I am a music aficionado, an avid concert goer, who thrives on the energy and the high such events hold. It was the second time in my life I would attend a show alone. In fact, both these times had occurred since my arrival in Massachusetts. I felt defeated.

Half way through the show I received a text. You can come if you want, it read.

I needed to go back home, shower, change clothes, feed the dog, maybe even text the dog sitter.

I had no decency left in me.

I drove quietly, this time more aware of the hold this man had on me, aware of the loss of ascendency on my life, my thoughts no longer belonging to me. And it made me wonder, if like the skidding of a car before impact, my loss of control foreshadowed a death of some sort.

A warning of death coming.

CHAPTER TWELVE

Two friends from Montreal were planning to visit me within the next two weeks. The thought of it comforted me with the promise of peacefulness. I did not know if I wanted to include Patrick in their visit. Part of me wanted him to see me, really see me, for the person I was, but the other part of me knew he was blind to any elements of my life that showcased my vibrancy.

I realized now the extent to which my light had been dimmed.

I had no choice but to face the ache emerging from my stomach, the place where all my thoughts converged, never leaving room for lies. The normalcy I dreamed felt unreachable. He barely remembered the only thing that truly mattered to him: my body. Why should he concern himself with my soul?

We both agreed I would go to his house on Thursday night, two days before my friends' arrival on Saturday. Patrick quietly acknowledged that, yes, it was best for me, best for us, to spend those two days together. I jumped each time I saw that word being formed by his mouth. Us. It made me feel almost respected. His tone of voice had been light and encouraging.

All would be well, I kept repeating to myself, as I drove to Lowell, with the music blaring to keep me from falling asleep.

I arrived at the usual time: 11:00 p.m. Stepping out of my car, I was immediately seduced by the Salsa music being played by the neighbors across the street. The night was warm and breezy. It was a dry summer night that felt soothing to me. Patrick and Alejandro were busy unloading the van and transporting their tools to the yard. I walked toward Patrick and briefly kissed his lips, before climbing the steps and entering through the side door. The house was unusually dirty, messy, and smelly. I hated the carpets, the black grease stains they harbored, a reminder that the men living in this house were juveniles in dire need of a mother. I quickly placed that thought far back, where I could not reach it. I headed to the bathroom to shower. I knew the drill. I also knew what I wanted. The warm air infiltrated the room, indicating that morning had emerged. I felt a kiss being gently placed on my cheek, opened my eyes and saw Patrick staring at me, oddly, with a cup of tea in hand.

"Here," he said, "for you."

I sat up and took the cup to my lips.

Such a delicate gesture coming from such a heartless man, I thought.

I smiled at him. The day would be good.

Amnesia, its make-believe power, so easy to cling to, still and forever a wicked ally.

Expecting my friends to arrive at lunchtime the next day, I was thinking it would be best for me to leave after dinner. I kept my options open, preferring not to share my plans with Patrick.

He and Alejandro departed together at 10:00 a.m. for Manchester. They were planning to return around 2:00 p.m. Again, I had the house to myself, a rare occurrence. Dawdling into each room, I made mental notes of potential improvements that could be made to this man cave. I imagined how I could modify the layout, and how gutting the bathroom would be my first project. I was now living proof of the human capacity to adapt. That, or I was now crazy. Really crazy.

With music blasting in the background, I allowed myself to surrender and feel the pleasure of being in the moment. More and more, there was a sense of belonging I was able to weave for myself when I visited Patrick. Energized by my thoughts, and alive with the desire to please, I showered and beautified myself. I was eager to prepare the night's meal, knowing the Sicilian chicken dinner and cherry clafoutis dessert would pave my way to the night I had in mind. I had learned that whatever hold I may have had over him was related to my ability to prepare exquisite dishes.

That, and my willingness to spread my legs, I suppose.

He hovered over the stove with curiosity and much circumspection, then swiftly kissed the side of my neck, something I had learned to expect. I had just removed the casserole from the oven and placed it on the stovetop to adjust the seasoning, when he started to dig into it.

What is he looking for? I wondered, irritated. He turned to me and mentioned something about how good lunch would be.

"Lunch... Shit," I whispered to myself. I had not thought of lunch. "Sandwiches," I threw out there, somewhat panicked. "But, your dinner is prepared," I quickly added, hoping to redeem myself. "All you will have to do is warm it up." His turn was abrupt, startling me. The usual low tone he employed reached a high pitch I had never heard before, warning me of a storm to come.

"Don't you know what time we have dinner in my country?" he yelled. I looked at him, not fully understanding the implication of his remark, as dinner would be ready in time.

"What is all the fuss about, Patrick? "I asked him. "Anyhow, I must leave tonight. Since you continually complain about not having time to cook decent food, I thought I would prepare dinner for you and Alejandro," I softly offered, having decided I would leave before dinner. He looked as though he was ready to pounce on me.

"No woman will come and cook for me only to disappear afterward, like a caterer, a stranger," he screamed. "If you leave, I will throw your food in the garbage, Isabelle."

I stared in disbelief. I had not seen that one coming. "Enough of this," I told him, as I walked briskly to the living room, safely distancing myself from the drama that had erupted. I turned around and quickly sat on the couch directly facing the open area leading to the kitchen. Feeling the sweat trickle down my temples, I dropped my head down between my legs, letting it hang, hoping the blood flow would abort the fainting spell I slowly felt coming. The relief was almost immediate, but, still dizzy, I stayed seated and slowly brought my head up, my eyes focusing on Patrick still standing in the kitchen. My vista offered an uncompromising viewing of the part Patrick was acting out. The chicken was being swung over the garbage pail, leaving me with nothing else to do but watch incredulously. Is he really going to throw my food away? I asked myself, staring at the casserole—the fucking meal I had prepared with such intent! Fuck this, I decided. I stood up and walked to him, unsteadied by my disbelief. "You call this love?" I let out between my teeth, my hand waving the fetid air floating above the open garbage pail. "Fuck you, Patrick."

Startled by my words, eyes ready to pop out of his head, he grabbed my hand, leading me back to the couch and forced me to sit. The coldness of the leather was perfectly fitting, given the heat that had taken hostage of my body.

"No," I told him, getting up again, barely containing my tears. Without a word, I gathered my purse and the few items of clothing I had brought over in another bag and left, this time, through the front door, something I rarely did, as Patrick always insisted on me using the side door leading to the garage.

Patrick remained seated.

Once inside my car, I let go. What the fuck just happened? I wondered. My breathing, shallow and loud, the only company, the only witness to this confusion of mine that shouldn't be. There was a weight on me, coming from above, as if an invisible someone was lurking. I felt it, like we all do, this sensation of being observed, spied on. I stretched my head, peeked through the car windshield and caught sight of the tenant living on the second floor. She slowly lifted her hand as if telling me she knew, smiled, then let go of the curtains she had pushed sideways, to see better, that which she had most likely seen before. The curtains swung softly and the voyeur in her shied away, leaving me to stare up, at the sky, at the wind.

I couldn't go.

I can't go, I thought. Mad, tired, feeling weak, this emotional farce, its strong and toxic roots extending to all of me.

INHALED

I got back out of the car and climbed back onto the front porch. I knocked on the door and waited. When he opened the door, his sternness was still present, deadening his facial expression. It was now 5:00 p.m. Friday night.

"If we are to end our relationship, it cannot be like this," I mumbled tearfully, cowardly. At that exact moment, Alejandro and Jocelyne appeared, behind them the shuffling of feet, the sound of children laughing. "We have guests," they happily shared, leaving Patrick and I speechless.

I took my bags, walked inside the house, my shoulder brushing against his arm.

Alejandro and I set the table while Jocelyne played in her bedroom with her newfound five year-old girlfriend. We added placemats, as a family of three would be staying for dinner. The Latina woman before me had just been released from prison. Prison. Upon having her face punched by her then husband, she had knifed him to death. As Patrick shared this information, seemingly amused, I pinched myself for the third time that day. Such an edifying entourage I thought, fully aware that any human had limits to their willingness to adapt, and that the path of most resistance came with untold consequences.

What exactly did I need to finally understand?

Patrick was preparing his usual dishes, and, as if nothing had happened, proudly displayed my chicken casserole, positioning it in the middle of the table for all to admire. We took our seats. While our guests brimmed with excitement at sharing our meal, I braced for the shallowness of Grace that was about to be said.

"My God, bless this meal, bless the hands who have prepared it. Help us drive our lives in the right direction. And, remove all negativity from our minds. Amen," he prayed. As I listened to those empty words, I felt my stomach being remolded by new levels of acidity flowing into it.

Unable to articulate my refusal to eat, I stared at the plate Patrick was filling up for me, as he always did.

"Eat," he ordered, provoking an uncomfortable silence at the table. Humiliated, I could not look up at anyone and motioned to bring the chicken-filled fork to my mouth.

"Isn't this dish wonderful?" he inquired, suddenly animated, serving the guests second portions of my chicken. "Isabelle, such an incredible cook, really," he added.

I looked at him, nauseated from disbelief. The same scenario unfolded when my clafoutis was presented. But, this time Patrick upped his theatrics. As we crossed paths in the kitchen, I stared at him as he smiled and winked at me. He knew that I knew. Grade A Nicaraguan shit is what he was.

"Not too sweet," Patrick underlined. "It reminds me of a dessert we have back home."

Fuck you, Patrick. Fuck you, I thought.

After the guests left, I washed Patrick's truck and hosed down the top of his car, welcoming the mindless distraction. Going around the truck, I turned and noticed Alejandro doing the dishes, while Patrick spoke to him. They simultaneously looked at me from the small kitchen window. Patrick smiled.

"Alejandro tells me you are the best option," he nonchalantly said in my ear, as he penetrated me gently. "He loves the way you cook. He looks up to you, you know." I ignored the nonsense coming out of his mouth. I had enjoyed the reprieve from the suggestion of Alejandro joining us in the bedroom. I had not been able to articulate a word since dinner. It was as if the air, all of it, had been punched out of me. But here in this bed, I was resuscitated, revived by sexual CPR. Abandoning myself to his slow rhythm, I could not ignore how this moment violently contrasted with the unkindness the day had brought me.

The orange glow of his Himalayan salt lamp was highlighting his cheek bones and darkening his brown eyes. This face, his face was the only reason I was still here with him, tolerating the intolerable. I found solace in his body. I plunged my tongue into his mouth, wanting to drown in it. Feeling a moment of empowerment, I asked him to turn around, this time aching to lead the dance. He resisted, but did as I asked. I parted his legs, as I painted his body with my eyes, settling on his butt cheeks. Caressing them, I parted them slowly, bringing my face to the small of his back, where I started moving my tongue around, circling down toward that division, narrowing my attention to that place. My saliva was lubricating his orifice, my lips hugging its contour. On hands and knees, I demanded. And, he obeyed, enabling me to strike his cock as I pursued my hungry quest to reach his insides. I stopped suddenly, my desire to feel his skin on mine now dominating my senses, and rolled on my back. His eyes were questioning, but he simply moved on top of me and resumed our lovemaking.

"I love you," he said, caressing my cheek in circles to announce the imminent blow that would leave the residual redness on it he so loved to see. "Get us some water," he added as he firmly hit the side of my face. I had become used to this fetish of his, and simply closed my eyes, satisfied with the satisfaction I, myself, was procuring him. "Then, knock on Alejandro's door. Naked," he let out.

Shocked, I was unable to gather any form of resistance.

"You will go to him, and without waking him up, you will place his cock inside of you." The surprise had paralyzed my will to flee. He pushed me out of the bed, making me fall to the floor, forcing me to get back up. Again, he pushed me, this time toward the door, and out of the bedroom.

Whipped by the coldness of the house, I decided to turn around and come back into the room. Silently, I slid back under the comforter.

"Go get your own water bottle," I told him with disdain, feeling the weight of his glare on me. So much of our communication had become nonverbal, I was now acknowledging. But, the only competent communicator was me. And then, looking at him, reading his facial expression, I knew I had won, I knew he was going to leave me alone.

The next morning, with our legs intertwined, my head uncomfortably boosted by his thick torso, we lay in bed. We had both tacitly chosen to ignore the perversity he had so openly displayed the night before. I would address that with him later. It was 10:00 a.m. I got up, quickly remembering my Montreal guests would be arriving in less than two hours. I needed to get going.

"Can you give Jocelyne a bath before you leave?" he asked me innocently, peeking his head in the bathroom. In a rush, I looked at Jocelyne, noting the grease that had slicked her hair.

"Fine," I agreed, taking Jocelyne's hand.

I shampooed her hair with efficiency, leaving me enough time to eat breakfast with Patrick. Seated at the end of the dining room table, sipping the tea he had brewed for the both of us, I told him casually he needed to clean the bathtub.

"Your daughter's bottom sitting on top of that scum…Surely you can see it needs to be cleaned, Patrick," I noted, peeling the chipped nail polish from my nail. Feigning to ignore my remarks, he pointed to my purse, placed on the dining room table.

"The brand is Coach," I told him, with a smile. "I bought it at the Tokyo airport on a layover to New York."

He picked it up and threw it back on the table. "Money," he let out. "You are just about money."

CHAPTER THIRTEEN

Upon arriving home, I checked my phone. I had heard the numerous texts coming in while I was driving, but, this time, I had decided to ignore them. I sat down at my dinner table, with Jackson at my feet, and started reading. I was bombarded with a barrage of insults, a seemingly never-ending sermon.

If you think my bathtub is so dirty, you should do what any decent woman would do, and solve the problem. Clean it. His spitefulness pierced me. I literally folded in two and, gagging, ran to the toilet to throw up. What my body was expelling had to be venom. I was the victim of hate indigestion.

Thankfully, I had been mistaken about my friends' date of arrival. They were arriving Sunday. I had one more day. This was a blessing, as the distress I was feeling had rendered me dysfunctional. The liquid surging from my eyes was abrasive to my brain, setting the terrain for a migraine to form, another one. In spite of the torrid heat, I slept under the covers, wanting to halt the chills creeping through my body, wanting to disintegrate, wanting to disappear.

I had neglected to honor the negative space that was part of Patrick's being. I had neglected to acknowledge the details that would have made my understanding of him complete. I had failed to acknowledge the breathing space that made Patrick's existence possible, oblivious to the elements supporting his strange equilibrium. My focus had been on him all along, obliterating everything else around him, etching his contours with nothingness.

The surge of joy I felt when I saw my friends walking toward my door jolted me out of my fog, creating a small buoy on my horizon. I could see it, I could feel it, but I already knew I would not be able to reach it, let alone hold on to it. The fatigue was drowning me.

These Montreal friends were the first ones to travel my way. I was grateful for their concern, love and kindness, but I ached to be with Patrick.

My throat was tight, and I felt faint. I mindlessly prepared some cappuccinos before deciding on the activity of the day. I was debating between visiting Brattleboro or Northampton. We all agreed on the latter. Art galleries and drinks at the Northampton hotel would define our sunny, summer afternoon. Somehow, I emerged. I went beyond the act of existing.

I stepped outside the house to call Patrick, while my friends were setting the table.

"Will you be joining us for dinner tonight?" I bluntly asked, hopeful.

"No," he said, "I won't." His voice, so soft, so detached, so uncaring. They knew about Patrick, but what I had shared was minimal. With a fake smile hanging on my thin face, I told them a little about his controlling nature, blaming it on his Latino ways. I wanted to shield myself from being judged, to hide the big, fat shame I was carrying on my weak frame. They did not buy my lies.

Months later, they would recount that they had not slept well during their stay. They had sensed danger by the uneasiness of my moves, by the marked hesitations with which I would punctuate my speech. They heard the restraint with which I sprinkled a few pieces of information. They had read beyond my tiny, kind decoys meant to keep their attention away from my truth, my sad reality.

Seated on the floor beside the toilet bowl, I managed to let him know, between episodes of emptying my stomach's content, that I wanted out of this scurrilous relationship. You are abusive to all around you, so yeah, I'm done, I texted. Then, I blocked his number.

Despite the heat, I still opted to walk the four miles that separated my house from downtown Northampton. I was on my way to my mindfulness class. It was a private class, and it would be my first contact with the concept of mindfulness. I had high expectations of this meeting, but mindlessness would prevail. I wanted out of the present moment. I wanted to find an exit to the outside. I wanted to flee the bowels of mind-fuckery he had created. I could see that my teacher was feeling overwhelmed as she was trying to direct me, amidst a deluge of tears, to concentrate on the present.

I am so sorry, I was thinking.

So sorry.

My bedroom was the only space I felt safe. This was ironic, since most of the trespasses against me had occurred within its confines. Still, in my room, I could simply be. I let myself fall onto the bed, coming face to face with my laptop. I chose to watch a movie that failed to capture my attention, yet again. An Ambien is what I needed, the little oval pill that acted as my blue blanket. Just as I was about to slide into a drug-induced sleep, the phone lit up on my night table, startling me. I stared at it, fearful. It was 10:30 p.m.

It must be Alice, I told myself. Looking at the screen, I realized it was a text from Alejandro.

Are you available to help me study for the roofer certification exam? he wrote.

Is Patrick dumb enough to pose for his son? I wondered. Alejandro had a GPA of 3.7 and an IQ twice that of his father. He did not need my help to study the particulars of this trade. Roofing? I was puzzled, feeling the effects of the sedative enveloping me. Closing my eyes, I sensed my breath slowing down.

The noise of the phone hitting the floor woke me up. I picked it up and felt its vibrations in my hand. No caller Id.

"Alice?" I asked, sleepily.

"No," he answered. "Open up."

As I walked to open the door, I was thinking I should get in touch with Stephen King to tell him, "Yes, the boogeyman does exist. He lives in New England, predictably so. But surprise, the boogeyman is a bronze-skinned, dark-haired, balding, five-foot-ten, 170-pound Latino. He roams the highways at night, from the wheel of his beat-up red Dodge Ram. Warn the neighbors. If your cell phone rings after 10:30 p.m., beware. Do not answer.

And heed the sound of keys clicking on your windows. Just know that when you hear them, it is already too late.

Seated on the kitchen counter, legs crossed, in a state of shock, I watched him gesticulate his humiliation away. He was leaning against the stove, furious. "How dare you accuse me of being abusive!" he yelled.

I looked at the time, red numbers on the stove that caught my eye. It was 1:30 a.m.

He had driven here from Lowell for a chance to disprove his guilt. It was not the Ambien pill that was quieting me, no. Each time he visited me, I was impressed by the time and energy he was infusing into me. Into us. It had a hypnotic effect that exacerbated the sedated feeling already circling inside me.

"Patrick," I softly articulated, "you mistreat everyone around you. Jocelyne, Alejandro, me—all as objects you can disrespect, toss around, and even replace. You are abusive," I repeated confidently.

He energetically negated and denied my assessment, while pacing back and forth across the kitchen. To my satisfaction, I could hear his tongue unable to fully glide inside his mouth, its movement broken by the pastiness that had formed there.

He's like a cottonmouth, I suddenly thought. The reptilian kind, the only kind.

He was nervous. I was making him nervous. I was the source of his despair. The left corner of my mouth lifted. I knew I had him where I wanted him. He was suffering, of that I was certain. But what I saw next, transfixed me. His agitation betrayed something I could not identify. I sensed he was torn, that he was wounded, that I had wounded him. His eyes, that of a stranger, had a ghostly presence that permeated the air I breathed. They were shifty, looking to hook onto something. And then a rush of guilt assaulted me. Our story so far had only been a long series of misunderstandings, I told myself, wanting to believe it was true. He has love for me. His presence here means there's some substance uniting us.

The power of autosuggestion, my main power.

INHALED

I didn't come here to fuck, he suddenly spat out, his eyes now alive in mine.

And I looked at him. In these moments, the man lived inside a disequilibrium so profound, dug in by wounds I had inflicted. My words, like shovels with razor sharp edges. The depth of them opened a space for me to rule, momentarily giving me the illusion I thought was real–that I was in control. Worthy and capable of obtaining what I wanted.

A body, and hopefully, a soul.

We will see about that, I told him, won't we?

My appetite had almost returned to its normal level, giving me a feeling of renewed energy. I felt as though Patrick and I had finally reached an equilibrium, like a reprieve where sanity dictated a new way of being with me. The softness, the quietness of a presence that felt real. I knew that balance with this man was precarious, at best. But the taste of it gave me hope.

CHAPTER FOURTEEN

Alice would be finishing her theatre camp in two days, August seventh. I was planning to leave for New York on the sixth. Patrick was now working in Charlestown, New Hampshire, about two hours from Lowell. His business was still fragile, and the bidding volume was low, which is why he was accepting contracts so far away from his home.

Busy gardening, I felt my phone vibrate in my pocket. Pulling it out and reading the message, my spirits immediately lifted.

Join me for dinner tonight in Charlestown, it said. I remembered then, he had mentioned he would often sleep inside the house he was renovating to reduce his time spent traveling. Going to Charlestown fit perfectly with my schedule, since it would only add an hour to my drive time to New York.

Yes, I texted him, it's doable. I will be there at 6pm.

The day was crisp and the roads felt like velvet, something only a Montrealer could fully appreciate. Meeting Patrick in Charlestown felt like going on a vacation.

How my standards have changed, I thought.

It took me just over an hour to get to the site of his renovation project. It was a typical New England house with gray siding and white trim. I parked my car on the gravel road beside his Dodge Ram. I stepped out of my car and realized he was standing there, in his stained jeans and polo shirt, with his tool belt hugging his waist, quite eager to greet me.

"You came," he shouted happily. "You came!"

I smiled, not quite understanding his surprise.

"I told you I was coming, Patrick," I said, taking my overnight bag out of the car. He then took my hand and led me to the front entrance, unable to keep still, wanting me to appreciate the work he had accomplished. I was impressed by the quality of the work, his precision, and obvious organizational abilities.

Again, he took me by the hand, this time leading me to the second floor where we would be dining. The space welcoming me was empty except for the inflatable mattress placed in the middle of the room. The pièce de résistance.

I walked around, my kitty heels catching the loose fibers of the cheap wall to wall industrial carpet, as I absorbed the reality of the sleeping arrangements. These moments of rare, but sudden lucidity, always felt like a slap on the face. They highlighted how far away from my comfortable life I had now come, how my standards had been demoted to the bottom of Maslow's pyramid of needs. Unfortunately, for me, reality floated away the minute Patrick touched me.

He placed me against the wall, covering my mouth with his, whispering Spanish love words I did not understand. There were no distractions, no emergencies. It was only the two of us, fully present to each other's needs, fully acknowledging the gift we had given ourselves. Did I know this man?

Placing me on top of the mattress, he looked at me silently for a few seconds with his head retracted somewhat, as if to see me more clearly. "You came for me," he articulated. "Now, this really is love," he added, looking into my eyes with bewilderment. The moment was strange. His eyes were abnormally enlarged, giving a look of genuine intensity. Or, maybe it was only the illusion of genuine intensity.

I chased my discomfort away and redirected my thoughts to the fact he must have miscalculated the distance separating Charlestown, New Hampshire, from Northampton. It was only a little over an hour's drive. He must have overestimated the time it would require for me to get to him. That, in itself, was odd. He knew the roads. And these towns, these highways were his stomping grounds. But, most troubling to me was the comment he made regarding the proof of my love. Until that moment, it had not occurred to me that his inner notion of love might be absent, or warped, at best. Could it be he's on a hunt to collect expressions of an obscure emotion he calls love? Is he rationalizing something only the heart can measure? I wondered.

There, on a sad and dirty mattress, in an empty house, located in the middle of a small New England village, I touched upon the message his eyes had released. His eyes, the gateway to his soul, had failed him momentarily. They were revealing his true self. They were revealing what would take me another year to fully grasp.

The mattress, with its lack of firmness, added to the playfulness of our lovemaking, by enabling us to try positions we had never tried before. The mattress provided no balance, no stability, no point of support. The mattress was him.

A garbage bag containing blankets acted as my kitchen chair, inducing another invisible slap to my face. I sat, watching him silently prepare our meal, filet of sole, avocado salad, tomatoes, and, of course, the sacred rice and beans.

Facing one another, we ate slowly, listening to the town's church bells ring us into the evening, confirming I would have to leave soon for New York. He insisted on cleaning up and doing the dishes, leaving me to lie on the mattress, wishing for some sleep to bless my night.

The candid moments we spent together on that day, August 5, 2016, held a peaceful quality I had never experienced before with Patrick, and never would again. My fears, my anxieties, had been forgotten. In fact, I had touched hope. I had believed. I should have known better. I should have remembered that, yes, preceding a storm, the charming feel of a lull's spell.

Alejandro mentioned Patrick's birthday was coming up, on August the 12th, to be exact. Patrick had asked for a white vanilla cake, specifying, he did not want chocolate. His obsessive aversion to black had often manifested itself during my time with him. Even Alejandro's skin color, darker than his father's brownish-black tone, had been the subject of Patrick's overt criticism. I often witnessed, in silent disgust, the manner in which Patrick would display his racism. He would denigrate Alejandro's essence, an essence whose roots Patrick failed to acknowledge, as they pointed to his own. Patrick's repugnance for the color black infiltrated much of his everyday life. It dictated simple choices, such as the color of his towels and kitchenware, but surprisingly, never his clothes.

So, mindful of his preferences, I prepared him a vanilla cake, in the shape of a heart, and waited for him. Time passed. It was getting late. Disappointed, and too tired to wait up, I sent him a picture of the cake, turned off the lights, headed to my room and went to sleep.

He arrived at 6:30 a.m., preceded by the usual call. I opened the door and saw him appear in all his entire splendor. Dressed in a tight-fitting gray T-shirt and jeans, he had come to claim his prize.

CHAPTER FIFTEEN

It had been a long week. Alice and John were in Montreal, and I had planned on spending it in Phoenix to visit a friend. Instead, I chose to stay in Northampton, to avoid being bombarded by Patrick's lethal, venomous texts. More importantly, and as much as I feared it, I sensed an opportunity was surfacing.

I had counted on the month of July, while Alice was at Tisch, to truly position my relationship with Patrick. Many times, Alice had expressed her desire to meet him, but I had resisted. I knew my hesitancy was a reflection of the fact that I had some wisdom left in me. This reluctance to introduce Alice to Patrick had been the only rope bridge to my sanity. I had to honor my self-distrust.

On our way to New York, at the beginning of July, I had explained to Alice that I did not know where my relationship with Patrick was heading. I stated that, upon her return at the beginning of August, I would reconsider.

I remember looking at her, my eyes shifting between her and the road ahead, when a thought violently snapped into my mind, Alice is the grounding force. She makes clarity possible. But, the month of July had failed to provide me with the information I was seeking. How would this crucial coming week provide me with the pieces to make everything flow? How would I fill the spaces, the holes, and push forward, whatever forward meant?

Patrick arrived, as usual, quite late, preceded by a phone call stating he had arrived. I bounced off my bed and quickly went downstairs to open the door, as always, full of anticipation.

"Hi," he simply said, as he grabbed my waist, pulling me tightly to him. "Upstairs we go," he simply added. It was one of the most puzzling nights we had ever spent together. It was as intense as Charlestown had proven to be, but with a newfound restraint his opening line had not prepared me for. Mindfully sharing his time with me, he highlighted how our bodies were made to fit into one another's because spooning, the 55 position, was so easy and effortless for us both. He said it confirmed our lives were meant to have crossed, superimposing themselves neatly like two building blocks. Atypically, there was no lovemaking that night, just the strange comfort of his strong and silky arms, a comfort unable to soothe the rejection I was feeling.

And there is violence inside these arms; there is hostility etched in each fiber of his muscles, I suddenly thought, lying there with him. A vivid contrast to the soft, smooth envelope that is his skin. Patrick's sleep had always been a mystery to me. It seemed so easy, in fact, too easy, for him to leave me there, with my eyes fixated on the ceiling. I tried to move away from the thickness that was his chest, a thickness feeding a neck pain, but his arm reached me and pulled me over, closer to him, as always. Unable to follow my dreamer, I remained immobile, thinking, absorbing the moment. As much as I yearned to be with him, wishing for the now not to escape us, I still felt the urge to stop it all, to flee for safety.

He left again, early in the morning. Maybe, I was thinking, this was the last time he would grace my room with the scent of his Chanel Blue cologne on his overly washed body. Or maybe, for me, Chanel Blue would induce spontaneous vomiting for the rest of my life.

I woke up with a migraine, a stiff neck, and a body consumed by pain. I reached for my Zomig, the only medication capable of soothing my pain, reentered my bed and waited for the medication to hit me. I fell asleep.

The light in the room pulled me out of my torpor. My shades had rolled themselves up somewhat, letting the sun in. My head felt better, but I knew dizziness would fill my day, slowing me down. I stepped out of bed carefully, so I would not fall, and headed to the kitchen to eat my breakfast, two doses of peanut butter toast. While eating, I rewound the previous night's mindfulness coaching class in my head. I also noted that Patrick, knowing very well I was walking back in the dark from that class, had not called to see if I had made it back home all right, if at all. Selective worries. Selective control.

The day passed slowly, as had most days that summer, slow, painful, uneventful seconds that created slow, painful, uneventful moments. My immigration status had stunted my mobility, forcing me to depend on Patrick's limited availability for my release from boredom. He made me feel oxygenated, resuscitated by the love rushes, reanimated by the anticipated moments of savage sexual encounters.

And it hurt to know, deep somewhere, that I was starving for something I couldn't name, because I had never tasted it—a meal, a real one. I had been fed crumbs most of my life, I would come to understand. Crumbs of care, crumbs of understanding, crumbs of compassion, crumbs of love. My mother, John, now, Patrick. All hard-core crumb givers I had tolerated and loved.

At 7:00 p.m. I got ready for bed. I showered, blow dried my hair, and lathered moisturizing cream over my body, eager to feel the loss of consciousness.

My sleep patterns had become erratic at best, of that I was very aware. It was worrisome. The pace I was keeping and forcing on myself was akin to raping myself. I knew I needed my days to be structured with regular meals, my nights with regular sleep patterns. Yet, I was recklessly ignoring my needs, disregarding the impact on my health, both physical and emotional. This man was making me ill. My addiction, like all addictions, I now came to understand, was killing me. I turned off the lights with that thought in mind. Just as I was about to put my head on the pillow, my phone lit up and vibrated. Once again, my heart stopped.

Come whenever, he wrote.

Whenever was now.

I arrived at Patrick's at 12:15 a.m. on the 19th of August. It was a Friday night. The drive had been difficult, as the anticipation transformed itself into a subtle feeling of frightfulness. The music pieces I chose for the trip were neutral, meant to attenuate the disturbing sensations that were twisting my stomach. How long had I been living with this tightness? How long was I going to sustain this relationship? When was my body going to kick my heart into submission?

I walked into his room, relieved to see Patrick was as tired as me. He showered first, as usual, and came out of the bathroom with a solid erection. I made no move toward his shiny member, thinking that this was where our relationship had arrived. Normal sexual intercourse frequency was making its way, I was hoping. He fell asleep as quickly as usual, snoring into his pillow, while keeping me tight to him.

The morning offered us moments of closeness similar to the last time we had been together, spooning. As his arms enveloped me with strength and softness, his hand in my hand, his fingers laced into my fingers, I looked at the contrasting colors of our skin. My petite white hand held hostage by his large brown one, had always been a point of conversation for us. He loved the way I placed my hand inside of his, just as Jocelyne had started to do.

Holding onto me solidly, he caressed my forearm with his fingers, kissed the back of my neck and whispered tenderly in my ear that he was happy with me. It was a velvet-like moment only two lovers could devise and share, deeply felt and deeply received. Such a heartfelt statement on Patrick's part should have calmed me. But, it did not.

These intermittent moments of tenderness remained the most complex moments for me to integrate into my psyche. They were dispersed randomly, amidst, what had now become, a chaotic relationship.

The next day, as Patrick left with Alejandro, he stated he wanted me to stay home. "I want you to behave like a perfect little princess," he said seriously, looking at me. It should not have made me smile, but it did. I waited for their departure, got out of bed, and grabbed the robe that was hanging in his closet. It was an off-white robe he said he bought at Marshall's for a bargain, three for the price of one. Oddly, this robe was clearly a woman's garment. I had noticed it a few weeks before and that had been his answer. Apparently, it was a sale not to be ignored.

I walked into the bathroom, disgusted. It was the bathroom from hell. There was a stench of mildew that even the smell of bleach could not mask. It was a bathroom that belonged in the sugar shack my grandfather owned in the northern part of Montreal. I kept staring at the absence of a ceiling, where wood beams, wires, and exposed plumbing hung precariously over my head. The bathtub, where I washed my body, was filthy. This bathroom could have and should have been my compass. I had willingly ignored this inukshuk, this marker that had been veiled by the storms of my heart, the gusts of his confusing signals. But today, this bathroom was revealing itself as a mark to be recognized. Its repugnant smell, its open pharmacy, with an array of feminine products present since my arrival, disturbed me more than usual.

I blow dried my hair, put on my white jeans, my black silk halter top and shoes and fled to the Market Basket. I had not chosen the menu yet. I would improvise. I had branded myself as an exceptional cook and today would again confirm my culinary hegemony.

For Patrick, food preparation had become pivotal to the respect he held for my presence in his life. Food, and the swiftness of its preparation, I had understood, was crucial to him. In another life, the one I was leaving behind with John, the preparation of meals had always been my sanctuary. Over the last few months, the physical and mental exhaustion had acted as an impediment to my desire to eat and therefore to be at the helm of any kitchen in a consistent manner. But today, part of my seduction of Patrick was rooting itself in my ability to stun him with my culinary prowess. The game was on.

My presence, among the Latino patrons at the market, made me feel like a tourist each time I went. I smiled at everyone. I was happy. I was on a mission to please, to impress, to finally fit in. I had decided on a Greek-themed meal, zucchini and lemon rice soup, tzatziki, marinated lamb and some fruit. It would be a memorable lunch. Of course, my presence at the Market Basket did not go unnoticed. Was I still an anthropologist studying her subject? Had I been demoted to tourist status? Or had I become a native? A voyeur. A vulgar voyeur was what I had slowly become.

I unlocked the door with Patrick's heavily loaded set of keys. Of the 25 keys on his set, only four were required to get into his house. When he gave me his keys that morning, he gazed at me with a slight veil of concern. This was the first time in seven months he had allowed me to use his keys during his absence. The privilege I felt became almost orgasmic.

I entered the house, walked by the four boxes of old stamps Patrick had found in the basement of a house he was renovating—stamps he had asked me to sell, convinced he would make a fortune—and began unloading the grocery bags. Once done, I walked to his television, picked up the controller and chose a YouTube channel dedicated to Bebel Gilberto.

The food was ready to be transformed, and the musical ambiance had been secured. I was ready to perform my magic. With delight and levity, I prepared the soup, the tzatziki, and the meat. As I was washing my hands over the kitchen sink, I noticed two women outside. They were loading boxes into a Honda 4x4. They seemed to have come from Patrick's basement. By now, I had abandoned the idea of probing Patrick for details. I knew too well his answers would always be vague and encrypted. Always. If I wanted answers, I had to be a patient hunter of information. Still at the sink, I now recognized one of the women as the second floor tenant Patrick had just evicted. The other lady was unknown to me. I examined this second woman, attentively. My eyes squinting, I was somewhat confused and animated by curiosity, but mostly I was struck by how thin her legs appeared to be. I could not help but wonder at her age, as I was not wearing my glasses, but from a distance, she looked to be at least seventy-two years old. Her hairdo, short and coiffed, in that old aunt style, was slightly off-putting.

"Judge Judy," I heard myself say. "She looks like Judge Judy." The door opened slowly, and I realized, I had absentmindedly left it unlocked. A Latina, had just walked in. As I introduced myself, she scrutinized my whole being. I could tell she did not know I was Patrick's girlfriend. It was odd. Then again, Patrick was so secretive.

"Patrick's novia," I said, introducing myself. She hesitantly smiled, introduced herself as Valeria, Patrick's sister-in-law, and apologized for coming into Patrick's house unannounced. Seeing an opportunity to dig deeper, I offered her to join me for tea. "Stay," I said already pouring water into the kettle. I felt nervous. I felt the need to leave my mark, to impress her, to let her know that I was the one, that I was here to stay.

I was trying to reconcile all these thoughts in my head. I knew they were abnormal. I stared at this woman I wanted to impress. Her dark hair was covered with a net, food leftovers decorated her cheap pink blouse and her garlic breath was crowding my nostrils. A part of me found this scenario completely ridiculous. This isn't me, I thought, staring at the Latina woman in front of me. This can't be my life.

Flashes of my past sprang to mind, as I quickly rescanned my immediate environment. But still, I was shaking, feeling the netted woman held some form of power and control over me. Feeling that she could influence the direction my life could take. Stop shaking, I told myself as I prepared her tea. Stop. Here in front of you, stands an opportunity.

Valeria warmed up to me quickly, highlighting the surrealism of the moment. It was as normal as I had ever felt since starting to date Patrick. She infused a lightness into his home that I had been dying to feel there. This feeling of normalcy was making me lightheaded. It seemed to confirm that Patrick and I were finally on the right path, that stability and predictability would become constants in our lives, and would speed up the welding of our bonds.

"How long have you been dating Benjamin?" she asked, looking at her tea.

Benjamin, I thought. He uses both names, Patrick and Benjamin. Again, the unease. Again, the rationalization.

"Since January of this year," I replied. "We met shopping at the Burlington mall," I lied. Patrick had been firm. I was not to disclose we met on Tinder. And so, she was charmed by my lie.

She discovered I was a business and life coach, and rapidly delved into her marital distresses.

"He cheats," she said, "with my cousin back home in Puerto Rico. I am so unhappy. I stay for my children. I do not know how to leave, or if I can at all." Then she stiffened up, saying she should not talk so much, as Benjamin was probably recording our conversation. We both directed our eyes to the camera installed behind her. She shrugged it off, leaving me to wonder.

Upon finishing her tea, I walked her out. We gave each other a heartfelt embrace, kissed and promised to meet up again for tea some time before the end of the summer. I had made my mark.

As I began to reenter Patrick's house, I saw the second-floor tenant, Araceli, again.

"Isabelle," I offered, extending my hand. I kept wondering about the real story behind her eviction. Had she really skipped her payments, as Patrick had vehemently affirmed? I decided to bluntly ask her. After all, the meal was ready. I could let the afternoon continue its social course.

"So, look," I said firmly, "Patrick tells me you do not pay your rent on time, is that the case?" She turned to me, obviously shocked.

"You have two minutes?" she asked, visibly irked by my question. "Come upstairs. I will show you something." I followed her up the steep set of stairs, feeling hypnotized by the foreshadowing my mind was somehow identifying.

I stepped into a living space that was clean, tidy, and open. The color palette was a mix of turquoise, white and pink pastels. It was very feminine, unlike her. While somewhat pretty, with straight black hair, small, dark beady eyes, a delicate nose and thin red lips, her petite frame was stalky. Unlike many other Latinas I had met before, her loose-fitting clothes betrayed a penchant for comfort, a preference for the practical. She invited me to sit at a table in the middle of a well-lit kitchen. As I waited on my chair, somewhat shifting my body, she opened a white cupboard door and retrieved 12 money orders. She laid all of them in front of me, pointing to their dates. I took my time and scrutinized the documents. I could read that all, except for a few written a day or two after the expected date of payment, complied with her lease. I flushed.

I got it.

I quickly saw the lies Patrick had told me and, most probably, to the other puppet, his son. She saw my confused state and understood I had been fed a different story.

"Benjamin wants me out of the house," she explained. "The rent he is now asking for and knows I cannot pay is creating the perfect excuse and opportunity for him to remove me and renovate the apartment to house more than one tenant," she added. More money was the bottom line.

"I see," I said. An uncomfortable silence set in, but not for long.

"You know Benjamin dated Patricia, right?" she asked, with calculated poise. I turned toward her, caught off guard.

"Who the hell is Patricia?" I asked.

"The previous owner of the house," she firmly stated. "The woman I was helping earlier to remove her belongings from Benjamin's basement," she specified.

"The old lady," I reformulated with what must have been a very incredulous expression. The image of that thin woman surfaced in my mind. The hair. The short, dry, curly black hair.

"Yes," she said. "They dated for three years, until the sale of the house, basically." I stared blankly at the money orders in front of me. He had told me the owner of the house had died, and that her children, once traced, had declined to repossess their mother's belongings. I remembered that moment vividly. It was the eighth of February. It was the day I had come over for my four-day stay.

He had brought me to the basement, proudly showing me, what appeared to be a collection of theatre costumes. You could see they were very old and had been handmade with exquisite craft. The basement was full of artefacts from another time: game boards, sewing patterns, furniture. He even let me have a purse I thought was retro-cool. Patricia's purse.

"But, that's not all," Araceli softly continued. "There are other women who come to visit him." Seated at this other table from hell, my heart sank to my heels. Shaking, yet again, I took out my phone, pressed on my Tango app, looked for Lydia's profile and showed it to her.

"Is she one of them?" I asked with a shaky voice.

"Yes. Yes," Araceli said, "she came one night when you were sleeping here at Benjamin's house. She knocked on the door for a long time, then left driving her usual blue van." And without missing a beat, she added that once, after my departure, another woman, this time in a gray car, had come to spend the night. At this point, I was not hearing much anymore. I was deaf, but for some ringing in my left ear. Pressure will do that to you.

My brain was in overdrive, my synapses connecting the dots at the speed of light, my energy directed at making sense of what I had intuitively suspected, but had chosen to ignore.

"Araceli, please call Patricia and see if she wants to meet me here as soon as she can," I requested. Araceli immediately called her.

"Patricia is on her way," she confirmed.

I got up and started toward the stairs.

"What will you do?" she asked, obviously worried.

"I will leave and go home," I told her tentatively, feeling faint. She escorted me to Patrick's door, watching me helplessly play with the lock, unable to figure out which key fit. Feeling the lock release, I pushed and opened the door, entering the house. The four boxes containing thousands of stamps were looking straight at me. I picked up a box and started, in a zombie-like state, to scatter the stamps everywhere, all to the sound of Bebel Gilberto's Bossa Nova.

For some reason, I started dancing to its rhythm, in a trance-like state, emptying all four boxes with surprising control. I suspected I was probably being recorded and did not want to give him the satisfaction of seeing his prey disjunct.

Then, I turned to his bedroom. As was typical, I had made his bed that morning. He had commented the previous night that no one, in fifteen years, had folded his clothes the way I had done two weeks earlier. The last one had been his mama.

Fucking, mama.

Well, well, I thought. I opened each and every drawer, took out the clothes and threw them everywhere on the now stripped bed.

INHALED

I walked to his daughter's bedroom and grabbed the book I had given him as a birthday present, ten days earlier. The book was on the child's bed, beside Patrick's pants, socks, and boots, an oddity I chose to ignore. He must have started to read the book as he was putting his daughter to bed, and decided to sleep by her side. I remembered, a sting in my heart, how he hated to sleep alone.

No…more…book. I'm leaving nothing meaningful to this man, I told myself, ripping the pages, one-by-one, as my sinful gesture tugged at my heart. I was murdering my favorite book, a coup de coeur I had shared with a man I thought I loved, my favorite book of all time. It happened to be written by the Spanish author, Carlos Ruiz Zafon. Sadly, in addition to the clothes and the stamps, there were now sprinkled pieces of this epic novel littering the floors.

I then took out my phone, chose the video option and recorded my own masterpiece. I could have done more. I could have created so much more damage. I felt tempted to pour my soup on his clothing. I knew if I did more, I could expose myself to some legal trouble. I knew far too well Patrick's love for courtroom dramas would pull me into a public arena where the spotlight would be directed at him, the so-called victim. I had noted how animated he had become when talking about the possibility of bringing his second floor tenant, my new friend, to court. No, I would not give him the opportunity to shine at my expense. Never.

Standing on his balcony, his keys in my hand, I was fuming, thinking of throwing them into the Merrimack River. It was now time to text my Nicaraguan punk that I was leaving him and his petty little world.

While I waited for Patricia to arrive, Alejandro called me unexpectedly, imploring me not to leave the house. He insisted there was a plausible explanation for the chaos that was unfolding. I was crying, suddenly feeling the weight of the situation sitting on my chest.

"How could you be in on what your father is doing? You are his accomplice, Alejandro … I am sorry," I told him. "I cannot stay," and I hung up. I was baffled by the call I had just received. It was his son. He could not be that infatuated with me.

As she approached, I fixated on her thin silhouette, wondering what else would be revealed. She walked toward me with surprising vigor, holding her car keys in one hand, while clenching her stomach with the other. She was coming into focus now, allowing me to fully see the person, who, throughout the morning, had stoked my curiosity.

"Hi, Patricia," I said timidly. "My name is Isabelle."

"What's the matter?" she asked, her eyes betraying her curiosity.

"Well, a nor'easter is on its way," I offered. I then dove into the afternoon's discoveries, exposing the truths I had uncovered. As I talked, my eyes were detailing her facial features, her skin tone. It was almost hypnotizing. She was whiter than white, the translucency of her skin revealing her snaking veins. Her eyes, a striking pale blue, lightly contoured by an equally light shade of green, looked like mine. Her thin shape, her feminine and refined demeanor, complete with her thick Bostonian accent, was overwhelming. I could not believe what I was seeing. She was a much older version of me ... of me.

Araceli joined us at the side of the house, and there, repeated the stories about the women who visited the house when I left, when I was there, when I was securely tucked away in Northampton. Evidently, the distance had procured Patrick the safe space to pursue his many deceptions. I cried intermittently, as I was being consoled by both Patricia and Araceli, their genuine compassion highlighting the mediocrity of Patrick's character.

I could see Araceli was feeling the weight of what was unfolding. She feared Patrick. She was understanding the maliciousness behind her landlord's intentions. Knowing Patrick was on his way, she retreated to her apartment, leaving Patricia and I walking together toward the front of the house.

There, we sat on the cement ledge bordering the sidewalk, letting our legs dangle.

"We went out for three years," she shared, with sadness. I looked at her, leisurely reexamining her features. She was beautiful, but she still was much older than Patrick and older than me. It was challenging for me to see the physical attraction she said he had for her when they were together. Maybe her grandmotherly aura made it difficult for me to imagine the two of them together. The mismatch they must have formed screamed at me. She described to me an intimate relationship with him that lasted three years. "The closeness seemed to be genuine," she said. "The conversations would be long and satisfying, just like the laughter," she added.

"And...the sex?" I risked, hesitantly.

"A lot of it," she replied, proudly. What she then shared, troubled me. As if it was possible to be even more troubled. She recalled a particular month where he had visited her every night. "He would walk into the living room, drop his pants to the floor and have me right there on the carpet," she shared. "Sometimes he would do that while his son was waiting outside in the car. He would then shower, dress, and leave," she added, shaking her head. Never, during their three year relationship, had they spent the night together. Never. It disturbed me. She thought she had had a relationship, but a relationship must abide by certain criteria, one of which is a physical intimacy that goes beyond the act of having sex or watching television. The act of sharing the night together will often consolidate that feeling of intimacy so dear to many women. I was puzzled by the fact that this woman had not picked up on the absence of such closeness. But she held the certainty, in her mind and heart, that their liaison had been a legitimate one.

She believed they had been true lovers, bonded by the promise of a future together. Who could blame her? He would mention the possibility of marriage. He would call her in the middle of the night to check her whereabouts, like he had with me. His repeated and continual surprise nocturnal visits were enough for her to validate the status of their relationship. My heart felt for her. She was another victim whose reality would have to be reevaluated yet again.

Again, because thinking she already knew everything about his life, I revealed the existence of Jocelyne, his young daughter, the child he conceived two years prior to their meeting, a child whose existence he had voluntarily concealed from her. She listened, in complete silence.

Patricia had left Patrick when she found out about Lydia. Patricia's daughter had attended a barbeque get together where both Patrick and Lydia had been present. When Patricia's daughter asked Lydia why Patrick was there, Lydia replied they had been going out together since "forever." There was hesitancy in Patricia's voice as she was sharing these recent memories with me. The recollection of her shared past with Patrick was making her travel a path that, as of now, would take her further into the deep woods of suffering and disillusionment. Her pain was easy to measure. Her breathing had become shallower, consistently so. The skin of her neckline had become wallpapered with red blotches. Beads of sweat had started to pearl where her hairline met her forehead. It was right then that he appeared from the back of the house.

Patrick was obsessed with secrecy. His display of cameras, both inside and outside the house, his visceral inability to tolerate the sight of opened curtains, the spite he held for his neighbors, all portrayed him as a controlling man prone to bouts of paranoia. He would always prompt me, in his thick Spanish accent, to speak softly, motioning with his index finger pressed on my lips to keep quiet. He would always remind me of the importance of not discussing anything out loud in public.

The scene waiting for him then, as he walked toward both Patricia and me, displayed nightmarish elements that would trigger his fear of transparency, fueling his latent irritation at being exposed.

The expression on Patrick's face was one I had only seen on rare occasions. His eyes were conveying a look of both concern and madness.

What the fuck is happening? was the question they were clearly asking. Our eyes locked. He continued that strange stare, creating an acute uneasiness in me. I felt my body congealing. This was where my incessant pursuit for transparency, the demystifying of my own intuition, had led me, this final act unfolding on an unkempt, debris-filled, Latino front lawn. I had unwittingly staged a very public scene.

I could hear the cars passing behind me, Latino music blaring from their bass-only radios. I could feel them slowing down, the drivers, all Latinos trying to get a glimpse of these common theatrics so entwined into their culture.

I could almost sense their smiles saying, It's your turn buddy, good luck …

I was the first one to break the silence. I cleared the lump in my throat, slowly raising my water bottle to wet my dry lips.

"You told me Patricia was dead, Patrick." No reply. "Not only is she alive … you dated her for three years? Patrick … and Lydia … she was seen here recently, with her children," I added.

With raised eyebrows, he yelled that he had never dated this crazy woman. He gesticulated and pointed at her as if she had committed an irreparable crime. I could hear—as I had heard all the other times I confronted him with the possibility of ending our relationship—the dryness that had settled inside his mouth. Our mouths now were two desert storms heading for an inevitable collision.

Patricia, I just noticed, had become paler, seemingly paralyzed by what she had heard. He had just publicly denied the existence of his last three years with her, negating their history, their past and everything they had been to each other. She lovingly scrutinized his eyes, looking for some logical explanation, hoping to hear him acknowledge the lives they had shared. But no, his body had stiffened, spite, and annoyance animating his arms, as he was busy shooing her off his property.

She pushed back, questioning his denial with a hurt I could taste, coming from her trembling voice. Listening to them bicker, I turned around and spread wide both my forearms on the top of the car roof, resting my head on its edge. As I turned around to face the spectacle still playing on that stage, Patricia's paleness startled me. I walked toward her, noting Patrick had walked into the house, and told her to let it go, that I believed her, that engaging with him was futile.

I took her in my arms, slowly easing my grip, but leaving my arms wrapped around her shoulders. I felt her frailness, her vulnerability. She was stunned, and it worried me. I walked her back to her car and said I would call her later that night. She got in her car and left, and as I watched her leave, I wondered if she was going to reach her destination.

I walked back, slowly this time, with fury and disgust tangled inside my chest. Patrick had returned, standing on his porch, his ugly unpainted porch. His eyes were alive with a bruised ego, whose only purpose was to mask his false detachment, conveying a sense of concern, but deadened by the shallowness of his understanding of what had unfolded. He had just returned from inside the house. The stamp tableau I had created obviously did not agree with his perception of aesthetics.

"How could you do this to me?" I asked him, understanding fully how futile my question sounded. "Knowing what I had gone through with John, how could you? How could you prey on me with such callousness?" I could not control the volume of my voice anymore. I had so many words to vomit. His eyes quickly scanned the neighborhood and then he walked back inside the house.

"We are over," he spat before closing the door.

"Really, asshole? You think?" I shouted.

PART THREE

CHAPTER ONE

How I made it back to Northampton, I do not know. The roads I had driven so often had suddenly become a strange series of exits and turns. It was a maze only my GPS could solve. I knew I was in shock. I felt the cold sweats, my rapid heart rate, my trembling hands. Adrenaline was keeping me from leaving my lane, but I knew I had to pull over. I had to stop. I needed to center myself.

As much as my brain had registered the factual buffet I had just been served, confusion had still set in. The words and stories I had been fed over the months were now resurfacing, tangling in my mind.

My gullibility was shameful.

How could I have been so naive, so fucking trusting? I wondered. It had been all laid out for me to see, the innumerable inconsistencies, always quieted by loving words, placed at the right moment, as we were fucking. I was now seeing his gaze floating over my face, focusing on my eyes, and hearing him warn me, as he held my wrists up with one hand, warn me not to do anything crazy.

Him waking me in the middle of the night just to repeat tenderly how much he loved me, when all the while Lydia was still around, and Patricia was not too far away, not to mention the gray car.

Mind fucking.

I made it home and stepped out of my car, grabbing my overnight bag, and all the rest of the belongings I had managed to collect from Patrick's house. My hairdryer had, over time, represented a strange symbol, one of finality. Somehow each time I had felt like leaving him, I had thought of the hairdryer. Removing it from his house was akin to removing him from within me, my life. Often, I had kneeled on his bathroom floor, opened the cabinet door that would fail to properly close, and I would stare at the device that was always plugged into the wall outlet underneath the sink. So many times, I had left Patrick's house, fighting the urge to leave with this device. And that day, well, I had. I had pulled out of him, a failed outlet.

The minute I entered my house, Patrick called me. He was on his way to a restaurant with Jocelyne and Alejandro and had the audacity to put Jocelyne on the line.

"Isabelle, why did you make the big mess?" she asked. Unable to make small talk with a four year-old, I asked her to put her daddy back on the line. Patrick was trying to explain that all that was said to me that day was a lie. "Alejandro is upset at what Araceli said. He thought that all was going so well until then," he said.

Yes, I thought. The truth has a way of rearranging the lies sometimes. Nothing like a witness to fuck with one's story, liberally paraphrasing Mark Twain in my mind. "Fuck you," I said. "And, die ..."

After hanging up, the text messages began. Again, he denied, negated, and blamed. At one point, he said to call Lydia, so she could corroborate his story.

All right, I wrote, send me her number. And then I waited.

I am driving. I cannot send to you, it read.

Right. Of course. I knew how to retrieve Lydia's number, anyway. Suspecting she was still part of his life, I had looked up her phone number back in June. I did not have the courage then to call her, thinking I was the one imagining the worst. Patrick was always so convincing with his explanations. Now, things had changed.

The surreal moment I had wanted to create was now at the tip of my fingers. Heart racing, palms sweating, I dialed, hoping Patrick's version was going to hold and that everything had just been a misunderstanding of epic proportion. She answered, her voice feminine and assertive.

"Lydia?" I asked with calculated kindness. I wanted answers. Pissing her off was not going to help.

"Yes," she replied, immediately concerned.

"I am sorry to call you like this. My name is Isabelle," I blurted out, stalling for a few seconds. This was a strange moment. It was a moment I had avoided for so long. "Up until today, I was dating Patrick...Benjamin Rodriguez. Is it possible you were as well?"

Time had seemingly stopped for us both, as silence etched its way in. Is she going to hang up? I wondered.

The volume of her voice increased as she began her interrogation. First, she wanted to know where I had gotten her number.

"Google," I told her.

Second, she asked me when I had started seeing Patrick.

"January," I said.

Third, she wanted to know where I had met him.

"Tinder," I replied.

And just like that, the gates of my own hell opened and, I supposed, it did for her as well. The heart of the barricade that Patrick had constructed to contain his secrets was yielding to the flow of polluted water. Sewage, it seemed, had a way of pressuring its way into anything, pushing until it could spread itself everywhere.

"We met on the app, Bumble, in January 2015," she confessed with a sigh. "Our relationship slowed down during the last Christmas holidays." It appeared I had been the rebound. I then remembered the unanswered knocks on his door, that first morning we had spent together at his home. "Can you believe he never bought anyone Christmas gifts? Nothing even for his four year-old?" she went on, uninterestingly. "Jocelyne kept repeating that Santa had not come for her." Yes, I could believe it. I had been the recipient of his stinginess, and a witness to his neglect. But, I did not care to hear the recitation of flaws I had personally experienced. My understanding of the situation had met its own boundaries.

I could hear her, as though she was floating above my body. She explained that they had kept in touch until the beginning of the current month, and he had insisted, no one was part of his life, that he was single. My heart sank as I heard this. He had denied my existence as well. He had confined me to the perimeters of his shitty, little makeshift house.

"I was aware of a feminine presence," she stressed. "I saw a blue pair of Tory Burch sandals in his bedroom closet and a woman's Cartier watch on his dresser."

"Both mine," I confirmed.

"And then, the other toiletries," she added. "Didn't you see the question mark I left on one of your deodorants?" she asked.

"No," I answered in disbelief. "Never."

The next question was the one I needed answered. "Lydia, were you sexually active with Patrick during this time?"

"Well," she said bluntly, "he did fuck my brains out on Valentine's Day."

"Well," I replied, as jealousy began inserting its novel hold on me, "I had him in the morning."

Having declared battle, she then added that once in June when he fucked her, he quickly ejaculated because he could not hold "his wad."

I surrendered. I did not want to hear any more of this vulgarity. His wad? Where had I landed? Amidst the trashy waters to which she was carrying me, I was still swimming fairly well, treading with stamina through the sludge. I did not know how I kept it together.

All right, I thought, time to share. Time to even the layer of hurt she was willingly spreading on me. "Patricia and Patrick dated for three years," I informed her. "They dated while he was with you. Their final fuck was last December on the floor of his cellar."

Dead air followed. Will she be able to bear the weight I'm shamelessly placing on her? I was asking myself. And yet, surprisingly, that is when we started to bond. We both quickly understood that we had been dealing with a player, and a pathological liar.

While I was speaking with Lydia, Patrick was texting me. Unbelievable. I informed him with great pleasure that I was on the line with Lydia. He stopped texting.

I heard her. She was barely crying, but I heard in her voice, the poignant disbelief of a broken dream.

"We spent so much time together ... meal times. We were a family," she offered softly.

My mind needed time to absorb that piece of information. Meals had always been the focus of Patrick's attention. He wanted a cleaner, and Lydia cleaned houses to earn extra money. He wanted a cook, and Lydia operated as a caterer in her free time. I could not help but wonder why he would pass on a woman like her. She offered everything he desired. She was white as snow, brandished waist-long reddish blonde hair and shone gem-like eyes. Flashes of him trying to pull my hair as we fucked appeared to me just then. He craved long hair. Mine was short. This Aryan-Latino had hit his own lottery with Lydia. Why spoil it?

Seeing that Patricia was calling me, I asked Lydia to defer our conversation to the next morning. We needed to process all this information. She was a step ahead of me in that regard, as her process was about to come to its inevitable conclusion, to surely leave him. I was still battling the pull of denial, incapable of acknowledging the existence of deception and extreme betrayal.

Patricia, like Lydia and me, was dealing with the pain the day had revealed. As she shared the details of her relationship with the man she called, Benjamin, I came to understand that she had also been the victim of a deeper kind of fraud.

I got off the couch, walked to the kitchen, opened the refrigerator door and zoomed in on the bottle of champagne.

"Fuck the migraines," I decided. I opened the cabinet and took out a champagne flute. Then, I grabbed the bottle, popped off the cork and filled my glass until it overflowed. I took my first sip. It was dry and it was cold and it was soothing. I sat down on the living room floor to enjoy it. Then, I got up, chose a Madonna CD and danced all night, until I emptied the bottle.

Waking up the next morning proved harder than I expected. The nausea, induced by both the champagne and the aftermath of my discoveries, had drilled its way into the whole of my digestive engine. I was in disbelief. I was humiliated. I had been royally fooled. I had ignored my intuition, my little voice. It had been telling me, so many times, that I had to leave. That something was foul.

Paralyzed in the middle of my bed, with Jackson at my feet, I dissected the previous day's events. I could not do it for long though. I felt it coming. It rarely happened, since my stress was usually exulted through painful migraines.

The slow lava-like fluid was making its way through my esophagus. I felt its sandpaper-like quality rubbing against the silkiness of my soft throat tissue, warning me I would not make it to the toilet. The hot mess, now pouring uncontrollably to my feet, was christening the arrival of a newfound awareness, the very real departure of my surprising naivety.

I took a shower, which provided me some temporary relief, but it was my coffee that saved the day. I sat at the dinner table, sipping it, feeling the liquid partially alleviate my mouth's pastiness. Rubbing my temples, my eyes closed, I thought of Lydia and of our conversation the night before. How I envied her position—the detachment from Patrick she had managed to carve, both physically and emotionally, however relative, was something that felt unattainable to me.

I was remembering how she had asked me to become friends on Facebook 30 minutes into our first encounter, a request I had felt was odd, considering the situation we both were facing. Not trusting her yet, I had refused, and she had understood.

I decided to call her one last time, needing to have her story, with its own intricacies, to dilute mine. Our phone conversation was shorter this time. There was really nothing more to add, nothing more to say. We both agreed, we were simultaneously fucked, mind, body, and soul.

CHAPTER TWO

Even though I had blocked Patrick's number, the emails were still pouring into my spam box. I knew I should pull away from him completely, but this was the only channel of communication left for me to spray my indignation. I wanted him to suffer, to bleed, to die.

I love you, I read. You are the only one. Always have been. You are my life, Isabelle. None of what you were told is true. Come to dinner with me tonight. Let's start again. I will explain everything.

Seriously? I thought.

It was becoming clear that although we were both acting in it, he was the main character of this sick play. He used the drama to carve a space for himself, where he could feel alive. I was caught between the outrageousness of his falsehoods and my desire for this chaos to all be a mistake. I was hoping that all of this had not really happened. I wanted to believe that the man who had held me in his arms, who had sworn allegiance to my body and my mind, who had gushed words of adoration, while we passionately fucked, had actually been truthful. I did not want to believe he had been preying on me for the last eight months, scheming behind my back, and callously and coldly orchestrating a ballet of moving targets.

Exhausted, I could no longer pursue this mindless exchange. I was fighting to keep some perspective and to not be lured into the details of his disillusioned universe. His was a world filled with half-truths and self-deception. His life was a dysfunctional circus, where clowns could not elicit smiles, where trapeze artists fell to their deaths, where knife throwers killed their wives.

And I needed to leave the circus master's chambers.

I need to go to the police, I first thought, as I opened my eyes in the middle of the night. I had just remembered that he could still, somehow, be monitoring my phone and my whereabouts.

He had just commented, the week before, on the number of hours I had spent on my phone in the last 6 weeks—72 hours, apparently.

He had often quoted to me a few of the texts I had written to John, oblivious to the damage such an intrusion in my life, such a breach of privacy, could inflict on me, and on us. He had called me once, while I was driving back to Northampton, gleefully pinpointing my location.

"Hi, Babe," he said. "You just finished gassing up and exiting to the I-90, I see," he added with a chuckle. All these facts were mushrooming in my mind, emerging to the surface.

Moreover, Patricia had disclosed a disturbing fact that was still circling in my head, further highlighting my need for protection. She had shared that when she and Patrick shopped together, he would innocently put his items on the conveyor belt and look away, openly pressuring her into paying for his merchandise. She had also described how, upon entering a retail store, he would physically distance himself from her. She felt he had wanted to hide the fact that they were together. I knew he had. So did she.

Most disturbing of all was the financial fraud. Over the course of their relationship, she had lent him a total of 20,000 dollars. She had even paid for his car, just three days into their relationship, to supposedly improve his credit rating. His goal was to qualify for a mortgage, so he could buy a house—her house—which had just been repossessed by the bank.

The police officer attentively listened to my story, as I wondered, what is this man thinking? I was such a sorry sight. I had hidden puffy eyes behind sunglasses and was aware of my dried lips as I articulated my story. A story, that I, myself, had difficulty comprehending. I listened to my options.

"One option," said the officer, "is to get a restraining order. The other option is for me to call and tell him not to come to your house or to contact you through any means."

A restraining order. I should opt for that, I thought. It seemed the surest way of stating the seriousness of my decision to have no contact with him. "Call him," I finally said, unable to gather enough conviction to legitimize a restraining order.

Leaving the police station, I walked to the parking lot, across from Northampton's city hall, to retrieve my car. It felt like I was suspended from the concrete world, disconnected from my surroundings, the blinding sun adding to my disorientation. Blindness. I knew the potent relief it could cast on one who was not willing to see.

John and Alice were scheduled to return from Montreal at the end of the day. In addition to the pain I had been feeling, I had the added hurt of knowing that Alice had not tried to reach me all week. John had taken her to his brother's house, where dinner with her cousins had been organized. I felt so alone. I had been abandoned by my own daughter, whom I had protected from John's emotionally dysfunctional family. I was apprehensive. I feared my own behavior had changed me into a helpless individual who had willingly abdicated her parental duties. Alice's lack of communication with me over the last week, coupled with a few pictures she had sent from her cousin's picturesque home, tugged at my vulnerable heart. I was weak, unbalanced, and afraid.

The week was trickling down slowly, with each and every minute spent thinking of what had been revealed on the weekend. I felt trapped in Northampton more than ever. I had nowhere to go and no one with whom to really share my hurt. I needed support. I needed my friends to distract me from my pain, to anesthetize me. I needed their presence to attenuate this feeling of emptiness.

I felt misunderstood. No one with whom I shared my distress had fully comprehended the depth of my misery. I had been toyed with and emotionally abused. That was true, but I had also fallen in love. It was a desperate love that had been molded by a master manipulator. Instead of supporting me with unconditional love, they rained judgment on me, adding salt to my gaping wounds. Moreover, the growing feeling of isolation clumping in my stomach was interfering with my parental judgment, adding to my perceived inadequacies.

Shamefully, I had let Alice become my confidante. This unusual choice highlighted my thirst for support, no matter where it stemmed from. I did not want her to misinterpret my strange behavior and obvious despair as rejection. Her feedback momentarily validated my perceptions. She shared that she was starting to integrate my distance as something to take personally. I looked at her porcelain and perfectly oval face, her wide brown eyes, her plump red mouth. She was beautiful. And, suddenly, I remembered, as we were walking together in downtown Northampton, throughout my conversations with Lydia, she had alluded to the possibility Patrick may have been targeting Alice as well. I felt like throwing up, suddenly reminded of my other beautiful daughter's existence.

One week had passed since I had last seen Patrick. I could not breathe properly. All I had left of him was the lingering pain from the last time he had bitten the inside of my right palm. All I needed to do to invoke his presence, his touch, was to press on that meaty part of my flesh and wait for the physical sensation to follow. And so, I did.

I was desperately trying to hang onto every second I was not with him. The battle raging inside me was one I had to win. If I gave in to temptation, I would be returning to his simmering, burning hell of a house. I would be returning to an empty place that invited only unbridled carnal consumption in exchange for my life.

But is a relapse but an opportunity to taste the forbidden?

One last time?

One last moment?

To learn even more?

I reached him by email.

What will you do with the pictures?

Our memories are stored in my brain, he texted. That's better than anything.

Eyes glued to the computer, I hovered over the words. Our memories. Had all this really happened? My memories had been altered by this emotional plastic surgeon, all of them modified from their perceived perfect state and meaning. Before finding out the extent of this man's sickness, I had taken solace in the thought that we had at least touched and shared some of our truths and that I had been stroked by the brush of lust and passion at an opportune time in my life. By way of intense lovemaking, where fingertips were the conduit appeasing our mutual fears, anxieties, and desires, I had seen a future with him. Now these memories were empty shells where hollowness meandered.

One week into my weaning, stepping out of my fog, I decided to take Alice to Northampton for dinner. If nothing else, I had to try to infuse some form of reassurance into her life. I was overwhelmed with maternal guilt and my parental inadequacies.

What a fucked up mother I had become.

As I pulled away from Alice's school I checked my emails. I could not believe what I read. My immigration lawyer had sent me a PDF file from Homeland security. The file stated that my status as a nonimmigrant had been granted. I quickly arranged for Alice to stay at her friend's house for the week, and then I hurried home to pack my bags. Life was finally turning around. I was now allowed to escape my New England prison.

I kissed Alice goodbye. She knew how dear my Montreal friends were to me and how much I needed this time away from Northampton. Yet, she wished I would stay. It was not so much that she wanted to be with me, but that she wanted to be in her own room, inside her own house for this first week of school.

"Tough it out," I heard myself say to her, without one ounce of guilt.

But there was one thing I had to do before I crossed the border, though, and this, I kept to myself.

I stepped yet again, into my car, absent to everything that mattered to me. Grief is a different animal in the kingdom of pain. The road it brings you on is wide, its distance from the core of you, difficult to assess. The trigger of it, an ordinary instant that can morph into remarkably mediocre ones. I had become the queen of that kingdom where my grief, like a wild salmon jumping rapids it was drawn to, needed to land to that place where it would spawn.

More grief.

And yes, she would have died knowing where I was headed, just as all who looked at me crawl for love from the comfort of their so-called compassionate understanding, would have.

The drive to Charlestown was a short one. I parked my car in the driveway, stepped out, and strutted down the gravel driveway in my Christian Louboutin heels and blue and white striped Max Mara dress. It was hardly an appropriate outfit for a worksite. By wearing designer clothes, my intent was to make my reentrance to Montreal, the return to my hometown, a symbolic one. Here though, my intent was to seduce and provoke.

I walked slowly toward the back door, guided by the sounds of hammers banging inside the space that had been divided into three distinct sections. First greeted by a Dominican worker I had never met before, I quickly spotted Patrick. He was busy measuring a wall to his left.

The initial sight of him paralyzed me, leaving me standing there, inches away from him. It had been ten days since I had left him.

He reached for my body, wrapped his arms around my waist, and gripped me tightly. "What are you doing? What happened?" he asked with a warm smile. "I love you. You know that," he whispered, as he sucked my mouth with the vigor of a man about to eat his prey. It would become obvious to me, eventually, but too late, much too late. He was the fly and I was the meal he regurgitated, seemingly liquefying my flesh, making me so easy to consume, time after time, again and again. Tastier is what I became not only to a mouth, but to eyes eager to see me hurt, to see me suffer, to see traces of pain live inside my eyes.

He took my hand and led me to the second floor. It was the same area we had christened at the beginning of August, a month before. I stayed silent, speechless. My inner thighs were aching for him, pouring wetness onto the insides of my thighs. My body was pulsating. Still unable to talk, I simply stared at him as he impatiently removed my dress, my bra, and my underwear. I helped him out of his jeans.

"Keep the shirt?" I asked, wanting to expedite his presence inside of me. We fell to our knees. The industrial carpet, the only thing furnishing this empty room, barely broke our fall. He slowly controlled my descent as he glided into me, molding himself to my swollen contours.

"It feels tight, yet so malleable," he whispered, as he motioned in and out. He held my face tenderly, repeating words I had heard before. They sounded so truthful.

Pressed for time, thirty minutes later, he dressed quickly, and said, he needed to go back and finish his work. He looked out the window overlooking the yard. "Park your car at the pizzeria," he told me, smiling. "The inspector will arrive in fifteen minutes. I'll meet you at the restaurant once he's left." He then bent to caress my cheeks, first rubbing them with his hands, then with his lips. "See you in a bit," he whispered in my ear.

I detailed his silhouette with renewed scrutiny as he left the room and headed down the stairs. Looking around, my naked back pressed against the carpet, I could feel dampness had humidified my skin. I got up, feeling liquid dripping down the small of my back and walked to the shower. I opened the faucet to wash my face, slightly turning my back to the mirror. There, in the middle of my back, a flesh wound had erupted. From it, blood was trickling.

"The carpet," I mumbled, remembering the abrasive heat I felt as Patrick forcefully planted himself into me. I had ignored the uncomfortable sensation, or maybe I had just dismissed it as another mark, another scar to develop, another form of proof of my dependence on pain to feel alive.

As if in a daze, I showered, then dressed, slowly feeling my weightlessness disappear, momentarily understanding I had willingly reentered a dangerous zone. I made sure to block the uneasy sensations wanting to flood my brain. If I let them in, I would burst into tears.

I walked around the second floor, reacquainting myself with the corners of a room I had explored before with Patrick, spotting a stain we had left the last time we had fucked on the carpet. Eyes fixated on the stain, I picked up my purse and mindlessly walked downstairs and out through the yard to reach my car. Just before turning the ignition key, I heard his footsteps moving the gravel around, as if to warn me.

"Hey," he said, as he stretched his arm through the open car window to place his hand in mine. His soft eyes were pleading for me to believe him, as he said, "I love you. I'll see you for lunch."

Smiling back, I said, "OK."

The pizza place was empty, but for a couple of teenagers sipping their cokes as they toyed with their pizza crusts, reducing the overbaked, dried dough into small crumbs. I ate my pizza in a daze, bothered by the fact that Patrick had not let me see his driver's license.

When he paid the cashier for lunch, I had playfully ripped it from his hands, but he had overpowered me. He had denied me access to a seemingly innocent document. How I hated myself for being there, for having given in, again. I looked at him, noting the lightness of his demeanor.

"I will see you at the end of the day," he said. "Stay here if you want." Then, he grabbed my cheeks with his hand, squeezing them tightly, forcing my lips open and dropped his saliva into my mouth. Watching him leave as I cleaned myself up, I wondered if tranquility would ever settle in my stomach. Unable to ignore the nausea forming inside me, I got up and walked toward the bathroom.

While Patrick was busy finalizing his day, I drove around the area and discovered Claremont, a quaint little town nearby, that seemingly had more happening in it than Charlestown. I spotted a restaurant with neon lights spelling, Tavern on the Square. A restaurant bearing the same name also existed in Montreal.

"Couldn't be," I smiled to myself. "We'll have dinner there," I decided.

Patrick quickly showered, as I had pressed him to hurry. It was 9:00 p.m. and something inside me told me we were running late. I was trying, as always, to infuse normalcy into our dynamic. Our relationship was so much about sex. If I were to go back to him, I needed more. I wanted more. Yes, truth's embrace, its perennity, the promise of its coming. He hopped into the passenger seat of my car, his face now stern. I knew that face. It was a face filled with contempt and envy. It was a face, which a few hours before, had looked different on a loving man. The mercurial nature of his character was surfacing for me to clearly see, but I did not care, I didn't want to care. I wanted normalcy. I wanted to pretend all was sane, that I was sane, that *he* was sane, that this impromptu outing was just a routine moment—a normal one. I had ached for that moment, and had needed it. And this time, I would have it my way, my blindfolds, silky and tight—the blocker of light—strapped around my head, this neo lady justice who would ignore the essence of the man, his toxic petulancy.

"Slow down," he told me dryly. "The cops are everywhere." I barely acknowledged him, as I slid an INXS CD into the player. Something had startled him, I noticed. I watched him squirm on the edge of his seat, eyes glued to my car's screen.

"It couldn't be!" I thought. The song title, appearing on my monitor, evidently stirred something in him. It was called, "Devil's Party." I let him remove the CD, aware of the volatility that was threatening to impact his behavior. I could escape the darkness that surrounded my car as I sped to our destination, but here inside of it, darkness had formed, this one, inescapable. I parked the car across the tavern. As I stepped out onto the sidewalk, he grabbed my hand to lead me across the street. The roughness of his touch always surprised me. If there had been a living soul around, the contrast we were offering would have been noticed. I was dressed up enough for the Ritz, while Patrick was in his washed-out, dirty jeans.

An hour after leaving to dine at the venue I had chosen, we were both lying on the mattress, starving. The tavern's kitchen had closed just before we arrived, and since all the other restaurants in the area were also closed, we had not eaten. The city girl in me would never get used to this aspect of rural life. We silently prepared ourselves a quick sandwich and headed back to our floor mattress to eat.

The room was dimly lit by the yellowish oven light that gave the industrial space a contrasting velvety ambiance.

This is camping, I thought to myself, and I hate camping. Truthfully, the idea of sleeping in that shit hole again had lost its novelty. I wanted a hotel room. Even a sleazy one would have done.

We started talking. It was a conversation serious enough to command his full attention.

"All lies," he insisted. "Nothing you were told is true. I never fucked Lydia after I met you. She is the one who has been after me, all this time. She's been after me ever since you came into my life. You think I could have sex with a woman after I caught her fucking a man whose face was deformed?" he went on to say, as I absorbed the oddity of his statement. "I could never, ever have sex with a woman who can't control her urge to fuck when drunk," he let out. I was about to ask him about the gray car and the woman who had been seen at his place on the fourth of July, when his phone lit up.

"You have six messages from Lydia," I pointed out with elation. At minimum, he would now have to reveal some small bit of information, thus piercing the opacity that had woven itself into our relationship.

Watching him read Lydia's latest texts, I recalled the many times he had commanded me to hand him my phone. I knew he had switched the sim card on my phone, and had monitored my activities both on the road and on my computer.

"Show me?" I asked, pointing at his phone. He looked at me with surprise, evidently not wanting to play my game. I insisted enough for him to finally show me the content of the six messages. They were all pleas for him to come back to her, imploring him to give them another chance to form the family they both eagerly desired.

As I read her desperate attempts to draw him back in her life, I felt sad. Sad for her, and sad for me. Desperation, it seemed, was a state he was able to manufacture in us both, poisoning love with it, almost artfully. She reminisced about their past together, emphasizing the fact she had no friends in her life. No one like him. The pathos was real.

"I want more," I suddenly told him, my appetite whetted. "Give me your phone so I can scroll up to the very first conversation," I insisted. Both our hands were now on his phone, pulling in opposite directions. He then scrolled up frantically. His impatience was so displeasing to me. He did let me read a few extra exchanges, highlighting how he barely responded to all her very lengthy texts.

I did catch a small phrase he had written her. It caught my eye because it was a phrase he often used to describe me. "You are my little typhoon," he would say, blaming our physical distance for the creation of a violent storm-like disequilibrium in his life. It seemed he had more than one storm on his front as he had referred to Lydia as his little hurricane. Unknowingly, it seems I had dated a weatherman. I stilled, feeling alone, there with these thoughts.

Abruptly, he ripped the phone out of my hand. "Enough," he firmly said. "You will have to trust that the rest of the exchange is just about the same."

I looked straight up at him. How could he possibly ask for trust? And yet, evidently, I had made the choice to return, despite everything that had been revealed. Yes, he cheated. I knew he had. His denials did not affect my certainty of that. His lies were imprinted on my brain and guts. He thought I believed him, and I would let him think that for now.

I suspected his relationship with Lydia had wilted into an after-thought. That it had ended. He had promised to cut all contact with her—he had told me so. That's good enough for me, I thought, as I let him pull my underwear off.

It would have to do, after all, I was there again, with him. Wanting him. Wanting more.

The morning quickly rolled in on us. My sleep, again, had been restless. I left in a hurry, with Patrick handing me an apple for the road. I placed my sunglasses on my head to truly take him in, the morning sun contouring his bronze skin I loved so much and needed to nourish me.

At all costs.

And what of Alice?

I turned the question around inside my head, until I felt it drop from my mind. Then, I stared at the fruit I was holding in my hand. It was red. It was shiny. An invitation to bite.

Apples had so often defined my departures from Lowell. Gifting me an apple to eat on my way back to Northampton formalized the end of my stay, his signature gesture, I realized. I had become a new Snow White, the incarnation of a woman whose only asset was the color of her skin. A woman caught in a twisted version of the Brothers Grimm's storyline. Patrick, my failed prince, permeated with the evil he should have been protecting me from, was intent on annihilating me, his perceived rival. The mirror, its role, had remained, predictably so, pivotal. Patrick could spend one hour each day examining himself meticulously in front of his bedroom mirror, I reminded myself. Consulted obsessively by Patrick, its reflection somehow must have confirmed this man's sense of grandiosity, feeding an inner dialogue that validated his actions and rationalizing their consequences. I could now hear the words that must have circled inside his mind, words describing the vital need for him to suck the oxygen from the blood running inside my veins, their prominence irresistible.

I stopped to fill up at a gas station twenty miles from Charlestown. John and I were still using our joint credit card, so I did not want him to know where I had been. Since he was still getting the Visa statements, he knew where I went and how much I spent. I basically had two controlling men on my trail. I could not wait to be divorced and done with John and, somehow, I sensed Patrick would also be exiting … eventually. But, now was not the time for this exit to happen, to be absorbed. No, not for me.

Not another exit.

I wasn't ready yet.

My life then, its past, its future, two nonsensical bookends reeking of emptiness. I wanted unseen, ignored. Because I couldn't look backwards any more than I could look ahead. Only the absolute present, lethally parceled into palatable pieces of existence—the only leftover of life I could handle.

And that leftover was him.

As I drove north, a familiar landscape unfolded before me. It was breathtaking. The sight of the Adirondack Mountains quieted my anxieties. They represented to me, the promise of a freedom I had not felt in so long. I was anticipating the shower of love and care, I so craved. I needed to be held, to be seen, still, as human worthy of what I was at my core, in spite of what I felt I was becoming. I needed to be filled by people who knew me, who had known me. Mostly, I needed to interact with normally-wired humans.

The Canadian customs agent, who greeted me at the booth, was a woman I somehow managed to make genuinely smile. This was a feat in itself. I told her I was returning home for five days, after having been imprisoned in Northampton for five months. My joy was palpable, almost contagious, as I watched her contain her laughter with difficulty. She handed me my papers with a wink, and voilà, I was home.

Gastronomical dishes, fine wines and lovely music, marked my stay. But, one major problem surfaced on the first day of my trip. I found out my immigration papers, while allowing me to stay in the United States for another three months, did not hold if I left the country. Bluntly put, I was at the mercy of the American rednecks managing the US-Canada border. Their decision would be final. There could be no appeal. How had my lawyer neglected to tell me I would jeopardize my status if I left American soil, even with this document in hand?

"There is nothing we can do," my lawyer now told me over the phone. "You will have to take your chances at the border." It seemed I had no choice but to embrace my time in Montreal, while praying to the Gods of immigration to let me back into the States. I was painfully aware of the challenges that would follow if I was banned from returning to Northampton.

Alice, I wondered, and she was heavily on my mind.

While in Montreal, I spoke with Patricia almost daily. She kept obsessively replaying each part of her relationship with Benjamin, a.k.a. Patrick. She focused on all the details, all the vivid moments, weaving them back and forth in her mind, until she had created her own believable reality. Much the very same as I was doing myself. The two of us.

Patricia's neatly woven world had blown up in her face that fatal day when I, and my truth-seeking obsessions, revealed all. The disillusionment we were both facing was stripping the ground beneath each of us. She was the strong one, though. She was the one who had given him an ultimatum when she found out he was leading a double-life with Lydia.

"Her or me," she had told him. Luckily for her, Lydia had been the chosen one. I did not tell her I had seen Patrick. I did not want to cause her more hurt, but mainly I did not want to be seen as a fool, a consenting one.

My last night in Montreal was spent at Simone's. Simone had been part of my life now for seveteen years. She was a friend I truly loved, a friend who displayed a rare form of authenticity, a friend whose fearlessness charmed me. Tall, with short blonde hair, she had eyes so intense, they compelled you to stop and notice the moment.

We spent the last night, before my return to Northampton, with her family. She had organized a sumptuous dinner with a couple I had yet to meet. I was feeling unwell. The real possibility of being refused at the border was dawning on me. The consequences of being refused reentry would be disastrous. How I hated John, at that very moment, wishing he had died. Simone held me as I cried on her shoulder, reassuring me that all would be fine, that I would make it to Alice.

Patrick's behavior that night added a layer of unwelcome trouble. He had called relentlessly to check up on me. He wanted pictures of me, every other minute, seeking proof of my location to soothe his jealousy and quench his need for control.

Still, the evening was filled with sweet moments of laughter and music, providing me with the release I needed. I recorded Simone's husband's rendition of "Long Train Running" and sent it to Patrick. I wanted him to understand what my life here was all about. What I was all about.

My internal dialogue, negative at its core, was killing me. I was creating catastrophic scenarios that were now seeping into my sleep. Unsurprisingly, I woke up nauseated, fearful of the day ahead. I now had to face the inevitable confrontation that was awaiting me at the border. I left quickly, unable to eat anything, my stomach tight, my heart pounding. So much was at stake.

I decided to opt for the New York-Canada border. The Vermont-Canada border had an awkward aura about it, to say the least.

With three cars ahead of me, I texted Patrick with shaky hands, while I waited in line. I kept caressing my documents, ready and available on the passenger seat, focusing on them, wishfully. I was sweating. My heart was pounding. I kept thinking of Alice, alone in Northampton, of the power these right-wingers had over me. Unable to successfully discard all the catastrophic scenarios filling my mind, I simply stared ahead and did what Patrick had, for once, relevantly suggested I do. Pray.

When it was my turn, I rolled down my window, dreading to face the gentleman who was asking me for my passport. There was no fooling his kind. He was trained to pick up nervousness of all types, and I was as easy to read as an open book. And so, after asking me where I lived and spotting the documents spread out on the passenger seat, he directed me to the main office and politely asked me to park my car in the designated area.

I had failed.

Teary eyed, I walked into a building that held about twelve service counters. A busload of people had just arrived, keeping all the customs agents busy. I heard my name being called out. Lucky me. It was a woman agent.

"You are clearly living in the United States," she said, obviously happy to lay down the law. I pointed to the copy of the Homeland Security document stating I was authorized to stay in the United States until November 30th. It turned out they had never seen this type of document. Never. Ever. I explained that because I had permission to temporarily stay in the United States, I did not know I was not supposed to leave the country. I went on to say that I had gone to Montreal to visit my ailing father, and that it had been five months since my last visit there. More importantly, I added, I was in the United States to accompany my daughter, who was currently attending a private school in Deerfield.

"Sit down, ma'am," she suddenly told me, unfazed. "I will call you in fifteen minutes." I felt like a feeble little mosquito about to be squashed.

For seventy-five minutes, I observed a team of agents looking over my documents, from all sides, it appeared. They were reading the file my immigration lawyer had built. I could hear them argue and laugh, oblivious to my presence. My document was to them what a new disease manifesting itself on a patient was to a team of doctors. My document and I were, at best, a bureaucratic curiosity to challenge their rigid minds and, at worst, a case study gone wrong.

The customs agent walked to the counter and waved me back. Expecting to be defeated, and drained of my ability to stay grounded, I dragged myself to the booth. I had no emotional strength left.

"We will let you in this time, ma'am, but there is no guarantee the next time will be the same," she said, delighted to give me a sermon.

Good enough for me, bitch, I thought. I will not be leaving your country again, for a long while.

Walking back to my car, and thanking the gods I had prayed to, relief spread to my chest, as I slowly became aware of my changing luck. I opened my phone to see Patrick had been texting me. He was worried by my sudden silence. And I asked myself, when was the last time anyone had worried about me?

Please let me know what is happening, he had messaged. I called him. He tried to grasp the intricate parts of my story, asking if I needed him to write a letter stating that he had enough funds to financially support me.

"I will write an affidavit," he kept repeating, "I will. And you will stay here, with me, you are never going back."

I said nothing and stepped into my car.

I walked slowly toward the backyard, watching him intensely working in his makeshift outdoor station. Allowing myself time to observe him in his environment, I noted he was wearing a red sweatshirt and a pair of jeans accessorized with his tool belt. My desire for him was impossible to ignore. What a strange turn our relationship was now taking. I wanted to believe his excuses, his explanations, and his newfound adoration for me. My phone had been lighting and buzzing with attention for a week now. It made me feel wanted.

Adored and loved.

I had been chosen, eclipsing all others—me.

I was the one.

I believed in him and I believed in us.

And, yes, I felt, he believed in me too.

Love at all costs.

The day was typical of a late summer day, the warm air cooling itself as the sun started to slowly fade, leaving its rays to slide between the loosely knit poplar branches bordering the Charlestown property. Both of us acknowledging our need to seek warmth, and we quickly moved upstairs to the sexual campground we kept staging.

Leaning against the wall, he nonchalantly pulled me toward him. I felt him, all of him.

I wanted it all, and he knew this was the part I enjoyed most, when he would take my face between his rough hands and let my hair become dampened by both our mouths. The kissing was long, the teasing of his tongue pleasantly artful and sensual.

He was preparing the terrain admirably.

We decided tacitly to forgo the use of the mattresses, acknowledging the adequacy of the carpeted floor to which he now pulled me. He lifted my skirt, removed my panties, and stared greedily. Simply dropping his jeans to his ankles, he then inserted himself, everywhere, the fullness of him unavoidable, satiating my appetite.

As usual, we talked while we played.

"You know, I know," I told him. "You know I am using you, as well," I said breathlessly.

He stopped and looked at me. His eyes amused by my remarks, he simply caressed my cheek and delivered a soft blow. "Really?" he asked, panting. "You really think you want to play this game?"

As if detached from myself, melting into the now, I simply ignored his question.

"Thank you for coming," he said to me, as we dressed. "I needed this, and I needed it from you."

Yes, you needed me. You needed relief, I was now repeating to myself, as he dropped me quickly at my car, in a rush to head back and finish his day's work. How polarized my thoughts appeared to have become.

How could I reconcile the feeling of being wanted with that of being used?

This was no ordinary return home. The fog had now been lifting, albeit slowly, over the last two weeks.

I knew who he was. I knew him more than he knew himself.

Yet, after all that had been uncovered, I loved him.

His touch.

His words.

I loved him still.

All the possibilities. All the possibilities of us. One day.

And yet, the incongruity of it all, the physical and emotional incoherence being held in my body, was tugging at me.

Was I still willing to play with the devil … even the devil I knew?

Right now, the only truth I felt was dripping between my legs.

CHAPTER THREE

I had clarified my purpose in life during my time in Montreal, away from Patrick's mind-fucking games. Through the disclosure of his betrayals, lies, and fraudulent behavior in the two weeks preceding my trip to Canada, I realized how far away I had stepped from myself. The focus had now become clear. I was here in New England for Alice. I had conducted an internal audit of the last eight months and the conclusion was clear. I needed to change paths. If not for myself, for Alice.

I had lost almost twenty pounds, had gone through seven urinary tract infections, battled six episodes of bacterial vaginosis, and my fibromyalgia had reemerged with renewed intensity. But, the collateral physical damages could not compete with my state of mind. Confusion was part of my everyday life. Patrick had gotten into my head, pulling the strings that released the right number of hormonal cocktails to keep me hooked on him.

Now, standing in the middle of my kitchen, disheveled and tired, scanning the messy counters, I knew my life had been out of balance, that it needed to be fed, reshuffled, and whipped back into more than a pseudo-existence kept alive by an addiction. Mindful of the precariousness of my state, of the urgency to interfere with the slow decay threatening my body and my mind, I had started focusing on other interests, including, attending Alice's soccer games, advocating for foster children with special needs, and volunteering for emotionally abused women. My appetite returned, and I was incorporating physical activity into my schedule again. Meeting normal adults had an almost instant grounding effect on me. A curtain had been pulled back, revealing the existence of quietness and peacefulness.

Yet, I ... had ... returned ... to ... HIM.

Alice did not know Patrick had returned to my life. I wanted to protect her from my twisted reality, unsure of my own burgeoning sense of stability. Now that it was September, school had resumed, allowing for our morning rituals to provide us the physical space to bond. The car, again, was my ultimate ally. There, with nowhere to go, no choice but to acknowledge each other's energy, we sang the songs that had become part of our thirty minute drive to Deerfield. Our evolving playlist would become, in time, a musical artefact documenting our New England adventure.

To pursue my relationship with Patrick, I had resorted to lying to Alice about my whereabouts. I created false venues to visit, false events to attend, and non-existent people to dine with. Stealthily sneaking out of the house at night had become part of my masterful routine. The challenge was two-fold. I had to dupe Alice, but I also had to dupe Patrick into thinking Alice liked him. I had drawn a line between the lives of our two families. It was a boundary he wanted to cross, but one I denied him. To secure my continued relationship with Patrick, I now knew the importance of making him feel like Alice accepted both him, and the idea of us, as a family unit. I was relying on the magic of deceptiveness to quell my insecurities, while using Alice to quell his own.

I was learning to survive to my own self.

Saturday night had rolled in, and, as usual, I was waiting for his signature text to give me the signal to leave for Lowell. But, that night I felt unusually comfortable with the thought of staying home. A level of trust had emerged with us, a level that quieted my fears of betrayal, a feeling that diminished my need to go to him and look for indications of deceit.

To keep moving forward with this relationship, I had to trust, I had to let go.

His text, late as usual, came in around 9:30 p.m.

I left, swiftly anticipating my delicious and addictive drive to him.

INHALED

He had arrived home, maybe 10 minutes prior to me. I entered through the opened door and walked into the unlit living room. Visibly exhausted by his day, lying on his couch, work boots still on, he motioned for me to sit beside him.

I approached and kissed him softly on his cheek, smiling at his unshaved, patchy beard.

"Baby, I'm so tired," he mumbled, eyes closed.

I looked at him, suddenly moved by this Latino immigrant who deployed so much effort to make a decent living for himself, Alejandro, and Jocelyne. I sat at the other end of the couch. In stark contrast, I was wearing a gray A-line jumper dress with my favorite pair of turquoise John Fluvog shoes. My elegance, my sense of style, defined me. It was something I felt I could never deprive myself of, for doing so would precipitate the decline in my stock value. He liked simple, he had repeated to me so many times, but I was not simple, nor would I ever be. I knew this puzzled him, my individuality most likely a threat to his absent sense of identity. Moreover, my integrity had its priorities. I could fuck him in my house while my teenage daughter was on the other side of the wall, but hell, I would never compromise my stylistic integrity.

Another familiar ritual was then set in motion. I removed his first boot, the left one, his damp sock welcoming my well-manicured hands. I started to massage his foot the way he loved, clamping with my nails at all the right places, firmly pulling his toes, scratching with strength.

Performing my magic, I was suddenly recalling what Lydia had shared with me. She too, had performed this service … and so much more. I quickly erased these thoughts, reminding myself that I was the one with him now, here in this shitty living room.

These moments were my gateway to him, his life, his past. There, I was capable of lulling him into a hypnotic-like state that could pave the way to some truths.

"Lydia hates you," he suddenly blurted out, surprising me.

"Hates me?" I repeated, remembering how my last conversation with her had been quite amicable, considering the circumstances.

"She is jealous," he stressed. I could understand that, but I also remembered how she had told me she was finished with him. Yet, there had been the texts and now she was upset.

"You are still in touch with her," I remarked, annoyed. "I asked you to stop all contact. I told you that she was using Jocelyne as a pretext to keep you in her life. You haven't blocked her?" I asked, concerned.

"Yes," he replied, staring at me, "I have now."

Switching to his right foot, I decided to steer the conversation in another direction.

Iraq. Let's talk about his time spent in Iraq, I thought, noting he had the makings of a killer.

"I was better than a sniper," he stated with suspicious pride. Turned on, I started laughing, thinking of my cousin Cecil's affirmation of being easily seduced by guys with big guns. How her and I both would become giddy when the subject of guns emerged. From there, we somehow managed to head to the bedroom. So big guns, like chocolate and oysters ...

Tangled in his bed covers, I pretended to sleep, not wanting to reproduce our night's performance. We were savvy at creating our own brand of knotting when we fucked, our own brand of sadistic lovemaking, I reminded myself, my head hurting. Yes, somehow, I had become adept at his cruel ways, allowing the pain to fill the void, I so often felt.

That morning, my body ached. The night before, he had pulled my arms behind my back, with much strength, in fact, too much strength, providing him the taunt stability required for me to absorb his multiples thrusts. We had incorporated other novelties into our lovemaking, too.

Patrick, from the onset of our relationship, had introduced me to the practice of being hit. Midway through a lovemaking session, he would lift up my head and gently start to draw circles on my cheek. It was his way of asking for permission to hit my face. And I would nod him in.

No, I didn't mind. I was starting to love it.

Because it filled, not a void, no—it answered a want.

To feel nothing.

To feel everything.

All but not me.

I had allowed myself the pleasure to feel pain, but the night before, I was the one who demanded to produce the blows. I wanted his face to now become my own canvas to mark. Straddling him on the chair we had brought in from the dining room, and motioning up and down, I slapped him. I was now remembering the look in his eyes as he had absorbed that first hit. Feeling empowered by my new-felt sensation of control, I had then decided to deliver a second slap, while unable to withhold my laughter. That is when he had stopped my arm, mid-air, halting my third delivery. Laughter had not been invited to the party. He had turned me over violently and planted himself inside of me, uncompromisingly. There was a price to pay for allowing such punishment to be carried out. Reviewing the night's exploits, rubbing my temples with my weak fingers, all I knew was that I needed my medication.

I felt his kisses on my forehead, my cheeks. A tender, "I love you," was whispered and then the door closed. I opened my eyes, seeing Jocelyne was there beside me, breathing lightly. I got up, swiftly, looking into my bag for my Zomig migraine spray. I walked to the bathroom, my bladder crying for help, needing release from the pressure it felt against its inflamed lining. From the toilet seat, a vantage point to the open pharmacy in front of me, I slowly scrutinized its contents. I had photographed its moving pieces, in my mind, over time. Victoria's Secret products, numerous women's deodorant that had come and gone and now, relieved, all I could see were the products I had brought in January. But then, something caught my eye.

"Hey," I said on my car's Bluetooth, as I drove back to Northampton. "How was your morning?"

"Good," he replied, distant. "You seemed so comfortable when I left you this morning," he said.

"I didn't hear you leave," I lied. "So, big day ahead?" I quickly pursued.

"Normal," he replied.

There was no time to waste here. He could hang up at any moment. I dove in. "Who wears contact lenses in your home?" I asked squarely, followed by a short silence. "There is a huge bottle of contact lens solution in your pharmacy," I finally specified.

"Oh, that" he said with the speed of lighting. Alejandro's girlfriend. I'm never home. I don't know what the fuck is going on anymore in my own home," he screamed at me. That was true, I knew it for a fact. He knew I was listening, waiting to see where I would be spinning from there.

"Gotta go," I told him.

Whether his explanations were true or false, I understood how the absence of trust would continue to mark this relationship. I needed to be vigilant, to play with care. But how long would any sane person want to play this game?

Once home, I texted Patrick that I made it home OK, reminding him of how he had had his way with me the previous night, and asked again, who wore contact lenses in his family. I was not going to let that one go. I received no replies.

After lunch, I headed to the shower, dressed and brought Alice to Marshall's for some shopping. She thought I had gone out the night before to meet with Patricia and Araceli in Worcester.

"You know, the sisterhood," I had said. I felt relieved she was not asking for any details regarding what we had done. I had lied to her enough, and frankly, I did not feel I had the creative capacity to offer a believable answer. I was brain dead.

After dinner, while Alice was working on her college applications, as I headed to my bedroom, contemplating my next move. Out of curiosity, I was again, creating an agenda.

Patricia, I needed to call Patricia. I knew I had to be mindful of her delicate state as well. She was a lonely woman who really had been left for dead. Wasn't that what Patrick told me? I thought that she had died? Understandably, the part she would never be able to digest, let alone metabolize, was that Patrick, or Benjamin, as she knew him, had eclipsed her from his heart and mind, denying her very existence then and now. So, when I thought of how much value I was adding to her healing process, I was not sure anymore. But, I needed her.

INHALED

Still seated on my bed, I decided to reactivate my Tinder account. Within five minutes, his profile appeared, sending heat to my face. He was roaming the cyber pathways again, looking for more skin. In fact, he was looking for a tall, smart, white girl, with blond hair, blue eyes, who likes to cook, travel, and loves sex ... being skinny is a bonus, he had written.

What the fuck had been my bonus?

I was going fishing for new information. It was only 8:40 p.m., Lydia would still be available.

If you want, call me, I messaged her, don't hesitate. I know this is unusual, but I feel we could help one another. I respect your silence and won't push. The truth is I did think we could help one another. I had seen her helplessness in the texts she had sent to Patrick. I had heard her cry when, only three weeks before, I had revealed my and Patricia's existence.

I placed my phone down and waited.

At 10:00 p.m. Patrick texted, Kisses.

I ignored it.

At 10:20 p.m. I heard the beep.

What happened, she wrote.

I cowardly explained that I had been seeing him again.

I understand, she replied.

I know you do, I wrote back.

By the way, she added, another woman has called me. Did I tell you last time? She is the one who bought him that stupid orange glowing lamp in his bedroom, plus most, if not all, the furniture in his house.

Yeah, I thought, the orange light that sprayed the walls with the ambiance of a bordello. The light all the girls must fuck to.

She added, "He once told me he was going to New York for a weekend, when in truth he had spent the weekend in Worcester with her. Jane is her name," she revealed.

I was trying to take this all in. So, he had bought his house at a discounted price, financed by the owner of the house who he was body and mind-fucking. And then this girl, Jane, he obviously used for her furniture magic. Lydia, I failed to see exactly what her purpose had been. Patrick had once compared her to a working horse. He loved her roughness, the way she could whip up a meal. So much had been about food. At some point in his life, he must have known starvation, I thought.

I am curious, she asked, why text me?

Well, I wrote, I just want to know how you two left off. He says you hate me. I would like to understand.

I was about to learn one huge lesson. Never assume abused victims want help from the other woman, even if the other woman is trustworthy, intelligent, and well-intentioned. Her patience had clearly been tried.

I don't give two fucks about what is going between the two of you, she wrote. You have no life, obviously, and that is why you are still dating him. Can you not see he is a player, and an imbecile? He texted me yesterday and this afternoon and called me twice in the middle of the night this week, she continued.

Why the attitude? I asked, stunned by the viciousness of her words and the harshness of her revelations.

Well, I'm not used to being referred to as plump, she wrote.

I exploded in laughter at the absurdity of the exchange. In light of his quest for white, skinny girls I had ridiculed Patrick's choice when Lydia's physique had been revealed to me. It had been meant to mock his lack of consistency, not her voluptuousness, which I found quite appealing and sexy. In all objectivity, Lydia, while displaying a penchant for the common, was still somewhat attractive, her long and thick strawberry blond frizzy hair the only strange addition to an otherwise quasi-symmetrical face.

The only problem was that she was now standing in my way. Whatever smile had unwittingly drawn itself on my face was now disappearing. I had been sucked into a parallel universe that had no relevance to mine. I had entered a world laced with vulgarity, and it was nauseating to admit.

Yeah, she went on, you, your arrogant demeanor, your skinny body, your hair extensions, your beautiful face. Don't fool yourself, do not act as if you are not being used, because you are getting used, you are being exploited. For the sex, the pussy you offer him at will, for the care you provide to his daughter, for the meals you prepare and whatever else your sorry Canadian ass can bring him, she wrote. Remember, she added, I was the first one to have him and you followed, like the other clueless bitches. And believe me, there are many more of you out there.

Hmm ... his first? I'm not so sure about that, I thought, immediately understanding I had to end this now.

Apologies, I texted, hammered by the trashiness of the exchange. I felt my core had been whipped, scraped by the turpitude with which my life had been injected. Lydia was shedding light into the abyss to which my integrity was shackled. The steadiness I required to pull myself from the obscurity was not there. I was frail, unreliable.

I had to make one last call.

This was now my second real attempt at leaving him. The first time, about three weeks earlier, had left me with a multitude of truths and lies to untangle. It had left me in a state of shock, allowing layers of trauma to pile up on me. Yes, I had expected to find something, but nothing so twisted. The pain then spread evenly throughout my body. The numbness was short-lived, as if allowing me to process the truth in its full splendor. But, I had failed to stay the course. I had returned to my torturer, fully responding to the pull of his well-crafted words, celebrating his adoration of my mind, my body, my soul.

It was all my fault. I had reinitiated contact when I texted him to diligently dispose of any digital evidence of our lovemaking sessions.

Now, I felt different. Yes, I was hurting. The humiliation was setting in. But now, I was in control. I was starting to reconnect with myself. It was within my reach to move on, as I so wished. I smiled at the unveiling of his latest fumbles. I had allowed my intuition and my humor to have their fully-earned space in my mind. I could now see the shadow my strength was casting.

CHAPTER FOUR

The first few days following my self-release, I was elated. There was an incredible high stemming from having been the one to dictate the end of this toxic relationship. I had punished him. I had taken myself off the menu of his girls to fuck.

I had left his harem of fools.

But … the haunting cravings for his touch. I needed. I had to have. Images of our time together would burst forth in my mind without warning. At the most awkward moments, my face would flush, my heart would race and my insides would become moist with an unsettling desire to be taken.

To fuck, yes. But there was more I wanted, more that would never last, more that had never lasted.

But I still craved it.

Over a period of three weeks that felt like an eternity, Alice would be the cold shower necessary to stun me back to life.

My appetite was not fully back, but my sleep patterns were returning to some degree of normality. Healing was on its way, I kept repeating to myself. I knew what I needed to do. I needed to restart the default mode that Patrick's presence in my life had pulverized. I needed to activate my self-care systems. I was slowly taking everything in, becoming myself again.

As I walked downtown in Northampton, I suddenly remembered, my Swarovski necklace, Alice's mattress. Shit, I told myself. Shit, shit, shit. I wanted to recuperate those two items from Patrick's home. This was not a ploy to see him. I just did not want to be part of the funding machine that was financing his lifestyle. I texted him that I wanted him to either leave them on my driveway or leave them in Charlestown for me to pick up.

And so, the following Saturday morning, at 6:40 a.m. I was awakened by a text. Your possessions have been placed in your driveway. Merry Christmas.

I got up, opened the front door, stretched my neck and saw a garbage bag, onto which a smaller bag had been placed. I picked up the bags. Once inside the house, I checked their contents. In the large, heavy-duty garbage bag, was the mattress, folded in two. In the small bag was an envelope containing my blue Swarovski necklace. A baking pan was also returned. The only problem, the baking pan was not mine.

My second week without Patrick remained bleak, despite the inroads I knew I was making in my own healing process. I filled my time with outings and resumed my mindfulness classes. The heaviness I was carrying was slightly offloaded by the time John arrived at the end of the month. Part of me was happy to have access to a familiar face. There was normalcy in his flawed persona, something I welcomed, like a wicked balm. But his desire-filled stares were uncomfortable to witness, to absorb. I would never be able to reciprocate the desire they expressed. The flame of that desire had burned out years ago. I decided to open a bottle of white wine, something I rarely did. The talk was light and mostly concentrated on his time spent in Argentina with our daughter, Catherine. Catherine had still been refusing to speak with me. It had been four months, now, an eternity. She could not accept that Patrick, another man, had made his way into my life so quickly after the break up with John. Catherine's reaction was a tragedy for me. The pain her silence and absence were inflicting on me was boundless, deadening another portion of my heart. The heart fracture her reaction had caused would have to be addressed in time, with time.

John, Alice, and I sat down and shared dinner together. The essence of our family was somehow still intact. Alice's willingness to share her week, as well as her laughter, was refreshing to hear. Following our quickly eaten meal, we all cleaned up, and from there John and I headed to the living room. Oddly enough, he offered to massage my feet. I stared at him, recollecting how I had often been a slave to Patrick's feet. It was now time to collect, I thought, to let things come full circle.

John picked up my feet, happy to touch me, any part of me it seemed, and made his way up my calf with his hands. I felt all of it was wrong. I knew he wanted more. I knew I didn't. But a switch had been flicked, some collateral damage that would never be healed. And, there he was in front of me, displaying a form of kindness that I needed.

And I needed to experiment.

Another experiment.

Playing with a husband I didn't want.

I took advantage of the lightness of the moment. As I had often done in the past, I shared with him the details of my absurd relationship with Patrick. He was quick to comment on my lack of judgment. Just as quick, I reminded him of his relationship with the Asian bitch with borderline personality disorder who he had shacked up with in Taipei. I had evened the score, albeit unintentionally.

My head was spinning. Thoughts of Patrick returning to my mind, were instantly knotting my stomach. I needed to sleep it off. John followed me to my bedroom, unexpectedly lying beside me. Earlier, I had proposed we watch a movie, but the wine had sedated me. How unfair of me. It had to be Patrick's influence, I was thinking. How else could I justify being so self-centered and oblivious to John's painful desire?

John's ultimate failed attempt at reconquering his space in my bed left a bittersweet expression on his face.

"Have I not told you, John, that if and when I were to leave Patrick, I would not return to you?" I whispered, my head spinning, clutching my pillow.

As I closed my eyes, relieved, I heard his footsteps disappear behind the door he had just closed.

I woke up somewhat late. Thankfully, despite the wine drinking, my sleep felt restorative. Together, John and I headed for coffee, away from Alice's ears. Why we always chose the same local coffee spot in Hadley to stage our arguments was baffling to me. We talked about Catherine, again. Unable to hold my pain and suffering at the thought of being so disconnected from my daughter, I abruptly left the Esselon café and headed to my car. There I sat on the passenger seat and I cried. John tried to pull me to him, but I did not want to be held by him, and so I pushed him away.

There, in this New England parking lot, I felt as though I had saved my family from a brutal car crash, absorbing the shock of the impact, dying to let them all live. I was in Northampton for the sole purpose of Alice's schooling. John's indiscretion had provoked a tsunami of events in a place I could not escape. I had walked blindly into a wild man's arms. I was a prisoner of the United States of America, unable to seek the help and support required to pull myself up. Amidst all this, my crazy mother and deranged sister had teamed up to let me know, flatly, how they thought I had fully deserved the wrath of John's six-month affair. The dam I had become was, at its core, losing its seal.

I saw him leave the next day.

His jeans now too big, floating, hiding the contours of his waist and his legs.

His shoulder slouched.

His gaze pulled by the ground.

He had left.

Following John's departure to the JFK airport, Alice and I started to make plans for the evening. We were both relieved he had left. The burden of his awkward presence in our small house was finally gone. As much as his stay had been somewhat helpful in distracting us from our respective anxieties, we needed to reclaim our space to make sense of our newfound appreciation for the progress we both had made. I had not felt better in months, and neither had she. We were both looking forward to the first Clinton and Trump presidential debate. We prepared our popcorn and giddily headed to the couch.

Once the debate ended, Alice went up to her room, leaving me on the couch to play with my phone. Quickly, not wanting Alice to catch me in the act of swiping left and right, I saw his profile appear. Nine miles away it said. I swiped left. It was now time to go to bed.

Just as I placed my head on the pillow, I heard the familiar sound indicating a text had arrived. It took me a good twenty seconds to figure out who was texting me from KIK, an app I never used and had completely forgotten about. The text was from a user called, Patrick4always.

The second I responded, I knew I had returned to the hell I had skillfully untangled myself from. His words were artfully pulling me, patiently showering me, his victim, with adoration. Proclaiming his innocence, and blaming scorned women for trying to keep us from moving forward, he stated how he loved and missed me, how he could not go on without me.

He pleaded for me to give him another chance. Uncertain of what had just happened, and feeling the force of my addiction setting in, I closed my eyes and fell into a restless sleep.

I woke up frightened. My dreams, usually riddled with complex layers of indecipherable meaning, were now frightening me with their clarity. Somehow, my subconscious wanted to warn me. The dream had been so simple, so boringly simple and common. The maze in my dream was delineated by gray brick walls that intertwined and folded into a middle. I carried a feeling of powerlessness and despair. The doors would open and there, each time, Patrick was waiting, stoically ... with a knife.

I quickly prepared a second cup of coffee, as Alice started walking out the door, toward the car.

How would I pretend, again?

I am driving with you on my mind, was the first text I read after dropping Alice at school. I have unblocked you. Please call me, I read next, noticing he was using another phone number in addition to the usual one.

When I called, I could not get one word in. He professed his love for me with words meant to melt me, words meant to ease the insertion of his tentacles into my heart. My brain had stopped functioning. I could feel it getting stuck. If only it was in neutral. I had become hypnotized, unable to respond to the deluge of his ardent love manifestations.

"When can I see you?" he pressed, breathlessly.

Fixating on the road, my only obstacle, I remember thinking, How can I sneak him into my room without Alice calling the police?

I had to call Patricia to help me manage the rush of adrenaline that was taking hold of every cell of my being. I needed her to help me stay on course and manage the hurdles I had just created for myself and willingly placed on my path.

"Hi Patricia," I said. Immediately sensing my despair, she quickly warned me, I needed to stay away from him.

"He wants your money, Isabelle. He will do anything to marry you," she insisted.

I could not help but laugh at the fact that I had, in the past, actually entertained the thought of marrying him. "It will never happen," I told her, half-convincingly. I tried to calm her down, reassuring her that I would be fine. This was why I called her, to let myself know that I would be fine, that I was going to emerge as the winner of this sick game.

Araceli was next. Having not been evicted, she was still living on the third floor of Patrick's house. She was my sim card, my in-house spy, except she was unaware of her role. I was ashamed of myself for manipulating her into feeding me the information I required to keep my senses in control. She shared with me that on the previous Thursday, Patrick had brought her to court, yet again, stating that she had not paid her August rent. Everyone in the courtroom had been surprised when Araceli produced a copy of the money order for that month. Patrick apologized, explaining he must have misplaced the original, not caring how this made him look like a fool.

"Oh! And his girlfriend," she added, "you know the one driving the gray car? Well she was there, Thursday night. I saw her leave Friday morning."

The gray car. I had yet to demystify its existence, its significance in my life, in his. "Well then, thank you Araceli. Talk to you soon," was all I mustered.

Alice rushed to her study room. No words had been exchanged in the car, but I knew she suspected. I had unwittingly trained her to sniff out her mother's loss of self-control and self-respect.

She would need to accept it, I rationalized with expert mental malleability.

I would deal with her in the morning.

Seated on the front yard stairs, I felt the coolness of the outside air. It was the type of coolness I had missed while living in Taipei. I had always equated fall weather with a feeling of rebirth, its cocooning pull, the precursor of renewal. Sipping my Chardonnay, looking into obscurity, I waited for his car headlights to announce his arrival, wondering what type of cocooning my evening had in store for me.

And then I heard it. It was the sound of a car parking at the edge of my property. I looked frantically for the dog's muzzle. Jackson could not screw this one up, I thought, somewhat panicky. I stood up and left for the kitchen.

Patrick stepped into the house as I was pouring him a glass of white wine. I casually handed it to him, without saying a word. I led Patrick back outside, as I knew it was the only way the dog would calm down. Standing together at the front entrance, looking at the dog, we waited for the right moment to answer the longing that had marked our time apart. We watched, with contained impatience as Jackson ran around the front yard.

Patrick slid his familiar rough hand into mine.

The gesture, almost poetic in nature, had felt so true, so real, making me sink into that known space where all time stopped.

Heading back inside, few words had been exchanged, and we had managed to avoid eye contact until their inevitable collision created that instant pull. He grabbed my waist and placed me against the bottom cupboard, just in front of the kitchen sink.

"How can you not know I love you?" he asked me with incomprehension.

Remaining speechless, I let him firmly take my chin in his left hand, press his mouth against mine, suction my lips, bite my teeth. The silkiness and plumpness of his lips were creating sensations I loved so much. He knew what I liked, and he was applying his knowledge of me, to me.

I indulged myself, letting go.

He walked to the dining room table and took my phone. "Have you been using Tinder?" he asked, abruptly.

"Yes, I have Patrick. I have had one date," I specified, almost proudly, as I opened the page to my twenty-one matches. I needed to hide the despair that had been haunting me, to pretend the strength and aloofness he saw in me was real. His posture tightened, his expression hardened. In silence, he was seemingly assessing the quality of the men I had chosen and of the ones who had chosen me. He randomly picked a conversation, read it, then placed the phone down in my hand.

"Time to go up," he said.

Yes, it was, I thought.

We tiptoed up the stairs, as Alice's study room was adjacent to my bedroom. I switched on both noise makers, and then closed and locked the door behind us. I moved to the bed, lay down and watched him empty his pockets and remove his jeans and T-shirt.

There, I felt the guilt already setting in. What I was doing was wrong.

Not just because it would make the next separation even more challenging, but because Alice would be a witness to her mother's descent into a black hole … once again.

The Montreal poet, Leonard Cohen, said that it is the crack in us, in everything, that lets the light in. Eyes fixating on Patrick's balding head, I felt the certainty that somehow, it is how darkness escapes as well.

The night continued on, with me feeling alone, so very alone, sleepless and full of doubts.

So many questions.

Patrick offered an addictive, venomous solution that was filling the hole at my core.

Is it the acidity of the venom that has opened this hole? Or was the hole already there? I wondered.

And yet, for all of this, Alice was paying the price. Closing my eyes, the only certainty I felt, remained in my stomach. I should not have answered. I had let him in again, the destructive torments he would again breathe into my life, a life I was trying desperately to repossess.

I finally found sleep, hugging myself at the waist, as if trying not to let go.

Of me.

I watched him get up, the darkness unable to hide the contours of his body. He began tending to his chin hair. How his body monopolizes much of his attention, I was now acknowledging. I remembered how, in Lowell, he meticulously tweezed his chest and eyebrows and shaved his groin. And when he showered, it went beyond the lathering of his body. It was as if each time he intensively scrubbed, a layer of skin disappeared, much like a shedding snake, I now concluded with unease.

"Stay in bed," he whispered in my ear, as he prepared to leave. "You need your rest."

"Yes," I replied, allowing myself to slide back into sleep, Alice still on my mind.

I felt the solitude glide into an acute loneliness. This void I was trying to fill was simply enlarged by the presence of a man who wanted to fuse with me, to swallow me until I could no longer breathe on my own. He did not even care to hide his true intentions.

"I want to put you in my stomach," he repeatedly had said. He wanted to be my life support... and then kill me.

Of that, I was more and more certain.

My back was firmly embedded in the mattress. In my dream, I turn my head slowly to the right and open my eyes and I see it approaching, and yet, I cannot move. It seemed to be the size of a basketball, with wool-like texture, but unidentifiable. It appears to be steadily rolling toward me, but its trajectory still feels tentative. As it approaches my face, my eyes come into focus and the image that reveals itself to me, leaving no room for confusion. This woolly ball is composed of millions of daddy-long-leg spiders, collectively swarming toward me. Incapable of moving, paralyzed, I see the creatures approach my face, understanding I had no exit.

Drenched, I sat up in bed, sobbing, my head in one hand, my other hand caressing my cheek.

CHAPTER FIVE

It was the second of November. My cousin, Cecil, was set to arrive the next day from Spain. I had asked Patrick if I could sleepover at his place in Lowell, since it was only thirty minutes from Boston's Logan airport. That way, I would arrive rested to pick up my cousin.

"Of course," he had said. "I will be sleeping with my workers in North Walpole, but I will make sure Alejandro leaves the keys inside the empty toilet tank outside by the garage."

My plan was set. I headed to the CVS Pharmacy and began choosing various toiletries I had no use for. I would be planting them under the bathroom sink and also in the bathroom closet where feminine products would appear one week and disappear the next. How often, from the toilet's vantage point in that bathroom, had I analyzed the contents of the cupboard. I would note the new shampoos, conditioners, and deodorants magically dance their deceptive dance.

In addition to planting items in the bathroom, I would also conduct a test in his bedroom closet. I would leave a little striped dress I bought at Marshall's to hang among his shirts, his pants, and that off-white feminine bathrobe. Inside the pockets of that robe, I would place a piece of paper with my name and number on it. Yes, I knew then, I was entering another dimension.

And that night, the deviant in me slept peacefully, there between the sheets of another deviant. I looked around his room, catching the reflections on the wall of the candle burning in the corner, by his commode. His mother, I thought, here with me, now. Her with him, here, always.

A fully dressed body, still cold from the night air, landed firmly on my back, its arms forming a circle around my waist. Startled out of my sleep, I managed to disengage from the forceful embrace and turned around to face him. It was 5:30 a.m.

"Hi, Babe," he whispered as he undressed, unable to say more, in his trance-like state.

I looked at him, unsure of how I should react. Where did he get his energy from? When did he sleep?

Then I pulled him to me, there in between sheets made for the deviants that we are.

As I got ready to leave for the airport three hours later, he grabbed my hand and twirled me in the dining room, dipped me, making my head tilt back. "Look at you," he whispered. "You are white, so beautifully white."

It must be true, I thought, because at that very moment, exhausted, I felt like a ghost.

He dropped me to the ground and playfully kissed me as I lay thinking of what I had devised. I stood up, placed a kiss on his cheek and finished getting dressed.

I wanted to flee.

Cecil was on my mind. The levity I hoped she would bring, pushing me away from his place.

On my way to Boston's Logan airport, magically, everything about him left my mind, my morphing into another version of him, also, leaving my mind.

So far, I had concealed Patrick from my friends, the friends who had been made aware, at one point, of the hurtful betrayals and lies Patrick had subjected me to. No one could understand all the dynamics at play here, the shame, the sexual pull, the wishful plans. Unfortunately for me, I also felt the need to hide Patrick from Cecil. It was difficult to tell Patrick he would not be able to see me, while my cousin was staying with me in Northampton. He was furious with me, but even more so with Cecil. I lied, telling Patrick she was not feeling well and that she came to my home for some peace, and that his presence would be disruptive for her. I just did not want Patrick to be seen, heard, or felt. I also wanted to protect him from Cecil's venomous tongue.

Her opinion of Patrick was tainted by her own experiences. She had been married to a Latino for twenty-five years. She despised everything about Patrick, angered by the hurt he had put me through. Had I exposed him to her infamous sarcasm and sharp inquisitions, Patrick surely would have left me. I could not take that chance.

I needed my relationship with him to last a few more months.

I needed it to stretch out my own agony.

I still needed to get my fix.

I secretly escaped from my house, twice, and met him at a hotel near his work places in North Walpole and Charlestown. Both times, as foreseen, Cecil reacted to my absence with much virulence, leaving me no choice but to legitimize my decision to bluntly lie to her. I felt guilty about my lies and denials, yes, but I was now used to living with them, albeit, shamefully. In all honesty, I knew those two occasions could offer me time to gather and collect more information on Patrick. I felt there was something more than a man wanting to collect girls for the sole purpose of caressing and penetrating their bodies.

While at my house or his, Patrick would typically undress in the bathroom, leaving his jeans and their contents on the floor. During my second encounter with Patrick, while Cecil was visiting, I seized the moment. As he was showering, I caught a glimpse of his wallet. It was sitting on the night table of our motel room. I froze. I did not have much time. It took me two minutes to uncover what I wanted to know before he realized his mistake. He stormed out of the bathroom, naked, wet and dripping, eyeing me with suspicion. He did not know, I now knew. Inside my body, I was dancing, feeling victorious.

He had told me at the onset of our relationship that he was thirty-nine years old. He had lied. He was not eleven years younger than me, as he had affirmed. The age difference was only five years. He was forty-five years old.

His driver's license also revealed another new detail. I had baked him a birthday cake at the beginning of August. The date on his driver's license read August 30th.

How many cakes did he eat that month? I wondered.

While I was lying on the bed, contemplating the full meaning of my find, Patrick came back out from the shower naked, but this time, fully dry. "What were you doing before?" he asked with unconvincing nonchalance.

"I don't understand what you mean." Kissing, him, occupying his mouth, is my only way out, I thought. Aware of his suspicions, I let him roll us onto the bed, mindfully distracting him from his concerns. Plunging into the moment myself, I felt all life's worries slip away, leaving nothing but the very primal energy fueling our sexual desire.

Alice was busy preparing her college applications, while at the same time coordinating the numerous auditions she would be attending in January, February, and March. Our mother-daughter bond had regained strength as she had witnessed my energy level increase.

Convincingly, I infused into my life the belief that all would be fine. If I believed, so would she.

On Tuesday, Patrick had visited me for an impromptu, quiet dinner. The next day, he had his epiphany, a revelation he felt the immediate need to share with me, to impose on me. He called me, wired by the content of his thoughts, as I was driving back from my lawyer's office in Boston.

"You are the woman for me," he was repeatedly saying. "I love you. I love the way you talk. I love the way you walk. I just think you are for me." His words had hit their mark. Maybe, as fucked up as it appeared, maybe he was the one for me, too.

Saturday arrived, and I felt happy, still seduced by his sudden awareness of our potential as a couple. During that same call, he had mentioned he would enjoy going to the movies over the weekend. This, in itself, was an oddity as he would proudly and often say he did not care about anything social. I had anticipated the outing and had planned accordingly, making space for us that evening. But, the weekend had arrived and he was now unreachable.

INHALED

Unsure how my day was going to unfold, I finished the dishes, looked at my phone, and saw I had finally received a text from Patrick, complete with a picture of himself looking distraught. He had failed his latest site inspection. Therefore, he had to work all day and evening. It worked out fine with me, I realized, as my repeated absences meant my house had been neglected. More time with Alice could not hurt either. But deep down I did not like the change of pace to my weekend, a pace he himself had set.

I will see you tomorrow, I texted him, insecure.

I met him the following day at 3:00 p.m. His house was tidy, I rapidly assessed. I entered his bedroom and noticed his orange lamp had disappeared. When I inquired about its whereabouts, Patrick took my hand and started gently kissing the side of my neck.

"As I was cleaning, I accidentally pushed it off the dresser," he said. His eyes were unflinching. His kiss was uncompromising.

"OK," I said, eyes still open, looking at the empty space on the dresser.

"Ven aca," he then insisted as he pulled me to him. "We have two hours before Alejandro comes back."

He gently brought my white Ralph Lauren dress over my head and then removed my tights. His mouth first attended to my stomach, his tongue lingering above the pelvic area. Everything about him was unrecognizable, I remarked. The languor, the lasciviousness, the desire to really feel the moment, was now inhabiting his every push into me. He had decided to savor me, and the pressure of time felt relative to us both. I closed my eyes and absorbed this newfound lover.

For the next two hours, we moved slowly in and out of each other, creating the space necessary to refuel. We had become two dancers, moving on the dance floor that was his bed, the newfound rhythms captivating me. When I closed my eyes, images of my childhood emerged, bringing me back to that very first orgasm. It was as if I had been brought to the essence of what lovemaking ought to be.

"This is good, Baby," he murmured inside my ear. "You have taught me to make love, Isabelle. Like an adult."

And I wondered, staring above his head, so shiny, a body pressing against mine, watching the light kiss the ceiling's fissures, about the meaning of it, the strangeness of the comment.

CHAPTER SIX

Driving purposefully toward Lowell the following weekend, I wondered what the closets would have in store for me. I needed to see if the objects I had strategically placed in his house a few weeks earlier had been moved. The week before, I had forgotten to check, replaced, or if they simply had stayed there, motionless, as I so wished they would. The uneasiness was slowly mounting inside me. I was disturbed by the thought of having opened a secret channel of communication with the other woman whose presence in the house I suspected.

On Sunday morning, I waited for Patrick to leave for work. Once I heard the sound of his truck back from the driveway, I got up, headed to the bathroom, and opened all the closet doors. Nothing had moved. Only traces of my presence remained.

Okay, I thought, it was time for breakfast.

"Would you like to go to yoga?" Alejandro offered, seated at the table, eager to break my routine. His face, so stern, so serious, so wanting to please me. I knew my presence in his father's life puzzled him. My interests, my age, and my background all clashed with Patrick's rigid profile. Aware of my simmering discontent, and understanding the continuous compromises I had to make to stay with their father, Alejandro feared my imminent departure. He had suggested yoga with much empathy and compassion, hoping it would help structure a routine for me. Sadly, I knew he could relate to me in that regard.

"Sure," I said mindlessly. "I don't have my workout clothes with me, though." Then, I suddenly caught myself thinking, Ah. The striped dress could do, the garment, more of a body suit than a dress won't constrict my movements, and, with some tights, it'll do, I decided.

I headed to his closet to look for it. One-by-one, first with containment, then with nervous despair, I slid each of the garments hanging from the rod in his closet, looking for my dress. It was not there. I frantically looked everywhere else I could think of. It was gone. I felt the blood leave my face. I felt my heart racing. I picked up the phone and called Patrick.

"My dress, where is my dress?" I demanded.

"What dress?" he quickly asked.

"The dress I left at your house three weeks ago. Where is it?" I pressed.

"It has to be somewhere," he quickly stated.

"Why the fuck would it travel to some other spot in the house?" I asked.

"It will turn up, eventually," he responded. "Look again." And just like that, as I looked for the dress gone missing in action, Jocelyne, called for my help. But it was not Isabelle she was repeatedly asking for. It was Clarissa.

"What's your name again?" she nonchalantly asked me, unaware.

"Clarissa?" I asked, as I lifted her up and looked into her brown eyes. They were two slits.

"Clarissa, I need you to give me a bath," she repeated.

Looking at the old, brown, eternally unwashed bathtub, I cursed at myself. The gaping hole in lieu of a drain, the old ceramic tiles hanging off the walls, the absence of a ceiling where all plumbing and wiring hung above your head, all of it, I had ignored. If I had been smart, I would have taken the hint and left the first night, never to return. Self-pity will do that to you. It will manipulate you into doing things you never thought possible. And more. What a productive day it had been, so far. First the dress, then the name, and now a phone. Yes, I had just found a phone, hidden amidst a pile of bunched up hand towels I found tossed, nonchalantly, on the top shelf of his hideous bathroom closet. The closet from hell. I stumbled upon the device when I was looking for a towel for Jocelyne. Finished with her bath, she had been standing there, hoping the shivers of her little naked body would communicate the immediacy of the problem to be solved. She looked at me, both feet planted on that blue cotton rag, acting as a carpet. Oblivious to Jocelyne's trembling, I subtly reacted to my impromptu discovery. Wait here little girl, I thought, I'm not leaving just yet.

What a coincidence. Or is it? I wondered. I maneuvered the device down from its position on the shelf, hiding it neatly under the towels. On quick glance it looked like a Galaxy 4 phone, covered in a blue plastic case. I had to be careful. Jocelyne was an observant little girl and a mouthy one as well.

Patrick had both of his phones with him. I knew that. I had reached him at both numbers that day.

What was this phone all about? Why here? Why was it not with him? I wondered. I turned my head toward the naked child beside me and placed the phone back on top of the closet shelf, between two brown towels.

Dirty, nervous, and evidently volatile as I had just heard him snap at both his children, Patrick rolled in at 10:30 p.m. Seated on his side of the bed, fully dressed, I let him kiss my cheek.

"Is everything all right?" he asked. "You almost made me have a heart attack today," he added, with pleading eyes. I looked at him as he removed his jacket. I was scanning his face for a glimpse of sincerity, hoping to catch him default from his core-filled lies. I had devised the moment that would follow.

"Patrick," I said with intent, "the only way to diffuse my suspicions is to show me the contents of your phones." Show me the content of your phones. How many times have I wanted to ask him that question? I wondered.

He walked to the dining room and sat down at the end of the table. I was in tow. He looked at me under the glaring light of the bulb hanging over us. Motioning that he would comply with my demand, he took his phone and zigzagged his password on the screen. But then, he placed it on the table, face down. "No, Isabelle. No one will ever order me like this. Not you. Not any woman," he said, his eyes now wide open. "I will share the content of my phone when I feel like it."

Fabulous, I thought.

The only thing needed to end this relationship was a farewell fuck.

Home from Patrick's, I parked in the driveway and got out of my car. I grabbed the bags containing my belongings and went inside. Déjà vu. Quietly, I walked into my room, throwing my coat on the seat at my bedside. Sliding under the duvet, I decided to keep my clothes on. I knew it would ease my morning with Alice. As I felt myself slowly slip into what would be another agitated sleep, my hands mindlessly made their way to my neck, looking to play with my necklace, my 5,000 dollar Bulgari necklace. I opened my eyes. I had left my necklace in Lowell.

I remembered then, that Patrick had removed it and placed it on the carpet, right beside his rosary.

The meeting was set to take place ten days later at his house, on a Tuesday afternoon, at 4:00 p.m.

I retrieved my necklace, and re-signed my kiss of death.

CHAPTER SEVEN

My second winter back in North America was now unfolding. There was snow, a fair amount of it, and the cold was not too biting. It was an indicator that sleep might come easy tonight, as the colder temperatures usually meant less fibromyalgia pain. My Christmas tree was up and fully lit and I was playing holiday music in my home now every day. I was aware I had artfully crafted an atmosphere meant to numb my feelings. I was doing what I could to survive.

I had planned to spend another weekend at Patrick's, knowing Alice would be at a friend's house in Petersham.

Another guiltless treat, I thought.

Patrick and Alejandro left early in the morning, leaving me to leisurely sleep in until 10:30 a.m. I got up, and slowly began lurking around the house, examining its known contents, searching, always on the lookout for something. On the kitchen counter, a small note was waiting for me atop a cup of star anise and cinnamon tea.

I love you Isabelle Rodriguez, it read. I smiled, as I picked up my tea and let the spices release their flavors onto my tongue. Again, surprised by my capacity to adapt to his rudimentary surroundings, I walked back to the bedroom.

His dresser had a total of nine drawers, with the three drawers across the top being smaller than the rest. One of the larger drawers was dedicated to my belongings. I sifted through the other drawers, something I had done in the past, of course, but it was something I felt compelled to repeat.

In the middle top drawer, I found a familiar velvet pouch. Patrick had showed it to me a few months before. He had found the pouch, oddly hidden, in the pocket behind the driver's seat of his car. Inside the pouch was a heavy, gold ring set with a small diamond.

"An engagement ring I should have given Jane, but never did," he said amusingly.

"Yes, Jane," I thought. He had acknowledged her existence, but denied Lydia's allegations that Jane had given him any furniture. But, she was irrelevant to me, for now. I emptied the pouch onto the dresser's top, knowing by its weight that its content had changed.

I looked at the numerous pieces of jewelry before me, delicate earrings set with amethysts, small hoop earrings, a tiny children's bracelet, and a few other items that had newly been added to the loot bag. What caught my attention the most was the watch. It was a woman's watch with a flexible silver bracelet, and it looked old. It was old. Turning it around slowly, examining it with an anthropologist's minutia, I saw there was a name engraved on the back. There was only one thing I had to do. Call Patricia, I thought.

From my seat on the bay window, I saw her approach, walking vigorously, and understood the youthful vibrancy Patrick must have felt upon meeting her.

"Patricia, hi," I said with a smile, kissing both her cheeks. I had not seen her since that fateful day in August, but somehow, though the circumstances differed, our adrenaline levels had remained synchronized.

She sat down quickly, her clear blue eyes alert, looking at me with unmasked inquisitiveness. "What happened, Isabelle?" she said, toying with the cup of coffee I had just placed in front her. I observed her with attentiveness. She had a thin frame, more apparent this time, reminding me of Patrick's fixation on this type of physique. I suspected he must have decided upon first meeting her that she would become his first fantasy fuck of a skinny white girl. Ignoring that she was at least thirty years older than him, he was probably secured by the thought that, having been widowed for ten years, she was not at risk of transmitting any sexual disease. He must have decided, on the spot, to seduce her when they first met at the Santander bank where she had worked as a branch manager in Lowell. She had been the perfect, innocuous prey.

"Patricia, I think you need to see this," I finally shared, emptying the black velvet pouch onto the pinkish melamine table. I spread the jewelry out evenly for her to see. Her eyes lit up, their blue color transforming into a sea of turquoise. She took each item in her hands, as I had done in Patrick's room, and examined them with unabated interest. I observed her silently, as her head bent over her newly returned possessions, noticing her teased hair, standing straight up, fixed with spray, exposing the whiteness of her scalp. I stared for a long while imagining the odd sexual couple they had formed, still unable to digest images of their lovemaking she had described to me back in August.

"I don't know," she said, trying to remember if he would have entered her room and stolen them during one of his numerous nocturnal visits to her apartment, two years before.

She was distraught. I was now regretting my gesture, however kind my motivations had been at the onset of my discovery. Was it necessary? I wondered. Moreover, had I been truly motivated by kindness, or had I simply been on a mission to accumulate more information for my own personal, clearly unhealthy, curiosity?

After a tight embrace, we said our goodbyes, promising to keep in touch. I watched her dangle the pouch as she walked to her car, wondering if Patrick would notice it missing.

It seemed I would still need to perform.

Sunday morning proved to be one of the few lazy ones Patrick and I had enjoyed together in a long time. He had stayed in bed with me, electing to spend the day at home with his children, hoping, with Alejandro's help, to install new windows in his house. Closeness, proximity, and intimacy had converged, stopping time, over-stretching it, momentarily erasing my doubts, eliminating my habitual confusion. But there in his arms, I also felt tortured by the thought of what I had done the previous day. The extent of my deviousness was difficult for me to acknowledge and accept.

While still naked under the covers, and talking about the day's upcoming activities, we heard some noise coming from the front entrance of the house. Tacitly agreeing to ignore it, we continued our conversation, until we noticed the noise was moving closer to us, settling on the other side of the bedroom door. We should have listened to Jocelyne's soft voice warning us, but we ignored her as well.

The door opened slowly. Expecting Jocelyne to walk in and join us in bed, we looked on and smiled. But, no, in her place, walked Patricia.

"Isabelle," she started. "How can you possibly still be here?" Unable to respond, stunned, I instinctively pulled the covers higher up to my chin. She then turned to Patrick, looking down at his equally stunned expression, and just stared at him. Her eyes momentarily betrayed the hurt, the disappointment, and the love she still had for him.

"Where are the rest of my belongings?" she started. "My Lladro figurines, my crystal glasses, my Freemason tray," she insisted, her distress mounting. She then went on to recite all Patrick's wrongdoings, enumerating his transgressions, one by one. Patrick's face had paralyzed into an expression of cluelessness. I could not look at him. If I had, I would have laughed myself onto the floor. Seated on his bed, with his mouth half-open and his back against the headboard, he was trying to understand what had just happened. He was obviously struggling to make sense of the very strange situation that had landed in his bedroom on a quiet Sunday morning.

Patricia and I both knew the story that had brought her there, and that story needed to remain a secret. The only way for me to minimize the possibility of Patricia exposing my scheme was to create a diversion.

"Patricia, go to your car," I interrupted. "I will meet you there in five minutes," I said with firmness, afraid the truth would spill out of her mouth. She looked at me, as if suddenly understanding the turmoil she was causing.

"OK," she simply replied, rapidly turning around and leaving the bedroom.

Still caught in his maze, Patrick watched me in growing disbelief as I rapidly covered my naked body with that off-white bathrobe I hated so much. As I was slipping it on, I could not help but think of the number of women who had most likely worn it. I wondered, then, if my business card, which I had inserted inside the robe's pocket a few weeks before, had reached another target, another victim. Feeling solely the soft inside of the garment, my hands met nothing. My card had vanished. Another mystery to solve. But, not now.

From his window, Patrick saw me run barefoot through the snow banks outside his house. I was skipping over huge piles of snow and my feet were piercing the thin layer of ice that had settled over the soft snow. I quickly opened the car door and turned to Patricia, my mind razor sharp. There, for twenty minutes, we squared off under Patrick's bewildered gaze.

"How can you still be here?" she asked, her eyes questioning.

Again, I saw the hurt and pain they carried. What the fuck have I done? I thought. "Look," I told her, "I know what I am doing, Patricia. And, yes, I'm still here. I will be for a little while. But, do trust me," I added. "All this has a point."

"How the hell did she get in?" I asked him, as I walked back in, feet bloodied, red, and frozen.

"Well," he said, pointing to his recording device, "while reviewing the video, I was able to see the door had been left open, most likely all night."

"So, after spotting my car and giving in to her need to confront you, all she had to do was push open the door," I blurted out, upset at his nonchalance.

He looked at me, still shaken, unable to explain.

We ignored the day's events and resumed our routine. Patrick was installing new windows in the house. Alejandro, after having walked through the house burning sage, started studying. Jocelyne was watching Frozen.

We all were in shock, of course, but, in an effort to redeem myself, I made every effort possible to distract us from the earlier occurrence. My solution, as always, was to transform food into a feast.

Tuscan lamb stew, complete with a creamy polenta and Caesar salad would do the trick, I thought. And, why not a Tiramisu? I felt inspired. My detective skills had yielded more information, taking me to new levels of understanding, allowing me to glimpse into a portion of Patrick's defective mindset. He could appropriate objects that did not belong to him without shame or remorse, self-administering justice he thought he deserved.

What slight had he perceived from Patricia? Of that, I was not sure. What I was certain of was that my culinary magic would work to offset our odd morning. I, too, it seemed, was able to script and control flawlessly.

On my way back to Northampton the following morning, I reviewed the events preceding my departure. At Patrick's request, I had called Charlie, herself a lawyer, to ask for her legal opinion on Patricia's uninvited intrusion. I chose to speak to her in French, so I could talk freely.

Patrick, observing from afar, was irritated by his inability to understand the French conversation taking place before him. He knew, far too well, that some matters were being hidden from him. I was aware that Patrick and I were forming a reckless team. The drama I had created on my own was somehow acting as a bond, unifying our twisted perspectives.

As I turned on to my street, I saw John's black Audi, and realized he was now back from Taipei, something I had forgotten that morning. I was remembering how Patrick had asked me the day before I left if John was sleeping over at the house tonight.

"No," I had lied swiftly. In truth, I wanted John to sleep at our house. The house always frightened me. It was located at the end of a cul-de-sac, where, at night, darkness engulfed it. So, yes, I wanted him there.

That evening, Alice and I witnessed John's typical inability to blend into our routine. He imposed his own living habits without being aware of its impact on our lives. It was an acute reminder of our marital shortfalls. Our family was decomposing at its own rate, and there was nothing I could do to stop the process.

Annoyed by John's presence, I left the table, wanting to reach the comfort of my bed, before having to fight John's proposal to massage my feet or any other part of my body. I felt shame and resentment. I should have sent him to a hotel and ended his misery.

At 6:00 a.m. texts started to roll in.

Who did you sleep with last night? Why did you lie to me? You slept with him. I know. I saw his car parked behind yours, preventing you to leave if you had wanted to. He is dangerous. And your lights were on all night. And the toilet was flushed throughout the night, as well.

Nah, it can't be, I thought. I wrote back, Patrick, what are you saying? How can you imply such a thing? Where are you? Did you follow me?

Yes, I did, Isabelle, he replied. And if you don't believe me, go see for yourself. I left a scratched lottery ticket beside your mailbox.

Unlike the Sunday before, I did not run out in the snow in my bare feet. I took the time to boot up and slip on my coat. Slowly, I walked the icy path leading to the mailbox. The sky and the ground seemed to melt their respective whites into one another, forming a milky entity. My eyes were looking, focusing, zooming in and out, until they saw it. It was lying in the frozen ground. Flashes of fluorescent green were pulling at my eyes. The ticket was there, where he said it would be.

I do not know how and why these troubling behaviors did not shake my sense of security. How had I become immune to the craziness displayed by his behaviors? How much more of his digressions was I going to rationalize? How could I confuse control for love and care? Desperation and hope were the only answers. I must have been craving a sense of belonging somewhere.

Crumbs of them.

I must have hoped for the annihilation of my own hopelessness.

I removed the top of the tin, shoved my hand inside the container, looking for what was left of the tea leaves I had brought from Taiwan the year before. I dunked the tea ball inside my cup and waited for the water to change color.

Waiting, a power being diluted by time, diminished by it, its own fuel.

I looked out the patio door. The wind was blowing hard, a vertical fall of snow pushing against the structure of my plastic house. I took a sip of my tea, Oriental Beauty. Again, I thought of the story of The Three Little Pigs, and wondered about the both of them, John and Patrick. About their ending with me, and if it would it fit the original ending of the fable?

Would I boil the wolf and eat it?

The snow kept falling, and Christmas was coming, and I knew I was the same as the year before, but worse.

A shadow of a shadow.

Patrick was working up north, and we were keeping in touch regularly, via texts. On that Wednesday evening, he and his workers were planning to sleep at a motel in Berlin, where they were working. That way they could save time and ensure constant progress was being made on their project. In the middle of that night, he had texted me he was eating crap with his workers, and that he was not comfortable sleeping with them. I miss you so much, he had written. I will try to go and see you tomorrow night.

The next morning, somewhat tired, I helped Alice and John get ready to leave for a Christmas holiday trip together. Observing their excitement, I, by contrast, felt distraught at the thought of spending my first Christmas alone, in a country I could not leave. I knew I could not rely on Patrick to lift my spirits and provide me with the magical Christmas I needed.

After seeing Alice and John leave, my feeling of loss, uncertainty, and abandonment was acute. The hair salon, I thought, anything to help me regain some self-esteem.

Patrick had hinted at the possibility of coming over for dinner. Following my return, familiar with his proverbial lack of punctuality, I took my time preparing a meal of beef stew, caramelized carrots, and pasta. Simple enough. I was expecting him to arrive at his usual time of 10:30 p.m., some three hours later than promised. I was completely surprised then, when at 7:30 p.m., I heard keys knocking against the window of the front door.

The night would be good after all.

There was playfulness. There was tenderness. There was desire.

There, together, I thought we still had a chance at creating a relationship that would transcend our past, a past that somehow was accumulating darkened memories.

"Let me take a quick shower," Patrick said.

Absent-mindedly, watching him enter the bathroom, something caught my attention. I noticed his phone was on the floor, beneath his jeans. It was unlocked.

I looked up at the closed bathroom door and asked myself the same question I always did. How much time do I have?

I quickly picked up the phone and pressed the button to light the screen. I was nervous, my hands trembling. I was momentarily disoriented as this was a Samsung and I owned an iPhone.

Where should I start? Messages? Recent phone calls? I wondered. I opted for the latter. I opened the drawer of my night table, took out a pad of paper and a pencil and wrote down two recently and repeatedly dialed numbers. I was pressed for time, not wanting the humiliation of being caught. I looked at the messages, but saw nothing out of the ordinary. I closed the screen and replaced the phone under his jeans.

Patrick opened the door, walked in, body steaming.

"Give me a kiss?" I asked him, as I pulled him in.

Our meal together that evening, was surprisingly pleasant, different. The discussions surrounding our respective childhoods and past marriages had depth and humor and he seemed genuinely interested. He shared his love for Spanish guitar, which he quickly put on Spotify.

The authentic intimacy of our interaction had taken me by surprise, whipping me into a trance-like state.

He left the next morning, at 5:30 a.m., as usual, kissing me lightly and leaving me to rest.

"I love you," he said, as he stepped out of the room.

I took those words in and somehow, this time, they soothed me into a comfortable sleep.

At 10:30 a.m. he called to see how I was and to tell me that he loved me. He told me how he loved making love to me, that I was his life, his everything.

Yes, it made me smile, it made me forget.

I got up, feeling rested and invigorated by all the attention and love I was receiving. As I walked to the bathroom, I suddenly remembered I had checked his phone the night before. My God. I have phone numbers to play with, I thought, my heart pounding with excitement and dread.

I will find nothing, I kept telling myself. Nothing.

Before I began, I still managed to take the time to make myself a coffee. Wrapped in my bathrobe, wearing knee high wool socks, I sat cross-legged on my chair and dove in.

Should I dial the numbers directly and take it from there? I asked myself.

No, I thought. My coffee was kicking in. I'll do a reverse look up first.

I went on the site, registered and paid.

The first phone number I found was a number linked to a Latino individual living in Springfield. Instinctively, I did not wish to pursue my inquiry with that one. Instead, I decided to concentrate my efforts on the second number.

Staring outside my window, the ridiculousness of my situation was catching up to me.

Where has my self-respect gone? Just how far am I willing to go, and why? And still, I wondered. Carrying feelings of guilt and shame, I typed the second number into the allocated space and pressed the send button. And, then I saw it—the name. The name that fit into a rhyming story, only this story could inspire, exposing the star, Jocelyne, the fallen gatekeeper.

Not, Clarissa, sweetie, I thought. Felicia. Felicia Lancaster, I read.

"Hi," I said, with a sturdy voice. "Am I speaking with Felicia?"

"Yes," she hesitantly said.

I breathed deeply, as flashbacks from August, when I had learned about Lydia and Patricia, invaded my brain. I apologized in advance, explained that my calling might seem odd, but was it possible she was dating a man called Patrick or Benjamin Rodriguez? The pause I expected never came.

"Yes," she said rapidly.

Yes. Yes. Fuck. Unbelievable. Or, is it really? What the fuck did I expect? Somehow, I stayed collected, visualizing my adrenal glands as permanent Pez dispensers working on overdrive inside me.

"Well, well, we are dating the same man," I shared, the voice in me quieted by a feeling of victory. "When did you meet him?" I asked finally.

"Last April," she said, her voice trembling. "We started dating last April. Seven months ago."

Seven, I thought.

"I just left his house this morning," she added with care.

"What?" I asked with incredulity.

"Yes, I slept there last night. I prepared dinner for Alejandro and Alejandro's girlfriend, Lisa. He wasn't there. He told me he was sleeping at the motel with his workers," she added. Her voice had now become a breathless whisper. I was the messenger from the land of the broken and the duped. "I have to call him now," she said, and she hung up.

Of course, you do, I thought, understanding too well the significance of what I had revealed to her.

She called me back thirty minutes later, still breathless.

"He denies everything. He says not to believe anything you say," she shared.

I sighed. Of course, Patrick. Denying is part of your religion, the same religion that will bring hell to your door. You can kneel and pray all you want in that shitty little corner you call a shrine, an homage to your late mother. Surely, you must understand that your prayers cannot be answered. You fucked me on our first night, face down on the floor as I was head-to-head with the burning candle and cross that frame your mother's face. How many women did you sacrifice on that altar? I wondered.

For the better part of the week, Felicia and I stayed in touch as Patrick continued lying to us both. The only anchors to the truth, resided in our respective stories. She was stronger than me. I could sense it.

I called John, begging him to call Patrick and ask him to leave me alone, to not contact me. He did as I asked. But what I needed was to be removed from Northampton. And, that was impossible. John had refused.

Five days had passed since I had finally identified Felicia as the other woman in Patrick's life. The woman who had found my dress. The woman who had confronted her lover, only to be placated by her own tailor-made set of lies. I was caught in the familiar haze I had felt each time I had left him. The desire to be with him, the desire to flee, the internal dilemma, always so present, palpable even. I was alone. But, this time my loneliness was exacerbated by Alice's absence, an absence I hoped would be buffered by my volunteering at the local soup kitchen in Northampton.

Merry Christmas to me, I thought.

And I heard footsteps, someone climbing, a someone who only knew how to fall, and take me with him.

"I am sorry, I am sorry, I am sorry," he said, as he jumped on the bed and grabbed my face.

Tears were running down my cheeks.

It was 2:30 a.m.

It was time to orchestrate, yet another, farewell fuck.

My head on his shoulder, crying profusely, I knew I had to let him go, despite his numerous pleas asking me to stay, to go back to Lowell with him.

"No," I told him. "It ends here." Both seated on the bed, him staring blankly at the wall, me listening to George Michael music, we stayed silent.

Patrick, I could see, had zoned out of reality, and gone into his own angry world.

I had called Child Services on him ... for the second time. He had just been informed, two days before, on Christmas Day, of the content of the second complaint I had placed with them. I had shamelessly called them the first time, the previous November, after witnessing Alejandro's aggressive nature with his sister. He, like his father, would often force feed the child and slap his hand on the dining room table to make her finish her plate, inducing in the child a state of terror so compelling I had felt obligated to intervene, albeit secretly and, yes, deceptively. Imploring them to stop using such terrifying strategies with Jocelyne had not worked.

The latest denunciation had been triggered and legitimized by what Felicia had shared with me. Through our phone calls, I had discovered that Jocelyne had been joining Patrick and Felicia in bed. This had most likely occurred with the other girls he had been dating, too. Jocelyne had the habit of sliding in beside us during the weekends, and Patrick loved to make love in the morning. A pillow placed between her and our naked bodies had been sufficient to ease his mind.

I remembered my discomfort when these sessions would occur, with the child sleeping by our side.

I knew it to be wrong, of course, but the pull had been too hard to resist.

Alerting Child Services had been my way of redeeming myself, now that I knew for a fact that his bed was a sexual carousel.

Despite my dizziness, I headed to the kitchen and prepared a coffee. After a few minutes, he entered the room, grabbed me, placed me against the wall, held my face and again begged me to follow him back to Lowell. His eyes plunged into mine.

For a second, I hesitated, and then I managed to open the front door, let him out and watch him walk across the ice crusted pathway to his silver Mazda. I could feel my strength weakening. I closed my eyes, wishing his disappearance away.

Felicia and I were still in contact. She shared that Patrick confessed he had made a mistake and that he had told me, by phone, that we were over. He also told her that I was a depressed mess and an unfit mother, pointing to the alcohol incident, Alice had been the victim of in April.

"All lies, except for Alice's incident," I told her, as I reluctantly shared that he had come over to my house to try to lure me back into his life. It was the same way, it turned out, he had tried to lure her back to his place, under the pretext of recuperating her belongings.

Felicia and I decided to meet at a bar on Pearl Street in Boston. It reassured me. With her with me, by my side, close enough to weave a feeling of safety, I would wait for my time in Massachusetts to expire. She would be my anchor, my savior.

But she withdrew from our rendezvous, at the last minute.

I can't, she had said, it's better for me.

How I envied her, her ability to detach, to let go. Patrick was mind-fucking with her, confusing her to the point where she understood the best thing to do was to remove herself from all elements of the saga, and that included me.

I remained in my bed, a glass in of red in my hand, and listened to the sound of my silence.

My quest had never been to seek revenge against the other women. No, like a madwoman, I had simply longed for the truth. My mind was playing tricks on me, bringing unknown feelings of paranoia to the surface. I had thought then, that a form of jealousy was the culprit. I say "a form" because I had never been the jealous type. Maybe at times I had felt envy, but no, jealousy was foreign territory to me.

My determination to find the truth had been propelled by a need to annihilate the uncertainty my life had become. This is what had led me to expose these women and the relationship they had with Patrick. First, it was Lydia. Then, it was Felicia. Two pasty-white, fleshy bodies, that provided a canvas for my Latin beau to leave his marks on.

They had all left him when they discovered they had been used, lied to, and cheated on.

They had all abandoned me.

It was the 30th of December and it was cold.

John and Alice had returned from Montreal.

Again, unable to spend time with John, his wanting me, his inability to surrender, I left.

From my standpoint in the lobby of the hotel, it was easy to detect Patrick's feverish state. His brisk movements betrayed his nervousness.

I watched him come to me, walking with intent and focus, controlling his posture until he sat on the sofa, looked at me, and simply kissed me fully on the mouth.

He took me by the hand and led me to the elevators.

No words were spoken.

He swiftly removed his clothes, as he stared at me, commanding me to do the same. He pushed me aggressively onto the bed and inserted himself, like he had done a million times before. Staring at the ceiling, I had escaped his presence and I was thinking of John, at home with Alice.

John had reserved the room under his name, believing my lies, believing I had decided to sleep there to give him and Alice some space. He was reassured by the thought he had left a message on Patrick's voicemail, asking him to stay away from me and Alice.

But, no. I had renewed my twisted vows.

I had sworn I would not bring him along into the New Year, my new year.

I had promised myself I would hold fast.

In the middle of the night I woke up in a panic. Patrick, as usual, had been sleeping the sleep of the dead. I looked up at him and felt my throat tighten. I felt trapped.

What the fuck had I signed up for, again? I wondered. I woke him up. "I want to talk," I said. "We need to talk about what happened....About your betrayal....Betrayals." I wanted him to clarify his position, I wanted to hear that he was sorry.

But the dawn would not be a soothing one. He resisted and minimized, letting anger take over. He was pissed ... annoyed ... at me. Imagine that.

Felicia's last text was vivid, echoing in my head, tattooing my mind with a fair warning. You will never find solace with him. Yes, anguish was what he brought freely to my life.

We had a quick breakfast in the dining room of the hotel, while we watched the muted television. But then, our voices, with the lack of containment our respective tones betrayed, disrupted a couple seated nearby, prompting them to leave. They closed behind them, the only door capable of buffering the nonsensical conversation echoing through the cafeteria. Looking at Patrick's stern face, I knew I did not want to head home to Northampton and spend New Year's Eve with John and Alice. But, I did not want to spend it alone either. I had a choice to make.

We got into our respective cars to leave. He followed me to the gas station, as he had asked. From there I led him to the fastest route back to Lowell. Suddenly, aware of the very real possibility of never seeing him again, I improvised a stop at the local cafe on Leverett road, realizing too late it was a ploy—my ploy, to lie to myself. To create unnecessary turmoil. To throw confusion on what appeared to be a very clear situation. I had led him to the road that would have initiated my freedom from his grasp, but it was I, who now, would follow him.

He had called. I had answered.

He had begged. I had caved.

At that very instant, I knew what I had simply become—another version of him.

The Latino music surrounded us and erected a frontier his friends and family could not cross. Having decided to celebrate New Year's Eve with him, I navigated through the thickness of his relatives' accents, pretending to understand them, when, in fact, I was barely listening. We were mingling at our own pace.

We danced in front of my newfound, extended family. They all stared at the couple we now presented ourselves to be. The part in me that had seemingly been simmering, waiting for the right role to come along, was here, and I was ready to perform.

Happy 2017.

CHAPTER EIGHT

My stomach was in perpetual knots, either because I ached for him, I craved him, or I mistrusted him. In the end, my body was in a state of constant disequilibrium.

Paradoxically, I felt alive, more than ever.

I somehow had a self-generated sense that moving toward the fire was essential, to feel the heat brush against the outer layer of air that protected my skin, as both a warning and an invitation.

The second snow storm of the season had made its way to the east coast. We still managed to go to the Sunday market, an activity we had wanted to do with Jocelyne for a while now. There, through the dozens of outlets that formed a maze, we walked, the three of us, Patrick happy to introduce me to all the people he knew.

The stinginess he usually displayed had become effaced by a sudden urge to spoil both me and Jocelyne. Purchasing boots, jeans, and toys for Jocelyne, he offered to buy me two dresses. One black, one white. In spite of their price, at twenty dollars each, they did give out an elegant feel. Looking in the mirror, appreciating his look of approval being reflected, I wondered where and how he had developed such an acute sense of style. He had spent most of his life in the slums of Managua and from there had left for Spain to be deployed to Iraq. It was puzzling.

Walking to his truck to head back home for dinner, he turned around and decided to immortalize this moment using his phone. A heart-warming photo of me and Jocelyne was taken by a very animated Patrick, whose demeanor had stayed consistent throughout the day. That energy was transferred to our table, where, after having eaten pasta, we placed Jocelyne in front of her computer and headed to the bedroom. There, I received my send-off. I was to leave for a seven day New York visit with Alice. Audition season had arrived.

Alice had chosen to apply to fifteen acting colleges, which meant fifteen auditions, all in the Big Apple. I love New York. I was the quintessential city girl, caught in Northampton, Massachusetts. Evidently, while the thought of escaping the countryside was quite enticing, leaving Patrick behind tugged at my stomach, my ultimate barometer. Even though we were already living an hour and a half from each other, I was convinced the additional distance would morph itself into a deeper emotional detachment.

I cursed John as I felt the parental burden weighing solely on my shoulders, again, blaming him for not letting me indulge in my own twisted love narrative. Moreover, because of John, I had no choice but to play a game I feared I was ill-equipped to win.

I had asked John to take me away from Northampton during Christmas. It would have been the only way for me to leave this game intact. But no, failing to understand the stakes at hand, he had declined to shield me, the high target, from the reach of the sniper my lover had revealed himself to be. But at least I now knew a game was being played. I knew its rules. Would that be sufficient?

I hated texting. It had become the leash keeping me from enjoying the freedom I hungered while in New York, preventing me from reconnecting with the adult in me. He kept texting me, asking me for pictures, proof of location, proof of submission, proof of faithfulness.

At the beginning of my trip, he had also sent me, via text, two links to articles he had deemed relevant for me to read, one article on the subject of happiness, and how to achieve it, the other, horrifyingly explained being skinned alive, step-by-step. I had stared at both articles, lying on the hotel bed, mouth opened, questioning Patrick's motive.

WTF, I had written back. But, he had replied nothing. I had decided to simply ignore my unease and incomprehension for now, planning to discuss the disturbing content with him at a later date. And then, in the middle of the week, the texting, the attention, all of it stopped, leaving me free falling into fearfulness and abandonment.

My reaction was immediate and predictable. The morning of my return to Northampton, while waiting for Alice's last audition to finish, seated in a stress-filled waiting room, I texted him.

I don't trust you. I want out.

Driving to him, I went over the conversation we had before I decided to head for his house.

"It's a shame really, when you know how much I love you," he had told me over the phone. "I have done nothing wrong," he had pleaded. "Nothing."

Yes, there had been a sense of authenticity in his voice, but mostly, I was surprised to admit, it was despair, soft and touching despair.

"Did you shower?" he asked, upon my arrival.

"This morning," I risked, exasperated by the question. To him it meant I needed to wash again, so I complied and hopped in with him—me, but not my words, so recently spoken, 'I don't trust you. I want out.'

He turned me toward the opposite end of the tight space, making me grab the towel handle placed inside the shower. I felt the pressure of the soap on my back, my armpits, my inner thighs, down the anal divide. Nothing about this was sexual. The goal was clearly to get me clean. He turned me, so I could face him. He gripped my jaw and there, with no room to escape, he whispered not to ever, ever leave him again.

"You and I," he whispered, "we will die together."

CHAPTER NINE

The dental surgery had me in a state of pain so brutal, I needed to add oxycodone to my already increasing list of pain medication. While the daze it put me in was welcome, my unsteadiness was difficult to hide or tame. That was how, from the top of my stairs, not having noticed Jackson, I stumbled and fell. The left side of my face, mostly my nose, had taken most of the brunt. I was in pain and frightened by my reflection when I saw myself in the mirror. Seeing the swelling gain momentum, I quickly iced my face and lay down on my bed. I took two Advil pills and fell asleep.

For 24 hours, I willingly disappeared from the Earth. Finally, wanting to halt the cascade of texts Patrick was sending me, I decided to send him a picture of my face. The picture should have done the trick. It should have kept him at a safe distance, helping me create the space I needed to mend. I did not want anyone to see what I looked like. A storm had hit the east coast again, and the winds were picking up. That should also have been a deterrent to him. But, no.

He insisted, "You need food, you need to gain strength, mi amor."

I pleaded, literally, for him to stay in Lowell, claiming I was concerned for his safety on the blizzardy roads. I did not want him to see me so obviously vulnerable. I had wrapped a bandage around my swollen face to ease the swelling. My eyes were bluish black, swollen to the point of bursting. Everything in me was expanding. I needed space.

He arrived at 11:00 p.m. with bags of Goya-brand products. Seated on the bottom of the stairs with my beaten face, I watched him put all the groceries away in the kitchen.

A Latino grocery store had landed in my kitchen. I could not believe it. The storm had gathered some strength. He had braved it for me, with all these gifts.

Our synchronicity had returned, highlighting the emergence of genuine companionship for each other. He had stayed over, letting our night pour into my day. His touches, his caresses, his words were convincing me to travel back to Lowell for the weekend.

Our hands were intertwined throughout the whole trip. We stared ahead, concentrating on the snowy roads.

"It is surreal," I shared with him. "Me, the French-Canadian girl, fresh from an Asian tour, dating a Nicaraguan construction worker living in Lowell, Massachusetts."

"I know," he said with a wider smile. "I feel the same."

My aim had been to spend the weekend in Lowell with Jocelyne and Alejandro. But, Saturday morning, the throbbing in my head could not be ignored. Unbelievable pain, coupled with mind-blowing nausea, had invaded my body and I had no medication there with me.

Patrick quickly assessed the situation, delegated his work responsibilities to Alejandro and called Valeria to babysit Jocelyne. All this was seemingly done out of concern and care for me. He helped me put my coat on, insisting I wear a hat, grabbed the keys to his truck and led me carefully down the outdoor stairs.

"Quick," I said to him. "I am dying here."

Lying on the messy backseat of his Dodge Ram, the tranquility of his truck surprised me. I was discovering other parts of him. I wondered if he knew how his behavior was affecting me now, here. Oscillating between pain-filled moments and the joy of still being with him, I kept asking myself if this time—this time, finally, we would successfully bond, all the previous transgressions, left behind, and gone.

INHALED

My head heavy with pounding hotness, my neck stiffened by knots that had rooted themselves at the base of my skull, I stretched my arm, my hands, my fingers to the front seat, across the armrest separating us. There, he met me, gently taking my hand in his. Over the next hour, every so often, he would gently squeeze it, telling me repeatedly that he loved me and that he was happy. Music, the revelatory tool, the instrument that exposes the soul, soothed me. The music he chose to play, then, in the truck, highlighted some filaments of incongruity. To my complete surprise, amidst a few contemporary pieces, the music of Sweet People and Richard Clayderman emerged with all its nauseating mediocrity. Moreover, he seemed to enjoy its melody, whistling and swaying his head to the rhythms. The music lover in me was disturbed—amusingly so.

I felt the final turn, as the car swayed gently on the ice. I looked up, recognizing the thin tree branches parading above our heads, indicating we were approaching my house.

He parked the car, opened the door and helped lift me up from the backseat. He watched me, surprised by my sudden outburst of energy, climb over the snowbanks with wide, almost heroic steps. Once inside, I kicked off my boots, walked in and started running up the stairs to the bathroom. I opened the cabinet, found my medication and quickly sprayed it into my right nostril. Walking straight into the bedroom, I let myself fall onto my bed, untidy but feeling safe.

The smell of food, the familiar perfume of coriander, cinnamon and star anise brought me back to the world of the living. Unsteadied by the medication, I went downstairs and was welcomed by a man drenched in his thoughts, concentrating on cooking in my kitchen. John had never prepared anything, but peanut butter toast for me. What I was seeing had never happened to me before as no man had ever graced my kitchen before with any culinary sense.

While I had been sleeping for two hours, Patrick had prepared a bulgur pilaf-like dish, a red bean stew, a chicken noodle soup and, of course, an avocado salad. I was moved.

Exhausted from my pain, Patrick was almost spoon feeding me at the table. I knew then I had a decision to make. I had exposed myself to him like never before, and he was still here. No more games needed to be played, I was concluding. Thirteen months into my relationship with Patrick, after having subtly directed the house traffic and camouflaged his presence, managing both Patrick's and Alice's movements to avoid a collision, I decided it was time. As she walked in from her school getaway, I let Alice meet Patrick for the very first time.

I saw Alice politely shake his hand and heard Patrick articulate the welcoming of her presence into his family. Then, my heart was triggered by a sudden uneasiness. I vividly remembered the first time he had seen Alice's bedroom, 12 months before. After opening her bedroom door, Patrick had first taken a step forward, then, a firm step back. His stance had changed. His body had displayed a newfound alertness. His eyes had narrowed. I still did not want to acknowledge it, but I could have sworn I had then detected the sides of his nostrils briefly pulsate as well, taking in the hormonal perfume that was lingering in her room.

Alice, having shaken Patrick's hand, removed herself from the kitchen with controlled disgust. Without acknowledging her simmering disdain for his presence in our house, in our life, he grabbed me by the waist.

"I am happy," he told me, clueless.

I should have been happy, too.

Patrick insisted on coming to see Alice perform Macbeth. I could tell she was a bit uneasy with the idea, but not enough to refuse. No one from Montreal was making the effort to come and see her perform and John was in Taiwan. She wanted her own audience there, as well. She wanted to show her school friends and cast members, that her acting had managed to strike some interest, within her own personal circle. I did, too. So, the third and last showing provided Patrick, Alejandro, Jocelyne, Alice and me the opportunity to gather and admire her strong rendition of a very complex character.

Once home, it all came together, unexpectedly. The girls fell in love with one another. Jocelyne watched Alice's each and every move, while Alice was equally mesmerized by this little person who, maybe, one day, would become her sister. Alejandro's innate shyness was quickly disarmed by Alice's willingness to make him feel comfortable. He, too, held the potential to become the brother, the older sibling she had always wanted, since Catherine had abdicated her role a long time ago.

While the children were bonding, Patrick and I prepared the meal together, dancing, to the sound of Reggae music, drinking champagne, celebrating Alice's stellar performance.

There, suspended in time, amongst the ruins of past memory, was the sketch of a family.

Set in New England's idyllic countryside, Alice's school was a beautiful establishment. It was located at the top of a hill, surrounded by acres of land. We had been immediately charmed by the conviviality of its staff and student body. But, the IB Mandarin classes and equestrian program had been the central reasons we had chosen the school.

She had started to ride at the age of eight, unafraid of the large animal's size, genuinely intrigued by its willingness to be tamed. Learning to trust herself and her horse, and to establish a constant dialogue between them, Alice understood the power this type of partnership promised. We had seen her talent for riding surface, but mostly we had recognized how the presence of riding in her life had quieted her anxieties.

Over the years, jumping had become her main focus, pushing her further into the technical and physical challenges of the sport. She would often talk about the feeling of freedom she would get from being momentarily suspended in the air with her horse. Of course, throughout her life as a rider, she had also gained experience through a series of improvised dismounts, none of which had physically injured her.

But, days before the March school break, during a regional competition, her horse had refused to jump. It halted in front of the obstacle, abruptly switching to the side of the wooden structure. While she tried to control her fall, the horse started to buck, expelling her small frame into the air, resulting in a brutal fall. She had the misfortune to land abruptly on her side, fracturing her collar bone, two ribs, and a wrist.

At that moment in time, our relationship, while somewhat polite, had become strained by Alice's eagerness to see me leave Patrick. This was in spite of my efforts to formalize my relationship with Patrick, by introducing her to him. Leaving Patrick was something I was not ready to do

I had planned for Alice to spend her March break, back home in Montreal, but now that she was physically immobile, those plans had changed. It was a change, of course, I wanted to ignore.

I would care for Alice. And, I did. The Isabelle way.

One week after her accident, on a mild March evening, Alice and I walked to Northampton's local pub for dinner. There, I unapologetically downed two rum-based cocktails before Alice's amused eyes. Walking back home together, giddily, for once simultaneously happy, she held me tightly in her arms, controlling my unsteadiness.

Yet again, Alice had become my source of direction.

With Alice having gone to bed, I sat on the kitchen counter, my legs dangling, I listened to the sound of them hit the cupboard doors, a noise that soothed me. Mindlessly, I sipped some water and thought of how I had drank too much, of how I hated the feel of my throat, parched, as if scrubbed by fear. From where I sat, directly facing the entrance door, I saw it move. The lock. I saw the doorknob turn. And then, I remembered. My keys. I had forgotten I had given Patrick a set of my house keys. He slammed the door open and appeared, as if dazed, as if not there, and marched quickly toward me.

And I saw he wasn't seeing me.

Ven aca, I heard again.

Pushing me against the stove, he unbuckled his belt while keeping his mouth pressed against mine. Still undressing, we hopped to the living room and facing the staircase fell on the only piece of furniture in there, a black leather swivel chair.

I had sold much of the furniture in preparation for my move to a smaller house in Montreal. My immigration status only allowed me to stay in the United States until the end of May, barely allowing me time to attend Alice's high school graduation.

INHALED

The emptiness of the room momentarily brought him back to where he thought he wasn't, destabilized him. He sat me down on the one-seater and spread my legs, stretching my panties to the side. As I saw the upset in his eyes at the truth of my departure sinking in, he slowly inserted himself into me. While looking straight at me, his hands parting my lips a little further, moving his fingers, adding to the pleasure of the penetration, wildness was inhabiting our motions. There was no restraint, only synchronized fluidity. There, long, languorous strokes brought us to the culmination of a soft climax for me, a full-bodied one for him.

Exhausted, we climbed the stairs to my bedroom and let ourselves fall onto the bed, surprisingly skipping the ritual shower. As my head hugged the top of his shoulder, I heard him fall to sleep at 4:00 a.m. I, on the other hand, remained wide awake, electrified by the intensity of our moment, unable to find rest.

At 6:00 a.m., his internal clock woke him up, always so punctual. He got up and showered. Eyes opened, I squinted with pain, my bladder feeling as though it had been labored by waves of suspicious warmth, my head dizzy, my legs rag-like.

Suddenly remembering all the times he had prepared me tea, all the times he had sat by my bedside to greet me as I had opened my eyes, I now felt the urge to return the favor. I wanted to please him, to make him a cup of hot chocolate the way he liked, to show him how much he meant to me, that, maybe, I was the fool he wanted.

I got up, slowly heading down to the kitchen, placed the chocolate powder and milk in a cup and put it in the microwave to be heated. After 90 seconds, I removed the cup to test its temperature. It still felt too cold, but as I was starting to feel unwell, I left the cup on the counter to go sit in the dining room. The back of my neck was getting clammy, droplets of cold sweat were dripping along the middle of my back, and I felt dizzy.

"Amor, there is not enough chocolate in my cup. Where are the pouches?"

I heard him ask, understanding my concoction was not chocolatey enough. I motioned to get up, feeling the need to correct my mistake.

When my eyes opened, all I saw was his face on which two acute arches had been drawn, looking at me with a seriousness I had never seen on him before. Lying down on my back, in front of the staircase, I understood then that I had fainted, that for the first time in my life, I had lost consciousness.

"For ten minutes," Patrick told me. "I thought you were dead. Your skin was so cold. I thought I had lost you," he continued, seemingly in shock. "I caught you as you were falling down to the ground and carried you here," he added, incapable of hiding his worry.

As soon as I regained consciousness, he left my side to wake Alice. "She has to know. I can't go to work and leave you like this," he insisted, while climbing the stairs. I tried to object, but, ignoring my protest, he woke her up and brought her downstairs. She knelt by my side and stared at me, confused.

"I am OK," I told her, "Don't worry."

Patrick wanted Alice to call an ambulance.

"No," I said. "No need, I am fine," I pressed, unaware Alice had become pale. Wanting to return to her bed, she tried to climb back up the stairs, but again he was quick, catching her, as she too fainted. Lying still on the floor, I watched in disbelief as Patrick carried Alice to the couch to check her vital signs. The minute she regained consciousness, he returned to me, caressing my head and placing a kiss on my forehead.

"You girls need a man in this house," he said half-smilingly.

I looked at him. The man was distraught, moved, clearly. By what? I didn't know. Me? The thought of losing me? Alice and her need to be held by a father she didn't have access to? What would have anyone thought, I asked myself, dizzy, and weak, but still aware. There were changes, concrete ones, observable ones, in him, in his holding of me, my life. And it made me wonder about the hope that can lie inside all movement. And at the core of it, of change, the right to a second chance.

I swallowed, my saliva thick and dry, and motioned for his cup.

Feeling better, Alice joined us on the floor, placing my head on her lap, as Patrick spoon-fed me the hot chocolate that had been meant for him.

After my quick breakfast, he carried each one of us back to my bed, kissed the both of us, and left for Lowell.

Lying in my bed, by Alice's side, I felt time slipping. Disoriented, unsure of what I had seen and felt, I kept asking myself if I had orchestrated my own fall. The recurrent urinary tract infections, the dehydrating effects of the antibiotics I was taking, my lack of water intake, the wine, the lack of sleep, had all played a role. My loss of consciousness, had, in effect, fed on itself, guided by my own recklessness and naivety.

It had started as a personal dare, had it not? I thought I could walk that fine line between control and abandon. Moreover, I thought I did not need a safety net. An over-confident tightrope walker is what I had become.

I felt the sleep settle in my body, and holding Alice's hand, in the middle of my bed, I wondered, what had he done while I was on the floor, passed out? Had it lasted more than ten minutes?

And why had he moved my body from where I had fallen?

Why?

CHAPTER TEN

Alice needed to go to Boston to buy a dress for her upcoming graduation. I informed Patrick, ahead of time, that we would stop over for dinner on our way back from the city. He was tentative in his response, but I left him no choice. We would spend the day shopping at Macy's and Nordstrom Rack and from there we would drive to Lowell.

The house keys were waiting for me, as they had been since January, inside the empty water tank of an old toilet in Patrick's junkyard. As we walked inside his home, the full impact of Alice's presence there hit me. I had tried to prepare her for the visual images the house would surely imprint on her mind. I had warned her. The warnings were not enough to shield my little bourgeois teenager from the bleakness of this dungeon. Expressions of disgust and misunderstanding were dancing on her face, there for me to see.

Patrick arrived on time, equally curious and flattered by the fact that Alice, my daughter, had finally made her way into his house. Proud and amused, he gave Alice a tour of "her" home.

"When your mother and I move in together, you will room with Jocelyne," he firmly stated, as he pointed to the girls' bedroom.

Alice turned to me wide-eyed.

"Isabelle did share, didn't she?" he asked her, suspiciously.

"Of course, I did," I lied to him, and to Alice, telepathically shooing away the incisive looks I was being subjected to by both parties involved. Talks about our tentative future had animated many of our conversations, but I had not divulged any of it to Alice. I had to keep my options open. Swiftly, I managed to reorient the conversation to the more pressing matter, dinner.

The three of us drove to the Market Basket and from there, we decided to pick Jocelyne up at her mother's apartment in Lawrence. I navigated my way into the narrow streets of the city, guided by Patrick, the seediness of that area inescapably unsettling. Rushing to my destination, suddenly, a car cut in front of us, forcing us to a stop. A drug stop.

With my car forcibly immobilized, I looked over to my left and saw the driver of the car that had stopped us. He was a tall, dark Latino, unremarkable in all other aspects, whose Spanish I did not understand.

Patrick, alert to the impending danger, successfully declined the drug offer and firmly demanded they unblock the road. We had driven in this section of Lawrence so many times before, without any unwanted encounters.

Why did Alice have to be with me this time around? Why did she have to witness the extent of the depravity I'd been playing in? While my children had been raised in luxury, I had still made all the necessary efforts to protect them from the trap overabundance can set. We had chosen to live in a middle-class neighborhood, had driven second hand cars and encouraged friendships from all walks of life. Visiting Lawrence, however, was taking things too far. Here, only trouble existed. Trouble and danger.

I had fucked up once again.

Jocelyne, upon entering the car, was happy to see Alice. I was reassured, by the obvious fact, that Alice was happy to see her, too. Listening to them talk was heart-melting. Watching them through my rearview mirror, I smiled and wished for someone, somewhere to make this moment a lasting one. I was ready to resume my life, here, with a man whose Machiavellian penchant seemed to have faded away, while under my wise influence, my loving presence.

It made me believe, again, in the possibility of us.

Alejandro was away in New York, visiting his mother, Desiree. To fill the void his absence created at the table, to provoke a sense of interconnectivity, we sent him a photo of the elaborate meal before us. We miss you, the text read below the image. We then said Grace and feasted on the meal that Patrick, had himself, prepared, salmon, rice, plantains, yucca, shrimp, red bean stew, and avocados. It was a colorful spread, meant to seduce and impress. More pictures were taken, this time of Alice embracing Jocelyne.

Together we all washed the dishes, cleaned up the house and decided to stay in, changing our plans to go out and see a movie. The girls then spent the whole evening playing with dolls and tea cups, while Patrick and I sat on the brown couch to watch the news. There, I touched some of it again, happiness.

The following morning, I woke up quickly, remembering I had to drive Alice to Northampton. My plans were clear, take Alice back to Northampton and return to Lowell. Jocelyne would come along for the ride. Before my departure with the girls, Patrick had called from Manchester, asking me to leave the keys in our secret place. He needed to get some paperwork for the bank and was set to return home during the morning.

Saturday was banking day, an unmissable event in his weekly schedule. And so, upon arriving in Northampton, I got a panicked call.

"Where are the keys?" he asked.

"Shit," I thought. "I forgot to leave them," I told him. He remained calm, as I told him I was dropping Alice off and returning to Lowell immediately thereafter. He called back a minute later to let me know how he had been able to get in without the key.

"The window," he said.

Later that day, back in Lowell, I was seated on the brown couch. He shared that my mistake with the key had surprised him. "Maybe you thought I was coming back to change clothes or something," he said suspiciously.

Reciprocating with a similar skeptical gaze, I found myself pondering the strangeness of his comment. He had thought I had purposefully kept the keys with me, choosing consciously to ignore his demand to leave them in the toilet tank.

"My niece is getting married this afternoon," he continued, casually ignoring my sudden discomfort at his comment. I had met her, Emma, at the New Year's Eve party— the party I had attended with Patrick after finding out about Felicia, and then recommitting to him, once again. Emma was a beautiful and voluptuous Latina who had just immigrated to America. I was now learning she was also four months pregnant.

Sad, I told myself. Still, I understood, even condoned, the ploy for her to accelerate her immigration process.

"I can't attend the celebrations," he told me. "I need to pay my workers tonight. Take Jocelyne?" he asked while stroking the side of my face. Bent over his foot, kneading his heel, I thought about how his absence from the reception would be perceived, but more importantly, I wondered, momentarily, about his true motive. A really strange bird, really, I thought, weighing my options to attend the party without him or stay at his house for the evening. In truth, I was invigorated by the prospect of an outing, a rarity in this man's life, and quickly started to prepare both Jocelyne and myself for the event.

Finally, yes, I told myself, it'll be a family party where, yet again, I can ascertain and validate my presence in this man's life.

Valeria's small house was spread over one floor only, the kitchen area first greeting you from the entrance, then leading to the dining room area and finally the living room space. As I entered, I realized I had a problem. There was a production underway, a Latin production. Gold-colored garland hung everywhere from the colorful walls that framed the small rectangular space. As I stepped further in, I saw against the back wall of the dining room, a tall, multilayered cake sitting at the center of a long table.

Continuing to quickly scan my surroundings, I was blinded by the bling flashing at me from every direction.

While intimate, with maybe fifteen guests attending the ceremony and reception, every one of the women there, all Latinas, were dressed to shine, literally. What Patrick had omitted to tell me, was that the wedding would be celebrated there. Louis's and Valeria's house was the venue. I scanned my attire, suddenly feeling self-conscious. I was wearing jeans and a black turtle neck.

"No, not this time," I thought, deciding to leave Jocelyne behind and return to the house to change. It was imperative.

Upon my return to Valeria's house, proudly displaying my reception attire, I approached her, offering to serve the plates she had individually filled for each of the guests. Examining the contents of the plates, I smiled to myself. Rice, beans, chicken and avocado. I was, after all, on known territory. Oblivious to my offer, she quickly voiced her displeasure at Patrick's decision to decline the invitation and not attend the celebrations.

"Doesn't he understand that family is important?" she asked rhetorically. It seemed I had been successfully desensitized to what appeared to be a clear breach of protocol, if nothing else. The last time I had seen his niece, Emma, the bride, was at Patrick's house a few weeks back. She and Patrick had retreated to his bedroom.

Patrick insisted I join them to discuss some family issues, away from the nephews and nieces running around the house. While holding me tightly by the waist, seated on the bed facing Emma, I had seen him display his allegiance to what he termed, "the flesh extension of his late brother." Emma was the incarnation, the embodiment of his brother. Patrick had repeatedly said, he was the follower.

"If you need me for anything," he had told Emma with insistence. "I will be there." Now, his absence from this very intimate gathering was beyond strange. It exposed another incoherence that both Valeria and myself had noticed. It reassured me–I wasn't the one to see.

Valeria would prove to be convincing, more convincing than me. Invoking Emma's admiration for him, her unconditional love for an uncle she wanted to be part of her life, Valeria unknowingly pressed on Patrick's weakness. Adulation is something he could not fight, its pull irresistible.

And he arrived, alert, commanding.

Sitting by the table in the dining room, I saw how quickly he zeroed in on me. He walked toward me, barely acknowledging Valeria's obvious desire to speak with him, and kissed me with feigned indifference, making me smile, almost timidly. He promptly sat by my side, lifting my bare leg to place my ankle on his thigh, his fingers firmly wrapped around the contours of my narrow joint. He made this small gesture, as he targeted the other men's gaze on me, almost defying them to look on.

"Have you met Isabelle?" he asked them arrogantly. "My Canadian girlfriend," he stated proudly, taking my hand to place a kiss on my palm. His message was clear. Mine, it said.

I had become a trophy, the kind you add to the top of your cardboard box.

But I was at the top, wasn't I?

I could tell the men's demeanor betrayed their discomfort. They were staring at him, unsmiling, almost fearful. I was reminded of the silence that had ensued as he had walked into the small house. And beyond strength and power, there had been something else.

We left the party at around 11:30 p.m., Jocelyne in his arms, me glued to his waist, his arms unavoidable, his embrace non-negotiable. As we entered the house, he immediately put Jocelyne to sleep and motioned me to head to the shower.

"I will see you in bed," he said angrily, walking to the kitchen, "The food Valeria served tonight was crap. I need to eat something." Vaguely puzzled, I stepped into the shower, recalling how the food that had been served had been impeccably prepared and tasteful.

Let him whine on his own, I thought, hoping his grumpiness would be short lived.

Sliding in beside him under the covers, my body still damp from the shower, I told him about an awkward moment I had spent with Eddy, the groom, at the party. "I don't like him," I told Patrick. "For the first time in my life, I felt scared and physically vulnerable in a social setting. I felt as though I needed protection," I added. "I tried to make small talk with Eddy, before you got there, while you were off paying your workers, but the guy turned weird on me."

I explained to Patrick, that early into the exchange, Eddy had bluntly told me I was asking too many questions. It had completely caught me off guard. At first, I thought he was joking, but then I realized I had committed some sort of transgression. Feeling concerned by his agitated state, I politely extracted myself from the conversation, then moved away from him, feeling violated. As I was sharing my story with Patrick, I could see his eyes had become dilated, his gaze sustaining a firm intent. I had shared with him, seeking his comfort. Strangely, I still felt like I was in danger.

Sunday was spent baking with the children, a heartwarming ritual I had become addicted to. Jocelyne was always so eager to bring her child-size chair to the kitchen counter, Alejandro, pencil and paper in hand, would be ready to document my baking steps.

Imagine, I thought. He could Google all of this, but he chooses to shadow me instead. Me, the promising embodiment of gustative nirvana.

This was the family I wanted.

The night before, as we had entered the house after the party, Patrick had mentioned to me that he had seen Alejandro arriving from New York. When Patrick returned to change his clothing for the party, he had apparently seen him. So, all day I asked Patrick about Alejandro's whereabouts.

"I don't know," had been his only reply. "I have been texting him all day. He must have left early this morning."

Dinner was approaching and still Alejandro was nowhere to be seen. Something was amiss. We proceeded, eating Friday's leftovers without him. I bathed Jocelyne and placed her in front of her computer, to watch her favorite movie, Frozen, again.

Comfortably seated on our bed, the subject of Alejandro's girlfriend came up. Patrick hated her. He hated her skin color, her Dominican roots, her education, everything about her.

"Look," he almost spat out, "black colored grandchildren. Who wants that?" At that very moment, I heard it, the knocking on the window. I stared at Patrick, knowing full well who it was. I got up, fuming, nauseated by Patrick's racist comments, and opened the door. Alejandro, holding a small suitcase, greeted me on the other side, the expression on his face begging for one thing, no drama.

Patrick had followed me to the door, so, as I turned around, I inadvertently pushed him. I headed to the bedroom and waited for him to close the door behind us.

"What the hell, Patrick? Why did you tell me that you had seen Alejandro last night when you obviously hadn't?" I yelled.

"I saw his shoes in front of his bedroom door," he innocently offered.

It took a good two seconds to wrap that explanation around my brain. "You told me you saw him," Patrick. "That you saw him, his body," I firmly stated. Had he seen a fucking ghost? I was asking myself, maddened by my own blindness. "Why lie about that, Patrick?" I asked him, my mind racing. What was the motive? What was his motive? I played all the events leading to this moment. The comment about me and the keys. And then, last night. Had he, in fact, gone and paid his workers, as he had affirmed? I made a quick calculation. And I allowed myself the right to think, this lucid thought I hated to hear bang inside my head, a pounding that could kill. There would have been no time for him to fuck anyone between the time he had left his house and his appearance at the party. So then, why lie? I asked myself.

Patrick thought our argument was futile, but I persisted. He finally had to yield something. He had to admit he had created a story, however trivial.

"So, yes, I lied," he blurted out. "What does it really matter, Isabelle?" he asked, his gaze floating blindly above the stained white carpet. "Whether it is true or false, it has no bearing on your life," he continued, his tone animated. "Why does it really matter to you or to anyone else?"

I listened, flabbergasted, studying him, thinking about his unapologetic rationale. I understood he maybe had lied for the thrill of it, or so he implied. In the unlikely event that his statement was true, how does such aggression possibly integrate with widely held social norms?

Who the fuck lies for nothing but the pure enjoyment of it? I wondered. "Manipulating my reality is fucking with my perceptions and fucking with my perceptions is fucking with my life," I bluntly told him, fuming.

Seated upright, back against the headboard of his bed, his face had transformed into stone. Both his eyes were now squinting. He said nothing.

INHALED

Lying in his bed, with Jocelyne safely sleeping in my arms, I remained troubled by what he had confessed. I felt Patrick come and place a kiss on my cheek. I looked at him, his eyes wide open, searching for reassurance that I would stay, that all was well.

His eyes ... I thought.

My mind's eye now held its own matrix table, where I could correlate each of his facial expressions with a probability of deception. It would take me sometime to realize that this latest data entry could only be indicative of one result. I had been duped.

The lull ended abruptly. How I had rocked myself to our bedtime stories, soothing myself into the illusion of safety. We had each infused our story with our own signature projections. Mine were rooted in sweet and fertile soil, while his were directly linked to Lucifer's garden. Our respective acts, so brilliantly delivered, amazed me.

It was now the middle of April. I had to survive until the end of May, my own personal expiration date. If the relationship was going to end, it would be my choice. He had never left anyone, and he would never leave me, of that I was certain. All the others had left him, their decisions helped along by the lies I helped expose. I had stayed in my quest to test, hope, and pretend. Whatever decision I was going to make, I wanted it to be final. I had repossessed the keys to my house, where he had kept them hidden, in my assigned drawer. No more impromptu visits to my bed at 2:00 a.m.

I fell asleep to the sound of my vibrating phone. I soon awakened though, pulled by the visceral need to check my texts.

The keys, he asked. Where are they?

CHAPTER ELEVEN

I had a lot to do. Alice's graduation ceremony was only three and a half weeks away and the day after that, the movers would be arriving. Our move would be a three-day stint, whereby John, Catherine, Alice and I would momentarily become a unit, once again, before each of us would head back to our respective lives. Catherine to her now husband in South America, Alice to New York, John back to Taiwan, and me to Montreal. I could not help but pause at the sight of our burst family, manifestations of soft shrapnel sent across the planet. What had become of us? As my eyes scanned the chaotic house I was leaving, my throat tightened. There had been so much drama in this synthetic box of a house. So much drama, it was sickening.

Fifteen days had passed since I had left Patrick, yet again. It was time, I thought, seeing the end of May approach, a deadline that was a lifeline. And my feelings had not changed. The emptiness, desire, and cravings I felt were fluidly interchanging places in my mind, my body, and my soul, tucked away somewhere. I knew this familiar road of pain, but that was not making the weaning process easier to manage. I was hoping this time, I would finally pass the test.

I just needed to pass.

I ached to reach the point where I could finally heal from the sickness both John, the origin of the downfall, and Patrick, the symptom of it, had touched me with. Yes, they had both concocted this disease, and only distance could help cure me.

At that moment, what I feared most was Patrick's violent and unwanted intrusion into my life, and even more so, into Alice's life.

Alice's graduation held the promise of a shining moment for him. It was a moment where he would victoriously stand by John, feigning a humble camaraderie between them, while flanked by Alejandro and Jocelyne. Twice, he had asked me to confirm her graduation date and provide him with details of the event. Aware I had obliterated his fantasy, I feared he would show up, uninvited, at Alice's graduation. He had become so territorial of me, projecting his own violent proclivities in an attempt to scare me, to keep me at his heel. I did not trust his judgment, and because of that I had arranged for my private investigators to secure the school premises during the ceremony.

How very normal, I laughed, inside my head.

And now, three and a half weeks had passed since the last time I had seen him, a milestone I had never reached before. Maybe, it was because I knew this time, the time frame had already pointed to a certain breakpoint on his part, maybe because that same point coincided with mine, but I felt it coming.

I sensed him.

My Bluetooth rang at 11:30 p.m. while driving from an evening out in Petersham. On my car screen, it read no caller ID, and I assumed it was my father calling from Montreal.

"Amor, amor," he said. "Do not hang up. I trusted you," he hurried, knowing I could hang up at any second. "Why did you leave?"

"I'm with Alice in the car. I can't talk," I bluntly stated. "Let me call you once I get home in fifteen minutes," I said, as I hung up. I had no intention of calling him back.

When I turned onto my street's cul-de-sac, I saw his Mazda was parked in front of my house.

I stared at Alice's petrified face.

I gave her the house keys and told her to head inside. "It will all be OK," I reassured her. I turned around and saw him step out of his car. I walked toward him, slowly, while he waited. He was wearing that brown leather jacket I hated so much. I made a conscious effort not to look at his face, while I placed my head against his chest. "Why are you making it so difficult for me to leave? Why?" I asked him, stepping back. "Let me go," I pleaded.

"I need you," he said. "I do not want to go back to dating all those girls. It is you I want," he added seriously. "No one else."

Do I sense some honesty in here? I thought. It was as refreshingly manipulative, as it was timely. How much more pathetic can we get? I asked myself. And the feeling of no longer being able to understand what I was sensing.

All in me was a blur.

"We can't work it out," I told him. "I am leaving at the end of next month. It'll be complicated. We can't sustain this. And, I have no trust in you," I specified, motioning to see his phone. He handed it to me, albeit reluctantly, sustaining contact with my eyes.

On his SMS I could see a text from the night before.

I like your skin tone, it said.

Thank you, he had replied.

I can't reprimand him for anything from the last three weeks, can I? I wondered. I looked at his WhatsApp. January 5th, 2017. Katerina Weinstein. Another fucking one, I thought. I want you to show me how to handle a gun, it read. Followed by, I miss you.

Miss you too, was Patrick's reply.

I lifted my head to solicit a response from his eyes. He looked at me with fake innocence.

"The English teacher my sister is using back in Nicaragua," he explained. "She tried to hook me up with her. I am not interested." So swift, so fluid. "I replied out of politeness," he added.

. I took his hand and told him we needed to walk. I ignored the soft drizzle that was now falling on us. As we reached the street lamps, we both stopped to face each other.

"Ven aca," he said, as he pulled me to him. "Your eyes," he said, mesmerized. "Look at you, your paleness."

I let him take my face in his hands. I let him lick both my cheeks. I could hear his breathing. I could feel it land on my lips. I really did not care anymore. I knew I was going to be stuck with him until my moving day. I just feared the pain that would come with it … and Alice.

The house was completely dark when we entered. The dog was gone now, I reminded myself, as I climbed the stairs as quietly as possible. Two weeks earlier, I had driven Jackson to the shelter. Another sad casualty I was now deeply regretting. There would be no room for him in my Montreal apartment, and even if there had been, Jackson would have become a burden to my lifestyle, I shamefully had to admit.

John came to mind. His absence. His delegation of all things made of conscience and lucidity. His lack of concern for me met, me there, in that house now darkened and silenced by my emptiness, with a madman in tow.

How I hate you, I thought, the coward in you, the man– a different mad.

We headed to my bedroom, the original bedroom I had shared with John. He struggled impatiently to find the light switch. I brought my index finger to my mouth, signaling him to keep the noise level down, Alice was asleep and my noisemakers had already been packed.

He was in awe, yet again, as if seeing me for the first time. Always so strange, that feeling of being rediscovered—a magical act I never knew I was performing, to disappear and reappear, albeit unwillingly.

He is now completely here with me, I thought, as I watched him strip down. I too had undressed swiftly. His demeanor had changed. He almost had a loving look about him. His shield, protecting him from the truths I fully had exposed, was now gone.

The main truth, that he would hold onto that night, yet again, as I let him insert himself between my thighs, was the intensity of a feeling I still didn't understand.

Taking in his thrusts, I sensed the wave of pleasure approaching its dropping point, as my feeling of shame was reaching a newfound elevation. Stay the course, I told myself as my mouth was being swallowed. You will win the next round.

The final one.

Yet, again.

In the aftermath of our make-up sessions, I would sometimes have the effervescent feeling that comes with the promise of change. I felt truly invigorated by the presence of Patrick, by my side.

"You are spending the day with me," I told him with enthusiasm. My naivety would never cease to surprise me as I saw him quickly dress and tell me he needed to go back to Alejandro.

What I had kept.

All I had.

The proverbial now.

The past, I had to forget, the future, ignore, to survive my own madness.

"He is alone with Jocelyne. I must go back," he said, obviously feeling the need to specify. "We will leave my car here," I heard him say. "Come with me to Lowell for the day and we will drive back tonight," he insisted. This was more than I had expected.

I opened Alice's bedroom door. I could see she was still asleep. "I will be back tonight," I told her.

"Whatever," was her only reply. The unfolding of her middle finger would have felt more loving. I looked at her, her petite silhouette, covered by the blood stained duvet, its whiteness compromised by the reveal of John's betrayal. Traces that would have to go, the visible ones. I closed the door behind me, numbed by her pain, distraught by the flash back.

Any yet, I went.

Let's go, I told him.

On the way back to Lowell, Patrick and I stopped to buy a pack of Poland Springs water bottles, the only kind he drank. I had tried to explain to him how the water in those bottles had been rated as one of the worst among all the water brands. It seemed his stomach was allergic to all, but Poland Springs water.

"Nothing else will do, Babe, nothing else," was always his response.

At the counter of the 7-Eleven convenience store, where we had purchased the water, a few girls had been standing behind us in line.

"Did you see how they were looking at me?" he asked, with a smile, as we returned to the vehicle.

Looking at him, I was struck by the magnetism he knew he exuded. His deep awareness of it, was itself a weapon. Reviewing the scene inside my head, I remembered the link to an article he had sent me the year before. It explained how women perceived a man's desirability, how the number of women gravitating around him would help garner a certain capital of attraction.

Yes, I thought, he was a temptation laced with shiny barbs.

Our talk in the car had been light. I described to him the sumptuous dinner my friends had prepared the previous night, describing in minutia, how everything had been executed.

"Oh," he said nonchalantly. "It's your car I must have crossed on my way to your house, yesterday."

"But it was only 3:30 p.m.," I told him. "You were parked at my house at 11:30 p.m.," I continued, slowly understanding, he had spent most of his day trying to find me.

"Yes, Baby, I went to your house three times yesterday," he confessed.

Stunned by that revelation, I was unable to articulate a reply.

I barely heard him whisper to himself, "Yes, I needed you to return to me."

I parked my car near the side door of his house. He got out first, seemingly in a rush to meet Jocelyne, who was waiting for him at the top of the stairs. When she realized I was also there, she extended both arms to me, as she vigorously tried to wiggle out of his embrace. It had been two weeks since I had unfairly removed myself from her life without warning. As he brought Jocelyne over to me and put her into my arms, I caught his look. His eyes had shrunk to two little beads directed at me. He was brimming with jealousy, obviously disconcerted by the outpouring of love Jocelyne was giving me. I ignored his glance. I was tightly embracing Jocelyne, who was now glued to my shoulders.

"I missed you so much, Isabelle," her little mouth breathed down my neck. Caressing her hair, I then lifted her up to my eye level and kissed her cheek.

"I missed you, too, baby girl," I said, feeling my heart melt. From the corner of my eye, I could see Patrick, still on the porch, observing the scene with obvious contempt. He failed to understand his daughter's love for me. He saw her as a direct threat to the place he held in my life.

Then we all heard it, the plea in her voice.

"Please Isabelle, don't leave me again."

CHAPTER TWELVE

"Music down," he ordered, his eyes closed. I turned to him, stiffened by the demand, keeping an eye on the road, so I would not miss the exit sign. I did not say a word.

I did as I was told.

The bouncy demeanor I had had throughout the day had now been diluted by a good dose of disenchantment.

We slowly walked up the stairs. Thankfully, Alice was already in bed sleeping, unaware of our presence in the house.

He headed immediately to the bathroom, eager to shower first, insisting I follow him. As he stepped out of the shower, I decided to stay a little longer, suddenly feeling the need to relax on my own, away from his presence. When I reentered the bedroom, Patrick was already in bed, discontent on his face. He was staring into a void, unblinking, but focused. I chose to ignore his demeanor, as I slid in beside him.

In the morning, after he left, I pulled open the drawer of my night table. I then understood what had upset him. During my two week hiatus from our relationship, I had started to believe that Patrick could pose a danger to me. Ever since I could remember, I had always kept a metal baseball bat hidden under my bed for protection. But, it had suddenly felt inadequate, insufficient, leaving me no choice but to turn to my famous Japanese knife. What was it that upset him most? I wondered. Was it the knife, or the title of the book it had been placed on? My laughter surprised me. The fact he had kept it to himself as we were making love was, in itself, astounding. The sight of a weapon, placed on a book entitled, Setting Yourself Free from a Psychopath, would have killed my desire to fuck.

Kill. No pun intended, I mused.

I had resigned myself to spend as much time with Patrick as I possibly could. I vacillated between what I wanted to see, and what was, and capitulating, I had chosen to delve into the experience. A new form of blindness. Since, John and Catherine were here for Alice's graduation and to help with the move, I had the freedom to fully be in Patrick's life. Patrick had asked me to stay with him, while John was in Northampton. He feared John's jealousy would turn violent. John, however, had never shown exaggerated manifestations of jealousy. Clearly, Patrick was projecting onto John his own predisposition toward jealous rage.

I pretended to go along with Patrick's twisted view of John's capacity to hurt me. I smiled at the irony of the situation. It was John's presence in Northampton that had secured my place in Patrick's home. And, mostly, always had.

I was scheduled to spend ten consecutive days with Patrick. It was a luxury, really, considering we had spent the last 15 months seeing each other once or twice a week. I calculated it took 1,945 hours of driving to make those encounters possible. Excluding the occasional long weekend, we had spent approximately 350 hours together during that time period. My math skills had always been approximate, but I knew this much, our relationship's rate of return was a deficit… in every way.

Our mornings in Lowell began at 6:00 a.m., with Patrick sitting on the edge of the bed, phone in hand, coordinating the day's work with his employees. He would then shower and groom to the sound of Latin music coming out of his phone, followed by a breakfast of hot chocolate and a Hawaiian sweet roll, his favorite.

Before leaving for the day, he would come back to our room and hand me a cup of tea. It was his love potion, star anise and cinnamon formed an olfactory trigger cable of creating amnesia-like symptoms in me. He would then kiss me on the cheek and I would lie in bed for another hour or so.

"See you later, Baby," I would hear.

Following his departure, I would leisurely roam the house and prepare meals, while listening to my music. I felt carefree. I felt alive.

And, sometimes, yet again, in these moments I chose to squeeze, I believed it would last forever.

We would have dinner around 7:30 p.m. each night, always preceded by the dreadful Grace. Force feeding was also part of the table's dynamic. "Eat," he would order. "More," each time.

Following dinner we would habitually go to the Home Depot store. His lack of planning meant we regularly had to run to that store to get construction material. I once made the mistake of refusing to accompany him on one of those trips. Alejandro had then stepped in, making it clear to me that I should go and to not question his father. His eyes had conveyed the essence of his message, you will not win. So I went. And there in Home Depot, a simulacrum of Latino-land, I would quickly be reminded of my trophy-like attributes.

It was apparent the Latino hardware store was the place to show off your shining property. Firmly grabbing my waist as we walked through the aisles, he would unavoidably immobilize me, pivot my face toward his and plant his tongue inside my mouth for all to see. See him with me. There, amidst the nails, the Gyproc, the tools ... there ... I was priceless.

Jocelyne joined us on the weekends, attracting the cousins who lived three houses down. They would liven up the house with the music of the family I was aching for. Fully aware of the compensatory nature of my attraction to the vibrancy of the Latino family values, I surfed its rare occurrence in my life, suspecting its wave would soon find a shore, that it would die there on the edge of the harsh gravel beach Lowell had been.

Leisurely activities were non-existent, except for some television, usually watched in Spanish.

"Time to put on my Spanish brain," I would say, making him laugh. His laughter at this joke was always curious to me, as his brain seemed devoid of humor, and my little joke, clearly not that funny. My attempts at introducing him to television shows such as, The Tonight Show or The Late

Late Show with Stephen Colbert, became failed missions. His reaction to American culture was always so visceral. It was difficult not to see how he despised the country he had chosen as his home.

The one activity I ached for was the one that opened the gate to his mind and body. It was bait in its purest form. He would initiate it by calling out my name, in a low voice my ears had been trained to listen for.

Then, I would wait for his uncompromising, "Ven acá."

Wherever I was in the house, I would drop everything I was doing and make my way swiftly to him, aware of his eyes detailing my silhouette. The ritual was hypnotic. I would sit beside him and proceed to execute the foot massage.

"Clamp, Baby, clamp," were my orders, and I would execute them diligently. Like food, massage was a currency, a currency whose value was stable. I, therefore, applied myself.

During those ten days, everything flowed in our bedroom. Trust had taken root in both our minds and our bodies, I thought. His back, the usual forbidden area, had now become accessible. Patrick would allow my fingers to stray everywhere across his back, letting me feel the texture of his scars, their varying fringes, their distinct depths. I was now permitted to confirm their existence, and acknowledge the damages the Iraq war had left on his otherwise perfect body. Inside those walls, the dialogue was strong, while fusing would feel as though we had entered a new plane, a new universe, a universe we were co-creating. Every so often he would ask me if this was real, if I truly loved him. I remembered then, a year before, when comfortably lying against me, my arms resting around his chest, watching television, he had asked me a strange question. His head slightly tilted, he had asked me if I really loved him. The insecurities had been real, but their manifestation fleeting. Unexpectedly, now, they had reemerged, joining us in the bedroom.

"Will you really marry me?" he asked, his eyes welded to mine, the tone so hesitant and frightened, even I saw and heard his concerns. I was always astonished by the depth from which his insecurities appeared to stem. If he only knew how authenticity could help him obtain what he so wished, how owning his vulnerabilities would crush his impetus to lie and make-believe. From his perspective, the clothes did make the man.

I had remained silent.

John wanted to meet with me to discuss elements of our separation, another subject of discord I needed to address with Patrick. But, it would have to be managed my way. As he lay on top of me, slowly moving in and out, he told me that no woman of his should maintain any form of contact with her ex-partner. I had to be swift and apply the manipulative techniques he had taught me so well. I told him I had no choice because the meeting had to do with our assets.

"John's family's sailboat is stored at Marble Head harbor, so John and I have to meet there to assess whatever needs to be assessed," I had told him. The story had sprouted in my brain with such ease, my words flowing, my voice finely tuned, my body language the embodiment of coherence. I had amazed myself. I was fully understanding, again, the intoxicating sensation deception provided its master.

Simultaneously, Patrick had reintroduced the topic of Alice's graduation, pushing for more information, wanting me to confirm his presence, and his children's presence, at the event. I did not want him there. It was not his place. I knew he did not belong, but, I could not tell him my real intentions, not now. It would ruin everything.

"You should direct your attention to Alejandro's graduation," I pointed out to him with a smile.

I showered, put on a dress, and applied makeup. As I was about to leave the bedroom, he took hold of my arm and firmly placed his hand between my legs, visibly bothered by the lacy underwear he was feeling.

"This is mine," he told me. "Mine." Immobilizing me, he opened a drawer and pulled out a pair of boxer shorts. "Put these on," he commanded.

I looked at him, amused. Disbelieving my own obedience, I playfully obliged. I was secretly savoring the peculiarity of the moment. I had placed Patrick on a well-chiseled precarious edge, a small nudge, combined with some drama, which was his essential nutrient, was all it would take. I opened the side door of his house, and stepped out onto the balcony, taking a moment to close my eyes. The air was warm, the breeze gentle.

Who would have thought revenge would have such soothing properties? I mused.

Another one full of promises.

Massachusetts had been my home now for twenty months. I had fallen in love with its towns, its valleys, but mostly, its coast. Places like Provincetown, Brewster, Gloucester, Manchester-by-the-sea, and Salem had seduced me. Marble Head, located not far from Lowell, presented itself as far more than just a destination, it held the promise of a pinnacle to the reckless, albeit mindful, journey I had now undertaken.

Sailing the east coast was something John and I had wanted to do for a long time. John had taught sailing, but had failed to pass his passion on to either Catherine or Alice. I, on the other hand, loved to sail. Thus, Marblehead had been chosen with intent. For John, I can only assume it was to charm his way back into my heart. Creating momentary illusions of a possible reconciliation was the only card left for me to use. I needed to secure my financial future.

Many of the weekends in February and March had been spent with Jocelyne. We had visited wintery beaches and drank hot chocolate. Alice had declined all opportunities to travel the coast with me, blaming her studies and homework load. And Patrick, well, Patrick never had the time. Jocelyne, with her thirst for stimulation and eagerness to explore, had made for a surprisingly pleasant companion.

"I'll miss her," I realized, driving through Salem to this new destination. The sadness was sudden and acute. Alice would soon graduate, my Visa would expire, and I would be returning to Montreal. My New England travels were coming to a hiatus.

A haze-like curtain seemed to spur from the asphalt's hotness. Through this curtain, Marblehead harbor revealed itself. It was beautiful. Somehow I was making some sort of reconnection. A piece of myself was here.

And it felt good.

INHALED

"I have something delicate to tell you," Patrick softly mentioned during his call. I had extracted myself from John's neediness at 4:30 p.m. Now, I was stuck in traffic on my way back to Lowell.

"What is it?" I hesitantly asked.

"My father died today," he suddenly let out.

I gasped.

That morning, as I prepared to leave for Marble Head, I noticed he had documents and passport photos scattered around a yellow legal-sized envelope on the dining room table. Earlier that same morning, we had indulged in making love, for a good hour. And as we had, he berated me about what my proper conduct with John should be, unconcerned, I could now see, by the death of his father, a man he spoke of often, in kind and loving terms. Concentrated on the road and lost in the morning's sequence of events, I barely reacted to what he was now demanding of me. "You are not to go back to Northampton while I am away," he said, ending our phone discussion.

Okay, I thought, here we go again.

The night air still felt warm and dry on my skin. This type of summer night made me feel lucky to be alive. But Patrick was there, beside me in the car, putting a damper on the moment. He asked me to turn off the music, asked me to slow down, told me which lane to drive in. I simply replied that it was my car and that I was the one driving him to Logan airport.

He sat in silence, sulking. "A sign of disrespect for the dead," he let out.

Shut up, I heard myself think. How about some respect for the living?

I parked the car in front of the airport's JetBlue doors and stepped out to kiss him goodbye. The voyeur in me was alert. I loved to observe him, the rawness of him, accessible now in his weakened emotional state. His eyes were always giving him away, betraying his true nature. They were telling me he was in pain. And, I shamelessly loved it.

Lightness surrounded Alejandro and me on the ride back home. A feeling of freedom filled the car, as we listened to the blaring music. Now Wednesday, I had forgotten his graduation was only three days away.

"I am so sorry your father can't make it," I told him, having overheard Patrick's return ticket to Boston was for Sunday morning. He looked at me, smiled, and said nothing. I was noticing him for the very first time, I realized. His strong hands, soft eyes, and muscular stature were all very striking.

How many times had Patrick brought him into our minds while making love, trying to weave my desire for his son? I suddenly noticed Patrick's fantasies had sanitized themselves. There was no more making love in Alejandro's room, there were no more stories of Alejandro masturbating with my underwear, which had now stopped disappearing.

I was remembering the last time, in February, for my birthday, when he had surprised me with a prop from Alejandro's room. While making love, during a long kiss, he had stealthily slipped a piece of cloth between our mouths. The smell of it had prompted me to immediately open my eyes. He then pinned me to the mattress and forced me to lick what was, to my horror, Alejandro's soiled underwear. His fingers, handcuffing my wrists together above my head, had immobilized me, leaving me to close my mouth as my only form of resistance. I was able to eventually escape his grip and rolled myself to the floor.

"Are you fucking nuts?" I had told him, breathlessly. "What is wrong with you?" I had yelled, in disbelief. "Leave the house," I had told him, disgusted by his incestuous inclinations. "You ever pull something like this again, I will denounce you," I slipped between my teeth.

I never did. But I knew that someday soon, not too far from where I stood, inside the moral turmoil I was feeding, I would, in a way, make things right.

For everyone.

Walking into my sinner's house, me, the object of Patrick's desire, with his son, Alejandro in tow, I could not help but wonder—would atonement be sufficient to support my path forward?

Patrick's absence was filling the house with joy. Lisa, Alejandro's girlfriend was staying over until Patrick's return. Despising everything about her, Patrick would never have permitted it. Alejandro, trained to follow his father's rules, tastes, and desires strictly obeyed him. He, therefore, would invite Lisa over only when he deemed it safe for her to be there. For the next three days, she and I would play house together.

Staring at the summer lamp I had bought for us at Marshall's the week before, I realized that, while trying to fool him into thinking I was electing to live with him, maybe I was fooling myself, too. All was a mess inside my head. And our interaction, my part in it, as I helped Patrick fold and pack his suitcase, had brought a feeling of added proximity to him. We were both dancing the dance. I believed his steps and he believed mine.

Lying on his side of the bed, I replayed the afternoon's short call in my head. He had called me as I was rushing out of the hair salon to meet with Alejandro and Lisa. Alejandro needed to buy a new shirt for his graduation and he had asked both Lisa and me to meet him in Boston. I had not heard from Patrick since his departure, two days prior, and had not expected him to call.

"I can hardly hear you," I said with a smile, listening to the children screaming in his background. He was calling from his sister's house, where the family was gathering after the burial ceremony.

"I want to change my life around," he yelled over the noise. "I want a new life. And you are part of that life, Isabelle." I stood there, phone in hand, in the middle of a parking lot, wondering how many epiphanies one individual could have in a lifetime.

From the surface of my sleep, I heard Alejandro open the door and leave the house, early in the morning. I knew some new construction project had to be coordinated, and that Patrick had instructed Alejandro to go to Nashua, but I was not sure if that was where he was going. Today was Saturday, his graduation day, I suddenly remembered.

What's my role going to be? What's expected of me? I asked myself, slipping into a semi-relaxed state, oblivious to the voices that had emerged from the back door.

"Hi, Baby," I suddenly heard. "I'm back," he said, placing a kiss on my lips. I turned to him, took his face in my hands and looked at him, happy. I had suspected it all along, but, had preferred not to create any expectations for myself. I was thrilled. Alejandro had kept the surprise a secret, proving he could be an accomplice to his father's good as well as bad deeds.

The day was beautiful, almost reminiscent of a crisp fall day, with clear skies and sun rays infusing the cold air with the right mixture of heat. The house was alive with pre-graduation preparations. Lisa was preparing lunch, Alejandro was finishing some work in the backyard, Patrick was dispatching work to the three workers lined up on the outside balcony and I was ironing the green dress I had chosen to wear for the occasion.

Jocelyne would not be part of the graduation festivities until the evening, when we would gather at Louis's, Patrick's brother's house. We were all set to fully celebrate Alejandro's day.

We walked hand in hand toward the tent, which was filled to capacity. Once seated, Patrick introduced me to his ex-wife, Desiree, for the first time. Short and stocky, with reddish dyed hair, she still presented a surprising air of poise and elegance. But, her face had surprised me. She had an unappealing overbite, a large nose, and a wandering left eye, that was challenging not to fixate on.

From the series of women I had been able to retrace, I could not understand what each had brought to him, besides the proverbial fucks he so craved. He valued beauty in its absolute form and none of them had displayed a sense of aesthetics that conformed to his standards.

That morning while putting on my makeup, I stared at myself in the mirror. I was tall, slender, with a beauty that had not yet started to fade. My eyes had remained strikingly green, my mouth had kept its fullness, its cupid bow intact, my nose was fine, my face, framed by curly auburn hair, was porcelain white. I was the total sum of the physical attributes he so wanted, yet, his past choices had revealed a penchant for the common, the vulgar, and the unrefined.

Still, I wasn't enough.

The oddness of Desiree's behavior had been obvious to me from the moment of our first contact. Her eyes, unable to focus on me, purposefully looked away. I was Patrick's novia and even though she had been divorced from him now for seven years, I could sense her palpable discomfort at seeing me. Of course, we could not rely on Patrick's awareness to help us navigate the uncomfortable moment. Instead of easing me into this new phase of our lives, he took his phone out from his inner jacket pocket, brought me tightly to his right and Desiree to his left. My jaw was crooked from the fake smile I produced, while she just plainly would not look at the camera. By placing the devious man in the middle of the Picasso girls, you had the oddest selfie ever taken.

"We have already celebrated Alejandro's graduation," he told me, with a stern look on his face. "And there is work. Much work to be done tomorrow," he added with obvious irritation. Doting, loving, caring Desiree was a sweet caricature of a Latina mother. She had hugged her boy, Alejandro, throughout the day, her eyes, brimming with an outpouring of unconditional love, Alejandro never leaving her sight. I sensed the jealousy, the envy, surfacing in Patrick, as he felt too much attention had been directed on his son, and not enough on him.

Patrick had paid for the lunch buffet and now cake was being served at Desiree's hotel room. The barbeque at his brother's house was yet to come. All the attention on Alejandro and everyone else, threatened Patrick's sense of self-importance. What was overkill from Patrick's perspective, was deemed necessary by Desiree.

Changing for the barbeque, I removed my green silk dress and jumped into a pair of jeans.

"Come on," I told him with a smile, as I placed my black wool poncho over my head. "Jocelyne is here, it'll be fun. Let's go," I insisted, animated by the need to socialize.

This was my third family event with Patrick. The familiar awkwardness hit me the instant I entered the asphalt backyard. Again, I noticed a shift in the ambience, the moment Patrick would enter a room. It was not respect. It was something else. Patrick would stiffen, while the others would salute him politely and then literally turn their backs to him. Unfortunately, whatever resentment he inspired was simultaneously transferred to me.

Throughout the rest of the week, I let myself soak in all the minute details of our lives together. There was tenderness, complicity, and shared silences, burdened by a fear I was certain we both felt. It was the fear of an unavoidable, painful farewell. I was aware of the space we had carved out for ourselves together. Those moments had been carefully sought out. I had wholeheartedly plunged myself into every second of the experience of living with him. On my way back to Northampton, I was questioning my true motives for prolonging the inevitable. There was so much fog clogging my mind. The steps of our conjugal dance seemed, and mostly felt, real. I wondered, did we each improvise out of spontaneity, or choreograph to deceive?

I arrived home in time to prepare for Alice's graduation, but I felt so far away from where I actually stood. I wanted to go back to Lowell and be with Patrick. It had been devastating to see his face when, the night before, I had informed him he could not attend Alice's graduation.

"John asked me to choose between you or him," I had lied. "He clearly stated that if you attended Alice's graduation, he wouldn't show up." He had looked at me, hardly able to hide his disappointment.

Alice's day, in contrast to Alejandro's, was cold and rainy. The feeling within me that morning, one filled with both, pride, at her, at myself, and shame—the shame that had polluted my way into this moment, the finality of it.

I wanted to drive to her school, since it would be the last time I would make the trip. For two full school years, I had been the parent who had driven sixty miles each day, with her by my side. I had been deprived of my family and friends, I had been preyed upon, I had endured so much. It was my right. I had earned the privilege to drive the last segment of our adventure, to guide the family on the roads that had woven themselves into my life, giving meaning to my existence. But John had decided otherwise and I had no energy to argue. He was, once again, showcasing his ineptitude at reading my needs.

Amidst the cascade of texts I received from Patrick throughout the day, I was still attentive to Alice's triumphant moment. My sense of purpose had finally been awakened, stoked from its ashes. This day had been the target all along, I reminded myself. My final destination had arrived, my mission had been accomplished. The only problem being, along the way, my sense of self had imploded.

CHAPTER THIRTEEN

Four days remained before I would leave the United States, and only two of them could be spent with Patrick. Yet, those two days I was able to spare for him were replete with intensity. The house was full, but I ached for intimacy and tranquility, hungry only for his arms. My last day in Lowell, while Alejandro was folding clothes and his girlfriend Lisa was playing in the living room with Jocelyne, Patrick, who was washing dishes, announced we were all going to the movie theatre. I wanted to stay home. I was resting on the couch, feeling physically exhausted and emotionally empty.

"The movers are arriving tomorrow morning," I told him, pleading for understanding. "I need my strength." Placing the last dish on the rack, he then brought me to his bedroom, closed the door behind him and knelt before me as he lifted up my skirt and pulled down my panties. There I was, standing up, looking down, watching his jaw motion slowly. He placed his finger inside me, not too far up, just enough to touch the right spot. He then added his tongue to the play, as he pushed my back onto the bed, my legs willingly parted. His tongue, wet and languorous, was moving slowly. He plunged completely into me with a newfound greed for almost thrty minutes. I loved the way he made me feel, but I was unable to let go, unable to release, so I faked it, wanting to put an end to his performance. Unaware, he lifted his head, presenting a mouth dropping with traces of me, satisfied by his accomplishment.

His eyes, unrecognizable, had become piercing. They had again transformed themselves into almond shaped slits, devoid of light. The portrait was there for me to see. A hyena staring at me would have been more comforting. The movie was showing at 10:30 p.m., and despite my numerous protests, I let myself be dragged along. Midway into the movie, I sensed it coming with dread, an oncoming urinary tract infection.

Fuck. Again, I thought. But this time, the pain was different. It was more difficult to ignore, prompting me to get up to go to the bathroom. As I emptied my bladder, the familiar smell filled my nostrils, confirming the presence of a serious infection. I slid back into my seat and informed him casually of my problem, hoping it would register with him at some level.

As we were walking toward the truck, he decided to take pictures of Jocelyne with the new handbag I had given her that afternoon. It was past midnight, and she was exhausted, so she was resisting. Patrick, oblivious to her needs, insisted she pose, smiling. He was demanding she perform as he wished.

Heartbroken, I witnessed the disrespect and lack of understanding he had for Jocelyne. He had thrown a cloak of invisibility over his daughter. How I had missed it, God only knows. But it was there, displayed for any caring soul to see. In front of us, complete terror, residing in her eyes.

Seated with Patrick in the back of the red Dodge Ram, as Alejandro was driving, I could not wait to get to bed. It was 12:45 a.m. and I needed to be in Northampton by 10:30 a.m. Patrick suddenly decided we should stop to get some food at the local Latino cantina.

Is he doing this on purpose? I wondered. I stared at him in disbelief. "All of us are tired," I risked as we stepped out of the car. So what, he said. And I thought, yes, so what, so what if I slip outside of myself, one more time, one last time. And I let him take my hand, let him lead me across the street to get to the eatery. Grabbing my bum, squeezing it firmly, he looked at me with pride. "Mine," he said.

I tried to smile back. "Take advantage of it while you can," I jokingly said.

INHALED

Slowing down our pace, as if entering a new dimension, I overheard him say softly, "Do not say that. Do not allude to that possibility."

But, it was the truth, I was thinking. I was leaving.

Once home, in disbelief, I saw Alejandro and Lisa set the table. It was 1:30 a.m. and I did not want to eat. I had been wanting to sleep since 5:00 p.m., and I was sick.

Feeling the need to establish his dominance, he sat me down on the chair, filled my plate and proceeded to feed me in front of the kids. The kids were now staring at me, fearing my reaction. As if this showdown was not sufficiently satisfying his appetite for control, he sat me down on his lap and brought a fork, filled with pieces of gel-like animal parts, to my mouth. I turned my face away abruptly and decided to leave the table. I had had enough.

With my teeth brushed and my body washed, I was the first one in bed. I had taken my daily dose of medications, including my usual antibiotic. I was hoping the latter would clear my infection and wishing the former would aid my sleep.

I felt myself falling into a comfortable sleep, when Patrick woke me up, predictably so. Hovering over me, I met his gaze. The softness it held was beyond anything I had seen him deploy before. I knew he wanted this moment to be special, as much as I did. But I dreaded what was waiting for me. He gently inserted himself, but the pain was too great. It was the first time I had refused intercourse with him. How timely.

"You don't want to make love to me?" he asked, completely taken by surprise, his look a pained one.

"I can't." I replied disconcerted by my refusal. In my mind, there was so many different ways I could have answered him that would have been more satisfying to him. My rejection was too blunt. Of course, he should have understood, showed empathy, cared. But this was Patrick, a subhuman, who sometimes resurfaced into the uncomfortable world inhabited by the vulnerable. He put on his boxers, slipped on a white T-shirt, and turned his back to me.

The silence, so uncomfortable and heavy, was looming over us, carrying with it a truth we both needed to face. But, denial has a way of seeping into one's mind like a parasite feeding on its clueless prey. We had plans, plans I had hidden from friends and family. I was going to move back to Montreal and settle into a rented apartment for one year, to establish my residency. This would, in turn, allow me to go back into the United States without any difficulty. John had arranged for me to travel to Asia in September to obtain my divorce. I would be free to get married in November. This was the plan I had repeated to Patrick each time he had questioned our future. And so, I strategically left a few items of clothing in the closet he had assigned me. Leaving clothes behind was the only way to stage the certainty of my return, securing myself an option. I needed to manage his perceptions without closing any doors.

I left the jeans, the shirts, the dresses, and the bathrobe in the bathroom and bedroom closet space Patrick had reserved for me, to quiet Patrick's insecurities, and to allow me to dream about the future. Still, he showed concern about the true possibility of my return.

"Leave me your Bulgari ring and necklace," he said, asking for some sort of safety deposit for my return.

"No," I bluntly refused. "Will you give me the rosary that belonged to your mother?" I asked with feigned defiance.

"No," he replied with equal bluntness.

Confusion, I had discovered for the first time, was a powerful tool.

I was all packed. Jocelyne was still in bed sleeping, Alejandro was studying at his desk and Lisa was reading on Alejandro's bed. I felt feverish, sleep deprived and overwhelmed with anxiety. I gingerly walked to Jocelyne's bedroom and kissed her on her forehead. "I love you," I whispered to her, feeling a tide rising in my eyes. How I will miss her, I thought. I then walked past Alejandro's room, smiled and waved to the both of them, unable to do more.

Patrick was silently washing the dishes, looking out the window. I placed my arms around his waist, laid my head on his back and let the tears run, freely. This was goodbye. But, goodbye to what? Of that, I was still unsure.

"Those who do not show their tears are the ones who suffer the most," he told me simply, motionlessly.

Maybe, I thought.

I left his house by the side door, overnight bag in tow. I did not know if and when I would come back. The pain I felt was unbelievably crushing, but for now I needed to regroup.

The movers are in Northampton, John had just texted, reminding me this was going to be my last drive from Lowell to Northampton. I would never again travel the now familiar road that had led me to this twisted relationship ... to him ...on a January night... seventeen months before.

When I arrived back in Northampton, the moving truck was parked in front of the house. I walked in, not acknowledging anyone. I changed my clothes and simply started packing with the workers. Distraction was my only panacea.

John was staying behind with Catherine to finalize the move. I literally had to be out of the country before midnight. It was the 30th of May, the date of my departure.

Finally.

Brattleboro, North Walpole, Claremont, Charlestown, Williamstown, Berlin and Montpelier were all unavoidable buoys that ironically marked the way back home. Those towns had been the stage of our sex frolics, where, away from our obligations, we had simply been allowed to be ourselves. I had forgotten about them, as it had seemed so long ago, so far away. I looked back in my rearview mirror and silently kissed each of them goodbye, knowing I would never return. I was aware I was leaving so much more of myself, here in New England, than I had ever intended. But alas, ahead, awaiting me, was my hometown.

PART FOUR

CHAPTER ONE

Entering our new home, Alice and I both felt a wave of relief. Finding this place to rent had not been easy. It was a large three bedroom apartment, beautifully located in the center of Montreal. Old, but with Victorian charm, it had immediately felt like home.

We quickly absorbed the city's energy, reacquainting ourselves with our visceral desire to fuse with its vibrancy. There was dancing for Alice, and plays, concerts, and restaurants for me. We nicely slid back into our old town. Like two, dried raisins plumped up by a Sauternes, or some other sweet wine, we came back to life—our lives.

The intensity of my final moments with Patrick had transformed me. I became hopeful. I was intoxicated by the possibility of establishing a life with him on the east coast, seduced by the thought of simply existing alongside a man whose differences had profoundly impacted my sense of self. Amidst the commotion surrounding my return to Montreal, I made the decision to commit to Patrick and to own that decision fully. I missed him, I missed his home, I missed the funkiness of it all. I would not hide the truth anymore, not from myself, not from the others. My goal was to complete the move as swiftly as possible.

What did that make of me?

To want him still?

Yet again, after everything?

In April, I had committed to a two week trip to Spain to visit Cecil. That trip was now three weeks away. Alice and I would be leaving on the 22nd of June to celebrate Canada's 150th anniversary with Cecil. She would be hosting a VIP event in Spain, and she wanted Alice and I to attend. I had not informed Patrick of my travel plans before moving, as I knew he would have disagreed. I had been manipulated many times, but the independent woman in me was still very much alive, or at least, awakening, once again. He would have to accept it as a non-negotiable part of our summer plans.

The extended time apart had infused some brightness and levity into my relationship with Patrick. However, the phone calls, video calls, and texts I was receiving at all times of the day had increased 20-fold. As much as I loved to see and talk to him, I caught myself wanting to ignore any sounds coming from my phone. His excesses burdened my days and nights, paralyzing me, impacting my quality of sleep, as he demanded I answer at all times. Moreover, it interfered with my social life.

Exasperated, one Saturday night, I decided to completely disregard his calls. What I wished for was to spend my evening alone, enjoying my new surroundings, reading in bed.

Book in hand, I stared at my phone, as it kept buzzing, non-stop. The texts then started to cascade. They were accusatory in nature, all of them. I picked up after thirty-two calls. Of course, I did not tell him the truth. My story was plausible though. I told him that while walking in the city, with my phone in my purse, I had not heard its rings nor felt its vibrations, and that I had then spent my evening with my friend, Simone. Whatever story I told him would not have mattered anyway. He would only stick to his version of the truth, that I was spending time with another man. Somehow I managed to reassure him.

"Always have your phone with you. That is all I ask of you, Isabelle," he finally asked sternly.

I repeated his words in my head, as I brushed my teeth. I could notice the fatigue being reflected back at me, as I stared in the mirror. I was discouraged, thinking my night would be another sleepless one. I felt tormented, both by the hurt of wanting him there with me, and by the hurt of being misunderstood. To hurt, I was bitterly reminded, was his intention.

I had experienced night sweats, ever since I could remember, but this was unusual, different. The sweaty film I felt on my back, around my arms and behind my neck felt thick, viscous in texture. I am drowning, I told myself, as I got up to get a glass of water. I felt the urge to moisten my pasty mouth and rehydrate my body. It was 8:30 a.m. I got back under the covers, hoping to fall back into a more restful sleep, but my phone caught my attention.

Fucking phone, I thought.

There were seventy-two WhatsApp calls.

On my way to Simone's I called him back. "Hey," I said with a forced cheery voice.

"Isabelle, why can't you pick up when I call?" he immediately asked. I could not answer, yet again, that I had not heard the phone. I could not say that it was absurd for him to expect me to answer my phone, while I was sleeping—even though that was the obvious truth, I had been sleeping. My voice was strange to my own ears. It was soft, and filled with disbelief and fear. The tone of my voice was a plea for him to listen to reason. But changing my tone, I was now realizing, would only send a signal that his primitive brain would be unable to decode.

"You are going to Simone's house," he said, repeating to himself, in a distant voice. "Call me from there," he said, as he hung up.

I walked into Simone's house, a haven of peace, quieting my nerves, diluting the hypervigilant feeling I carried with me. Everyone there was busy working in the backyard. Her son, the eldest, was raking the yard, her daughter was vacuuming the bottom of the pool, her husband was cleaning the barbeque. Simone was preparing lunch. The music was blaring in the background. She smiled at me. I had entered a sane space, a safe place, a place where no one would feed off of me.

How foreign all this has become to me, I thought, sadly. There is peacefulness and tranquility here. What a rarity.

"Hey Patrick," I said, looking into the camera, as I sat at the edge of the pool with my legs in the water. His demeanor had now changed completely. He was smiling warmly, visibly happy to see me.

"I feel secure when you are with Simone," he told me. It reassured me, which was the intended effect, I assumed. I walked around Simone's property, phone in hand and I introduced him to her son, her daughter, and her husband. I was following through with my intention of integrating him into my life. If anyone was to be introduced to him, surely, it had to be Simone.

"Hello," she told him casually, studying the Latino face appearing on the screen. Simone knew almost everything about my story with this creature. She had been a respectful sounding board, always reminding me to trust myself, just as Charlie had said. But I knew that in truth, they both had held their breath, and still did.

"It is an honor to finally meet you," he said. "Isabelle has spoken so much about you," he continued with his thick Spanish accent.

"Me, too," she replied, smiling. "When are you coming to Montreal?" she asked, now taking advantage of his presence here with us. "Come on over and we will host a pool party for both you and Isabelle," she laughingly offered.

I looked at her, touched. She was playing the game, out of her own volition. And when she did, I felt some form of validation take root inside of my wants. Simone's demeanor reassured me into thinking there was a possibility.

But I should have remembered that she and I were of the same make. That, she too, like me, could be fooled.

"Now," she said, as she turned to me, "this is normal."

I looked into her eyes. Yes, I thought, reminding myself of the seventy-two WhatsApp calls I had received. The new normal, I decided.

I am so happy that you are part of my life, I read as I drove back home from Simone's. *I love you, I love you, I love you.*

I love you too, I wrote back.

CHAPTER TWO

We had talked about him visiting me in Montreal before my trip to Spain. We had compared and discussed airplane ticket prices, train schedules, and bus routes on numerous occasions. It was, therefore, a surprise to hear him say he was no longer sure about his plans to see me. Blaming labor shortages, new deadlines and Alejandro's unexpected trip to New York, he told me he could not promise anything. Our conversation then became entangled with a slew of issues that had been festering in his brain, since my departure. One issue, of course, was the fact that we had not made love that last night in Lowell. Then, there was the fact that he saw me as the fish that had swam back to its ocean.

"I don't like the thought of you returning to a life filled with friends, when I have no one in Lowell," he had confessed, unaware of the anger that had infiltrated his admission.

I stopped listening, and I stopped hearing, as my stomach tightened. I had been in this position so often before, and I knew something was amiss. Too many highs, too many lows, had touched my time with him. I needed consistency. I wanted to flee, understanding this was yet another opportunity for me to let him go and to regain pieces of my dignity I had scattered all over New England and now Montreal. I had to end his machinations and inject the right amount of fuel into the fire he had started. And so, I indulged the role he had laid out for me since the inception of our relationship, that of the victim.

Do not come, I texted him. We are done.

Each time I had left him, I felt elation settling in. A sense of self resurfaced. And then, nothing. Again, I felt myself falling into the hell of unattended cravings.

I was set to leave for Spain in two days. I tried as best I could to keep my mind focused on my travel preparations. The challenge was real. I felt procrastination setting in, knowing Alice was observing me attentively. She, too, had been here so many times with me. How long would I hold this time, I could hear her ask in her mind. How long before her mother would give in again.

Amidst the emotional chaos I was drenched in, John finally agreed to a discussion concerning my financial future. I had been pushing for a meeting for so long, wanting to alleviate my fears and regain control over my entire life.

We met at a small park beside my apartment building. John's demeanor was soft, his tone affable, his carefully chosen words soothing. I was holding my breath, literally. We both sat down on the only park bench available.

"So, Isabelle," he ventured. "I am proposing 100,000 dollars per year for twenty years, plus forty percent of our company." Not expecting his proposition to be so fair, I started to cry, relieved. I could instantly see images of a promising future forming in my mind. We looked at each other, my eyes full of gratitude. His eyes held a different story.

He was pleading for something. More time. Another chance. A final attempt. Suddenly, I was understanding the possibility that his perceived kindness could be rooted in a ploy to get me back. Unsure of his true intentions and quite certain of mine, I got up, explaining my need to start packing. I did not want to be accused of manipulating him. I wanted him to understand that we were done.

Also… I thought, Patrick in mind.

INHALED

I hugged him, thanked him for his apparent fairness, and walked away, aware of his eyes on me.

I had gotten rid of Patrick, I had gotten rid of John, and my financial future was more certain. For a moment, the pressure on my chest was released. My breathing had resumed its normal rhythm.

I remembered then, that Simone and I were to attend a Red Hot Chili Pepper concert at the Bell Centre that night. My life had successfully exited its sharpest curve. It was now time to celebrate.

I woke up the following morning around 8:30 a.m. to the sound of Alice and Elizabeth, Simone's daughter. The girls had spent the night at our apartment and were now getting ready to leave for La Ronde, a Six Flags theme park. The mood was a cheerful one as the girls were both maniacs for roller coasters. Like me, I thought.

Dressed in my pajamas, coffee in hand, I kissed and hugged them goodbye. I stared at my suitcase, open and empty on my bedroom floor, acknowledging the mess around me. I knew Cecil's social calendar for us would be full, and it was unlike me to improvise my wardrobe, but I decided to postpone my packing.

Heading to the living room, computer in hand, the doorbell rang. Ten minutes out the door, the girls must have realized they had forgotten something.

There were three units in my building. Mine was accessible through the front entrance door. Guests had to ring the bell to be let in and climb a set of stairs before arriving at my apartment door. No camera or intercom had been installed in my apartment, so I had no opportunity to check the identity of the person at the door. I had to go down and open the front door myself.

Feeling lazy, I pressed on the buzzer, waiting at the threshold, and expecting to see Alice's silhouette appear.

"Baby, Baby," he said, "what happened?" His signature phrase. His signature question. He knew, very well, what had happened. It was futile for me to argue when my chemical relief was standing in front of me, at the threshold of my apartment. My restraint was weak, if not absent. He lifted me up and carried me to the kitchen, placing me on the counter, abruptly parting my legs. Holding my face firmly with his left hand, he unzipped his pants and let himself in.

The rhythm was familiar, and easy at first, only to pick up just before we both came. As his mouth pressed on mine, he lifted me up higher, holding me tightly, only to let me glide back to the ground, a ground I so longed to feel.

Lying in my bed, to the sound of him showering, I stared at the ceiling in disbelief. I was aware of the sedative effect his presence had on me. The efforts he had deployed to be with me, had induced in me, an amnesia-like state. Again. He had left Lowell at 3:00 a.m. and had driven five hours to me.

It has to be out of love, I thought.

The day was like no other. It had a dream-like quality. He accompanied me to my doctor's appointment, as I needed to have my urine tested, yet again, for a urinary tract infection. Exhausted, I placed my head on his shoulder, while we were in the waiting room.

Using his hand to press the side of my head to his, feeling the stroke of his fingers brush along my temples, I heard his voice, "I love this," he said. "I love our closeness."

"Yes," I said. "Yes, I know."

Later, walking through the streets of Montreal, with Patrick by my side, was exhilarating. To have him with me, wandering my streets, was surreal. How trivial choices and innocuous behaviors could now become entrenched with such deep meaning, was disconcerting to feel.

Back at my apartment we decided on dinner plans. He wanted meat, so I was taking him to an Argentinian restaurant near my apartment. Preparing ourselves for the evening, I let him help me choose a dress. This was something I had learned to appreciate about him. His clothing taste was surprisingly educated. How could a poor Nicaraguan punk like him have known the difference in textile quality or garment tailoring? Each time I had asked myself this question, images of rich women assaulted my mind, nauseating me.

So much of his past remained opaque, I reminded myself, while looking at the outfit he had chosen for me. Stories of his life in Nicaragua, of his training in the army, of his time spent in Spain, in Iraq, were all punctuated by gaps I had been unable to fill, even with the help of the private investigators I had hired.

Hand-in-hand at times, while tightly and uncomfortably held to his hip the rest of the time, we walked through the park toward the restaurant.

"This thing about trust," he casually started articulating. "It has to go away. What do I have to do to put your mind at ease?" he asked with tired eyes. I looked at him, stopping in the middle of the sidewalk.

"Everything," I told him. "Everything."

Approaching the door of the restaurant, we slowly realized it seemed totally dark and devoid of any activity.

"The restaurant burned down six months ago," one passerby yelled from the other side of the street.

OK, I thought, so the restaurant I chose no longer exists. I called for an Uber ride and decided on a famous steak house, Moishe's, a Montreal institution.

Arriving at our new destination, Patrick walked me up the stairs, led me to our table, and pulled out my chair. He decided on our order, then proceeded to lift up my leg and place it over his, a gesture so deliciously inappropriate and inebriating. "You are mine," he said, as he pulled my chair even closer to his own. "And you are, you are so, so beautiful, Isabelle," he whispered, as he licked my cheek.

And I wiggled out of his embrace, something I had never done.

Our Uber trip back to my apartment was filled with a new type of quiet. The driver, a Haitian engineer turned Uber driver, who, like so many others, had immigrated to Montreal, was observing us with a smile. My leg had again been propped up above Patrick's, exposing me quite indecently. As Patrick looked out the car window, moving his hand along my thigh, he parted my underwear and moved his fingers in and out with circling motions. My sexual stoicism surprised me. Observing him absorb the city life before him was enthralling, his stillness, so enticing. I had never spent a whole day with him before. Everything about his calmness was unexampled.

"So much French-speaking around here," he said, almost dreamily. My spontaneous laugh sliced the seriousness he had imposed on the moment. "Anyone can get by living in Montreal, just by speaking English," I reassured him.

He turned his head back to the window, his eyes narrowing, betraying an overactive mind. "French. Jocelyne will learn French," he whispered.

We entered the apartment, making sure not to wake up Alice, as it was now midnight.

"You are staying the night?" I asked tentatively as we were heading to the shower.

"I can't, Baby," he said. "My workers are waiting for me to prepare their day. I need to be in Manchester for 7:30 a.m.," he added.

I felt the withdrawal symptoms already seeping through my veins.

"I will need to leave at 2:30 a.m.," he firmly stated, stepping in the shower with me.

My iPhone alarm rang while he was already pulling up his jeans. The bags under his eyes, more prominent than before, seemed to have become a permanent feature of his angular visage.

Our tempo is killing him, as well, I thought.

I got up and threw my black cashmere bathrobe over my shoulders. I headed to the kitchen to grab an apple, two granola bars, and a bottle of water. I placed them all in his bag.

We slowly walked down the stairs to the front door. Outside, the neighborhood was unanimated. The sky was only lit by a few street lamps. The air was of a summery warmth, filled with a wetness I loved to feel, there on my skin. I walked him to his car, which was parked by the side of my building. My heart had diluted itself. It had lost its center. I wrapped my arms around him, unable to talk. I felt he had already left me, and left Montreal.

It was now 3:00 a.m., and I slid back into bed, toying momentarily with the idea of showering. I decided against it, preferring to let my skin absorb all of it, leftovers of him.

CHAPTER THREE

The ride to the airport was silent. So, too, was our flight to Paris. I could not bear Alice's interrogating eyes. No, they're not interrogating, I thought, they're demanding—demanding I choose.

"Him or me?" she let out with spite as we were waiting for our connecting flight.

As arrogance was my default way of being, I looked straight at her and firmly stated the person I would choose was going to be me, and only me.

"Cousin, cousin," I heard as we were walking down the corridor of the exit gate. There, I saw Cecil, waiting for us, all smiles. Her daughter, Chloe, surprised us from behind the door where she had been hiding. It created a commotion around us, startling all the passengers who had just deplaned. The enthusiasm emanating from this greeting was unsettling. It reawakened my long, lost feeling of joy—joy that, for so long now, had been numbed by restraint and mistrust. I fell into her arms, grateful for the laughter that would come to heal me and push me forward.

Constants, give me constants, I was praying. I need stability.

Inside the vehicle, we all started chatting and catching up on the latest happenings in our lives. I was relieved to see Alice smile. There would be space here for us to start working through the last twenty months of our lives. I knew we had a long way to go. But here, it could start.

Cecil's house was a large, three-story, Spanish colonial-style mansion. Its main entry was on the third floor. Entering, to the left, was a long corridor that led to three large bedrooms, two of which would be occupied by Cecil and me. To the right, was a large spiral staircase leading to the second floor. With its wrought iron railing and mahogany wood ramp, the staircase towered elegantly over the premises. The second floor housed the sprawling living room, kitchen, two more bedrooms, and a large outdoor dining area. The girls would be sleeping on that level. Everywhere you looked, marble greeted you. The hidden side staircase from the kitchen led to the first floor, a playground for gamers. It featured an in-ground swimming pool surrounded by luscious orange and pink Bougainvillea vines and a mango tree. I had entered paradise.

    I headed to the kitchen for a soothing chamomile tea, and there, while talking with the cook, I realized I had forgotten to check in with Patrick. In truth, I had purposefully chosen not to call him, wanting to create space between us, wishing this trip to yield the change of pace I needed to restore myself. I still called with dread, expecting the usual reproaches, the sermons, the inquisitions. Unexpectedly, the call was a short one, peppered by my own brand of sweetness meant to be bitter. How I could fake a fatigued voice, when I felt so alive, impressed me.

    The first week of our two week stay in Spain centered around Canada's 150th anniversary celebration. Cecil and her team had been preparing for the event for a year now. It was the main reason Alice and I were here. It was a great pretext to reunite four girls, aching to have fun.

    Cecil was visibly stressed, but we still managed to squeeze in a few activities, a fundraiser for single women held in an art gallery, a United States Independence Day celebration, a conference for women and leadership, where Cecil was the guest of honor, and a guided tour of the city.

    My connection to Patrick remained relatively fluid, the time difference seemingly unproblematic. My strategy with Cecil was the same as with Simone. I included Patrick in my conversations and when I video called, I made sure everyone in the room saw him and had the opportunity to speak with him. I wanted to see what my relationship could become when guided by healthy reflexes. I was following my plan.

INHALED

The days leading to the Canada Day celebrations somehow became laced with more calls from Patrick, both during the day and at night. He was now calling me in the middle of my sleep, every night, concerned about my whereabouts, my activities, and the new acquaintances I was making. I had usually interpreted this type of behavior as feelings he was projecting onto me. So, having now been triggered by Patrick's behavior, suspicions of infidelities filled my mind. I wished they would not poison my stay in Spain. Is he actually seeing someone else and worried that I'm behaving the same way? I wondered. It seemed unlikely. He video called me from his bedroom every night, and those calls could sometimes last two hours. I was seeing clearly, yet again, that his deeply rooted insecurities, fueled by his fears of abandonment had to be at the heart of his dysfunctional behavior.

I hoped.

The Canada Day celebrations had arrived, bringing with it an effervescent feeling, both Alice and I enjoyed tremendously. Throughout the extravaganza, I was able to video call Patrick, often, happy to be able to integrate him into my glamorous evening. Together, we listened to Cecil's speech, appreciating her poise, her stateswoman's presence on the stage, heard the band's renditions of Latin classics, and saw the Cirque du Soleil clowns perform their magic.

I wished Patrick would acknowledge my efforts to include him, and that my transparency would quiet his concerns. But, I had provoked the opposite. Following the event, he tightened his grip on me, randomly calling me twenty times a day, constricting my space, suffocating me, embarrassing me. I needed to remove the weight that had landed on my chest, again. If I could not do it for me, I had to do it for Alice, who was becoming increasingly agitated around me and my phone.

Desperate to regain a feeling of freedom, I put my phone on airplane mode and went about my day, occasionally checking my Facebook page. I had carved myself the space I needed to breathe properly, to be there in Spain with Cecil, Chloe, and Alice. I had strayed away from my master, and for that I knew there would be a price to play. I had lied to him. I told him I had suffered from food poisoning, following an outing to a local restaurant.

He had seen my Facebook page though, noting I had responded to a few of the posts that had appeared on my feed. He had become unhinged. I did not care. In fact, I enjoyed seeing him in pain, I enjoyed the fact he had become unhinged.

How many times had he led me into that horrible space? I thought.

I knew he was extremely busy with work. And, I knew his only concern at that point in time, was me, his polished plaything. I have him where I want him, in that in-between space, where uncertainty eats you alive and monopolizes your mind, I thought. The illusion of control, how intoxicating.

Our return to Montreal was only three days away. That night we attended a private dinner party held at the German Ambassador's house. Informal in nature, the evening had been quite intimate. The Ambassador to Germany was there with his gay partner, as well as the head of the UNICEF mission to El Salvador. The conversation was intellectually stimulating and instructive, the mood was light and jovial. Cecil, who loved anything Celine Dion, was controlling the flow of music, amusing us all with her unconditional admiration for the singer, who, coincidently, had been born at the same hospital as her, in Charlemagne, twenty miles north of Montreal.

I had placed my phone inside my purse, having decided not to put it on the table like the others had done. I had quite rapidly dismissed the thought of a video call with Patrick among these diplomats.

Who can blame me? I wondered.

While stepping into the limousine, I retrieved my phone from my purse. I was taking my place between Alice and Cecil, leaving Chloe to sit in front with the driver. Amidst the laughter, I looked at my screen and gasped. The number of calls received, showing on my screen whipped me back to my reality. I had received, in the span of one hour, eighty calls, all from Patrick. A heat wave hit my face, triggering an instant migraine.

Eight. Eighty fucking calls, I thought. There, stilled in the middle of the back seat, between Alice and Cecil, fear finally emerged.

INHALED

The WhatsApp call with him lasted two hours. It was two hours of brutal interrogation, where my answers were either deemed incomplete, unbelievable, or not worthy of being acknowledged. The torture was in the repetitive nature of his questions. He was asking the same, barely reformulated, mind-numbing questions, seeking answers that would never satisfy him. He knew I had put away my phone. He knew I had purposefully kept him from being part of my evening. I was guilty of everything of which I was being accused.

"Yes, I purposely kept my phone put away," I said. I wanted privacy, I thought.

But his latest concern made me question my own intelligence.

"Are you hiding me, Isabelle?" he asked.

I looked at him, tired. "Am I hiding you, Patrick? Yes, I am. And, when I am with you, it is me who is hiding behind you." We are a big disappearing act gone wrong because each time, we return, I thought.

The remaining two days in Spain, two days where he harassed me, his question, the same, relentless, Can I pick you up at the airport?

I did not want him to be there, fearing Alice's response, so I declined. Even though I missed him more than I wanted to admit, I was also exhausted from my stay in Spain. I needed to rest. Patrick visiting me in Montreal would be annoying, more than anything. Walking out of the Montreal-Trudeau airport to catch a taxi, I secretly, albeit momentarily, wished he had not listened to me. He never did. But curiously, this time, he had obeyed.

Stale reminders of our last night together welcomed me home. In my bathroom, there were towels lying on the floor, underwear half-hanging from the laundry basket and traces of his last passage. Exhausted, I set my bags down, quickly undressed, showered with the same speed as I had undressed, and slipped into my bed.

The following morning, on our video call, I noticed a change in his demeanor. The strangeness of his attitude concerned me. It was as if, all of sudden, his desire to see me had become manageable, very manageable. I felt my fears and my anxieties return. My throat tightened and my breathing became shallow. I had wanted to travel to Lowell to surprise him, but I feared the American customs agents would deny me entry, or worse. Alice would be attending New York University at the end of August. I just could not risk getting barred from entering the United States.

CHAPTER FOUR

An acute fatigue had taken hold of my body. Over the years, I had developed an intimate relation with pain and brutal tiredness, but this was deeper. I was rendered inert by systemic aching, and a continuously throbbing head.

I knew I was the architect of this construct that was now my life. Moreover, we had artfully co-created his image. My contribution to this fallacy was immense. I saw what I wanted to see, projecting my own goodness onto a hollowed shell. He, on the other hand, convincingly pretended to be someone he was not. It had become very clear to me, that without an us, there would be no him.

Still, I remained, as we continued to perform a chemistry experiment gone rogue.

Since my return from Spain, I had found myself lying in bed, unable to fall asleep, day or night, despite the heavy medication I was taking. Patrick's voice, low, vibrant, and commanding, was always ringing inside my head: I want to melt inside you, to swallow you entirely. I want a transfusion of your blood. I want to fuck you until death do us part. Until you are left like a ragged doll, spent, lifeless. That is what he wanted. He had told me so many times.

Unsurprisingly, one week after my return, I had another one of those dreams. It was so horrifying, I woke up in tears, heaving. In my dream, I had been decapitated. I was then playing with my head, like a soccer ball, at the bottom of a set of stairs in an empty white room. At the top of the stairs, Patrick, headless as well, was holding his own head, directing his eyes at me.

Seated on my bed, I was debating its meaning, pounding my fists against my chest. It was as if I had fed upon myself for so long, digging into my flesh, creating pockets of emptiness. There, in my bed, I was frightened by the state I was in. I was so weak I wondered if that was how death crept up on you. We had choreographed our own dance, a folie à deux, that was killing me. Obsession was not a state I could sustain forever. I had to leave … and soon.

Seated at the kitchen island, I reread my email, the light in the kitchen blinding me, as were my tears. I plowed through the moment. I had no choice. I had explained my dream to Patrick, my reasons for letting him go, and pleading for him to do the same. My hesitation was short-lived. I quickly pressed send and instantly felt both relief and euphoric sadness. I had been there countless other times, the pain each time so raw, deeply carving a stitch-resistant wound.

How many lesions can I sustain? I wondered.

I shared with Alice, again, convinced this time, I would hold and stay the course. She saw my resolve, I know she did. But she knew, we both did, that nothing was really over.

"I told him you hate him," I shared, with a tentative smile. "He is so focused on winning both Catherine's and your heart, he so wishes to be the head of this family," I added. "This should kill him."

She replied nothing, staring at me, unable to hide her skepticism. Because, there was nothing else to do, but wait.

Each time I had left him, I had turned to the internet for relief, seeking anything related to the subject of sociopaths or narcissists. I needed for my logical brain to step up and lead my heart. I had suspected Patrick was plagued with an incurable state of malignant narcissism, but I also fought that possibility, choosing to blame the machista culture he had been raised in to explain his misdemeanors.

INHALED

Sprawled on my daybed at 5:00 p.m., listening to Robert Hare discuss psychopathic character traits, I heard the doorbell ring. It had been four days since I had sent my email, and blocked him. Since I had left him.

He had returned.

I pressed the pause button on my computer, got up and buzzed the front entrance door open. I saw the back of his head first, then his face, as he had turned toward me. He must have come directly from work. His jeans were stained with the usual white paint, just as his hands appeared to be. My first reaction was to close the door, but I was not quick enough. He managed to let himself in. The expression on his face was one I knew so well, interrogating eyes, arched brows, mouth half-opened. It was a plea, another one, for me to come back.

I should have called the police. I should have left the premises. I should have done something other than let him in.

I should have at least varied the fucking scenarios.

I walked along the corridor leading to the kitchen, with him in tow. There, as I leaned against the counter, I explained the basic elements of our failing relationship, again. Our distance, our lack of trust, his sexual fantasies involving his son, his fixation on a threesome, his controlling behaviors, his numerous betrayals, my hurt.

The list was nothing new.

I felt in control this time. In contrast to my usual hypnotic-state during these reconciliation attempts, I felt a newfound tangible awareness. He, on the other hand, ignored my discourse. Instead, he told me he had tried to reach me. His sister-in-law had come to his house looking for me the day before, mistaking a neighbor's car for mine. He said he had asked her to call me, and that she had left me a voicemail.

"I love you," he said. "I do not want anyone else other than you," he added.

"Get some younger girl," I told him, pushing his chest away from mine.

But he firmly held onto my waist.

He was inescapable.

"We can make this work," he said, as he kissed my lips firmly, while grasping the nape of my neck. I was his kitten, it seemed, again. His efforts to win me back were so seductive, they nullified my so-called awareness.

"Alice is about to arrive," I told him, "so, let's be quick."

And we made love, yet again, meeting as if it was the first time. Like two girls skipping rope, we jumped out of our jeans and hopped into bed, our naked bodies meeting easily. Like usual, the release took hold of our intimacy, paved the way to a silence we barely knew how to interpret. And I felt it, that slip into a void. Then the doorbell rang, startling us both. There was no time to shower. My blouse would have to absorb the thick liquid dripping down my back. I let Alice in and retreated to my bedroom. I needed to hide him.

To hide all of it.

I needed to hide me.

Patrick and I opted for a restaurant we had both enjoyed the last time he had visited me. Hand-in-hand, we walked to Café Gentiles on Ste. Catherine Street, Patrick twirling, lifting, and turning me around as if we were part of a Fred Astaire production.

My mind was wandering. How many times, had he described parts of his life with acute detachment, analyzing his intrigue with unapologetic and strange pride? What has he scripted for the suspenseful story that our lives had become? More importantly, does he know the movie's ending, may escape him? That he may be unable to prevent its unavoidable conclusion?

Curiously, during our meal, my father called, asking me if I had an American address I could give him, so he could order a car part he wanted to buy online. I started to laugh, immediately struck by the synchronicity of the moment. I suggested, Patrick, a car mechanic, could take a look at my father's issue.

"OK, Dad. I will be there in an hour," I told him, happy that someone, other than Alice, would finally meet Patrick.

The encounter was fascinating for me to observe. Patrick replaced his hesitation with a will to impress. I saw him slip into character. His stance became firmer, his shoulders looked broader, his eyes became more sniper-like. He had grounded and intensified his presence. I could have sworn he had grown taller. Their handshake, a contest, a test, an inquiry of intentions, was epic. Their gigantic hands had firmly taken hold of each other's, as if welded by the seriousness of the moment, not wanting to let go until one understood the other's place in my life. Patrick, appearing to be surprised by my father's own charismatic presence, rapidly introduced himself as Benjamin. Patrick had been left behind, seemingly unworthy of the encounter.

My father was a man whose affability and humor had always helped him create instantaneous rapport with anyone he encountered. There with Patrick, my dad was charming. He poured the three of us his favorite rum, a Costa Rican bottle he had been saving for over a year.

Over the course of my time living in Massachusetts, I had shared with my father some information on my Latino's philandering ways. So, while the heat of the liquid spread to our throats and chest, my father, started to tease him, with kindness.

"So, Ben?" he asked Patrick, with blunt playfulness. "How many girlfriends do you have?"

Used to my father's twisted sense of humor, I was unfazed by the audacity of his question. I burst with laughter, unaware of Patrick's own reaction. Veils of seriousness falling on his face, his squirming body, were all cues I refused to acknowledge. This was part of our past, not our present, nor or future.

My father's concern was genuine, but the happiness I was obviously showing seemed to reassure him. So, too, did Patrick's loving demeanor. My father, like Simone and Cecil before, had been successfully seduced by Patrick's charms.

"He really seems to love you," my dad told me as we kissed goodbye.

I looked at my father and thought, yes, he does. In his movie, I am the love of his life.

Still wet from the shower, we dove under the covers, silently anticipating our lovemaking. This time, it was infused with tenderness and gratefulness for the evening we had spent together.

"I will buy your father a new phone," he started to share as we moved together, into one another. "Your father is using an old Blackberry. I will get him a new phone," he continued, kissing me deeper than usual. His typical roughness was transformed into tactile whispers, absorbed by our skins. The surrender was total. My men had liked each other, they had blessed me with renewed hope.

"It feels like I am making love to you for the very first time," he told me, softly. "Like we have just met."

I studied his face. His surprise was sincere, I could tell. The intensity of his declaration should have flattered me, it should have reassured me. But it didn't. I started to wonder, is the reason it feels so genuine simply because, being away from me he forgot my features? Is he unable to recall the contours of my body, the uniqueness of me? While these questions arising in my mind disturbed me, I let myself go and sink into him, hoping our sleep, however short, would provide me with clarity.

"I have to go. It's 2:30," I heard him say in my ear. I could barely move, I could barely open my eyes. How I hated mornings.

"I love you," I said sleepily. He kissed me and left quietly, cautious not to wake Alice.

Before falling back to sleep, I opened my eyes and saw he had left his rosary on my night table. I grabbed the wooden string of beads and rolled them around my hand. They had been impregnated with a mixture of his signature colognes, Chanel Blue and Mont-Blanc. I breathed them in, slowly. Fragments of him were embedded into each bead. I clenched the artifact to my chest and fell into a sleepless dream.

I reached Valeria, Patrick's sister-in-law, by phone the next day.

She was unaware of Patrick's visit to Montreal. She was unaware and quite surprised, actually. Patrick had shared with her that I had blocked him. "Isabelle doesn't pick her phone up when I call," he had complained, reducing our fundamental issues to a symptom.

"I told him that you are a reputable woman, an independent woman who needs to be treated with respect. I told him you are not his secretary," she said, recalling the conversation.

She went on to explain that Patrick had asked her to call me. But then, after displaying a lot of nervousness, changed his mind. This behavior startled her. And, the fact that it startled her, and startled me. It was out of character for Patrick, according to her, to show so much emotion for a woman.

"Wow," she had exclaimed to him, "you really love her." And, he had acquiesced.

"Love, true love, is rare," she had told him. "You might not find another opportunity like this in your lifetime." So many sudden truisms, surfacing in a world, regularly plagued by deception. But, I took the bait. Moved by Valeria's version, I started to believe—yes, I know, again.

Patrick and I were now in constant contact.

"Sleep with the phone close to you," he was still demanding.

And I obeyed.

Never had we been so close, never had I felt so relevant in his life. And yet, I felt irrelevant in mine and irrelevant to everything that surrounded me.

Alice.

We spoke every night while he drove home from work, our conversations filled with life projects and promises of a future waiting for me on the coast of New England.

"I hope you will come visit me and Isabelle in our new house," he had said over Bluetooth, to a friend of mine who was with me in the car. But, somehow mistrust reemerged. I suddenly imagined him talking to me as he was driving to see another woman, imagining him sending me another love song to quiet my concerns, artfully creating a deceptive moment. I tried to shake the images out of my head, but I could not. Paranoia had set in.

I needed distractions, so a week after Patrick's visit, Alice and I decided to have dinner at my father's apartment. Although my father had not seen Alice in a year and was tremendously happy to see her, he was visibly concerned for me. The contrast I offered from the week before was sharp. My paleness and thinness had now become visible, the deadness in my eyes unavoidable to see.

I had recently sinned. I had purposely left my phone on the bedroom floor, dreading its touch, its sound, its command. Part of me had wanted to flee his pull, but part of me wanted to tease him also, to provoke his controlling nature, to seek, in such immaturity, a false sense of love.

For such an elusive consolation prize, I would pay a price.

Telling him I had forgotten my phone, a half-truth this time, did not hold anymore, if it ever had. The texts he sent showed his agitated mind, as they hardly made sense. They were French Google translations of accusations. They were devoid of meaning, but aimed to make me feel guilty and incompetent.

The words were the words of a man held hostage by delirium.

The fatigue I felt was overwhelming, it seemed to slow every second of my day to a halt. I was sweating profusely, which was drying my mouth and imparting my breath with a repulsive, fetid smell. My heart, on a race to nowhere, was pounding inside my chest. It was the only thing left to remind me I was still alive. I had been unable to leave my apartment, or even my bed, since returning from my father's place, five days earlier. Something had to be done.

Disregarding the cracks in my body and the depression that was clearly setting in, I called Patrick and told him to anticipate my arrival in Boston within the next twenty-four hours. My fear of further compromising my immigration status had acted as a breaking mechanism. But now, I rationalized, it was better to test the waters by flying into Boston, before actually crossing the border with Alice, and risk being denied entry then.

I had to end the tortuous uncertainty I had imposed on my life. This play had to come to an end. I had to orchestrate a last verification.

Thoughts of our plans now flooded my brain. Discussions on his brown leather couch, as I massaged his feet, of my impending divorce. Our marriage. The growth of his company. Living arrangements for all our children. The temporary reorganization of the house until we purchased our new house by the sea.

INHALED

The indecisiveness that was polluting my brain had to be removed, and fast. I had to know more before committing to him and foregoing a life I could so easily return to. I had to carve momentum.

He, at first, displayed a reassuring exuberance, when I told him about my impromptu visit. And then, as if the information had pressed on a different set of neurons, he retracted and told me that, overwhelmed by work, he might not be able to dedicate as much time to us as he wished, and that it would be preferable for me to arrive on Friday. Since it was now Monday, the familiar feeling of mistrust was reemerging, nesting itself on my chest, straining my insides. My reaction seemed to please him. He must have heard the plea in my voice that fueled his moment. I chose to retreat and agreed to postpone my arrival to Friday.

The days leading up to my departure should have been filled with excitement. Instead, the familiar and delicious rush I usually felt was absent. It was replaced with an immeasurable level of fatigue that accompanied me wherever I went. There was so much I had to do to before I could safely cross the border. I needed to obtain my lease and all other relevant documents that would establish my Canadian residency and facilitate my entry into the United States. The process was exhausting. As I stood in line to obtain my health insurance card, I almost fainted. Set to leave the next day, I did not know how I would be able to sustain the five hour drive to Lowell.

Initially, my plan had been to fly to Boston. Showing a return ticket to the customs agent at the airport would have helped guarantee my entry, soothing my nerves. I changed my mind because it was costly. But now, waiting in my car at the Vermont-Quebec border, I wished I had bought the expensive ticket. Refusing me entry would deny me access to the truth I was so eager to expose. As I rolled down my window to face the smiling agent in the booth, my inside turmoil was obliterated by a convincing emotional lockdown.

I would be in Lowell, with Patrick, in four hours.

The scene I saw when I got to Patrick's house was puzzling, but not surprising. It took me a few seconds to decode the drama that was unfolding. Patrick, arms crossed, was standing beside Alejandro. They were both leaning against the side of the house, silently observing the police, who were having a discussion with someone who appeared to be the new second-floor tenant, Humberto. Having successfully gotten Araceli to move out, again, it seemed Patrick was having issues with rent payment

I got out of my car, leaving my overnight bag in the trunk and walked toward them slowly, with obvious curiosity. Alejandro timidly smiled at me, while Patrick's expression remained stoic. As he quickly kissed me, I smelled the nervousness on his breath, the putrefied odor I had so often detected each time we argued. Moreover, his usually perfectly tuned body odor had transformed itself into a sickening perfume. I was repulsed … at first. I watched and listened to Patrick explain his side of the story to the Latino officer. I, again, felt part of an intimate safari where preying on the predator allowed the illusion of safety to seep into my mind. The content of their conversation brought me back to reality. Patrick asked the officers to help him retrieve the rent money.

I turned to him and quickly tried to explain the obvious, the police were there because there was a physical altercation between him and his tenant, that it was a criminal matter, not a civil one. I made eye contact with both the Latino and the ginger-haired policeman. Looking at me, their eyes hinted at the same question, converging to one main point, lady, what are you doing here with this man?

I returned to my car, which was parked across the street, to retrieve my belongings. When I walked back to the house, Alejandro met me halfway to help me with my bags, while Patrick was still talking outside with the two officers.

Scanning the inside of the house, as it had been almost two months since I had last been there, something caught my attention. I saw his phone. His phone was on the dining room table—unlocked.

I must have stared at it a good thirty seconds, alternating my gaze between Patrick standing on the porch and the phone lying there in front of me. The temptation, the pull, was so hard to fight as I contemplated my chance to snoop.

Am I afraid? Or, is it guilt I feel? I wondered. My hesitation cost me. Patrick entered the house with his employee in tow. I had wasted my chance. When the worker left, Patrick came and sat beside me on the living room couch, with feigned indifference. He grabbed me by the waist, avoiding my eyes, bringing me toward him, my back to his chest. He gently turned my face and cemented his lips onto mine, knowing far too well I would easily succumb. Unfortunately, the kiss was cut short by his impulse to turn me around, his urge to take me from behind. The sudden change of pace unsettled me. I ached for softness. I had missed him, and my day had been a long one.

Too tired to resist his demand, I obeyed, placing my hands on top of the couch, facing the window and letting him perform the rest. With one hand he unzipped my jeans and pulled them down. With his other hand, he slid his own jeans down. His insertion into me was mechanical, as was the rest of the loveless act.

"Thank you," he said, as he arrogantly lathered my back with his milk. "I needed the release." Indifference could be contagious, because at that particular moment in time, I felt nothing.

I needed to go to the CVS Pharmacy, and evidently, this was deemed suspicious. He was questioning my motives and I did not feel like answering him—to him—more precisely. His need to control my whereabouts in such a trivial matter rendered me silent. Imagining the pharmacy as a dating rendezvous location, which is what he was obviously doing, was utterly ridiculous.

Insisting I needed some hair conditioner, when, in truth, I needed a refill of sleeping pills, I walked steadfastly toward the door.

"You can buy your conditioner at the Stop and Shop," he stated, with unconvincing nonchalance.

I turned to him, exasperated by his need to control, unwilling to confide in him my real reason for going to the pharmacy. I knew he sneaked into my medication bag regularly and I hated it. He had never acknowledged, nor understood my health issues. Moreover, my use of medications would most likely be held against me at some point. How I hated him then, and myself even more, for removing any hope of a restful sleep.

On our way back from the Stop and Shop, we decided to buy some fruit at his Latin food market. Whether he was entering my world, or I was entering his, it would feel surreal to me, maybe even to him. The incongruity of our relationship, impossible to ignore, would compel all the Latino patrons and employees to look at us. The Latina employees would observe Patrick with a mix of prudence, restraint, and curiosity. They must know him, I was thinking to myself, no one escapes his field.

We picked mangoes, tomatoes, and avocados with care, savvy even. How those little things had become the heart of his seduction, charming his way into my heart; worming his way into my mind. It was true, wasn't it? The devil is in the details, after all. Disguised by the aura of the numbing magic he applied to my senses, he was there for all to witness.

We were back in the kitchen, our stage, where our dance as a couple came into form, where our relevancies momentarily converged. Food, would always remain one of the main bonds tying us together, of that I was sure. We unpacked our bags and started to prepare a typical Nicaraguan menu.

While the crispy rice, I loved so much, was cooking and the salmon was poaching, I concentrated on mincing the coriander. He scrutinized the way I handled the chef's knife. He had seen me perform this gesture often, however, he seemed surprised each time.

Aware of his eyes on me, I managed to keep my hand steady, but I suddenly felt faint. Beads of cold sweat were now forming on my forehead, at the back of my neck, and even percolating between my shoulder blades. I placed the minced coriander on the side of my chef's knife. "Here," I told him, presenting the knife, "I'm done."

He stared at me, oblivious to the girl decomposing in front of him.

Still silent, eyes half-closed, I watched him lower his eyelids, and I listened to his vapid wishes. I had come back to the stage. I was again part of a scene marked by austerity, judgment, and dogma. Plowing through our dinner with a newfound detachment, I had repeated my performance, removing myself from his godless table, shielding myself from his graceless rendition of Grace. Again, I had pretended to pray, while instead, withdrawing from the falsity of the moment.

Jocelyne walked through the kitchen and the dining room, stopping at the living room threshold. The last time I had seen her was on a WhatsApp video call, following her plea to Patrick to speak with me.

Wide-eyed, a small timid smile forming on her thin lips, she observed me massaging Patrick's feet. Her eyes squinted, just like her father's, but her look was filled with pure adoration and visible relief. She slowly walked to him, understanding he had to be acknowledged first. She kissed him uninterestedly, only to come and nestle comfortably into my arms. I looked at her, caressing her head, playing with her ponytail.

"I missed you, girl," I lovingly said, feeling our complicity, our understanding.

She looked at me with her big, serious, brown eyes. "Isabelle," she said, "you left."

And I did all I could, my sobs muffled by her laughter, I embraced her.

Upon my arrival, I had expected to be greeted by manifestations of Patrick's joy. It was a wish I knew was risky to place. Again, I had mismanaged my expectations, it seemed. I just hoped the shower would somehow slide us back into the soft place I was eager to feel and renew.

"Turn around?" he softly asked. Dutifully, I placed my hands on the shower bar letting his sandpaper-like hands slowly prepare my body for the playfulness to come. The sweetness camouflaging his abrasive character, his artillery of choice, was to make me forget what I should never have had.

Continuing into the bedroom, our lovemaking eventually rocked us both to sleep. A sound one for him, a light one, as always, for me. He was holding me so tightly, so firmly, pulling me back to him, unaware, each time I slipped away from his grip. His vulnerabilities are keeping me here, I was thinking, as I let myself finally drift into a restful state.

My eyes immediately opened. My heart had changed its rhythm. "Patrick," I told him, "there is a phone ringing."

He turned to me with an expression I could not make out. He bent to pick up his phone off the floor and show me. "See," he said, pointing to his screen, "no one has called." And it was true, there was no sign of calls received.

Confused, I got up to check my own device, which I had placed on his dresser.

Nothing.

"It's the upstairs tenant's phone," he started to explain. "He places his phone on the floor all the time, sending the noisy vibrations everywhere in my room." Visibly tired, and worried himself, he turned on his side, leaving me to glue my nose to his T-shirt covered back. A back that had now stiffened.

"I could have sworn the vibrations came from our bedroom," I whispered to myself. "I could have sworn."

I had planned on taking Jocelyne to the beach, but my energy levels were still too low. Remaining in bed, with Jocelyne by my side, I checked my phone and saw Patrick had texted that he had left me one hundred and fifty dollars to do a more extensive grocery shop. This was a definite first.

Please have Jocelyne's ears pierced, also, he added. And so, Jocelyne and I spent the day together, shopping, baking, and acknowledging each other's presence, honoring our need to be together.

Patrick's demeanor had not changed, I reminded myself, as I saw him enter the house. The belief he exuded was clear. I own the ground I walk on, was the message he projected.

If only we were treated as subjects, the way a king would consider his entourage, with loving paternalism, I thought. But no, we're objects to him, things that can be placed, replaced, and disposed of. We're minimally humanized items and dehumanized humans meant to serve him. For some reason his condescending attitude and patronizing ways had now become more apparent. The distance he had created between himself, Alejandro, Jocelyne, and me only brought me and the kids closer, unifying us against our common enemy. We all were fighting to be recognized, to be admired, to be relevant to him.

The pawns would stay pawns and the queen in this chess game had temporarily retreated.

Was she displaying feigned or sincere powerlessness? Maybe she had retreated into a strategic pause, waiting, I thought. I needed to hope that was true, to hope she would perform, to fucking show up. After all, she had returned to the playing field to deliver a definitive move.

But was it going to be?

I felt his soft lips press on my cheek. "Wake up," I heard him say. I opened my eyes, lifted myself up from the mattress and saw the cup of tea he was handing me. Tea, he had made me some tea. "Drink," he said, placing the cup in my hands. Knowing I had no choice, I sipped one sip only, recognizing instantly the unusual nauseating sweetness. I placed the cup on the floor, its contents still brimming at the top.

A sweet poison, I thought to myself.

"I will see you later," he said as he walked to the kitchen.

"OK, Patrick," I murmured, holding Jocelyne closer to me.

"Pumpkin," I told her, as I watched Patrick's silhouette blend into the background, "today is beach day."

She squeezed my hand and fell back to sleep.

I quickly made breakfast, and Lisa and Alejandro joined us as well. I headed to the bathroom for a much required wash up session.

Stepping outside of the shower, I looked for my bathrobe, which usually hung on the hook behind the bathroom door. It was not there. Wrapped in my towel, I left the bathroom and opened my closet door. There, on the top shelf, above the hangers, was my white robe. Studying its placement, its inert shapelessness overhanging the edge of the shelf, it had a corpse-like quality to it.

It was meant to be hidden, I thought.

The familiar unease was reemerging. I turned around and decided to focus on slipping into my one-piece bathing suit. With its geometric segments to arrange and figure out, the technical challenge it posed redirected my attention from a hypothesis I wished to dismiss.

The car ride to the beach held a magic that all aboard welcomed. The lightness we had created was making all four of us touch a hedonistic-like moment. The music was loud and summery, Jocelyne was dancing in her car seat, lip-synching to songs she had never heard, making all of us laugh. Alejandro, his gaze floating over his own horizon, was seated by my side. Lisa was there for the ride. Whatever tensions held by her petite body, were now slowly untying themselves. The usually stern looking girl was smiling, a feat in and of itself. Under a clear blue sky, Salisbury beach would provide us an impromptu sanctuary.

Jocelyne held my hand as we walked the colorful streets of the beach town. The circus-like atmosphere was a caricature of how Canadians see Americans: arcades, fast food, and odd-shaped bodies that point to American excesses. I realized then, that I had become the heart of this family. Moreover, I had created for myself an alternate reality, a parallel life. Am I wishing for a rebirth or my own disappearance? I wondered. Confused, I did not know anymore, unable to reach my perfect in-between. I had to remember I was there, back in Lowell, with Patrick, for two weeks. My purpose was to leave the limbo I had single-handedly created.

Throughout the day, I took pictures of random moments of happiness and sent them to Patrick. His name had often surfaced during the day. We still all wished Patrick had joined our day, revealing the existence of a paradox we all felt, his absence was revered, his presence missed.

I had heard them in the past. Arguments followed by periods of silence. Him sulking, her crying. I could sense it again, discord between Alejandro and Lisa. Seated at the picnic table, Alejandro had refused, without any explanation, to hold her hand. Moreover, he did not want her to stay for dinner with us that evening. I knew the reason. We all did. The hurt she had been subtly carrying into the day, was now clearly etched in her squinty eyes, there, in the backseat of my car as we were driving back to Lowell. The public display of affection shown by Patrick and me, offered such a contrast to their behavior. And, then came her legitimate request.

"Can you move your seat forward?" she asked. "I have no space here in the back."

His scathing reply shocked me.

"No," he had said, "I am too comfortable." I examined him sideways, attentive to the situation, as I drove. He was the product of a sick environment, I told myself. Had the virus morphed into a more sophisticated version of the original strain? I pondered.

In the kitchen, I could see Alejandro had become stressed. Meal time was a cruel and unforgiving time in this house. There were standards to uphold, someone to impress. I took over, feeling protective, wanting to ease the stress and started to prepare the meal.

When Patrick walked in, the scene that greeted him had clearly displeased him. Jocelyne was watching, Frozen, Lisa and I were folding clothes, and Alejandro mindlessly playing on his phone. Aware of Patrick's discontentment, we remained still, leaving only our eyes to move freely, following his movements as if to assess the degree of danger we were all facing. The human composition we were forming lacked a main ingredient—food.

"Why wasn't my plate prepared when I walked in?" he asked me as he undressed, still fuming.

Fuck off, Patrick, I was thinking, and should have said. I explained that my strategy had been to leave the food out, so he could prepare his own plate.

"I walk in like a stranger in my house," he added, his anger palpable.

I looked at this man for whom, for no good reason, I felt love. I remained silent, lying on the bed, my back turned to him, pretending I was sleepy. But, I had become alert, more so than ever before.

When I woke up the following day, a small note was waiting for me on top of the office desk. A cup of tea was placed by its side. The note simply read, I love you, Isabelle Rodriguez. I stared at it, blankly, and placed it back on the desk. I looked through the stained glass window facing me.

The light coming through was bright, but I did not put my hand to my face, and I did not feel the warmth of it.

I had not planned anything much for the day. Jocelyne was gone to her mother's house for the week, and Alejandro was with Patrick, working in Berlin. Animated by a very deep desire to present myself as the prettiest thing Patrick had ever *owned*, I decided to get my hair done.

He had trained me well.

So far, I had proven, or at least, I believed that I had, been a woman holding culinary magic in the kitchen, a motherly presence in the house, and witching moves in the bedroom. I also had an image to keep, aware of the effect we both created in public. Everywhere we went, whether to the restaurant, to the movies, or to family parties, the couple we formed commanded attention. The reasons why, unknown. And yet, I felt that the dyad we presented to the world, and the attention we provoked, was a product that we had to upkeep. At the core of this attention, my value, my worth, pulled me to the surface of relative anonymity, validating my relevance to his life.

Looking at myself in the rearview mirror, I felt pleased with what I saw. My eyes, somehow, appeared greener than ever. They had come alive. Energized by my own pleasing, narcissistic reflection, I decided to stop at Valeria's house for tea.

"Hi, Isabelle!" she said with genuine happiness. "Come in, come in." Greeted by her daughters, who had already rushed to meet me at the door, I entered, recognizing the familiar scent of cinnamon and anise.

"Isabelle," said the youngest, "Jocelyne kept asking for you. We can't believe you came back to see her," they kept repeating, dancing around me. Looking at the little Latinas celebrating my return to their lives, I wondered, has Patrick pushed too far? Did he really intend for me to be part of his family? Does he understand how my departure would impact their lives? More importantly, do I?

Sit down, sit down, Isabelle, she quickly said, pointing me to a chair. "Let me get you some tea," she offered. Her niece, Emma, was on a WhatsApp call with Patrick's youngest sister, Adele, who still lived in Nicaragua. Eager to introduce me to this sister-in-law I had yet to meet, Valeria beckoned me to approach, insisting I join her on the call. I walked to the living room and bent down a little so Adele could see me on the screen. "Hey," I said, joyfully, relieved I had had my hair done. "It is nice to finally meet you," I added with a smile, animated by my usual deep need to impress.

I had expected a smile, an acknowledgement of some sort, but what greeted me instead was a motionless face, stilled by surprise, her half-opened mouth hanging, soundless. She was a pretty girl, not as gorgeous as Emma, the unaltered Latina version of Kim Kardashian, but nonetheless good looking.

"Hi," she finally was able to articulate. "It is nice to meet you," she added in a thick Spanish accent. Our exchange was short, our encounter odd. The language did erect a barrier, but her restraint and scrutiny could not be explained by the language issue alone. Instead of greeting me with the reassured expression of finally meeting her brother's girlfriend, she gave me a look of worried disbelief. I quickly ignored my discomfort, disengaged, and let Emma and Adele resume their conversation.

Back in the kitchen, sipping my tea, I half-listened to Valeria's marital challenges. She explained that her husband had slept with her cousin in their house. It was the main theme of their failed marriage. There was no point in trying to help. They all stayed. They never left. My mind was elsewhere, anyhow. I managed to extract myself from the barrage of information she was inundating me with. I needed air. I had to leave.

Upon returning home, I received a text from Patrick asking me to meet him at his secondhand electronic supply store, five minutes away. He needed me to bring the three hundred dollars he had left on top of the refrigerator, so he could buy a new phone.

I took the money, hopped in my car, and met him in the seedy store, where a group of Latinos was waiting for me to arrive. Patrick had obviously staged this display, observing and feeding off the men's reaction as I walked into the store.

He quickly settled on a new iPhone, insisting I change my phone cover as well, offering to buy me a new one. He had always been bothered by my Rebecca Minkoff phone case. He did not like its flowery style, or its obvious elegance, an elegance that often attracted many compliments. An innocuous comment in itself, it still puzzled me, the way he would criticize my style, my choices. Whether it was Coach, Chanel, or Gucci purchases, he labeled them all "crap."

"OK," I said, pointing at a basic silver case, "I'll take that one." What did it really matter, mine was fraying at the edges anyway.

I quickly hopped into my car again, and drove back to his home, followed by Patrick, who was now driving the black van that held most of his working tools.

"I am starving," he had said, just as we left.

I had turned around and simply smiled, as I knew the meal was ready.

"Man, it smells good," he exclaimed as we both entered the house. I was more than satisfied, I was proud. He looked over my shoulder, kissing the nape of my neck, taking everything in, the salmon with lemon sauce, the prosciutto and melon, the butterscotch pudding. The food I had prepared, the heart of my power, would again secure my evening, ensuring it would flow uneventfully.

He grabbed my face in his right hand and kissed me fiercely, the way he would when joy would take hold of his mind.

I had made him happy.

For now.

I knew I had invested in my evening, understanding how the impact of every little victory would be short-lived. Short-term investments were risky at their core, something I had forgotten.

I woke up on the Tuesday with a brutal migraine. Nausea, aversion to light, and jaw defying yawns had hijacked my senses, commanding me to stay in bed. I immediately reached for the Zomig spray I had placed on the floor, by my bedside, brought it to my nostril, pressed and inhaled softly. I waited in bed for the medicine to halt the pounding in my head, and along my temples, so I could resume my sleep.

I woke up three hours later, groggy but functional and quickly dressed, slipping into my black romper. I was going to drive to the local Starbucks, an upgrade from the usual, Dunkin' Donuts. As I walked toward the door, I grabbed my computer. That day, for some obscure reason, I had the urge to resume my writing.

The cooled air in the coffee shop felt good to my lungs and brain, reviving me. Standing in line, waiting for my name to be called, I remembered how this particular Starbucks had staged so many of my dramas, here in Lowell. It was here Patrick brought me the morning following our first night together. It was here I had expected him to discard me, almost eighteen months ago. It was here I had brought Jocelyne for hot chocolates, listening to her stories about Lydia and her Julian.

I got my macchiato grande and sat at a table by the bay window. Placing my computer on the table, about to start typing, I was suddenly struck by a piece of information that, until now, had somehow eluded me. Patrick, from the onset of our relationship, had held two phone numbers. Since our renewed commitment at the beginning of January, we had stopped using his business cell number. He had repeatedly told me he only used the business phone as a GPS.

However, on a few of our latest WhatsApp calls, I had heard a phone ring in his car, while he had been driving. Of course, the two or three times it had occurred, I had questioned him. He had claimed it was his worker's phone. Then, it had made sense. But now, there was a problem with his story. Something I was now remembering from the previous day, struck me. Between the time I had left Massachusetts in May, and my actual return, four days ago, he had repainted his red Dodge Ram truck and had gotten his business number written on its side.

How blind had I been willing to be?

My breathing became remarkably regular. I gently brought the cup to my lips and let the coffee glide down my throat. The stillness that surrounded my decision had been defined, I was sure, by the crispness of the air. I felt oxygenated, casino-oxygenated. I finally knew what I needed to do. I felt it. I knew the conclusion, the finale to this sick play was within reach. I knew my story was now ready to meet its fate. It was ready to be scripted, ready to be acted out. I had devised the beginning, I would devise the ending as well. I texted Patrick I would be late, to not expect me for dinner, and to not wait up for me. As he had done so many times before, he ignored a text that should have been a clear sign of trouble, a red flag warning him of a storm to come.

Another one.

I have had difficulties with a worker, he texted, leaving me feeling incredulous at the obliviousness he displayed.

Your days are always difficult, I replied, seeing his attempt at drawing pity from me.

I love you, he quickly responded.

Save your words, I wrote back.

I slowly walked back to my car, planning my next move, with uncanny calm. It was now 7:30 p.m. The wind was deliciously soft and sensuous, delicately caressing my skin, prompting me to forego the air-conditioning and drive with the windows down.

I parked my car in front of the house, aware he had arrived, watching him step out of his now white truck. He focused his blank stare on me.

"Hey," he said, containing his anger.

"Hey," I replied without lifting my eyes.

Entering the house, we both walked toward the living room.

"I don't feel like preparing dinner," I suddenly told him, reconsidering my plans not to have dinner with him, as I sat on the couch. He moved toward me and sat down, placing both his legs, as usual on my knees. How stubbornly defiant, I thought. I contemplated my next move and decided to give him what he wanted.

I might as well have fun and play my part creatively. I can pretend, I thought to myself. So, again, like I had done a hundred times before, I selflessly untied his boot, exposing the left foot first and removed his damp sock. I started massaging his problematic foot, understanding I had set the stage, yet again, for some truth to surface and for some lies to be uncovered. Not wanting to pussyfoot around the issues, I plunged right in. "Patrick?" I asked, firmly looking down at his foot. "Your business phone. You only use it for GPS, right?"

"Yeah," he said, looking straight at me, innocently. He suddenly got up to get himself some water, wearing only one boot.

Oh, you're good, I was thinking, but, equally stupid.

Returning with a glass of water, he stood facing me. A clear dare was inhabiting his eyes.

"You mean to tell me that you painted your business number on your truck, but only use it for GPS?" I asked with a carefully calibrated, honeyed voice. At this point I did not bother to listen to his explanation. I simply got up and with a wide smile on my face, I asked if I could see his phone.

Still holding my gaze, he reminded me of the last time, in May, I had asked him to show me his phone. "I told you it was going to be the last time," he sternly reminded me.

I looked at him, really seeing him this time, with his pale blue polo shirt, his fitted jeans, white paint everywhere. Somehow, there in front of me, he had become ridiculous. He had lost his physical luster. He was now, in all his mediocrity, taking his rightful place in my mind.

"But, that was a different phone," I told him, in an almost reassuring voice, my dismissiveness so convincing. Watching him leave for the shower, I weighed my options. Should I leave him tonight or tomorrow? I wondered. Having chosen to enjoy my evening, I committed to the idea of toying with my prey before abandoning it to a slow death.

I followed him to the bathroom. As I sat on the counter of his old vanity, I watched him step out of the shower.

I looked at him, as he was drying off, and asked with blunt playfulness, as my father had a few weeks back, "Patrick, how many girls are you chatting with at the moment?"

First appearing undisturbed by my direct line of questioning, he hesitated, betraying himself. "No one, of course," he said, eyes shifting. I smiled at him, knowing my mind was more restful now, my migraine gone, clarity finally emerging. I jumped off the counter, walked to the bedroom closet, put on the black patent leather shoes I had just bought in Montreal, and headed for the door, giving him the opportunity to dodge the question. More than ever, I was hungry.

"Taco night, somewhere in Haverhill," he stated.

"All right," I told him.

I was literally in the driver's seat, I thought, as we drove in my car to that Tuesday taco fiesta. I was high on my newfound feeling of detachment. My carefree behavior was making him uneasy…and that intoxicated me.

We entered the restaurant, with him holding me firmly by the waist. As usual, Patrick put me on display. This time, I was mindfully acting my part in this vapid show staging a togetherness that wouldn't fool.

I would follow my script.

We ordered our drinks, a margarita for me, a Pina colada for him. To my surprise, Alejandro and Lisa appeared from the front entrance of the restaurant. Patrick had not informed me they were going to join us. The kids were happy to be with us, animated by a lightheartedness they rarely showed in Patrick's presence.

I observed their interaction with each other, sadly understanding I was playing a central role in the happiness they were now experiencing. When I was there with them, they could unleash their laughter, share their jokes and enjoy each other's wit. I had been at the heart of their lives, that much I knew, for some time now. My light, what remained of it, a buffer protecting them from Patrick's scathing criticism and unrestrained harshness. I knew I had generated a sense of hope and excitement in Lisa's, Alejandro's, and Jocelyne's lives.

I turned to Patrick and gently kissed his lips, meeting his gaze. Pressing me against his body, and placing my knee on top of his thigh, he kissed me back, unaware I was rewriting the end of our tale. I let him kiss me, this time closing my eyes.

Breaking the edges of the taco shell containing my salad, I absentmindedly observed my surroundings, choosing to study the patrons laughing at the bar. Their happiness seemed so genuine, I caught myself thinking, hating the envy that had emerged in me, an emotion I seldom felt.

"You know, Isabelle," Alejandro started, watching Patrick disappear into the bathroom. "My dad is so centered when you are in Lowell, so different," he specified, his eyes pleading.

Watching him play with his own tacos, while I absorbed the significance of his statement, I wondered, does Alejandro suspect anything? Has he read my intentions? "How sweet of you to share," I simply replied, smiling, hoping no one had noticed I had morphed into one of them.

INHALED

Remorse and guilt had been stored somewhere deep in the folds of my brain and heart.

I, too, could deceive.

"Turn down the volume," he ordered me, again. "Why do you always have to listen to music when I am with you in the car?" he asked me, irritated.

Music, I realized, especially in my car, had become another of his rivals, competing for my attention. He knew the prominent place music held in my life. I abruptly turned off the music, without saying a word. It was a brisk gesture that startled me as much as it startled him. Rarely, had I allowed myself to push back against his unreasonable demands. In this moment though, I could tell I had made him uneasy with the irritated manner in which I had obeyed him.

Slowly, walking back to the house, the full meaning of what it was I was devising, started to weigh on my heart, on my stomach.

Unaware of my inner turmoil, unfazed by a deep silence that should have alerted him, he took my hand firmly. "I need to have a tire repaired," he told me, as he opened the door to the house. I followed him to the bathroom, unsure of what I was going to do. "Change your clothes, your legs are showing too much," he added, while brushing his teeth.

Looking in the mirror and down at my legs, I assessed the indecency of their exposure. I thought, yes, my rompers short, maybe a bit too short, but who really cares?

Still, starting to come down from my power high, I changed into my pair of Rag and Bone jeans.

I had obeyed again, suddenly feeling there might be something in our relationship to savor, even to salvage. My ambivalence about my trajectory was rearing its ugly head, unsettling the resolve I had had throughout the evening.

Patrick had become resentful of my sudden, disobedient outburst. It was now 11:00 p.m. To survive the next few hours, I needed to create an alternate personality, a temporary dissociative state that would shield me from my own emotions. Sadly, the anger we each carried, overshadowed the moment, interfering with our ability to truly connect and to enjoy, what I knew to be, our final lovemaking session. But, I was the only one aware of this truth. The disappointment was mine to bear, only.

His ego bruised, he touched me with undeniable roughness, imposing a distance between us. I had become absent, projecting myself into an unknown space, where I was nonexistent within my own body. The disconnect between us was real—our collision predictable. Had he known his membership to my body was about to expire, I was wondering if those last moments together would have been different enough to keep me from leaving Lowell. Uncertain and afraid, I fell asleep.

I missed him already.

At 6:00 a.m., I felt him get up. I heard the sound of him emptying his bladder. He came back to the bedroom, walked over to his dresser, pulled open a drawer and retrieved his phone—his business phone. He scrolled through it silently, unaware I was observing him. His shoulders were weighed down, as if he wanted to fold into himself. I stared at the lamp I had bought for his bedroom, a warped attempt to impart his room with the promise of exclusiveness. I had wanted to mark my territory with an object meant to imply the solidity of my presence in his life. I remembered now what happened to the girl who had given him the orange Himalayan salt lamp.

That, too, was a failed attempt, I thought, remembering how we had fucked under the soft glow it had cast over our bodies. He now had thrown a red T-shirt over my lampshade, to attenuate the harshness the light usually screamed on the walls. The red hue it cast, projected a lounge-like atmosphere. The final impact—still depravity. His room could never shake its innate tastelessness. I hesitated for a second, but, however imperfect the timing, I had to seize the moment.

"Patrick," I said, "if I were you, I would let me take a look at your phone." I lifted myself up, my back against the headboard, and waited. He turned sharply toward me, sat by my side, and aggressively showed me his phone screen. I tried to take his phone from his hand, but he would not let go. I looked at him, confused. "You told me I could look, so let me," I firmly stated.

"You actually want to look at my messages?" he asked, furious.

What part of this process does he not understand? I was thinking.

Clearly frustrated, he walked toward me and placed the phone in my hand. I only had it for a second, though. As I started to scroll down, he ripped the device from my hands and threw it across the room. The phone bounced off the wall, before falling on top of the mountain of dirty clothes, which had accumulated at the end of his bed. I stared at him as he picked up his phone. I wanted to pretend I was ready for this stare down, but I was feeling the hurt well up within me. I had had enough. "I don't want to see your phone anymore," I softly told him, getting out of bed. "There is no need to anymore," I concluded. I put my jeans on and slipped into the first top I could grab.

Under his gaze, I moved to the bathroom to retrieve all my beauty products. One-by-one, I uprooted them with calculated poise, freeing them from their perverse confinement in his closet from hell, clearing the way for his next target. I then proceeded to extract the star of the bathroom, my hair dryer. Pulling its cord out of the wall socket with mindful attention was like pulling a heart through someone's throat—my own. By removing that hair device from his house, I was, in effect, removing the only object whose absence would confirm the finality of my departure. For a brief moment, kneeling on the bathroom floor, hairdryer in hand, I stopped breathing.

I proceeded with feigned, but credible, conviction to remove from the hangers, on my designated side of the closet, all but the few items of clothing that had acted as stand-ins. The ones I was leaving behind, I just did not care for. Sitting on the bedroom floor, I packed my bags with newfound precision.

Patrick entered the bedroom, phone in hand, motioning for me to take it. I had not realized he had stepped out of the room. I took the phone, knowing all too well he must have deleted the incriminating conversations. Still, I decided to take a look. He was so confident I would not find anything. And so, I scrolled.

There was an Emma.

Where can I meet you, it read, with a smiley face terminating the question Patrick had written. I saw the date and time, April 15, 2017, 10:00 a.m.

That was the Saturday Alice and I had spent together at the hairdresser. I remembered it clearly, as she had to attend a party that same night, making me reshuffle my plans to drive to Patrick the night before. I had stayed and slept in Northampton. I looked at him, unimpressed.

"This is not your niece," I whispered.

I scrolled farther up, January 25, 2017, 11:00 p.m. Amor, princess, I am only asking you to send me a picture, I read, as he stood by my side. I looked at him, again.

A picture, I thought. He demanded proof of her whiteness. Amor, princess? Sweet nothings. Isn't that why they call them that? Because they mean nothing? I considered, as the overconfident look had disappeared from his face.

"We weren't together at that time," he scrambled.

"No, Patrick, we were," I immediately replied. "I was in New York with Alice," I reminded him, scrolling down my own phone to retrieve the loving messages we had exchanged half an hour before he had tried to lure in a new princess.

He had tricked me from the beginning of our relationship. His betrayal was immeasurable.

Everything, everything has been a lie from the onset.

"This is after Felicia," I finally screamed at him. "This, after you confessed to having made a mistake! This is after you promised me you would not place me—us, in a similar position again!"

He was now seated on the edge of the bed, staring at the ground. "But, I never met her," he sheepishly told me, his wide eyes betraying his altered state. I banged my fists against his chest, squeezed his jaw between the fingers and thumb of my right hand, trying to turn his face in my direction.

I need eye contact, I thought.

He resisted.

"I gave you everything, Patrick," I finally admitted, tears rolling down my cheeks.

And I had. Everything.

Yes, I oscillated between believing and pretending to believe, but those instants when I did believe, I was real and authentic. I became Isabelle Rodriguez, without restraint.

And I worked at keeping my replacements at bay.

I had played against the master of a game, a game I thought I had figured out. I had given him more than I had ever given any man. I had ignored, interpreted, misinterpreted, reinterpreted so many red flags. I had desperately wanted to see him as a man capable of kindness, empathy, and judgment. Mostly, I had wanted him to see me. We had projected visions of ourselves that could not withstand reality. And we had each created, constructing piece-by-piece, an image of the other.

How I had wanted his perfect body to be matched with a perfect soul. How can a woman my age, with my experience and maturity, be prone to believe such bullshit?

How?

I had made myself a willing hostage, bonding with my keeper like someone with Stockholm syndrome. I had fallen in love with a non-existing human, a dead man.

I just wanted, needed, a safe hiding place—a hideaway.

Instead, I'd was revealed, while he remained hidden.

Until now, I inwardly decided.

His gaze had returned to the floor.

Shame is what he is so fearful to feel, what he tries fiercely to conceal. It has eventually caught up to him, I thought.

He suddenly stood up to face me, and did, what he always did, each time I suspected something was amiss. He inflated his body, widened his shoulders, and stared, unblinking, into my eyes.

Seeing his reaction, I made a point of clearly articulating the next words that came out of my mouth. "We have no future together, Patrick. I am leaving. I am leaving you."

"You are staying," he ordered, after taking several seconds to absorb my words. "You are not leaving," he concluded. He brought me closer to him, and I let him. I also let him kiss me, for the last time.

I pulled away from him, finally feeling disgust inside my heart.

The seriousness of the moment was ultimately reaching him. "You don't want me," he mumbled, in obvious disbelief.

I turned around and let myself fall onto the bed, burying my head in a pillow, sobbing. I pulled away from him, something I had never done before. I had never turned away from his embrace, let alone his kiss.

To prevent my departure, since he rarely viewed an apology as an option, he removed my patent leather shoes, one at a time. "I expect you to be here when I return from work," he plainly stated, walking to the kitchen.

I remembered then, that while our drama was playing out, three of his workers had been waiting for him outside, seated in his truck. As he walked away, I lifted my head. I had to take one last look at him. He must have sensed the weight of my gaze, because he quickly turned around.

"Patrick," I told him, aware of the wound I was about to inflict, "for all it's worth, thank you for the sex." And then, I enjoyed the damage I had done. He was speechless. His face, now rock hard, marked my victorious moment.

Yes, I thought, he used me, but now, he has to contend with the very real possibility that I used him, too. I laid my head on the pillow, closed my eyes, and listened. I heard the sound of his footsteps as he was leaving, the door closing, the commands he was spewing at his workers and finally, his tires screeching.

Alejandro and Lisa had overheard the arguing. It was nothing new for Alejandro. He had been exposed to our outbursts before. During our fight, Patrick had motioned for me to tone it down, wanting to hide this new betrayal from Alejandro. But he underestimated the depth of the bond I had with his son.

Lisa came into Patrick's bedroom, clumsily trying to hug me. I stared at the clueless teenager in front of me. My pain had impacted her, and for a moment, I saw panic in her usually inexpressive eyes.

INHALED

"I cannot continue being humiliated like this," I slowly told her, resuming my packing.

I rolled my bags to the side door. Alejandro and Lisa walked up to me. "Come with us to the promontory in Methuen. Please, Isabelle? Before you go? It might help," they pleaded.

I looked at them observing me, their concern seemingly genuine. I could not refuse. "Let's go now before I change my mind," I replied, in attempted humor.

Leaving my belongings inside the house, I stepped into Alejandro's car with the new Bluetooth speaker I had bought for us two days before. My fatigue, and with it, a migraine, was reemerging.

The car ride to the promontory was filled with awkward silence. I felt shame, hurt, and despair, but deeper in my heart and mind, it was the humiliation that stung the most. As Alejandro parked the car, took the speaker and opened the door, leading us to the vista, I could hardly contain my tears. We all sat on the grass. There, with new age music coming from the device, and the Merrimack river as the focal point, I was trying unsuccessfully to meditate. I was now fully feeling the wound Patrick had inflicted on me.

"All a lie," I shared with them both, as I began crying profusely, my head in my hands. I then turned to Alejandro, and saw the pained expression on his face. He was visibly shaken. I have to tell him now, or I will never forgive myself, I thought.

Starting from the beginning, I described, in a general manner, the course of my tumultuous relationship with Patrick. They listened carefully, without interruption, drinking in all the elements of my story.

There is something I need to share specifically with Alejandro, I suddenly told them, while searching the photo library on my phone. Armed with the incriminating picture, I passed the phone first to Lisa, as if trusting her to soften the blow.

"Your father told me you were collecting my underwear," I finally shared. "That you were in love with me," I added. Lisa's expression was unexpected, a large smile appearing on her usually stern face. Lisa and I both knew, that the last time I had left Patrick, Patrick had told his son that I had left because of Alejandro—because I had fallen in love with him. Alejandro had shared this story with both Lisa and I back in May, when she had complained about strange things happening in that house. She was unable to identify what it was exactly that she had felt. This picture, the indisputable proof of Patrick's strangeness, validated her otherwise vague discomfort.

Alejandro frowned when he saw the picture. It was an image of a black lace bra laid on top of his duvet.

This is how my day is beginning. The problem is deeper than I thought. Have a good day, read the text from March 2016.

Alejandro looked at me, still speechless.

"Yes," I told him, "your father staged this. He wanted me to think you wanted me. He was trying to lure me into having a threesome with you," I added. I looked at him and smiled timidly. "I like you Alejandro, but not that much."

He smiled back, with a rictus that sent shivers up the back of my neck.

After leaving Methuen, the kids pleaded for me to have breakfast with them. A migraine had rooted itself in the back of my neck, spreading its pain to my stiff trapezius muscles. I had five hours of driving ahead of me, but I accepted. Alejandro cared for me, I knew that much. I also knew he had wanted me to stay to relieve him from the domestic burden Patrick would continue placing on his shoulders. Alejandro saw my resolve, though. He knew our farewell meal would be held at the dining room table. It was the table that had staged so many moments. On that stage, my last curtain call would be played.

We managed to swiftly wash the dishes, Lisa and Alejandro surprising me with their ability to detach from the drama, my drama. The talk was light. We simply focused on the activities they had planned for the day. Alejandro, placed the dish cloth on the kitchen counter and took my hand.

"Let's go outside," he said.

Unsure, I followed them. Standing together in the front yard, smelling the sage we were burning as the smoke floated around us, the three of us holding hands, we meditated for two minutes, facing the sun. Alejandro

INHALED

spoke gently, guiding our breathing, deepening our awareness of the moment. "Let the earth's energy guide our souls. Let our wounds be healed by the power of human kindness," he softly said. For the first time in this house from hell, located in Lowell, Massachusetts, Grace was finally said.

PART FIVE

CHAPTER ONE

Although music was my habitual companion, I temporarily replaced it with mindless radio programs. I needed distractions from my inescapable thoughts. All this was not accidental, I reminded myself, as I drove on I-89. I had chosen to pursue the idea of him, animated by a deadly curiosity, had I not?

I felt the images and the sounds that had marked my time with Patrick flooding my brain, a confused brain trying to make sense of the truths I now knew I had willfully ignored. I had been occulted by my own stupidity.

I was remembering how, two months into our relationship, Patrick had simply stated that our conclusion would be dictated by fate and that gravity was going to shape our reality.

"The natural pull to the ground, we cannot fight," he said. "Gravity always wins."

Clearly, we had both tampered with the concept, pushing its limits, infusing abnormality into its functioning, playing both puppeteer and puppet. I could see how his magnetism had offset gravity's normal pull.

It had brought me to the edge of my being.

I had stepped away from who I had been, and from who I had thought myself to be. But, I realized now, from my new vantage point, I was able to truly see myself. I could see my flaws, my needs, and my desires. I had revealed them both to myself and to the world. Moreover, I understood our illusive relationship was the product of our own warped inner voices.

Patrick's inner voice was marked by the nonexistence of complex and deep emotions regulating his behaviors. It was filled instead by primitive emotions of anger, lust, and envy, fueled by remorseless intent. I, simply, and shamelessly, ignored and shunned my inner voice, deciding instead to legitimize recklessness into my life. I had let myself become addicted to a collision of senses, in every way. We both had let our respective voids collide, enabled by a strong desire to quench the loneliness, whatever the price.

I had returned to Patrick at the beginning of 2017 because I had believed our previous failed script could be rewritten. I had fed my belief by fueling my denial of reality, protecting myself by negating, re-interpreting the truth, intermittently gaslighting myself with abandon. His deceitful behaviors had not deterred me from his toxic embrace. I had uncovered his many masks. Still, I never imagined his betrayals would be so far reaching.

All of it had been a lie, a ploy, a game. He had actively pursued other women, specifically white women, while maintaining the illusion of us. I had believed that our many weekends together in Lowell had held some authenticity. I had been willing to tolerate the possibility of betrayal in exchange for the comforts, both physical proximity and family interaction would bring. I had been willing to settle for these consolation prizes.

Those many weekends with Patrick, I now could see, had not been what they had appeared to be to me at the time. While Patrick was away working, and I was home with Jocelyne and Alejandro, he had done the unthinkable, he had not only pursued other women, he had fucked other women. I now also understood why he had taken so many pictures of me and the children. He had been building an image to present to the world, but more importantly, to the Massachusetts Child Services. Twice, I had reported him to those authorities, explaining the danger he presented to his daughter.

Twice, I had denounced him.

In hindsight, I should have been more suspect. Why would he go back to me, the woman responsible for making the official complaint? Ironically, as Alejandro had confided in me at the promontory, the social worker responsible for his case had stressed that family stability would increase Patrick's chances of having access to Jocelyne during the weekends. My disclosures had threatened the legal hold he had had on Jocelyne. How he must have hated me then, and most likely, still.

Patrick had wanted to prove there was only one stable woman in his life, me. I was the stability. Committed to his decision to paint a functional portrait of his otherwise sick family, he no longer had brought women home while Jocelyne or Alejandro were with him. But, he had to meet them somewhere. He had to answer his need to seduce, to lure, to catch, and to consume. While I had been cooking, cleaning and bathing Jocelyne, thinking these moments held some form of solace for me, he had been texting and fucking behind my back.

My understanding of it all was becoming boundless, here in this car, on my way home to Montreal. An awareness of boundlessness had flooded all my senses, highlighting the obvious, I could not avoid the unavoidable. I would reconstruct a new narrative, however painful it would prove to be. I would connect facts to form a sequence of truths, new truths.

What would become of me, at this point, I did not know.

Alice was surprised to see me enter the apartment. I had told her I would be gone for two weeks, but it had only been five days since my departure for Lowell. I kissed and hugged her, and placed her head in my hands. Looking straight at her, I told her that this time, I had left for good.

The void I felt in my stomach was physically painful and impossible to flee. Flashes of the last five days flooded my mind without warning, inducing panic attacks. I would hear the sound of Patrick's phone constantly vibrating in my ears, a sound that would haunt me for months to come.

Visions of his face suspended over me, would follow me everywhere I went. The morning I had left him, I was now remembering, I, too, had thrown his phone across the room after discovering the existence of his incriminating texts. His phone had been lost in the mess the room had become. He had needed that phone, his so-called business phone.

The fool that I was, I helped him look for it, for a good fifteen minutes.

As I was searching, yet again, for the device under his bed, I was vividly recalling how, looking up at him, he had told me he had found it. The devious look on his face though, told me he had never lost it.

It was that image—that devious look on his face—that I was stuck carrying, unable to push it from my mind.

For some reason, a flashback of my bathrobe askew on the shelf significantly impacted me. Surely, it had been removed to erase traces of my existence, paving the way for younger flesh to be consumed in that room. Obsessed with his looks, and more fearful of aging than most people, Patrick had begun dying his hair again, relying on the blackness of his stubble to attract young white-skinned girls.

Evidently, to Patrick, my flaws had become me. The object I had been to him offered no constancy, no stability. I was remembering now, how he had commented on my shaky hands, hands that once had mesmerized him, and the swell of their bluish veins. He would observe, with eloquent silence, but disapproving eyes, the shapelessness of my breasts, the threat of wrinkles hinting themselves around my eyes and my forehead. I had become a nagging reminder of his own mortality, the inevitability of his own death. He was a hunter seeking refuge inside the envelope his younger targets provided, allowing himself to caress older flesh when fresher meat was out of stock, soothing his need for release. I was certain of one thing, he would never really see beauty. He would remain forever untouched and fundamentally unmoved, by its presence. He had been cursed with a callous and remorseless mind.

An absent conscience.

To declare war on someone you feel love for is counterintuitive, akin to an act of self-mutilation. But, I had no choice. He would be back, of that I was certain. His last texts pleading me to stay, inviting me to see a concert, were indicative of his menacing shallowness, his incapacity to let go of his prey. He did not understand why I had left. He was puzzled by my reaction, obviously incapable of introspection. Now, three days after escaping Lowell, I knew I had to secure the position I had taken, by taking even firmer steps.

I had one thing in mind, and one thing only, I had to find a way to protect myself—from myself.

CHAPTER TWO

Seated at the end of my dining room table, I showed the officers picture after picture of telephone logs. I had kept it all. The logs were traces of his craziness, proof of his obsession, and manifestations of his numerous intimidations.

I, too, had had a plan, and I was now ready to acknowledge it. I had documented every misdemeanor, knowing there would be a time I would need to erect a permanent wall between us.

The police wanted me to write my story in the report.

"All of it?" I asked, understanding the weight of the task, as my mind traveled to that very first encounter eighteen months before. Exhausted, I forced myself to stick to the essentials. I was not sure my story would be compelling enough for the authorities and our legal system to take any action. The stalking, the harassing phone calls, and the covert threats would all have to be untangled and ordered into some form of substantial logic.

I handed them my report, and they took down his name, his phone numbers, and his address.

"What do you want us to do for you now, in the meantime?" they asked me.

I looked at them and understood the gravity of my situation. I had continuously dismissed my situation as being benign. "Call him," I told them. "Call him, and tell him to leave me the fuck alone."

Reassured by my apparent resolve, they nodded. "So many victims demand help only to run back to their abuser," they told me, very much aware of the abuse cycle's pull and push patterns.

"Not me. Not this time. I'm never returning," I decided.

Three times they called him. He never answered his phone. Each time they demanded he call back. He ignored them.

The detective in charge of my file was a woman named, Sergeant Detective Elise Perron. She had a firm voice and asked all the relevant questions. She was pressing me to establish the chronology of the phone calls and texts I had submitted as evidence of harassment. I needed to highlight and sort out the events that had occurred, while I was in Canada. Little of what had happened in Northampton and Spain would be admissible in court. Over a period of ten days, I spoke and answered her questions almost every day, until we both came to the conclusion we needed to meet at the police station. There, I sat down with her and produced a timeline. It showed the string of events that depicted the crazy behaviors I had allowed in my life.

While building my case against Patrick, I called Valeria once, hoping to get some clarity and understanding as to the role she had played in my life's screw up. She was shocked by the turn of events, unable to believe his true nature, disbelieving the extent of her brother-in-law's lack of morals. She too, had been manipulated and deceived into thinking he loved me. She had believed Patrick. She had believed in the sincerity of his intent. She had been completely certain that he had finally found his one true love. In broken English, she then began to reveal pieces of information she had willingly kept from me. She had wanted to protect him from his past, and from losing me. She recanted stories of theft and burglaries and that he had served jail time. With her poor English, I almost did not understand the reasons she gave for his last incarceration. The words I did catch, pointed to sexual assaults. "The charges were eventually dismissed," she told me, as if talking to herself only, "but I believe he was guilty."

The tightness I felt in my throat was instantaneous and inescapable.

INHALED

I left him with Alice in the apartment that time, when I took Simone's daughter back home to the South Shore, I was now recalling. I had left her alone in my apartment, while he was sleeping in my bed, for two hours, as I had gotten stuck in traffic. How I wanted to kick myself in the head. Alice. Alice. How many times did I place her in danger? How many times did I shove him into her reality, ignoring her emotional resistance, stampeding over her physical well-being? I thought with dread. And, what would his presence in Catherine's life have triggered?

I reflected then, on Alice's final IB dance project for school, inspired by my twisted life. She had choreographed an award-winning piece depicting the mind of a sociopath. I had pressed him into her life, making her stretch her limits, as I had been made to extend my own.

But, Valeria was not done. She had grasped the magnitude of Patrick's play. "Isabelle," she started, hesitantly, "I spoke with Patrick's sister, Adele, recently." A long pause ensued. "She asked me if you were the woman Patrick was dating for money."

I had suspected it all along, but now the final piece of the puzzle was in place. I could feel my heart solidifying. The landscape was complete. I was a high target, nothing more.

Freedom and revenge formed an odd couple, but I could live with that. That was, until I received a phone call that threatened the foundation of that combination.

"We cannot find any traces of him crossing the border at the dates you specified," the voice message said. "His name is not showing up anywhere." Seated at my kitchen table, my mouth agape, I felt my mind's volatility further pushed down into a tailspin. My world was collapsing, as I now realized he must have used an alternate name, or worse, another passport.

For an entire week, Sergeant Detective Perron had called me every day to tell me they had not yet found a match between Patrick's passport name and the individuals having crossed the border for the dates and times specified. If they could not confirm his identity, they could not issue the arrest warrant. This meant he could come back to me.

I called her back, pressing her to find a way to identify him. The following day, she called again. The customs agent had been bothered by her office's inability to successfully identify him. She had sifted again through the log, and found him.

Two weeks later, I received a brown envelope from the Justice department. It contained a document informing me that a criminal lawsuit was pending against the man who had been my manipulator for the last eighteen months. The barrier had been erected, my own fucking Mexican wall had been built. The name appearing on the document was the first thing that struck me. It was a name I had never seen in its entirety. Whispers of truth were now yelling at me. Patrick was, in fact, named Benjamin. Benjamin Mateo Rodriguez-Diez. It was a name I had never seen, belonging to a man I had never known.

Five weeks after having left Lowell for good, I was preparing to meet with some friends for an evening of dancing. Patrick was still trying to get in touch with me, even though the police had asked him not to contact me. He had coded all his messages, his own way. His anonymity was only relative, for I knew he was the one hiding behind the fake profiles and fake emails he had created. Because of this, thoughts of him easily swam inside my mind, leaving me to hang above an ocean of unanswered questions.

The day had been another struggle for me, and I now had thirty minutes to kill before meeting the girls. I had been bothered by his latest message which asked me to forgive him, to give him another chance. I felt compelled to pursue my investigation of Patrick, if only for a few minutes.

"Why not?" I had asked myself. It had been a good eight months since my last attempt to find him on the internet. I nonchalantly typed, Benjamin Rodriguez, expecting nothing to surface… but something did. It gave me access to a profile—his profile—for a good minute. Then, all the information disappeared from my screen. I sat in the dark, facing my computer, astonished. I then figured out it was because I had used a Canadian credit card and address. I needed an American address to obtain information from the site. I still owned an American credit card linked to my old address in Northampton. All would be good.

One of the challenges throughout my relationship with Patrick had been to not overshare portions of my screwed-up relationship with friends. I feared being judged, or worse, being labeled as plain, fucking crazy. This time was no different. I did not mention anything about my internet search and what it had yielded. I decided the dance floor would provide the only safe place for me to exult what I needed to exult. I decided perhaps karma required a little push. And the time to push, had maybe just arrived.

In front of me, sat a bowl of caviar, and a list of addresses and telephone numbers connected to his name. They were all temporary numbers, of that, I was sure. Only one email address was listed. It was one I had never seen. I knew of his LinkedIn account, but the Facebook one was under a different name altogether. I immediately proceeded to block him from my LinkedIn account, wondering why I had not done so before. I then turned my attention to the list of addresses he had lived at since he had arrived on American soil. Included with each listing, were the names of the occupants associated with the address. There she was. The elusive girlfriend had existed. Jane was, in fact, short for Janelle. And she, like Patrick, had a profile somewhere in the system.

Janelle's Facebook picture was blurry, making it impossible to discern any of her facial features. I tried to zoom in, but all I could determine was that she was short and stubby with dyed blonde hair.

Did she dye it for him? I wondered, unsure of why I still cared about such things.

I then looked at the long list of phone numbers associated with her profile. I got up, made myself some tea, and thought about my options.

To call or not to call? To write or not to write?

I assembled the courage to dial the first three phone numbers, but it was to no avail. They had all been disconnected. Unlike Patrick though, she had many email addresses.

I wondered, What are my chances of reaching her? " What are the probabilities I'll land on the right woman, and if I do, what will her reaction be?"

I picked the first one and introduced myself. I needed to camouflage my eagerness to uncover some truth and my impatience to face more truths.

I have terminated a relationship with a man named Benjamin Rodriguez, I offered. I believe you know him and would like to ask you a few questions. Maybe you have some of your own, I added. I would understand should you not be willing to respond. And if you are not the right Janelle, disregard this email. I exhaled as I hit the send button, imagining my breath carrying the message to a well of answers.

Seated on my bed, watching an episode of one of my favorite French television series, I had miraculously forgotten about my afternoon's internet search, when my phone lit up.

Where did you get this email, I read. No question mark. Just like a soft, but pressing statement meant to alleviate one's fear, while still demanding an answer. I could not admit to having used the TruthFinder site to locate her. I would have lost a potential ally. I found it scribbled on a piece of paper when I was doing his accounting, I lied.

How fluid those lies could now flow.

I stared at the response. I am his ex-wife. We were married for five years and have been divorced now for six years.

Five years? I thought. He had told me his relationship with Jane had lasted forty-five days. 'Forty-five days under the same roof,' he had said. I knew of the existence of Alejandro's mother, Desiree, but never had Patrick mentioned anything about another wife.

I quickly asked if she was the one, as Lydia had asserted, who had given him the furniture that now decorated his living room, dining room, and bedroom.

That wasn't me, she replied.

Did you ever live in Worcester (as Lydia also had affirmed), I continued.

Nope, she wrote.

Well, had he dated a Jane and married a Janelle? What were the odds? Were they the same person or two distinct bodies to fuck and play with?

Instinctively, I knew they were two. Rodriguez, did your barrel of girls to toy with have a bottom? I asked myself, already knowing the answer.

My exchanges with Janelle held a constant rhythm. She shared that she had left him upon finding out he had impregnated a young girl, Jocelyne's mother, while Janelle was still married to him. She explained that she threw him out of their Manhattan apartment, but not before driving from New York to Lowell, where Benjamin's sister and niece lived. She said, they had known all along about the teenager's pregnancy and had kept it from Janelle. I don't hold shit from nobody, she kept repeating in her emails. I believed her, suddenly remembering how Patrick mentioned a certain Jane coming for him from New York in a fit of rage.

Crazy puta, he kept saying. Upon Janelle finding out the truth, Patrick had escaped to his sister's house in Lowell. There, Janelle, gun in hand, found him surrounded by his family. There had been a fight, a physical one where punches were exchanged and shots had been fired. The police had been called, but no charges had been filed against either of them.

I felt Janelle's narrative belonged to me, as much as to Felicia, Lydia, and the rest of us, putas. In his mind, we must have formed one, singular person. Reading Janelle's emails, I understood that nothing about the women he had been with had stood out in his mind, one way or another. One person's qualities and flaws belonged to everyone, and no one in particular. The collage his mind had created was constantly morphing itself as he added new conquests to his life.

Which Jane had shown up at his door? I wondered. Both appeared to have had compelling reasons for committing murder. One, for having furnished a place she would never get to inhabit, the other, for having been cheated on stealthily, bringing their relationship to a point of no return.

Like me, they, too, had been violently humiliated.

The content of Janelle's emails was emotionally charged with anger. I am the one who helped Benjamin and his son obtain their American citizenship, she continued. I also helped him obtain his asbestos license. I was there for him when his mother died, she added.

I was struck by the vividness of her emotions, and that struck me with fear. Six years had passed, yet her wounds appeared so fresh.

Is this going to be part of my future, my recovery, as well? I wondered.

Sharing pieces of my story with someone who knew him was bringing me a hit of the drug from which I was trying to wean myself. She's a fix. A hell of a fix, I thought.

I wrote to her, how I now realized, I did not know anything about him, or his past. So many secrets, I feel as though I could have been in danger, I wrote her. Her answer sent electrical impulses to my temples.

He fled his country, she told me. I discovered the reasons he came to establish himself in New York. Isabelle, you were in danger. You are still in danger. The warrant of arrest will only fuel his drive to find you.

Her opinion's an educated one, I was thinking, as I stared at the words. Danger. What type of danger are we possibly talking about?

You must be young, she continued, he used to like them young.

My pride had been struck.

No, I responded with anger. Times have changed, I typed, biting my lip, now he likes them old and rich.

My decision to stay in Montreal had given me a focal point, a grounding force that saved me from my self-inflicted grief. Without Simone's presence and guidance at that time, I honestly do not know what would have become of me.

The day following my communication with Janelle, as I was preparing to take Elizabeth, Simone's daughter, to see Katy Perry, for her 18th birthday gift, I was surprised by my newfound vitality. The new antidepressant I had been prescribed was stimulating my appetite, increasing my restorative sleep, and improving my energy levels.

How interesting for me to stumble upon Janelle at this exact moment, I thought.

Life was somehow making sure I could manage the truth I so wanted to touch. I needed to know more. I needed to know why Patrick had fled his country. I had to ask Janelle. I had to make her spit out the reasons. I had given her the opportunity to inform me during our exchanges, yet she was clearly withholding that information. That puzzled me.

She reproached Patrick's family for their own lack of transparency, so why the opacity with me? I wondered.

Just before leaving for the concert, I quickly sent her an email. My curiosity, so difficult to contain, carried with it my unhealthy eagerness to not let go.

When you say he likes them young, what exactly did you mean? I feverishly wrote. How young were they? Has he raped anyone? Why had he fled? Why? I finally insisted. Why?

An email notification appeared, lighting up my phone's screen in the middle of the concert. Dancing to the rhythms of Dark Horse, I read her short, but telling reply.

Sometimes, she had written, sometimes, it is better not to know.

CHAPTER THREE

I had changed my phone number, and I had blocked Patrick, his family members, and Lydia and Felicia, from all my social media accounts. My weekly conversation with Patricia remained my only guilty pleasure. My sobriety was a relative one, of that I was aware.

Upon leaving Patrick eight weeks before, I had resisted rereading the text messages that had formed the core of our relationship. Those texts had been the only vessels by which my perception of being loved by Patrick had been built, maintained, and carried. Those texts, accompanied by a few pictures, were the only visible reminders of his passage in my life.

The silly Spanish love songs and the compromising pictures and videos he had sent me over the course of our time together, had become a WhatsApp casualty. I had lost them when I changed my cellular number post-Patrick. The remaining text messages formed a string going back to September 2016. For some reason, that morning I felt the need to reread them in their entirety. Comfortably seated in my office, looking out the window, I pressed on his name and took a deep breath.

I stopped randomly on a few messages, as I scrolled up to reach that very first message. My heart would either squeeze or skip a beat, whenever I reread one of the many love messages he had sent me. But then, as I reread all of them slowly and carefully, a few passages stood out, helping me connect certain events. Helping me reach some of the truth. They say there are no coincidences. If I did not believe that before, I did that morning.

Contemplating the string of text messages I had read earlier in the day, I was now re-examining some intricacies of the relationship with Patrick that had initially escaped my attention. The main part of my healing, so far, had stemmed from reconstructing the events that had shaped my story, and my knowledge of him. I knew so little of him and his life, which also meant, I knew very little of us.

What parts had been real? I asked myself.

Even those intimate moments, during our sexual encounters, had been distorted fragments of reality. As I reassessed the damaged character I had authorized myself to become entangled with, my stomach tightened. Even while with John, I had ached to feel the comforting presence of a man. A real man. I had wanted the physical sanctuary found in the warm embrace of strong arms—strong, in all aspects of the word.

Upon meeting Patrick, in the wake of my separation, my need for physical intimacy had been my main legitimizer for pursuing such a perverse relationship. I had thought, at the very least, it would answer my need to feel a connection, the connection oxytocin would secure.

Images of our lazy afternoons were now reappearing in my mind. There were afternoons where I would stay, firmly held in Patrick's arms, our breathing synchronized. These moments had been the illogical product of the events that had preceded them.

They had been moments framed by irrelevance—framed, by anything, other than something resembling strength.

I was now seeing the scope of his deceit.

He had staged manifestations of lovingness, and I had bought it. I had felt secure.

I had let go of any inhibitions.

The small fragments of recognition I thought I had seen in his gaze were actually slabs of denial and negation of my existence.

Now, more than ever, I wanted to uncover the face behind the mask.

I made myself some tea.

Star anise and cinnamon tea.

How very sad, but in my mind, I told myself, I needed to create the conditions that would help me travel back in time and guide me to the relevant stops.

Again, comfortably seated in my office, overlooking my street, I closed my eyes and remembered ...

I remembered how Patrick, in June, had planned to visit me in Montreal before my trip to Spain. He had changed his mind at the last moment, and it had unsettled me, prompting me to leave him, again. At that point, it had been three weeks since my move to Montreal and I had missed him.

His body.

His hands.

His mouth.

I was famished.

Why?

For the truth, I had created—the illusion, with me still.

Needing it still.

And what does that say?

I don't know.

All our phone calls, WhatsApp, and texting during that time, had told me my feelings were being reciprocated. In one of those text exchanges, we talked about John visiting my apartment. It had struck me as comedic, as a composition once again orchestrated by the master puppeteer. But thinking about it now, I realized it had held some depth.

I don't want to see John in your apartment, he had written. When I get upset ... there is a side of me, there are some behaviors that you do not know about, he had pointed out.

I was now remembering his suspicions the first time he had visited me in Northampton. He had refused to drink the fruit smoothie I had made because I had concocted it away from his supervision. He was seemingly afraid I had laced it with some drug.

I should have laced it with truth serum, I now thought.

During that first visit he had also placed a spoon on top of the doorknob of the front entrance door, creating an impromptu house alarm to warn us of the arrival of a jealous husband. John, he had been convinced, represented a threat, a violent one.

I absorbed the meaning of this memory and recalled the presence of the camera equipment he used in Lowell. Yes, I knew he had a paranoid streak. I had rationalized that everyone has some quirks. Now I realized, his paranoia went beyond his desire to control. He had something to hide. He was not trying to prevent the collision of his female targets, as I had first thought. Clearly, he had not cared about that.

We were all replaceable and disposable pieces of ass.

Always would be.

And besides, he would have loved the drama such collisions would have provoked. No, he had needed to efface traces of his own existence. He had proudly stayed away from social media and he had obviously used more than one alias. And his house, his assumed fortress, had to be defended.

But, from what? I wondered.

I realized now that one of his texts hinted to an admission of guilt.

If I ever crossed paths with John, he wrote, well, it would make front page news … I don't want to end up inside a Canadian prison.

Is this a joke? had been my stunned reply. I had thought it funny at the time, a distracting tactic to make Patrick's absence in Montreal more palatable for me. In truth, it was not funny at all. What I had not considering at the time, was Patrick possessed no sense of humor.

Now, another text came to mind, a warning I should have heeded. In January 2017, while I was in New York with Alice, Patrick and I were exchanging texts on the logistics of me moving into his house and bringing my furniture and other belongings with me.

Amor, let's make this happen, quickly, he wrote. I just don't know how much more time I can wait for you to be forever by my side.

By. My. Side.

His message included links to two articles. The first was titled, "Want to be happy? Give up these 15 things right now." Although sending something like that was out of character for him, it was innocuous enough. The second link, however, was completely shocking. The title of the article burnt in my brain was, "13 Gory details about what it's like to be skinned alive."

Skinned fucking alive?

WTF?

Staring outside my window now, I felt the weight of that memory and its potential significance. I had confronted him about that horrific link, as we lay in bed, following my return to him after yet another failure to escape his grip. Staring blankly, he claimed he had sent it, while ignoring the nature of its theme.

He had lied.

He had known what he had sent, of that I was certain.

Had he zoned out into an alternate state of being or had he dreamed it up to execute a long-wanted fantasy? How many times had he confided in me that he had seen his mother's ghost appear to him in the house, or that he had seen the specter of Patricia's dead husband dancing in the basement? How many times had he alluded to his ability to leave his body and travel inside his own house? Who exactly was this man? What exactly had happened?

I got up.

I needed more tea.

That tea.

I grabbed my phone and scrolled to the first week of April, a Thursday. And just like that, I remembered vividly, something I had completely forgotten, until now. My drive to Lowell, as usual, had been deliciously peppered with bits of anticipation, the way a bag of salt and vinegar chips made your glands squirt saliva when you were about to pop one in your mouth.

Patrick and Alejandro were in the kitchen when I arrived, and I immediately began to assess the culinary challenge for the night.

"Her crazy mother didn't bring a cake to class," Patrick told me.

"A cake for what?" I asked, nonchalantly, chopping the cilantro.

"Her birthday," he snapped.

"Her birthday? Just last week you told me her birthday was July 4th. That was after telling me it was in August," I snapped in return. Her birthday was in April, I had then found out. I turned to Alejandro, my eyes demanding an answer.

"He didn't tell you," he murmured, visibly stunned.

Throughout this exchange there was something else unfolding. More drama. I could hear Patrick complain. Something about a lie. This time it was a lie stemming from Jocelyne's mouth. I was now recalling what he had been repeating, over and over again.

"See, how I tell you never to believe anything she says? This girl is unbelievable," he said.

Jocelyne had apparently told her classmates that her father was agile at handling knives and that he had killed. This, of course, had prompted the teacher to call her mother, who had then called Patrick, in a panic.

Little Jocelyne loved to command attention, I was now thinking. This time, maybe truth had found its way out.

I had buried this event inside one of my mind's obscure drawers. I had thought it was too brutal to be true, a truth so bold it negated itself.

I had believed him.

I had believed that Jocelyne's vivid imagination was indisputable proof that anything she said should be discredited. My main concern had been redirected to finding out Jocelyne's real birthday, just the way Patrick had wished it would. It wove a solace, I was so desperate to find. His statement meant I no longer had to pester little Jocelyne with my questions, as I had then for almost eight months. It had been shameless behavior, but I could stop asking, stop believing, because, as Patrick had mentioned, she was unbelievable—until now.

Stretching my back on the floor, staring at the ceiling of my Montreal living room, I was now remembering what had ensued, the proverbial Grace from hell. I had stopped closing my eyes during the rendering of that so-called prayer at Patrick's house. It was an opportunity for me to observe him without impunity. His imperfect English, the seriousness of the prayer, the somber surroundings, the harsh lighting, a play on preying.

"God drive our life, give bread to even those who don't deserve it. Make sure no one is motivated by negative energy," he would say. I remembered how, as he had opened his eyes, I had given in for a moment, closing mine to the possibility he had committed a hideous crime. Jocelyne said he had killed with a knife, and I had ignored and dismissed it, just as Patrick had asked me to. But now, the facts were crawling to the surface of my mind, pushing up evidence I had wanted hidden.

Water had always comforted me, providing me a space where I could connect with myself and understand my feelings. Lying in my bathtub, my fingers puncturing the surface of the water, I took a deep breath and plunged back in time again, to the beginning of the year, January 2017.

I recalled Patrick's reaction when I had confronted him about Felicia. I was overwhelmed with hurt and did not want to carry the burden alone. I had wanted and wished for him to apologize, to admit the legitimacy of my suffering. But he had discarded everything, obliterating the tears, the slits and the scars his betrayal had inflicted on the whole of my being. I recalled, with disdain, that his chilling response displayed an uncompromising detachment.

"You are reacting as if I had killed someone," he had yelled, gesticulating. "She was a nothing, she was a spare. That is it," he had added, thinking it would shut me up.

She was a spare, I thought. Shouldn't that have told me everything?

"I didn't kill anyone. I didn't kill anyone," he had continued with renewed absence, as he slathered the bottom of his jeans with cologne. His efforts at trivializing his behavior had only highlighted the one word worthy of attention–killing.

Echoes of his flamboyant defense were now ringing in my head, but they had not deterred me from my pain. I knew the processes at work, the mechanics behind his deflections. I had hoped at that time, that he would have sprinkled crumbs of empathy on the moment.

My response?

"I love you."

He then took my chin in his hand, looked at me, and without warning, ripped my blouse off, buttons flying to the floor.

I had wanted the dust to settle, and it had …

In my mouth.

In my eyes.

Just not in my heart.

Patrick's mask was slowly sliding. The more I recalled, the more I was starting to understand I had underestimated his inherent character. That should have frightened me, but it had not. Not to its full extent.

Seated at my desk, toying with the cinnamon stick floating in my cup, disbelieving how I could have forgotten such potent information, I remembered the conversation I had had with the lady from Nicaragua, the year before, in Springfield. "Be careful," she had repeated, "be careful." I now felt her warning to be ingrained in reality, a truthful one. I scanned my memory, trying to retrieve her boyfriend's name. Morales, I finally remembered, Juan Carlos Morales, astounded by my mind's efficiency. As I had successfully done for Patrick and Janelle, I retrieved his profile on the same site I had access to via the internet. I read on, with uncanny restraint. I scrolled up and down, looking for a name that correlated her existence with his. Nothing. "Shit," I heard myself say. "Shit."

My mind had been stoked, though, releasing other pieces of information I had somehow stowed away. Something else was resurfacing.

August 2016, Charlestown.

While we were lying on our mattress, he had clearly stated that upon finding Lydia in bed with another man, he had been stunned by the man's elephant-like facial features. Many times, he had described to me with disgust, the man's large face that had greeted him upon entering Lydia's bedroom. He referred to the man as "baby elephant." Lydia's comments about that incident were also resurfacing. She had laughed when I shared that Patrick was not using his usual name, "Benjamin," with me. To my knowledge, he had not used the name, Patrick, before meeting her. I wondered why he had started using it with me and what she might know about it. I had to call her now, regardless of the potential slew of vulgar insults I most likely would be exposing myself to.

"Who is this?" she yelled, annoyed. "I don't know this number."

I took a deep breath, reminded myself of her unrefined demeanor, and reintroduced myself.

"Don't hang up, Lydia," I said. "It's me Isabelle. I need to ask you a few questions. Please give me two minutes."

"Make it quick," she said, impatiently.

OK, I'm in, I thought. I rapidly described the events following her disappearance from Patrick's life, the previous September. She listened, suddenly understanding I was never the rival she thought I had been.

"For my own sanity, Lydia, I need to understand what happened to him when he caught you in bed with another man," I pleaded with her.

"Isabelle, that night he trespassed into my home. He barged into my room, while I was with a man I had just met in a bar. Don't judge please," she hastily added. "He walked to my bed, punched my lover, picked him up from the bed and lifted him up against the wall. All the while, he was demanding I explain why I had chosen this man over him. He obviously forgot he had been unfaithful to me numerous times."

I listened to the familiar story, feeling her pain, remembering how she, too, had believed, hoped and given second chances.

"Then," she added, "Benjamin simply looked into the guy's eyes and asked his name. 'Patrick,' he said. 'Patrick is my name.'"

I had called her hoping to extirpate more information, information that would further help me understand and finally accept what I was obviously fighting to integrate. This piece of information, though, was unexpected.

I was now understanding that Benjamin had been marked by the vision of her lover. I had observed him while he meticulously tended to his hair—all of them, and choosing his clothes, slathering his body with Chanel Blue, or Mont-Blanc. I had witnessed Benjamin gazing at himself in his mirror, approving the reflection he saw. Having been replaced by someone he deemed a lesser version of himself, instead of soothing his sense of self, it seemed it had injured his fragile ego. He was obviously incapable of understanding how such a man could take possession of his property, Lydia, and how she could have allowed such a thing to happen. He must have retreated into a wounded, semi-psychotic state, like he had with me so many times before, and started using the name Patrick. And, I was the first one to be lured, the first victim, under his new alias.

"Lydia," I said, "I wish you the best and stay safe."

CHAPTER FOUR

Cecil had always been wary of Patrick, mindful of his kind. She had warned me to stay away, to not dig, to let go.

"I can't," I told her with determination. "Either you help me, or I fly to Managua," I threatened, aware of my attempt at blackmailing her. She hesitated, but acquiesced, contacting the head of the Canadian embassy in Nicaragua. She was, after all, my ally, my blood ally.

The person they assigned to me was an ex-Canadian military man who was heading the ad hoc security committee responsible for the training of dignitaries in the event of a kidnapping. Peter was his name, Peter Cowans.

The excitement I felt as I sat down in front of my computer was difficult to contain. I had access to a resource, an official one, who could help me dig deeper into Patrick/Benjamin's character, and his past. To understand Benjamin, I needed to know why he had fled Nicaragua in the first place. I placed my cup of tea on the table and pressed on the Skype name Peter had given me.

The face that appeared on the screen was at once, both friendly and inquisitive. He had big blue eyes, rimmed with a thick line of lashes. His smile, hesitant, revealed thin lips, above which was an equally thin and long nose. The obviously once squared jaw had rounded, giving his whole face a cherubic appearance.

"Hi," he said with surprising hoarseness. "You apparently have a mission for me," he said sarcastically. He must have been apprehensive, thinking I would be the distraction I threatened to be. I did not care. The small talk about the weather was short, as I dove quickly into the essentials of my story.

He listened carefully, noting on paper the elements appearing relevant to his search, and asking me for additional information where needed. He turned around and typed on another computer, located in the background, what I can only imagine was Benjamin's full name.

"Nothing is coming up," he told me bluntly, facing the screen.

Did he seriously think I was going to leave it at that and not pursue it any further? I wondered.

"I need this information," I insisted. "Try a variation on his last names, on his first names," I told him, annoyed by his apparent laziness. He looked at me for a good ten seconds.

"OK," he finally said. "I have a few contacts at the Prenzsa. Give me a few days. Maybe something will turn up."

"Good enough for me," I told him, unsure of his dedication to my cause.

"But, Isabelle, I warn you," he added sternly. "Don't hold your breath."

I had started to laugh upon hearing his useless recommendation. I now considered myself a static apnea champion, able to withhold my breath past the critical point, plowing through the struggle, tapping into my reserves. "Let me dive in. And, watch," I replied with a wink, before terminating the conversation, "I may surprise you."

On our next call, his voice had transformed, mellowed almost. But it could not hide the surprise and excitement marking its rhythm. "I'm not sure," he said. "It may be something. It may be nothing. But, it is all I was able to find."

The articles Peter found came from two different newspapers, El Nuevo Diario and La Jornada. Of course, I knew nothing about them, their political affiliations, their main market segment, their integrity.

The first one was dated June 14th, 2004. It was only four lines long, a small, barely noticeable rectangle lost on page sixty of the eighty page newspaper. Asking for specifications when I felt my Spanish fail me, I quickly read: "Two bodies have been retrieved by a local fisherman over the course of the weekend. The police have been alerted and are investigating the nature of the crimes."

"So," I asked Peter, impatience hinting itself, "I don't see the relevance. Where is the connection?"

"Read the next one," he started, "and keep in mind, Isabelle, that this is Central America. What you read may be true. And, when it is, it might be only partially revealed."

"My area of expertise," I told him with a smile.

This second article looked more substantial, and I needed Peter to translate some more. It was featured on page three of the monthly newspaper: "Local authorities have been investigating a series of murders in the vicinity of Managua. Since June, eight bodies have been retrieved, washed up on the shores of Lake Managua. For two months now the investigation has remained opaque. The details of the investigation were revealed at the end of September, when, during a press conference, the chief of police informed the population these murders are the making of one person. Six of the eight bodies have been identified. All belong to a cult, all bear traces of violence."

What the police had voluntarily withheld from the population, Peter was now telling me, was that the murders bore the signs of one MO, one motus operandi. Two suspects had been identified, Louis Marco Rodriguez, and Mateo Patrick Diez.

"It could be anyone," Peter quickly interjected. "Rodriguez and Diez are very common in the area. Hell, my wife's aunt is married to a Diez. And, I hate him." Still looking at me, clearly intending to downplay the moment, he added, winking, "It's probably him."

Canadian humor. So on point.

"I know those are common names, Peter. Lowell is full of them. I also know, that because there are no photographs, I will never be able to formally identify them. Him. But I hold the certainty that it was him," I shared. I had to share with him. I had to. Spread the burden evenly. Make it bearable.

"OK," he said, absorbing the information. "The chief of police is dead, but the investigative journalist, I may be able to retrace."

"Go," I simply said, "go."

The next two weeks, I spent with Simone and Charlie, waiting. Their company offered no consolation. I was inconsolable. And, I was not telling them about the investigation I was conducting with my newfound military partner. I needed to disconnect from the horrifying thoughts intruding my mind, both day and night.

"Isabelle," Peter said. "I hope it helps, but I know it won't. It won't be enough to make you feel secure," he added with a compassionate smile, his face on the screen showing signs of real and heartfelt desolation. "Alphonso Garcia is the journalist I was able to retrace. The only one."

"OK," I said, "go on."

"His investigation ruffled a few feathers among government officials. It turns out the two suspects identified in the article were linked to the general who was heading the military mission to Spain in 2003 and 2004. They were his sons."

"He told me his father was a fisherman," I was thinking.

"Their crime, it seems, had been religiously motivated, sadistic in spirit," he said. "Unfortunately," Peter continued, "they disappeared from Managua shortly after the article's publication. Garcia didn't want to confirm, but it was understood their escape had been orchestrated by the military and condoned by the president. He won't say more. He is too afraid."

After this conversation, I asked Peter to dig more. He and I had developed a good connection. We were united by the thrill of the ride. I wanted to know more. I wanted to know the details. I wanted to know the modus operandi. I was obsessed, really. And I think my obsession was becoming contagious. The police archives had yielded nothing. There were no documents, no informal notes, no signs of collaboration. We both agreed that a visit to the newspaper's head office might reveal some form of record of the event.

There, Peter ran into the head of the Current Affairs desk.

"No records," he said. "No paper record. But, I can tell you what I remember," he added, pointing to the side of his temple, "quickly."

All women. All young women. All young, white women. Blondes.

The newspaper's report had been inaccurate. While some of the victims had been identified as Mormons, the rest had been British and American tourists, all belonging to the same cultish faction. The paper had felt pressured to not disclose that information. The instructions the paper had received had been clear. Tourism was starting to burgeon, and the story had to be killed. More importantly, the government's link to the story had to be muffled.

All had been raped, all had been found in restraints. All had a two-inch square of skin removed ... from their left cheek.

"Cheek," I thought, remembering with visceral unease how, during sex, he would draw circles on my cheek, as a warning he was about to strike me. He could never get enough of mine.

Then, it really hit me. When I had uncovered Patricia's jewelry in Patrick's room the year before, I had also stumbled upon a large shoe box. It had been hidden behind a set of makeshift cupboard doors on a wall inside Patrick's closet. I remembered feeling my curiosity being satiated as I took out the box, and with shaky hands, lifted its cover. But, my anticipation had been met with disappointment. The box only contained pictures of a younger Patricia I had already seen, more of her jewelry, a birthday card addressed to Alejandro, and signed by Jane, an empty box of Kraft stuffing mix with Lydia's name on it, and a funny-looking necklace.

An image of the necklace was now reappearing in my head. It was a round wire with an improvised clasp. On it were five or six little square charms. The charms on the necklace looked a bit like varying shades of beige paper, but they were leathery to the touch. Now, I understood. It was a collar reuniting concrete memories.

A trophy—the hunting kind.

Now, seeing the necklace in a completely different context, I remembered something else, January 8th, 2016. "You want something to eat?" he had asked casually after we finished making love. I remembered it vividly now. It was our very first night together. I was high on lust and wanting more. I had been absent from my mind, too conditioned by my body's desire to numb the pain I wanted to escape ... John.

Patrick had insisted we stay naked after our lovemaking, and I had not cared. The carelessness I displayed most likely intrigued him. Looking back, I could still feel the coldness of the kitchen counter against the backs of my thighs. Cutting an apple, he had sternly looked at me over his shoulder, knife in hand. His gaze had held mine ... a few seconds too long. I know now what I had instinctively felt then. What I had known, but had dismissed. For a second, I had been a temptation ... an option ... a risk ... that he did not take. He had offered me, with precise intent, a piece of apple planted on the tip of his knife.

What had saved me? I wondered. The lighting. The lighting hitting my white skin had been my savior. It had uncovered the pastiness he so loved, exposing the veins snaking under my skin, the food his eyes needed in order to feed his sick mind.

I had been a keeper.

One of many.

Spare, or otherwise.

CHAPTER FIVE

"Drink up," Peter told me sternly, his eyes unable to hide his concern for the woman facing him. Swirling the ice that was fast melting at the bottom of my tumbler, fixating on the amber liquid that had warmed my throat, abrasively cleaning my insides, I understood his worry. Since my discovery in October, two months earlier, when I fully understood what Patrick had revealed himself to be, I had been unable to find sleep. I was still feeding upon myself.

"I am fine," I lied, unconvincingly.

Staring at the sea, trying to avoid the seriousness of the moment, I pondered. It had seemed a good idea. I had thought accepting his invitation to visit him in Nicaragua could somehow help me heal, that it would help me understand Patrick's past, accept the seemingly unacceptable.

The breathlessness I now felt told me I had maybe, yet again, pushed far beyond my boundaries. I had made the untimely and bizarre decision to leave both Catherine and Alice to prepare the apartment for Christmas, dismissing the bonding opportunity the pre-holiday season presented us with. They had both reintegrated themselves into my life, each at their own pace. Catherine and I had reconciled. Our sufferings had been met and understood, highlighting the possibility of a sustainable rapprochement.

Alice had started at NYU in September and was now completely immersed in her acting classes.

Alice's mind, and mine, had been stained by Patrick's twisted passage in our lives, and I knew only time would help us recover. I could feel our synchronicity remerging. Busy defining her life, her purpose, animated by the need to create her own space, Alice would resurface as her resilient self.

Still, in spite of the trust they had blessed me with, I had lied to both my children, once again. Supported by the belief I needed to protect them from my obscurity, I had lied for the sake of their emotional safety.

"Cuba," I told Alice and Catherine, as they watched me nonchalantly pack my suitcase. "I am going to Cuba. Alone."

I knew they had witnessed my need to rest, my need to simply be elsewhere. Detaching myself from the paradox the moment had connected me to and avoiding contact with Peter's eyes, I knew the compression I felt in my chest did not just stem from the guilt of my lies.

No, Peter, too, had been subjected to my newfound propensity to omit, my penchant to not disclose. I had not shared everything I knew with him. I had concealed, I had hidden. I had never mentioned anything about Patrick's closet, the shoebox and its gruesome content. The necklace, its composition, was known to me, and to me only.

"What are you going to do, Isabelle?" Peter asked me while pushing his back in the chair, crossing his arms.

Shaken from my thoughts, I turned to him, understanding the inevitability of the question. But, I could not. I just could not. Before closing my eyes, I took a mental screenshot of the blue before me, hoping the sea's sleek surface would transpose some quietness into my heart.

Let it go.

All of it.

All of him.

And in the quiet, darkest hours of my days, when I bite into my palm and summon the worst of me, I ask myself, still, who am I, now?

What will I become, and will I ever love again?

"Revenge, the sweetest morsel to the mouth that ever was cooked in hell."
- Sir Walter Scott